RIFKIND'S CHALLENGE

OTHER TOR BOOKS BY LYNN ABBEY

Thieves' World: Sanctuary

Thieves' World: Turning Points

Thieves' World: First Blood

Thieves' World: Enemies of Fortune

LYNN ABBEY

RIFKIND'S CHALLENGE

A TOM DOHERTY ASSOCIATES BOOK
New York

RIFKIND'S CHALLENGE

Copyright © 2006 by Lynn Abbey

This book is printed on acid-free paper.

Edited by Brian Thomsen

A Tor Book
Published by Tom Doherty Associates, LLC
175 Fifth Avenue
New York, NY 10010

www.tor.com

Tor® is a registered trademark of Tom Doherty Associates, LLC.

Library of Congress Cataloging-in-Publication Data

Abbey, Lynn.
    Rifkind's challenge / Lynn Abbey.—1st ed.
       p.   cm.
    "A Tom Doherty Associates book."
    ISBN 0-765-31346-4 (acid-free paper)
    EAN 978-0-765-31346-1
    1. Women heroes—Fiction.   I. Title.
PS3551.B23R54   2006
813'.54—dc22

                        2005034498

First Edition: August 2006

Printed in the United States of America

0 9 8 7 6 5 4 3 2 1

TO MY PARENTS,

whose support has never wavered

RIFKIND'S CHALLENGE

1

The brilliant orange sun sank toward the broad horizon of the Asheeran steppe. Sensing that another day had passed without a lightstorm, men and women emerged from a cluster of squat, round tents to begin their daily tasks. With shrieks of delight, a knot of children began a vicious game of tag with sticks and a fist-sized leather ball while their elders looked to their chores.

Though winter had ebbed and the snow had melted down to crescents, the air remained cold and dry with a stiff breeze from the south. Dust clouds hung in the near distance both east and west of the tents. In the west, ocher dust hung over the camp of a caravan enjoying Asheeran hospitality on its northward journey. To the east, a larger cloud marked the clan's near herd, consisting of some seventy mares, yearlings, and two-year-olds. The horses roamed free; the bond between them and the clan was strong enough that they never wandered far.

A smaller cloud marked the location of the sheep, which were equally important to the clan but eternally untreasured. Without the shepherds who braved the dangerous daylight hours to watch over them, sheep would wander to their deaths.

When the sheep had been safely confined in a roped-off pen and dogs set to guard them for the night, the shepherds went their separate ways. Two of them disappeared behind the largest tent. When they reappeared, they each held a stick carved to match the graceful curve of the steppe warriors' steel swords.

Not yet men and too old to be called children, the boyos strode past the knee-high mound of black stones that marked the clan's winter well. They walked until they came to a patch where the grass had been worn down to the soil. Without words, they heaped their cloaks and a lamb-sized water skin on the verge and began stretching and preening as young warriors had done since the beginning of time.

One boyo stood a full head taller than his companion. He had reach and muscle to spare, and a mane of ruddy-brown hair that fought free of traditional Asheeran braids. His clothes were mostly leather and garnished with brass studs that glinted in the declining light. He leaned forward slightly as he walked, always in a hurry, always in the lead. He could not bear to follow or absorb an affront.

The clan called him Cho, their word for "rust," because of his hair, rather than the name his mother had given him that was, at any rate, a foreign name. In a clan that could sing its bloodline back twelve generations, it was better to be called Rust than hailed by a foreign name. Asheerans would tolerate a foreigner, but never completely embrace him.

Cho took his stick in a one-handed grip and gave it a pair of fast swings; then he used his boot knife to improve the curve.

The other boyo watched and smiled. He was the clan chief's eldest son and his name, which had also belonged to his grandfather and his grandfather's grandfather, was Tyrokon. Tyrokon had the golden skin, the raven hair, and the anthracite eyes of the true Asheeran. A dozen or more gold beads were woven into his braids. His tunic was embroidered with crimson silk in ancient patterns that invited luck and wisdom. Before he'd learned to talk, he'd sat in his father's lap, absorbing wisdom as the chief rendered judgment. He rode like a burr on the wind, but his legs were too short for the rest of him and his ankles rolled when he walked. The infirmity didn't keep Tyrokon from lining up behind his practice sword or holding it in a way that said he had paid attention to his sword masters.

Cho went on the attack without hesitation and, like Tyrokon, his stance showed that he'd learned his lessons well. The rust-haired boyo fought at every opportunity, with sticks or swords, anytime, anywhere, with cause or without. Most of the men within the association of clans they called their Gathering had tested themselves against Cho.

Cho had a memory for warriors and a knack for picking apart their strengths, which he strove to neutralize, and their weaknesses, which he attacked relentlessly. When he sparred against Tyrokon—an everyday occurrence—Cho invariably came at Tyrokon's left, forcing the shorter boyo to defend from his right leg, his weaker leg.

Tyrokon sometimes delivered the telling blow. He was not without skill, finesse, or deception but, in the long haul, he wound up in the dirt more often than not. And Cho would be there, a heartbeat later, with his hand out, ready to hoist his friend upright for the next round.

This particular afternoon was not one of Tyrokon's best. He went down three times before driving beneath Cho's guard to land a blow that dropped the larger boyo, but even that victory was tainted: As Cho went down, he thrust into Tyrokon's right thigh. Had wood been steel, Tyrokon would have been crippled.

When they began again, Cho saw that Tyrokon was hurting. He could have eased up, could have taken the attack to Tyrokon's good side, but that wasn't Cho's way and it wasn't their friendship. Cho pounded hard, fully aware that every parry sent a tremor down chronically sore muscles. In the end, though, Tyrokon's fall resulted not from Cho's attack but from his leg's betrayal.

Too proud to massage his aching thigh, Tyrokon closed his eyes and momentarily ignored Cho's hand.

"Water?" Cho asked.

Tyrokon shook his head. "I'm ready," he insisted and levered himself to his knees. But his leg begged to differ with his mouth and he went down again.

Cho was as prepared to wait as he was to win. He needed water himself and turned to the heap of cloaks. That was when he realized they weren't alone.

A woman had joined them, coming from the open steppe rather than camp.

She was tiny—a handspan shorter than Tyrokon—and delicate . . . delicate the way the best swords were delicate. Her cheek seemed on fire in the sunset light. There was a silver crescent there, the mark of the goddess of the Bright Moon, the only god worshipped in the Asheera and bestowed only on those women She accepted as Her healers. Other healers were compassionate souls who comforted as they restored health, but not this woman. Standing still, this woman had the demeanor of a ger-cat on the stalk. Injury and illness were her enemies. She didn't heal; she conquered.

There was no guessing how long they'd had her for an audience, but while Cho watched, the woman began to clap loudly and slowly.

"No one learns a lesson better than you," she said when their eyes snagged.

It was not a compliment.

Cho ignored her. He retrieved the waterskin and offered it Tyrokon. The downed youth made another, successful, attempt to rise, but there was no concealing his right leg's weariness. He leaned against his stick-sword like an old man.

"Good evening," he said to the woman when she came onto the dirt.

"And good evening to you. Do you need that stick, or can I borrow it?"

Tyrokon steadied himself and surrendered the stick. The woman took it and tossed her heavy cloak aside.

"Your father know where you are?"

Tyrokon nodded.

"Your mothers?"

Tyrokon had two, the sister-wives of Hamarach who cherished their firstborn above all else. That he had not told them of his whereabouts or intentions was plain from the way he silently studied his boots.

"Ah, what do women need to know?" The woman shrugged. "No harm done, I think, but rest it a bit, will you? We accomplished little in that last healing, but I'd rather not see it undone completely."

"Yes . . . ," he replied, pausing where he might have offered a name or some familiar title.

The woman turned to Cho. "And you? What have you to say for yourself? Would you cross weapons with someone you *haven't* beaten a thousand times before?"

Cho's mouth worked silently. What he finally said—a simple "yes"—was clearly not the first thought that had come through his mind. He checked his grip on the stick and checked it again before retreating across the dirt. "Whenever you're ready."

The woman came on guard behind the practice weapon, transforming herself as she did. Despite her calf-length tunic and uncut braids, both women's custom in the Asheera, she radiated the calm fire of a veteran. Her balance was perfect. Her weapon was centered. Her face gave nothing away.

Cho, who attacked into weakness, didn't know where to start. He feinted toward her left side—her off-weapon side—hoping to create an opportunity.

The woman moved her wrists, nothing more; the stick canted slightly, enough to block any attack without exposing a flank. Cho feinted to her other side, with the same results. After his second withdrawal, he convinced himself that he had the sheer strength to beat the stick out of her slender hands.

He attacked straight ahead. Wood struck wood and she seemed to give way. Then momentum shifted. The tiny warrior enveloped Cho's stick and grounded its tip in the dirt. The downward pressure of her weapon stretched Cho's grip to the breaking point. He bent at the knees to free his stick and, before he knew it, he suffered an unwelcome wooden tap just below his right shoulder.

With steel, she could have sliced his arm off; even with wood, she could have broken it.

"Try again?" she asked.

Cho nodded, resolving, as he came on guard, that this time he'd wait for her attack.

After a long spell of stone-like patience, she twitched.

Cho would go to his grave believing he *had* seen a sunwise shift to her balance. And he'd swear, too, that he hadn't overcommitted his response. But—damn—this time the woman dropped low, which for her was very low.

She got beneath him and disarmed him with a wooden wrist slap that left his fingers tingling.

"Careless," the woman observed. "One more?"

Cho flexed his hand. Everything worked. He picked up the stick and nodded.

In their third go-round, Cho did everything right. He stuck with the basics, no tricks or displays of prowess. He drew upon his strengths—his height, his brawn, his reach—without expecting effortless miracles from them. He took the woman seriously, forgetting her size and her sex.

They traded futile attacks, then he got caught considering, for the smallest moment, what he'd do *next* before he'd finished what he was doing *now*.

That was all she needed. The next thing Cho knew, his weapon was spinning end over end into the grass.

"Not bad," the woman mused aloud as she returned her borrowed stick and collected her cloak. "When you give attention to the fight that is, rather than the fight that might be, or the one that used to be, you show promise."

Cho reminded her that he wasn't a wet-eared novice. "I won the red staff and a proven mare at the midwinter Gathering. Twenty bouts and I won them all."

The woman raised an eyebrow. "And used the same trick to win eighteen of them. That may get you the red staff but it doesn't get you the experience you need to fight when you're not fighting your friends."

She started walking toward the tents and never looked back. Cho watched her a moment before searching out his stick. He gave it a few swings when he found it, beating down a swath of grass.

"I hate her."

Tyrokon offered an alternative: "You're angry because she won."

"She has no right," Cho countered. "Where does she come off fighting like that? She's a healer . . . a *healer*! Isn't that enough? Does she have to have men's honors, too? Who does she think she is?"

"She doesn't have to think," Tyrokon said softly. "She *is* Rifkind. She does what she wants."

"Bloody damn Bright she does. Whatever. Whenever. I've heard the stories that she knows how to use that sword she keeps in her cave. But who believed it? A woman. A *healer*. I prayed for someone to call her out, but no one challenges *Rifkind*. Nobody says no to *Rifkind*. Nobody dares."

Tyrokon, whose father was chief over the clan's twelve families and the man with the absolute right to say no to anyone, stiffened slightly. When

he spoke again, it was to repeat what he'd already said, "You're angry because she beat you the way you beat everyone else."

"And she shouldn't have! She's a woman! Have you ever seen her practice? *Ever?* In all the years of our lives? Look at her! She's smaller than your
mothers! She's *old.*"

"And she's very good. Father says we can learn—"

"No, we can't!" Cho thundered. "Bloody Bright Moon—you saw her just
now. She barely moved and she had me covered like snow on the ground.
How did she do that? Where did she learn?" Cho took a ragged breath.
"Why didn't she teach me? Why couldn't she come out of her bloody
Bright cave just once to teach me? Name one time when she was there to
teach me anything?"

Tyrokon weighed his words. "She isn't charged to teach us how to fight.
She's our healer—more than *our* healer, she's the Mistress of Healers. The
Bright One has chosen her to pass the art to others. When she's not heal-
ing, she's teaching—"

"*Every* day? Every damn day? Never once has she thought, *I could help
Cho*—" The boyo caught himself on the edge of an ill-considered rage. He
took a breath and continued in a calmer tone: "It's different with you.
When your mothers brought you here, you couldn't walk and your old
healer had given up on you. She didn't; she stuck with you. But, everyone
else? Some fool gets drunk and falls off his horse and the alarm goes out—
Summon the healer! And the healer comes. She trained your sister, Amra, to
be your father's healer, but does anyone shout *Summon Amra?* Bloody
Bright no! It's *her* they want, and she comes. What about me? What do *I*
have to do?"

Tyrokon made no move to answer Cho's questions.

"Damn it all—she's my *mother!* All my life, I've made myself into the
best warrior I could be. She's known that; she's got to have known that,
even her. I've learned everything I could, from everyone who'd show me a
stroke or parry, and there's not one of them who could have beaten what
just beat me. Bloody Bright—who does she spar with? She's got to spar.
Nobody comes behind a sword like that without sparring every day. I'd
spar with her—"

Cho's voice disappeared. When it returned, rage had taken it.

"Why? Why doesn't she have time for me? How could she sit there in her cave—as good as every story we've heard—knowing my dreams? She has never budged. Answer me that."

"Well—"

"She's ashamed of me, that's why. She took off for the Wet-lands and made a name for herself. *Thank you, Rifkind, for saving our world.* Then she returns and sets herself up as a healer, as if she's never stood behind steel. That's good for you, Tyrokon. She's there for you. But me—I'm just something she brought back with her, somewhere between a trophy and a scar. She abandoned my father—I know it. And, when I was born, she couldn't wait to get rid of me."

"She sent you to my father," Tyrokon said with just a hint of warning.

Cho hesitated.

The calmer part of him, the smarter part—which was not, just then, in the ascendant—knew there had been no better place to grow than within Hamarach's tent. And even if Hamarach had not been as tolerant as he was powerful, any tent would have been better than a healer's cave. Healers—all of them, not just Rifkind—didn't share their lore with men. Something about a great betrayal generations upon generations in the past. Theirs was a woman-riddled society where *sons* were unnecessary and unwelcome.

Rifkind should have known that . . . should have known better than to bear a *son*.

In the end, Cho always came to the same conclusion: "She hates me."

"Rifkind doesn't hate—" Tyrokon corrected, but that was only another way of saying that Rifkind didn't love, either. She was fierce: fiercely loyal, fiercely protective, fiercely determined. Tyrokon knew those traits from the many times Rifkind had waged a healer's war on his twisted legs. But love, like hate, found no hold in her.

Rather than finish a statement that would fuel his friend's despair, Tyrokon changed the subject entirely: "She's headed to see my father. We could sneak up to the felt and catch their conversation."

Cho stared at the stick in his hand as if he'd couldn't remember why he held it. He gave a pair of half-hearted thwacks at the grass. "Yeah, why not. It's not like she'd *tell* me anything."

2

Rifkind strode into the busy camp, her eyes already on the largest of the tents, her mind rehearsing the announcement she planned to make to Hamarach, her chief, her friend, and her sometime lover. She heard her name called from the supper hearths and nodded politely, but did not look to either side. Hamarach's clan had been her clan since before her son's birth. There were no strangers among its tents, no one whom she hadn't laid hands on.

Healing was her passion and her duty. They called her the Mistress of Healers in Gatherings that stretched halfway across the vast Asheera. Back at the caves, she had students from west of the Death Wastes—

"Mistress! Mistress! Come, come quick. I beg you."

A woman in a worn tunic cut across Rifkind's path. She seized Rifkind's sleeve.

"You're here. The Bright One has answered my prayers. My daughter is dying."

Maniya, Rifkind thought, putting a name to the face as Maniya dropped to her knees.

"I beg you."

Rifkind could have freed herself with a twist of her wrist, but that was a warrior's knowledge, not a healer's custom.

Tears welled up in Maniya's eyes. The woman was a widow—and well rid of her husband, for that matter; Lukarad had been a preening cock of a man. No one but Maniya had been surprised when he'd gotten himself killed in a drunken quarrel. The Bright One knew how many children he'd sired, but Maniya was mother to only one of them, and she doted on that daughter.

Chresand was healthy enough, but saddled with her father's temperament: a born liar, and feckless, too. At seven, the child was a healer's nightmare.

"What does Amra say?"

Hamarach's daughter was all that a healer needed to be, though young still and reticent when she should be assertive—as in the matter of Maniya and her troublesome daughter.

Maniya's tears broke loose. "She looks and says nothing. I prayed . . . and my prayers have been answered."

In a perfect world, Rifkind would have freed herself and continued on to Hamarach's tent, confident that there was nothing wrong with Chresand that Amra couldn't handle—if indeed there was anything wrong with the child. But the world wasn't perfect and as confident as Rifkind was that she was in the camp on her own business, she could never be sure once her patron goddess had been invoked.

Concealing a sigh, she followed Maniya to a small tent on the camp's periphery. Two women squatted before the laced-flap doorway, pounding the herbs and wild grains for the dinner pot. They were easily twice Maniya's age and didn't conceal their scorn as Maniya led the Mistress of Healers through the doorway.

What little light reached the interior came in dusty shafts from the vent hole and the doorway, yet there was no mistaking silver-cheeked Amra, crouched against the outer wall.

Shouldering past Maniya, Rifkind knelt beside her former student and, as her eyes adjusted to the darkness, made a practiced study of the child. She quickly reconsidered her uncharitable judgment that Chresand was merely in one of her moods. The child's eyes were closed and fluttered for only the briefest moment when Rifkind pinched her forearm. Her skin was clammy and, though it was hard to be certain in the light, her lips and fingernails seemed darker than they should be.

"When you look from your *tal*, what do you discern?" Rifkind asked before offering her opinion.

"*Tal*" meant many things to a healer: a meditative state; the illusory place where she communed with her goddess; the point of invisible light that shone in the soul of every living thing; and the goddess-fueled source of her healing power.

"Venom—" the younger woman began.

Maniya cut her off immediately. "Venom! Bugs and snakes! As if I don't know my duties. The threshold herbs are fresh. I'm a good mother. *Nothing* here creeps or crawls! It must be something else. Tell her, Mistress, tell her she's wrong. The very light could have slipped down to strike my daughter as we lay sleeping."

"Nothing so dire," Rifkind assured Maniya. "The sky was clear all afternoon. A bite is possible—"

"Not in my tent! I sleep with my arms around her. Only light could have gotten past me."

"Children are willful," Rifkind said, striving for calm. "It's in their nature to misbehave." Then, before Maniya could object, Rifkind shot a warning glower that left the widow's jaw gaping. Satisfied that she'd restored a measure of peace, Rifkind turned her attention to Amra. "Where is the bite?"

"At her ankle." Amra drew back the child's blankets. "A single mark—a scorpion, I think. She must have a sensitivity to the venom."

"You know what to do?"

Amra nodded while sneaking a glance at the silent Maniya. "She was so certain. I didn't want to argue."

"You're the healer. You don't need permission to do the Bright One's work."

"I thought she would not find you and I would be done before she returned."

"You don't have to lie. You're Hamarach's daughter, Hamarach's healer."

Amra's eyes widened. To be sure, she was Hamarach's daughter, but Hamarach's healer? Not when Rifkind, Mistress of Healers, dwelt nearby.

It wasn't merely that Amra had inherited the temperament of Hamarach's quieter, meeker wife. Rifkind knew the length of her own shadow and the trouble it could make.

There were a thousand lessons that a healer didn't learn until after she'd received her crescent. Amra had just learned one; the last, perhaps, she'd learn from her teacher because Rifkind had learned a lesson, too. Or, considering the reason that had brought her to the camp, had confirmed a truth she'd suspected for a month.

Rifkind completed her journey to Hamarach's tent. The chief's two wives were busy hacking apart a joint of wind-dried meat and pounding wild grain. The warrior whose task it was to guard the chief's door stepped aside when Rifkind approached and let her enter the tent unheralded.

As Asheeran dwellings were measured, Hamarach's tent held the height of luxury: a great brass bowl for washing, a pillow-strewn pallet, carpets in bright colors surrounding a circular hearth, a half dozen wooden chests, and, between the poles, beneath an amber-glass lantern: a carved chair worthy of a Wet-lands prince.

Hamarach rose from that chair as Rifkind entered. "Was I expecting this visit?" he asked delicately after they shared a lovers' embrace.

Rifkind smiled as she shook her head.

They were well-matched. Hamarach had been a chief slightly longer than Rifkind had been a healer. His word was law among the families of the clan and respected in all the eastern Gatherings. Another unbidden thought entered Rifkind's mind: She would have to be a great fool to leave this man, this life.

"I've been having dreams," she admitted with a deep sigh as she collapsed on the cushions. "I had one this morning. I tried to convince myself it was indigestion—too many of those hot, little pickles." A bowl of sundried fruits sat beside the cushions. Without asking, she took a handful. Working healers—especially healers who brought others into the craft—were cursed with prodigious appetites.

"A bad dream?"

Hamarach joined her on the cushions, beyond arm's reach but close enough for conversation that would not be easily heard outside the tent.

"Bad? No, not ill-omened." And suddenly Rifkind was weary with the memory of her dreams. "I've been here longer than I've been anywhere."

Hamarach took his healer's moods in stride. "Since my eldest son was an infant."

"I've trained many healers. There's not a clan this side of the Death Wastes whose healer I haven't trained."

Hamarach nodded. "Your name is honored throughout the east and known in the west. When distant men come, it is not to make alliance with me, but to offer you their daughters for training. As I offered my eldest daughter when she came of age."

Rifkind stirred the berries. "Amra is a fine healer. The Bright One looks on her with great favor."

Hamarach narrowed his eyes. "You've come to tell me that you're leaving."

He was absolutely correct, but his perception took Rifkind by surprise. "Not *leaving*," she temporized. "Not forever. Black Rocks is my home. I have been having dreams, that's all. Dreams of faces. Wet-lands faces I swear I have not thought about since Cho was born."

There was one face in particular, but Hamarach didn't need to know that. Ejord Overnmont had been the most unlikely man to cross an Asheeran healer's path. After the ignominious deaths of Rifkind's brother and father, Ejord Overnmont had single-handedly restored her faith in men. She and Ejord had been friends and partners, but they'd never been lovers, as she was with Hamarach.

Ejord was *not* the father of her only child, whatever Cho believed.

Rifkind hadn't dreamt of Cho's father. She knew what had become of Domhnall—had known since before their son had been born. When Rifkind thought of Domhnall, she thought of a dead man and hoped that in death he had found peace.

"I wonder what's become of them. I don't know if I'm haunted by the living or the dead, but haunted I am. If I don't search for them now, I might be too late. Amra is grown. Tyrokon is grown . . . my son is grown. I feel my age, Hamarach."

She was all in earnest, but Hamarach found humor in her confession. "You may feel it, my dear lady, but you don't show it. I have known you for years and I tell you, you have not changed. There's not a strand of silver in your braids."

"Time passes."

"Time passes you by. It would not surprise me to learn that you've found some secret to keep yourself young."

Rifkind bristled. "That would be sacrilege. There is a natural span to all living things. It's in their flesh, in their *tal*. A healer may restore; she may not tamper. The Bright One forbids it."

Hamarach's brows arched. "You are *different*, grant me that, at least. You are like no one else. When you come to me, I am always delighted, but a little frightened, like a man who holds out his arm and finds a hawk alighting on his wrist."

"Never!" Rifkind laughed, hearty and sincere. The idea that she was a hawk! But Hamarach just stared. "What?" she demanded.

"I was just thinking—when I met you, you were still very much the paladin with your leathers, your weapons, and your righteousness. Then the paladin disappeared and you were a mother . . . a healer . . . Mistress of Healers. You became the heart of my spirit. Now, I look at you, and you've changed again, become something else; I don't know what. I have not changed; I've simply grown old. I ache when I stand. But you—there is a liveliness to you that I haven't seen for a long time. I swear, you are renewed."

"I tell you, that would be sacrilege! I live my days like everyone else and there have been a lot of them. I am the very opposite of liveliness. If I don't go now, I will become too old to even consider a long journey."

"A chief does not argue with his healer. But, tell me this: When did your dreams begin?"

"Not long. Since the new moon."

"Not a full month?"

"Barely. Why ask?"

"Because it's been a month since my son told me that you and he agreed there would be no more healings."

"Tyrokon's not a child anymore. He knew his opportunities had dwindled. We tried one last time, but there was only pain and the very real chance that we would weaken, not strengthen, his legs. In the end, it was his decision. It's time he made his own decisions."

"Indeed," Hamarach agreed. "It's not him I'm thinking of. It's you. I know you, dear lady. I know how you fight for every healing and how deeply you're hurt when a healing fails."

"It did not fail."

"Ah, I know that, and Tyrokon knows that, but do you? Do you know that there is no blame because my son will always limp?"

Rifkind said nothing.

"After he was born with withered legs, our healer wanted nothing to do with him. 'Expose him,' she said. But Idi, my dear Idi, would have none of that. She dreamt—women seem to dream more than us men—that she should bring our son to a forsaken well. They stole my best mares, she and her sister, and rode to this very place."

"Tyrokon was still an infant. There's so much more that can be done for an infant—"

"Not according to *our* healer. As I recall, she took one look at you, spat, and rode off without a backward glance. You did not make a good impression, dear lady."

"I wasn't afraid of your son."

"And after one healing, he crawled." Hamarach smiled at the memory. "How many times since then? I've lost count—but you always said there'd come a time when his bones would not respond."

"A child's *tal* contains the essence of becoming. By force of will, Tyrokon clung to that essence, but will is not enough. He's grown." Without thinking, Rifkind raised her hands as she might have if Tyrokon's legs had stretched between her and his father. "That's what I told him. We had come a long way, but we had come to the end."

"The end of a healing, Rifkind. The *good* end of a healing. You've finished training my daughter and healing my son. That doesn't mean you have to leave."

"I know that."

"Do you? First Amra receives her silver, then you can do no more for my son, and now you're dreaming of the Wet-lands. Are you haunted by the past . . . or the future?"

The question caught Rifkind off guard. "The past," she insisted. "I made a promise to you, to Tyrokon, to my goddess: I would do what I could, nothing would stand in my way."

"And, suddenly, nothing does. I'm not foolish enough to think a word from me will keep you here, but leaving is not necessary."

"I *am* dreaming about the Wet-lands. Why now and not before is a question I cannot answer."

"Very well then, when do you leave?"

"Soon," Rifkind replied—quicker than she'd expected, because it hadn't taken days to mollify Hamarach.

"Which way? I understand the Wet-lands are closer to the east and south, farther to the north and west."

"West. Due west—following the path I traveled before."

"Ah, that's unfortunate."

"How?"

"The Death Wastes lie to the west. Myself, if I wanted to get to the western Asheera, I'd go north or south first. The journey would be longer, but safer—if the goal is to find the living folk of your dreams, not join the dead ones."

"I'm prepared."

"You know best. It's unfortunate that you won't be traveling north. You could do me a turn . . . if you traveled north."

"If there's anything I can do—"

"No. Don't think about it. I can tell your mind is made up. It was a stray thought, scarce worth mentioning."

"What!? My mind isn't closed."

"You could travel with Tyrokon to the northern border."

Rifkind shook her head. "Tyrokon is going north . . . to the Wet-lands border?" She had not confided her dreams to Tyrokon and he, all too apparently, had not confided his plans to her.

"He's a boyo—not yet a man of wisdom, but a man in determination. He tells me he no longer needs permission."

"Permission to do what? Why is Tyrokon going north?"

"To smooth a path for Izakon," Hamarach said, mentioning the name of his second son. "He has pieced together what I never told him: He cannot inherit. While you were still healing him, the clan held its breath. But now that there will be no more healing, breath must be let out. The clan will not accept a crippled man, and even if the clan would accept him, our neighbors will not. You know the price a clan pays when its neighbors do not respect its chief."

Rifkind swallowed hard, remembering the day all her kin had been slaughtered. Her fingers stirred the berries, but her appetite, for once, had vanished. She'd never told Hamarach the full story. He knew it second-hand and had some of the details wrong. She'd never bothered to correct him, and saw no reason to start now.

"There must be a way. Izakon and Tyrokon—they've never been rivals—" Hamarach scowled.

Rifkind abandoned her protests. "But the *Wet-lands?* Surely there's some better plan, some better place."

"If you know of one, please share it with him, though do not be surprised if he does not listen. Tyrokon has been much taken with this Vendle of Roce who camps on our verge. From Vendle he's taken the notion that he can do good for us all by becoming a caravaneer himself. He means to go with Vendle to a city called Epigos . . . along the northern borderlands."

"Which is why you ask if I was headed north?"

"I could not ask for more—but you are going west."

"I could go north . . ."

"Eat with us tonight. Take Vendle's measure, then make your decision."

IN THE SHADOWS behind Hamarach's tent, Cho seized Tyrokon's sleeve. Tyrokon got the message. Both boyos sprinted silently from the camp to the sheep herd, where the dogs, recognizing them as shepherds, let them pass.

"You!" Cho sputtered. "Your idea!"

"There's nothing more she can do, not for the pain, not for the fact that I walk like a stone-blind drunk. A man who can't walk, can't fight—bloody Bright, you prove that every time we spar. And a man who can't fight, can't be chief."

"You don't have to beat me," Cho protested. "I'm your second. I'm your right arm, your right leg."

Despite the darkness, Cho knew his friend's shoulders sagged as he said, "A chief has to be first—before his second."

"You're Hamarach's firstborn son. You've got his wisdom—"

"Wisdom isn't enough. Think about it. Say, I was chief and you were my second . . . We'd be the target for every raid from every clan. You couldn't win them all, Cho. And it wouldn't be just you, or me, who'd suffer. I can't allow that."

"So? So, you're giving it up and heading for the *Wet-lands?*"

"The caravans are more important than raids now. If I guide a caravan—Vendle of Roce says it's a good life. If the healer—"

"Bloody Bright! To hell with Rifkind. If you can't stay here, neither can I. I *am* your second, Tyrokon. If you're a caravaneer, then I am, too. We go together."

3

The Asheera was a plain of extremes. The heat of its short summer could wither a man in a day, but the cold of its winters worked even faster, so the round tents were better at keeping heat in than letting it out. Though Rifkind had wisely nursed a single bowl of fermented mare's milk throughout her supper, as the hours wore on she suffered the usual drowse that rose in a crowded tent.

She'd made her initial assessment of Vendle of Roce from her healer's place beside Hamarach. The man was every inch a caravaneer. His skin was weathered to the same shade as the patchwork leather of his garments. He'd lost one eye along the way and covered the socket with a leather patch marked with a gilded serpent. Vendle was tall and lean, all sinew—a hard man to heal, if push came to shove. A hard man from any perspective.

Rifkind circled around to Vendle's side of the tent—the north side, where honored, but not completely trusted guests sat in the chief's full view. The three Wet-landers who'd accompanied Vendle to Hamarach's supper looked to him before making room.

"I hear you've told the chief's son there's a place for him in a town called Epigos."

"There's a place for everyone in Epigos," Vendle replied with a smile that revealed large, stained teeth. "I take it, from that crescent you bear, that you're Rifkind, Hamarach's healer?"

"Mistress of Healers, for Hamarach and beyond," she corrected. "I don't know this Epigos. Who is lord there, and which great lord does he serve?"

Vendle laughed and showed more teeth. "No blood lords, no spooks, either. No lords at all in Epigos. We serve ourselves, that's what we does. All of us who use the Vogoska Crease into Daria, we rule Epigos together."

Rifkind took a moment to absorb what she'd heard—what she *thought* she'd heard. Years ago, she'd been surprised to learn that the language Asheerans used to entreat their goddess—as opposed to the jealously guarded languages that belonged one to each clan—was the common trade tongue of the Wet-lands. Trade, which the Asheerans called the Voice wasn't the only language, not in the Wet-lands, not in the Asheera. The Wet-lands were an amalgam of many peoples, just as the Asheera was an amalgam of many clans. Roce, Vendle's homeland, was one of the southern provinces that were known for their lush fields, their shifty merchants, and the slurred, rapid twist they put to trade speech.

"Are you saying there's no lord in Epigos?" she asked, thinking she'd misheard. "Who provides justice, if there's no lord? Who settles disputes and sees that laws are obeyed and taxes collected?"

"No taxes. Didn't I just say, Epigos is a free city? If there's a problem, we solve it from council."

"What does the emperor say about your council?"

Vendle gave a look that, in other circumstances, other times, Rifkind would have answered with a knife. "The blood-damned emperor can do what he likes. He ain't no proper emperor. The thrice-damned Usurper kilt the last proper emperor and none knows what kilt the Usurper. There's a man sitting on the throne, right enough, but he's a shadow and his shadow don't fall far from his city, accounting on the Usurper and the plague."

"The Usurper's been gone for nearly twenty years," Rifkind said, meeting Vendle's eyes and letting him know she was not some barbarian to be gulled. "If the emperor's weak, then there are still castles, and where there are castles, there are lords—warlords, if not blooded lords."

The caravaneer gave her a calculating look. "Who're you?"

"Rifkind."

"But who's Rifkind? You speak if'n you'd been off the Asheera, into Daria."

"I rode with the Overnmonts when Lord Humphry brought An-Soren and his puppet down."

Vendle touched the gilt patch over his eye.

"That Rifkind was a witch," one of Vendle's seconds ventured into the lengthening silence.

"That was twenty years ago, if it were a day," Vendle snapped. "Any witch what rode with the Usurper would be a crone now, if she ain't be dead. Looking at you, there ain't no way you rode with the Usurper."

Rifkind met Vendle's stare with the frustration she felt whenever the truth wasn't enough.

"All right: The emperor's got no power, but men have to answer. There has to be a man where oaths come to rest and rule begins."

Vendle gave Rifkind a pitying look. "I don't know who tells you about Daria, but they tell it wrong. World's changed since the Usurper vanished. Yea, there's an emperor but he don't count for much. There're no great lords no more, only what you called warlords who take a cut of everything they can reach. There's the sea, for those who have ships, but there's no man building ships since the empire fell, not good ships. It's a bloody sight faster—and safer—for long trade to trek through here."

Another night and Rifkind would have listened politely and promptly forgotten every word Vendle said. The Wet-lands hadn't mattered to her since she'd left them . . . until now.

"Epigos is a place where caravans start and end?" she asked, and Vendle nodded. "A new city? Built since the Usurper vanished?"

Vendle nodded.

"And there's a place for a clan chief's son in the free city of Epigos? What sort of place? We're not traders."

"See—now you're wrong again. I bring what I need to please your chief, an' that's a sort of trade. Lookee there"—Vendle pointed toward the bowls stacked by the hearth—"when I started, all them were made of leather. Now, half's metal . . . and I brung 'em, one by one, for safe passage. What say, then, if I bring something, just for trading through the clans? And who'd know better what trades well amongst the clans than a clansman hisself?"

"You'd make him a peddler." Rifkind drew the Wet-lands' word from the depths of memory. When Vendle didn't argue, she had another question: "What's in it for you? No, let me guess—you fill the peddler's packs and unload them, too. There's profit at both ends of *your* trade."

Vendle's eyebrows rose, as if he'd been sure no tent-dweller could see through his scheme. "That's the way I started meself, an' I hain't done so badly. Enough to let out a few camels."

Tyrokon—*her* Tyrokon peddling from one clan to the next! And camels! Every family kept a few of the double-humped beasts; there was no denying that they were tougher than war-horses when it came to hauling the tents from one camp to the next. They throve on neglect—a good thing, considering their temperaments.

What Vendle proposed did not appeal to Rifkind at all, but she wasn't a chief's son with gimpy legs and no chance to succeed his father. She waited a while and made her escape from the tent. Hamarach followed her.

"You've taken his measure?"

"He's out for himself. What he's offered to Tyrokon benefits him most."

"Then he's not the man for Tyrokon."

Rifkind weighed her words. "Not necessarily. There might be a future for an Asheeran peddler."

She braced for questions. Trade might be the Voice of the Goddess but "peddler" was not a word Hamarach would know. She needed several tries to get the concept across.

Hamarach gave a thoughtful "*Hmm* . . . I sense risk. I would not welcome another clan's *peddler* prowling my camp."

"And I may not like what I see once I get to Epigos."

"You'll travel with Tyrokon, then?"

"I'll bring him back, if I need to, and we'll find another plan."

"My hopes are realized. Can you be ready to leave quickly? Vendle overstays his welcome."

"I travel light."

Wind blew from the north. Layered clothes were proof against it, but there was no point standing in the cold when a warm tent beckoned . . . or when it was time to walk home. Rifkind strode confidently through the

Bright Moon's light while her thoughts inevitably skewed back to the moments when she had left the Ashecra for the first time.

In those days the Bright One had been woven into every aspect of her life. She had never been alone or without direction. During her Wet-lands sojourn, she'd had face-to-face encounters with her shimmering goddess. Then she'd come home, taken up a healer's traditional duties, and *nothing*.

From the moment she'd accepted the challenge of healing Tyrokon, no matter how high Rifkind rose into her *tal*—and she could soar high enough to perceive her war-horse grazing an hour's walk away—she had been completely bereft of her goddess's presence. Even when she presented an apprentice for blessing and the goddess caressed the young woman's cheek, Rifkind was alone.

"WHO GOES?"

Rifkind's voice stopped Cho short and emptied his mind. He thought, from the shape of her silhouette, that she had gone for a knife.

"It's me . . . Cho . . . your *son*. I hear you're leaving. When were you going to tell me?"

"I hadn't thought about it." Rifkind shrugged. "There's no need. You obviously know everything."

"You would have left without saying anything?"

Another pause, as if talking to her son—her only child—was the hardest thing Rifkind ever did. "No. Our paths would have crossed."

Cho couldn't decipher Rifkind's thoughts any better than he'd been able to pick apart her sword strategy. She was his mother; she shouldn't have been a complete stranger. Yet she was, and had always been.

"It's easier this way," she said after another pause. "Who told you? Tyrokon?"

"Bloody damn Bright—*no*!"

"Do not blaspheme, not in my presence."

Cho made a fist and flexed it out again. He clutched his anger, but it burnt from the inside; he couldn't fling it at her. "Hamarach called Tyrokon and Izakon to him when he returned to the tent. He made an announcement: You and Tyrokon are going to the Wet-lands with the caravaneer."

"That can't be what he said."

"You weren't there, I was. He said you were going to find a place for Tyrokon with the Wet-landers."

"Hamarach wanted my opinion of Vendle; I've had more dealings with men like him. If I don't like what I find in Epigos, I won't let Tyrokon stay there."

"Bloody—"

"Watch your—"

"Don't you *dare* tell me what to say or do! You cut me loose the day I was born. And now you're taking Tyrokon away."

"Not me. This is Tyrokon's hatching. If he didn't tell you, that's for you two to sort out. I don't like it, but there's no liking or disliking the truth."

There were so many targets for Cho's anger: the chief whose word was law, the healer whose healings had fallen short, the friend who had chosen his fate but said nothing until it was almost too late. Only a fool would vent anger at a clan chief, and friendship was sacred. That left the healer who was also his mother.

"You lied. You never should have started what you couldn't finish."

"I never lied," Rifkind replied more calmly than he'd dare imagine. "Not to Idi, not to her sister, not to Hamarach, and never to Tyrokon."

"You lied to me! I believed you could make him whole. I believed he'd become chief and I'd be his second."

"When did I lie to you? When did I ever say a word to you about Tyrokon's healing?"

Trust his mother to think only of herself. "You're bloody Bright *Rifkind*. No one thought you'd *fail*."

"Do not blaspheme with my name. I'm no happier about this than you. Tyrokon and I had agreed there'd be no more healings, but I knew nothing about his plan to leave with the caravaneer until Hamarach told me. I didn't want to believe my ears, but they're right: A chief has to be the strongest man. Tyrokon would draw challenges like meat draws flies. Izakon must inherit without a shadow. Tyrokon's the one who thought of the Wet-lands, and if any part of what the caravaneer says is true, then Epigos may be a good place for him. I'll know when I see it for myself. I won't abandon Tyrokon."

"Damn straight you won't, because I'll be watching you." The black silhouette shied from surprise, perhaps, or shock. "You didn't think you could get rid of me that easily, did you? I *am* Tyrokon's second. I gave him my oath, and another to Hamarach just now, while we stood in his tent. No matter where Tyrokon goes, I'll be beside him."

"There's no need for this, Domhnall—" Rifkind began, using the name she'd given him, the name he did not use.

"Need? Bloody Bright, Mother—I don't *trust* you."

Though Cho couldn't see Rifkind's eyes, he felt their fierceness. For a moment he wondered if she'd slay him on the spot and wished he'd left the camp with a sword, then the fierceness vanished.

"I was going to say there was no need for you to come with us, but I'm wrong. Trust me or don't trust me, Tyrokon will need a friend, and he couldn't ask for a stauncher friend than you. We'll ride together to Epigos . . . somehow."

4

Asheerans measured their wealth in the beauty of their wives, the health of their children, the thick wool of their sheep, the edge of their weapons, the bits of bright gold and silver they sewed onto their clothing and, above all else, the excellence of their horned war-horses. Not one in twenty of the colts foaled each year bore the horn buds on its forehead; and they gelded those that didn't.

The bond between a man and his war-horse was a wonder to behold, and men kept that miracle to themselves. No woman rode a war-horse—tradition decreed that women should never even touch a war-horse for fear of breaking its spirit. But there were exceptions for every tradition and healers were the exception for war-horses.

Women with silver in their cheeks called a colt from the bachelor herd. The bond between a healer and her war-horse was more potent than the warrior's bond. A healer could find her war-horse while he grazed far beyond the tents, she could reach into his mind and experience the world through his senses. She had no need of a bitted bridle to guide her war-horse; reins were enough . . . reins and the *tal*-based bond of love and trust.

Rifkind, always the exception even to exceptions, had called the steady Turin while still a child stumbling toward her silver. The chestnut had shared her Wet-lands journeys and carried her back to the Asheera. When she took up Tyrokon's healing, she'd released Turin back to the herd and cherished the first of his budded colts.

After he had lived to a ripe old age, Rifkind had gone without a companion. A Mistress of Healers did not need to travel fast or far. Then a gray colt was drawn to her cave. Rifkind resisted, but the colt wore her down. She called him Banin, from the word for "pest," and he earned it. Yet, for all his mischief, Banin had potential. His jet-black horns weren't fully grown, but they'd achieved a length that gave him standing with his elders.

When he carried Rifkind to the chaos that was a caravan preparing to leave a camp, he claimed a place *with* Tyrokon's Assurin and Cho's Tein, not behind them with the solitary camel that carried their gear, and certainly not with the caravan. Predictably, Tein, whose horns were longest, took exception. There were two full nights of lather and bluster before the warhorses sorted themselves out and their riders could relax. After that it was hurry up and go slow, night after night.

"I'll be an old man before we get to Epigos," Tyrokon complained when another bout of broken camel harnesses delayed the evening departure.

Cho agreed. "If you didn't need Vendle of Roce to introduce you to his chief, we'd be there by now."

Rifkind said nothing. Her body was grateful for the slow pace. It had been years since she'd ridden hard. She ached down to her bones.

The drover boy slung the repaired harness between a camel's two humps. He loaded it with bags, bales, boxes, and the all-important water skins. Camels could go for days without water, not so the other animals or their riders. Together the camels carried enough water to sustain the caravan for four days, six in a pinch. Vendle promised a painful death to anyone who tampered with the skins, and no one doubted he'd keep his promise.

Vendle gave three toots on a small brass horn. The drovers guided their strings into two lines while Vendle's seconds set a perimeter against predators. Vendle himself took the vanguard. Rifkind, Cho, and Tyrokon rode well to one side of the parade, beyond the smell and dust.

The boyos rode with steel swords at their sides. Rifkind had a steel sword, too, though not the one she'd used before, but a serviceable weapon on loan from Hamarach. It was a man-sized sword, which meant it was a bit long for her comfort. As they weren't expecting trouble, she'd lashed it to the back of her saddle.

Hamarach's word was law to the clan's families and Tanacar, who headed the clan to their north, was known to host a caravan or two. Rifkind looked forward to visiting the old fox whose granddaughter was one of her apprentices. They weren't halfway to midnight when Vendle surprised them by veering the caravan due west.

Cho asked the unanswerable question: "What's he thinking? There's nothing but badlands and the Death Wastes in this direction."

Rifkind agreed. She planted the image of Vendle riding at the head of the caravan in Banin's mind and urged him forward.

Vendle had procured himself an Asheeran gelding, raw-boned, but not without spirit. Banin challenged first and the gelding replied in kind. Rifkind chastised Banin with stern thoughts and prudently kept a decent distance between them.

"We're headed toward the Death Wastes."

"We take the safe route."

"The Wastes are never safe. Tanacar will give us hospitality—"

"Never you fear, we use this route every time. You just ride behind Vendle. And—just so's you know—we ride by day now."

Between the fractious mounts and Vendle's slippery trade dialect, Rifkind hadn't caught Vendle's every word, but she'd gotten the gist: The caravaneer was on the outs with Tanacar and worried about raiders.

"We're still headed west," Cho groused when she returned.

"I'm starting to wonder if Vendle hasn't fallen out with everyone but Hamarach. There's a good chance that's why he's interested in having Tyrokon shuttle from clan to clan."

Cho grumbled something Rifkind was glad she didn't hear and Tyrokon said, "My father trusted Vendle."

"Trusted him more than other caravaneers."

Tyrokon absorbed Rifkind's correction. "I'll be glad when we get to Epigos."

"*If* we get there, at this rate," Cho said.

"Our pace could change. Vendle says we're to travel by day now."

Tyrokon asked, "Is that a good idea, as we get closer to the Wastes?"

"No"—Rifkind shrugged—"but I'm not one to criticize. When I rode away from my father's burnt tents, I headed straight into the Wastes. Crossed them with a single water skin. It wasn't a good idea, but I survived."

Belatedly, Rifkind recalled that she'd never shared that little detail with anyone. She braced herself for curiosity. They had a long ride in front of them, and no reason not to tell the tale from start to finish. Rifkind pared it down somewhat—she'd truly forgotten the smaller events—but left nothing out, not from embarrassment or pride and, for the first time, included the story of her first lover's death.

"You walked away from him," Cho accused.

"Domhnall was bound to the Well of the Black Flame. He couldn't leave it and we both knew it couldn't fall into the wrong hands, so we agreed to separate before the last battle. We won, but then the Landmother rose to level the battleground. We—the men and women who'd fought with me— were tossed about like seeds in the wind and, like seeds, we survived. When the ground quieted, there wasn't a landmark left. The Landmother had drawn the Well deep within her, and taken Domhnall with it."

"You could have done *something.* You could have *prayed.*"

"The Landmother remade the land," Tyrokon explained softly. "If your father was underground when that happened, he'd have been remade with it."

That wasn't what had happened. The Well had survived, a bubble deep within the remade land, and Domhnall had survived long enough to pierce his heart with her dagger. But—miracle of miracles—Cho seemed to accept Tyrokon's logic and Rifkind wasn't half fool enough to object.

Despite the boyos' chatter she slipped into a light trance from which she could ignore her discomforts. She had no awareness of a long and un-doubtedly unpleasant afternoon until Tyrokon touched her gently on the forearm.

"Vendle's given us a blast. We're done for the day."

Rifkind stretched and found herself saddle sore but headacheless. The threesome made camp a short walk from the caravaneers and, because they didn't bother with a tent, had it made well before the drovers had unloaded their camels or Vendle had gotten comfortable. Cho announced that he'd seen animal tracks and took his bow after a fresh-meat supper. Tyrokon offered to take their animals—the three war-horses and their camel—for water.

Rifkind didn't object. Using Banin's saddle as a backrest, she was dozing when Tyrokon returned.

"What he calls a seep, I call a cess," the boyo complained.

After a sniff at the liquid Tyrokon had sucked into their water skins, Rifkind agreed. She had skills she didn't share with the women she trained, skills that went beyond the healers' mandate and included such tricks as sweetening a seep, not forever, but for long enough. She knelt by the seep and rose into her *tal*. It took a while; she'd drawn a crowd by the time she reopened her eyes.

A few words of appreciation would have been nice, but changing water was the sort of trick that got folks burnt for witchcraft in the Wet-lands. What could be sweetened, could be just as easily soured and Wet-landers figured: better safe than sorry.

Vendle interceded and peace was restored before it was completely ruptured. The Wet-landers grumbled, made deliberate ward signs, and filled their skins without a word of thanks.

"To hell with them," Rifkind swore. She'd sweeten the water in their skins and the Wet-landers could drink sulphur. But when they came to her, all apologetic, at the next day's camp, she relented and plunged her arms into another foul-smelling seep.

The Bright One knew what Vendle had said to bring his men around but sweetening seeps was exhausting work, though Vendle made free with his suppers. After sweetening her fourth seep in as many days, Rifkind wanted nothing more than to crawl between her blankets, but first she had to tend Banin whose winter coat was coming out in great, itchy tufts. He craved the relief only her fingers could provide.

She leaned against the charcoal flank, plucked out a few tufts, let her eyes close—

"Rifkind?"

Rifkind knew it was Tyrokon's hand on her shoulder an instant after becoming aware of it, but that wasn't enough to keep her from leaping sideways. Banin shied and bolted from the camp, black mane and tail flying.

"I'm sorry. You weren't moving . . . I called your name and you didn't answer."

"I fell asleep on my feet. I don't believe it."

"Cho and I asked Vendle for a day's rest. He said no, that we've got to be in Epigos by Igote twenty-four. What's an Igote?"

Rifkind gave the boyo a lesson about Wet-lands time-keeping. Months were easy. Asheerans reckoned in months, though they gave them different names. Months begat weeks and weeks begat days, which Tyrokon understood, but in their cities, possibly even in council-ruled Epigos, Wet-landers mounted disks in their tallest towers and chopped their days into *hours*.

"What other surprises await me?" he asked incredulously.

"More than you can reckon. You'll get used to it; I did." Rifkind laughed. "And then it took a year or more to get used to being in the Asheera again."

Tyrokon shook his head. Rifkind guessed he was having second thoughts. She was having them, too. If he'd said the right words, she'd have split them off from Vendle's caravan, but he clung to his goals and she searched out Banin's saddle to sleep until she awoke.

A storm blew in after midnight. Great gobbets of icy rain striking leather and felt roused Rifkind just enough to realize that the boyos had erected the tent around her. She pulled her blankets tight again and returned to oblivion.

At dawn Vendle summoned everyone to his tent. The storm had peaked by then, but there'd be no traveling until it had passed completely. Rifkind had her day of rest and the Wet-landers broke out their dice, there being no better way, to their mind, to pass a stormy day than gambling. Rifkind warned the boyos to stay clear of Wet-lands games until she'd had a chance to teach them the rules and how men broke them.

Tyrokon accepted her advice and Cho resented it.

"I've never needed—or had—your teaching before and I won't need it now. I'm a grown man—a red-staff warrior. If there's learning to be gathered, I can gather it myself."

Rifkind didn't have the stamina for an argument. Besides, with no money to his name, there was a limit to the trouble he could get himself into.

5

Neither Rifkind nor Tyrokon needed Vendle's horn to know when supper was ready—the aroma drew them like moths to flame. Cho beamed when they crossed his path. He'd found someone to stake him in a game of sixes-and-sevens and, being on the receiving end of a lucky run of dice, had won himself a little purse of Wet-lands' coins. He unknotted the drawstrings. Rifkind laid a hand on his wrist.

"Not here."

Cho scowled.

"If you count your coins in front of the men you won them from, you're as much as saying you think you were cheated. That, or you're a fool in need of robbery."

Cho pulled his arm away. "Bloody Bright! You're jealous."

The attack was so far off the mark that Rifkind had to stifle a laugh before saying, "I'm telling you what you need to know if you're going to survive in the Wet-lands."

The boyo would have none of Rifkind's advice. He pulled Tyrokon aside and made a show of his winnings. Rifkind groaned inwardly. She'd have been better off telling him how to start a tavern-clearing brawl.

After supper they drew straws for the night watches. None of the Asheerans drew short straws, which meant Cho could introduce Tyrokon to the allure of dice. Rifkind retreated to their camp.

She knew exactly when the Bright Moon would rise. To be chosen by the Bright One was to know Her place at all times, even when She rested beneath the horizon. Dragging Banin's saddle away from the tent, Rifkind planted herself where she'd have an unobstructed view of moonrise.

I don't know what else I can do.

I did what seemed best. When I saw that I would become Mistress of Healers, I turned to Hamarach and he took my son into his tent. Cho had what I never had: a father he could face with pride, brothers who completed his life. I could not have done better and been Mistress of Healers. A choice had to be made—

The Bright Moon rose. Her light touched Rifkind's cheek. She closed her eyes and waited.

Thirty times or more, Rifkind sent students into the moonlight. Thirty times or more, she'd welcomed them back, with their glittering cheeks and listened, smiling, while they struggled to describe the indescribable. Undeniably, Rifkind was worthy of her title, but when Rifkind waited in moonlight, she got moonlight and nothing more.

In my day I was strong-willed . . . all right, beyond strong-willed. I was wild . . . but I served You. I gambled my life—I was young and didn't know better—but I served. I faced An-Soren and nearly lost my soul. I raised the Landmother and lost my future. I didn't know what to do, so I came home and—suddenly—there was a child with crippled legs. I took him as a sign. It was not the life I had imagined, but my imagination is wild, and I had renounced wildness.

I've been good.

And my son—the child of my wildness—hates me.

It does not seem right.

The Bright Moon climbed above the horizon. Silver-white light fell on Rifkind's face. It touched her cheek. By all that Rifkind had been taught and taught in turn, that touch should have been warm. It should have filled her with both peace and purpose. Instead she was cold, numbed and

aching, but she stayed her ground until the Bright Moon had risen so high
the light no longer touched her face.

It is not right.

A wise chief listens. Surely it is not too much to ask that You listen *to me . . .*

Moonlight fell behind the healer. Her face was in darkness. Muscle by
muscle, Rifkind willed warmth from her heart to her fingers and toes
Then, painfully, she dragged the saddle back to the camp.

The boyos were in the tent, already sleeping. They'd left a heap of blankets at their feet. With nomad expertise, Rifkind wrapped herself in wool
and fur and found space for herself between one softly snoring mound and
the tent's felt walls.

It is not at all right.

THE CARAVAN GOT UNDERWAY AFTER sunrise, still heading west toward the
Death Wastes. Day by day, the land had been changing. The broad, rolling
hills of Hamarach's holding had given way to steeper slopes and the occa-
sional upthrust of naked rock that Rifkind remembered from her long-ago
journey.

The steppes' grass had thinned to sparse gray-green blades emerging
from winter-killed straw and a thick-leaved ground cover that only the
camels would eat.

"We need grain," Cho observed as Tein mouthed the leaves and rejected them.

"Vendle's come this way before. He knows when to break out the grain."

Rifkind should have known better than to challenge her son, but the
words were out before she could stifle them. They scarcely needed an excuse to carp at each other. With neither warning nor explanation, Cho
handed the camel's rope to Tyrokon and clapped his heels against Tein's
flanks. He sped ahead of the caravan. Rifkind caught Tyrokon looking at
her from the corners of his eyes. She was on the verge of telling him to
hand her the lead rope and ride with Cho when her son came racing back.

"You've got to see this! There's a lightstorm ahead. A lightstorm like
nothing I've seen before!"

Tyrokon was game. Juggling reins and lead rope, he took off after Cho,
the camel bellowing at every step, but easily keeping pace. Banin, feeling

abandoned, struck out at a canter. Rifkind pulled him up. Lightstorms were nothing to gawk at. Cho should have known better. Prudent folk made a shadow and hid in it when a lightstorm roared—

Which reminded her that there was no roaring, no crash and rumble of continuous thunder along the western horizon. It would be a very rare lightstorm with no thunder. Prudent folk would still make themselves a shadow but Rifkind, rankled by her fruitless ordeal in moonlight, was suddenly not in the mood for prudence.

Banin caught her mood and leapt into a gallop. Braids, mane, and tail flying, they charged up the slope where Tyrokon and Cho waited. The crest offered a vista that was at least two days' journeying in breadth and, above the center of it, a swirling lightstorm.

Rifkind had seen more than her share of lightstorms and none of them matched the storm in front of them. The usual lightstorm was a single towering cloud, black on the bottom, dazzling white aloft, iridescent in between, and laced throughout with lightning. They were nasty tempests, but not so large that a good horse couldn't run crosswise from a storm's path. The Death Wastes storm was a broad wall of charcoal cloud, scarred with garish lightning, but lacking the iridescence.

"What did I tell you?"

Rifkind just shook her head. The sight of a storm so different from the others she'd encountered raised questions she'd never considered. What caused lightstorms? How long could one persist over a single place—because her gut told her the Death Wastes storm wasn't moving.

Unable to answer her own questions, Rifkind lowered her eyes and realized there was more to the crest than its view of the Death Wastes . . . or, rather, there was less. Not two strides ahead the crest came to a jagged edge. Looking right and left, north and south, as far as her eyes could see, it was as if some great weight had landed on the western side, tamping it down as much as thirty feet, revealing a cliff marked by horizontal layers in shades of brown and gray.

The Vogoska Crease.

With care, a person might descend the rock face, but it was an uncrossable barrier for their animals.

Tyrokon guessed Rifkind's thoughts when he said, "We'll have to turn north now."

Hoofbeats put an end to Rifkind's cogitation as Vendle's gelding joined them.

"You've spotted our storm," he called from a safe distance.

"You knew it was here?" Rifkind asked.

"As often as we've crossed, this storm has waited for us. Sure as the Crease for saying when to turn north."

"The same storm? It never blows off?"

"Can't say. What I say is, there's a storm waiting, 'cepting once."

Rifkind looked from Vendle to the storm. The caravaneer could be lying; he had the capacity, but he had no reason to lie about a lightstorm and seemed genuinely unsurprised by its presence.

"Can't be a good thing," Rifkind mused.

Vendle countered. "I tell you, there's naught to worry over. We hain't never had a storm east o' the Crease. It be easy traveling—sweet traveling now. Just follow the Crease, then follow the road. We be eight days' out of Epigos, ten, if we dawdle."

Vendle of Roce was done with dawdling. Sticking to a daylight schedule, he pushed hard while the sun shone. Riders were lucky if their feet touched ground twice between sunup and sundown.

Visions of grain flowed to Rifkind from Banin, grain and tired hooves. She patted his neck and assured him that there'd be grain when they stopped for the night. She made good on her promise, though not in the quantity Banin would have preferred.

The war-horse followed her while she collected winter-dried straw and the rare clod of sun-baked manure for the evening's fire. He was like a small child, pressing images of grain in delectable heaps against her mind.

Once, Rifkind caught a flicker of unexpected movement in the tail of her eye. She scanned the rolling hills, the scattered boulders surrounding the camp, seeking a source, but nothing moved, not even a ground squirrel. She touched Banin's mind—the war-horse's senses were in many ways sharper than her own—but his mind was fixed on grain. Returning to her collecting, her thoughts had circled back to the Death Wastes' lightstorm and what it might mean when a hue and cry erupted from the main camp.

By the commotion among the camels, some drover boy had lost control of an animal. At least, that was Rifkind's judgment until she spotted a handful of thin, dark streaks fly out from the boulders east of their camps.

Before her mind could say *arrows*, someone in the main camp began to scream.

Raiding a caravan—and Vendle's caravan had become the target of a raid—was not an inherently dishonorable act. But for the arrows, Rifkind might not have felt compelled to take sides against other Asheerans doing what Asheerans had always done. The arrows, though, changed everything. In the Asheera, a bow was strictly a hunter's tool, a food-maker, without honor when pointed at a man, any man, Asheeran or not.

Rifkind grabbed a handful of Banin's mane and vaulted onto his back. He sprang into a canter as the raiders launched another volley. One of the drovers went down with a scream and a string of panicked camels tore loose from their ground line.

Rifkind asked Banin for greater speed and he obliged.

Cho and Tyrokon had already claimed their weapons and were dashing toward the main camp. Tyrokon had his sword, but Cho had both his sword and his bow. Once honor had been broken, there was no reason not to return the insult in kind.

Rifkind kicked through her possessions; her sword, as luck would have it, was underneath everything else.

Banin remained beside her when Rifkind drew steel but he was a war-horse by breeding only. She hadn't trained him to use his horns against men; it hadn't seemed necessary while she was Mistress of Healers. She gave him a swat and sent him running from the camp.

Whooping like madmen, the raiders emerged from their hiding places. They'd slung their bows over their shoulders and drawn swords instead. There were seven of them—hardly a threat. Then a pack of mounted raiders boiled up, seemingly from nowhere, though Rifkind—who knew the tactics of raiding as well as she knew the art of healing—knew how easy it was to hide in the hollows of the deceptively flat Asheera, how wise to pin the caravan against the unscalable Crease they'd been following for several days.

This was no chance occurrence, not this far from a clan's wells. They'd been stalked by men who'd known exactly what they were about and where to find their prey.

In sheer numbers, the caravan had the advantage over the raiders, but most of the caravaneers were drover boys with neither weapons nor the skills to use them. Vendle's caravan faced doom as Rifkind sprinted toward the skirmish.

As she ran, she had time to measure exactly how long it had been since she'd fought to the death. A warrior who didn't practice wasn't a warrior, but the sword was comfortable in her hand, as if it had been days, not years, since she'd drawn enemy blood.

Without missing a step, she drew a long knife from her boot, to balance the sword in her right hand.

Her first enemy's attention was on the drover boys; he never saw his death coming. She ran him through, back to front, and kicked her sword free of his falling body.

In less than a heartbeat Rifkind had made a healer's assessment of an injured drover boy. He had a hacking wound to the neck and shoulder. Like as not, there was nothing she could do for him; the truth was, she didn't try.

Mounted raiders coursed through the camp, driving off camels, cutting down whoever got in their path. Rifkind caught a raider's eye; he raised his sword and charged. Rifkind used her knife to beat aside the sword as it descended, then brought her sword up, piercing the raider's flank. She felt the sword tip burst free between the raider's ribs, then, as the war-horse galloped on with a dead rider, her steel slipped free.

By then she'd selected her next enemy: another mounted raider who approached her with greater caution, greater determination. His bay war-horse was well-trained and he had mastery over it. The bay lowered his horns.

Only a fool would meet that charge . . . a fool or a healer. Rifkind shaped a single thought—*Up!*—and hurled it at the war-horse. With her thought in its head, there was nothing the raider could do to keep his mount's head down.

Rifkind held her ground against the charge. She crossed her knife and sword above her head to trap his blade as it fell.

For an instant, three steel edges ground together. Rifkind pivoted beneath the weapons. She hoped to disarm her enemy, but he clung to his weapon. Where his hilt went, his hand went, where his hand went, his arm followed, and his body after that, until he was overbalanced and tumbling.

Rifkind barely dodged his weight and weapon, but when he lay stunned on the ground, she pinned him there forever with a thrust between his ribs.

No one rushed at Rifkind after that third kill. She had to pick her enemy out of the swirling chaos.

Dodging a riderless war-horse and ignoring one of Vendle's seconds in a toe-to-toe battle, Rifkind looked for the camels. Raiding tactics targeted a caravan's camels: drive them away, strand the men, then pick them off. Already, Vendle had lost perhaps a third of his camels.

Rifkind chose a raider on a sorrel war-horse who'd just freed another four camels. She switched her weapons as she ran toward the sorrel and lobbed her knife at its rider's back. Her aim was off. The blade struck low, just above the kidneys, but that was good enough: The raider lurched in the saddle and lost control of his war-horse.

Panicked, the war-horse reared, dropping its injured rider. Retrieving her knife, Rifkind slit his throat where he fell.

Someone cried, "Away! Away, now!" and the raiders retreated into deepening twilight.

Rifkind sheathed her knife and grabbed the sorrel's reins. It was wild with fear and confusion and deaf to her empathy. One-handed, she struggled to climb into its saddle. Once there, she wasted more precious time exerting control. The raiders were gone by then; even the surviving archers had found loose mounts. Rifkind hauled the sorrel's head around as if it were a hornless gelding and banged her heels against its flanks.

"Not now!" another voice called, a voice she distantly recognized as Vendle's. "Let them go . . . or go after the camels."

As abruptly as it had kindled, the heat of battle drained from Rifkind's thoughts. She did not wrangle camels—though someone would have to, if Vendle was to salvage his precious cargo. Conveniently, she recalled the fallen drover boy of her first encounter.

She dismounted and left the sorrel with its reins dangling. If it had been well trained it would stand until someone claimed it; if not, well, that was no concern of hers. (Banin was nearby and unharmed; she would have known if he weren't.)

The boy hadn't died, but he would. The gouge was too deep and he'd lost too much blood for Rifkind's healing skills to save him. His eyes fluttered when she laid her hand on his forehead.

"Peace," she advised. He began to struggle and Rifkind realized she'd forgotten to speak in trade. "Peace," she repeated in a language he could understand. "The pain is fading."

She rose into her *tal*. Her touch was light. Mercy was a gentle art, gentler than healing, which was always a battle. The boy's *tal* was already loosening. It needed only the most delicate urging to slip free. Rifkind felt, rather than saw, the light that enveloped it.

"Is there anything you don't do?" Vendle demanded, and Rifkind realized she had an audience.

"Suffer fools. Heal camels. Where are the others?" she snapped, meaning the wounded.

Vendle led her to one of the seconds whose tunic was drenched in blood from a gut wound. She could heal that wound, with time.

"Any others?"

"None that need healing," Tyrokon said. He had a bloody bruise above his eye. Ugly and painful, it was nothing that warranted healing. "There's one among the raiders," he added, apologetically.

"Ours first," she said without hesitation. "Rig a travois. There's no way this man's riding a horse any time soon."

Vendle opened his mouth, as if to remind her that he was the one who gave the orders. "Mount guards," he commanded instead. "Find where they hid and see what they left behind. And round up those camels! Put out grain; that'll lure them."

Vendle had other orders, but Rifkind missed them as she rose into her *tal*. As healings were measured, this one was complicated, tedious, and inherently incomplete. The raiders knew what a healer could do and had smeared their weapons with ordure to thwart her. The sword damage wasn't the problem; it was the poisons the sword had introduced.

Rifkind did as much as she could and knew she'd have to do more. She descended with a sigh.

She was alone—except for her patient. The camp was busy. She didn't count them, but it seemed that most of the camels had been found and harnessed for moonlight travel. Vendle conferred with his able-bodied seconds around a small fire. There was no sign of his tent, no scent of a cooked supper. Rifkind went in search of her own packs where there was always a stash of dried jerky.

She needed to move and went in search of her dead. The drover's body had been carried off for burial—Wet-landers and Asheerans shared the same death customs in that regard. But digging graves in hard soil was backbreaking work and the honor had not been extended to the raiders. They lay as they'd fallen. As a healer, Rifkind closed a slain archer's eyes; as a warrior, she would do no more.

Her sword lay beside one of the raiders. She had no notion how it had gotten there and dark thoughts for each and every man who'd ignored it. As she retrieved it, the corpse of her second raider caught her eye.

He lay face-down and there was something odd about the way an empty scabbard rode across his back. No fall, not even a fatal one, should have hitched a man's sword belt up around his shoulders. With study, Rifkind realized that the dead raider hadn't worn a sword belt at all. He'd slung his sword as an archer slung his quiver. Had she seen him draw his weapon, she'd have seen him reach to his shoulder, not his hip, for the hilt.

As a warrior, Rifkind had always faced a dilemma: A full-sized sword required an extra thong to keep the scabbard from dragging; but a sword that was sized for her height robbed her of precious reach once the fighting started. The dead man's rig, with the hilt high and the scabbard across her back would solve a problem that had vexed her since childhood.

She undid the raider's rings and buckles, slid her sword into his empty scabbard, and slung the rig over her shoulders. As expected, it hung dangerously loose, but that was easily corrected. The important questions, the ones for which she sought immediate answers were: Could she draw her weapon and sheathe it afterward? The answer, with practice, was a resounding *yes.*

ON THE MOVE AFTER THE skirmish, Cho kept a length or two between his war-horse and his mother's. Banin had been fractious since they'd left the raiding ground. Rifkind's face had gone grim—grimmer than usual—with the effort of controlling him. Any time Cho got a twinge of envy, wondering what it might be like to share a deeper bond with Tein, he could shake if off by watching any healer—but particularly his mother—struggle to do with mind alone what was so much easier to do with a bitted bridle.

From a distance, it appeared that Banin had finally tired himself and Rifkind, too. His head was hanging and her shoulders were slumped, a posture made all the more noticeable since she had buckled herself into a dead raider's rig. Bad enough she'd had a sword sticking out of her saddle pack; now, suddenly, she was wearing it as if it were a quiver.

Cho didn't want to imagine how she'd manage to draw it but, sure as the Bright Moon shone down on them, she'd find a way . . . just as she'd found a way to kill.

"I can't get her out of my head," he admitted to Tyrokon. "I see her standing there, sword up, taking a charge."

Tyrokon grunted, which Cho took as agreement, then asked, "Did you—?"

"I couldn't," he confessed, grateful for the darkness. "Damn it all—I had my man . . . had him. He couldn't break my guard. I was better, and yet, I couldn't—"

"And I was lucky," Tyrokon admitted in the same confessional tone. "When I tried for a killing thrust, I laid open his arm . . . by accident . . . luck. He dropped his sword and ran. I—I went after him. That's when I saw her."

"We stopped, both of us. Like sheep. We stood there, letting our swords drag, because she'd let loose her war cry. Bloody damn Bright!"

"Did you see her cross her sword and knife?"

"I thought: *She's dead.* No way a woman—a little woman—could stand against a charging war-horse."

"Where did she learn to fight like that?" Tyrokon asked. "She made the war-horse balk, healer-like, and then she took his sword."

"Why didn't she go down? I outgrew her before I was ten and I couldn't have blocked that stroke the way she did."

"And she killed him."

"She killed four," Cho calculated. "Together, the rest of us killed three and wounded two more—not counting the ones that got away, like your man. She killed every one she faced, I think. She finally taught me a lesson. It's not about fighting. It's about killing. Next time, I kill."

6

After six days of struggle, Rifkind laid a hand on the brow of Vendle's gut-wounded second and felt him slip into eternity. A failed healing was doubly exhausting, first for the effort she'd put into keeping him alive, again for the despair she felt when she fell short. When Vendle didn't immediately assign a grave-digging detail, she gave him a glower that made him reconsider. Even so, the burial was perfunctory and Vendle soon had the caravan moving again.

Rifkind hauled herself to Banin's back. Her thoughts sank to the bottom of a mental well and stayed that way for the better part of a day and a night until, while she was staring at the ground, she noticed that grass grew on either side of the caravan but not beneath their feet.

"We've come to the road," she told the boyos. "We're near Epigos."

A bit later, they crested a hill and beheld the low, brown silhouette of the city. Rifkind would have called it a town, or a Gathering, for it looked to be about the same size as one of the seasonal camps where the clans came together. With each of Banin's strides the details became clearer: There was no wall, at least not around the town itself; there seemed to be a tall palisade in the middle of the town's western half. The palisade, and whatever lay within it, was the only structure of any size on that side. The rest of the half appeared to be low, rambling structures—stables and store-rooms, she guessed, with dirty walls and thatched roofs.

The east side was a jumble of roof lines, one or two of which ap-proached the palisade in height, though most were much lower. As they drew closer, a good many appeared to be Asheeran tents. Like any clan camp, Epigos was surrounded by its herds and, befitting its place between the steppes and the Wet-lands, there were also a few fenced-off squares where plants grew in tended rows.

There were other roads into Epigos, one from the southwest, another from the east, and, Rifkind assumed, a fourth that pointed north, into the Wet-lands. The roads they could see weren't carrying caravans, but isolated walkers and riders, one of whom headed straight for Vendle, conversed with him, then reined his horse about and headed back to the town at a gallop.

"What was that about?" Cho wondered.

Rifkind answered, "Epigos can see us coming, but they don't know who we are."

"Do you think Vendle told the rider about us?"

Neither Cho nor Rifkind had an answer for Tyrokon's question, but it gave Rifkind something to think about. She didn't have the sense that she was riding into a trap, merely the unknown, and that, with two boyos who'd never seen a building, much less a town, was worrisome enough.

When they were close enough that clothing had color and people had faces, Vendle motioned them to his side.

"You see that largish roof—the one with the vane atop? That be En-gelit's. That's where you wait. I'll come for you oncest I'm done with the Council. There're things I need to do first, so you be quiet till I come. You feed yourselves at Engelit's; they'll serve you there, but stay clear of the ale and wine. Your kind don't drink well. There's a watch up and it's no time for your kind to be causing trouble."

Rifkind shrugged off the slights. "Wouldn't we be better off staying with you?"

Vendle bristled. "You go to Engelit's."

"So, do we go to Engelit's?" Cho asked as they put a bit of distance again between themselves and the caravan.

Tyrokon answered with, "We shouldn't let him out of our sight. I don't trust him," which was the first time he'd said anything so blunt to Rifkind.

She wished he'd spoken up sooner. "Now's not a good time to start distrusting him. We've come this far, best we go along a little farther."

"He's planning something," Cho countered.

Rifkind didn't disagree. "Probably. If we keep our wits sharp, we won't be taken by surprise and a tavern's as good a place as any to get a feel for what we're into."

"What *I'm* into," Tyrokon corrected.

Rifkind had seen tougher towns in the Wet-lands, but Epigos, with its outer ring of Asheeran tents was like no other. The people who came out to watch the caravan's arrival were mostly Wet-landers with masked expressions. Men substantially outnumbered women and the only child she saw was a scrawny toddler that could have been a boy or girl.

Rifkind couldn't penetrate the emotions of most adults with her healer's empathy. The mark of adulthood was the creation of a psychic wall that hid a person's inner life. But children were all on the surface. She's hoped to learn a lot about Epigos from their naïve curiosity.

Within the ring of tents stood the buildings of Epigos, raw, but not quite new, as if they'd all been thrown up in a season or two. Every one of them could have done with a touch of color. A half-dozen men with a touch of color, the exact same shade of dusty blue to their tunics, swarmed around Vendle.

Livery, Rifkind thought and recalled how livery had appealed to many of the Wet-lands lords who'd loved nothing better than the awe that a cohort of identically clothed soldiers wrought on ordinary folk. Vendle had said there were no lords in Epigos, so it was his vaunted council that made the show.

The blue-clothed men escorted Vendle, with his caravan trailing behind him, through the palisade gate. There seemed to be no coercion on the soldiers' part, no resistance on Vendle's. Rifkind maneuvered Banin to see what she could of the courtyard the palisade enclosed. There was a good-sized central building that resembled nothing so much as a miniature wooden castle, but what truly captured Rifkind's attention were the many knots of men, all in dusty blue tunics and no few of them wearing their raven-black hair in long Asheeran braids.

"This city's mustered itself an army . . ."

In Rifkind's experience there were only two reasons to muster an army: protection or conquest. Conquest made no sense. The Asheera had nothing worth conquering; and as for conquering the Asheerans themselves, an army could squat over a well, but there wasn't an army big enough to squat over all the wells. So, Epigos's little army wasn't aimed at the Asheera, which meant its purpose was protection . . . of what? And with Asheerans among the ranks . . . from whom?

"There's more to Epigos than Vendle has told us. Let's visit Engelit's and see what we can learn."

There was no way to mistake the tavern. It was the largest, sturdiest construction on the east side of the town's solitary avenue. A full three stories high, it had slitted windows below its roof line and iron straps on its front door: more signs that Epigos had something to fear, something to hide.

They dismounted outside that formidable front door, leaving the warhorses ground-tied. Their camel was less reliable; Cho tied it firmly to a wooden post. Three stairs separated Engelit's door from the street. Rifkind ascended without a moment's pause and realized that the boyos had fallen behind. Glancing over her shoulder she saw the apprehension in their eyes. Their guard was down and their emotions were within reach of her healer's empathy. Never in their deepest nightmares had they envisioned a city—even a small, raw one like Epigos, a building, or a short flight of wooden stairs.

Bright Mother, was I ever so slack-jawed when I first left the Asheera?

The answer to that question was a resounding no. The same skills that powered her healing kept her centered in the midst of strangeness. The first time she had seen a city—a stone-built city, ancient and far more lively—she'd felt it as its citizens experienced it, and taken its novelties in stride.

There was little Rifkind could do for the boyos and nothing they'd appreciate.

Every head came up, every eye snagged on the Asheerans as they crossed Engelit's threshold. That in itself was not unusual when strangers entered a room. Rifkind strained her healer's senses to detect any threads of danger that might be weaving around them. She caught a sense of hostility that stopped abruptly: Whoever didn't like Asheerans knew what the silver in her cheek meant and knew how to retreat into his thoughts.

The best tables—the ones in the shadows with good views of the door and the bar—were taken by men who quickly went back to their soft-voiced conversations. With the remaining tables offering no advantage, Rifkind boldly selected one under the wagon-wheel chandelier. She pulled out a chair and watched in dismay as Cho threw his leg over the chair back, mounting it as if it were a war-horse.

"What?" Cho demanded. By way of an answer, Rifkind sat down in the accepted way. Cho's cheeks darkened, another dubious gift inherited from his fair-skinned father. "Oh, Bloody Bright."

Following Rifkind's lead, Tyrokon eased into a third chair.

A big-boned woman with pale eyes, loose blond hair, and a cinched bodice that made the most of an ample bosom sauntered over to their table. Asheeran women didn't show much skin, a combination of tradition and physical wisdom out on the parched steppes. The boyos had the wit not to stare, at least not for more than a heartbeat. The Bright One knew what they were thinking; Rifkind could have made a good guess.

"Last night's stew's three setas," the blonde said. "Four, with meat. We got west wine for another three. Home brew for one."

Cho blinked. He'd been gambling for copper setas and half-silver con-shas without knowing their worth. The prices seemed fair to Rifkind, though it had been years since she'd bought a tavern meal. She had a hefty purse sewn into her tunic and more secreted in her saddle: the savings of her Wet-lands years. It would be enough to feed the three of them and their livestock, too, for as long as it took them to get settled . . . assuming, of course, that Engelit's would accept a consha stamped with the profile of a Darian emperor who'd been dead for over twenty years.

"Stews with meat, all around, and home brew."

Rifkind was used to giving orders. She hadn't noticed that the tavern woman wasn't looking at her until the woman scowled. *So, that's the way of it: Epigos is a man's world* . . . The Asheera was, too, except for healers, and Rifkind, who was an exception, even among healers. She smiled her lazy smile—the one she used when she had a knife in her hand—and asked:

"How's your bread?"

"Good enough."

"A loaf, then, with the stews."

The woman headed back to the bar.

"They're *laughing* at us!" Tyrokon hissed when she was beyond earshot.

"And you've never laughed at a stranger? Ignore them."

The bread, when it arrived, was dark and day-old. The crust shattered when Rifkind tore it into fist-sized pieces, which she divvied up.

"Save a piece for the stew," she advised just before she bit into her share.

Asheerans ate with their hands: right hand to transport food from a common platter to a personal bowl, left hand from the bowl to the mouth. Bread, though unknown in the Asheera, was a hand-eaten food that the boyos warmed to quickly. Cho went so far as to grin as he tore into another chunk.

The home brew wasn't a problem, either. Mugs were mugs, whether sewn from leather or baked from clay. The brew itself was on the bitter side, but not unbearably so and the boyos, having nothing to compare it to, drank without difficulty or complaint. Then the stew arrived. Soup might have been a better description. Knuckle-sized chunks of carrots and leeks drifted in the thick, brown liquid. The promised meat was there, too, and a length of gray metal curving over the edge.

A spoon . . . because no one would think of eating soup with their fingers, at least not until it came time to sop up the last drops with a chunk of bread. And surely, after the chair, Cho would have learned caution from Tyrokon. He'd watch her use the spoon and absorb the lesson—

Not a chance.

With left-hand thumb and forefinger, Cho attacked his supper, going after the meat first. The soup was steaming hot; he jerked his hand back. The meat plopped into the bowl, sending brown splatters everywhere. Cho cursed vigorously and, at the other tables, snickers grew quickly into full-fledged laughter.

Cho's cheeks grew dangerously bright. His hand dropped below the table.

Rifkind had no time to think. She attacked, as was her reflex, but with healer's skills rather than steel. She ascended into her *tal* and exerted her will. It left her in heartbeat pulses: *Enough!*, *Calm!*, and *Quiet!*

Cho paled; he sat back in his chair as if struck. The folk around them fell silent, also. Tyrokon knew; if his eyes were any wider, they'd explode from his head. Cho, too, might have guessed. He shot his mother the evil eye, but, suffering under the weight of her will, it lacked force. For her part, Rifkind was light-headed. Imposing her will had been more exhausting than the most complex healing . . . and more effective than she'd dared hope.

She had a new weapon. Whatever else happened in Epigos, she'd have that forever.

She picked up the spoon and, after catching Cho's eye, scooped up a measure of meat and liquid. Reckless, but not foolish, her son matched her grip on the utensil and did the same.

7

"But Vendle said he'd meet us here," Tyrokon protested when Rifkind stood up from the table.

"We've had enough of dark rooms," she replied, which skirted her real concern: The force of her will wouldn't last forever and she didn't want to be in Engelit's when it wore off. "Epigos doesn't look large enough to get lost in. Vendle will find us."

With their war-horses and camel in tow, the trio ventured into the tent maze. They looked for the banners that would proclaim allegiance and found none. In turn, they were watched at every step by wary eyes.

"Where are the women?" Tyrokon asked.

Cho answered, "Hidden away."

Rifkind was inclined to agree with him. If there were any women. It was women's work to maintain the tents and hearths and, by the look of the tents and hearths around them, the work wasn't getting done. Every clan had its outcasts, men who'd come up against a clan chief and lost. Sometimes they found a way back into the chief's good graces; more often they disappeared. The fate of a man without a clan was no better than that of a horse without a herd.

Until Epigos?

Meeting the eyes that followed them, Rifkind could believe that the ragged tents of Epigos were home to outcast men. Tyrokon was not an outcast. He had his father's blessing . . . but how much would that matter here? Not only were the women missing, children were missing, too, and war-horses, jack horses, and sheep.

"Let's leave," Rifkind advised, and she was thinking of more than the tents. There was no way to settle Tyrokon in Epigos, no way that she could admit to his father.

Epigos was north. Glascardy, where Rifkind's dreams had impelled her—until Hamarach intervened—was west. Could she take the boyos with her to Glascardy? Should she? Or did honor and loyalty demand that she return to Hamarach first? They could sell the camel, now that they were beyond the Asheera, and make good time to Glascardy. Or the boyos could keep the camel and trek back to Hamarach on their own. They were old enough; they had the skills to make the journey.

"Healer!"

A woman's cry, came from behind. Rifkind spun around. With arms outstretched, the crier ran toward her from the perimeter, hopping and swaying with each stride as she favored her right leg. But it wasn't injury or pain that inspired the cry. Rifkind sensed a deeper panic and despair.

"Save me!" the woman pleaded when she was within arm's reach.

Rifkind caught her in an embrace. "I'm here." Already she had a sense of the woman's physical injuries: bruises—a lot of them. This woman had been in a fight, recently and more than once. Her limp came from a leg that, like Tyrokon's, had been weak since birth.

Healing bruises wasn't worth the effort and there was nothing Rifkind could do for the leg.

"What do you want?"

"Take me with you! Take me away from here."

Looking into the woman's eyes, Rifkind realized she'd misjudged the woman's age. Her face was hollow, her teeth mostly missing, but she was scarcely older than Cho and Tyrokon. It wasn't every man who cherished his wife the way Hamarach cherished Idi and her sister. Cruelty happened, but in a well-run clan, when it happened too often, the man was cast out.

Commotion followed the woman as men boiled out of the tents, led by one man in particular—a man as tall and broad as Cho with a stout, arm-length stick in his hand.

"Leave my wife to me!"

Rifkind couldn't do that. Pivoting around the now-terrified woman and confident that no Asheeran could ever be so lost in rage that he would strike a healer, she faced the charging husband with no weapon or armor save the silver in her cheek.

Neither blinking or flinching, Rifkind held her ground, even when the husband swung the stick at her head. She brought her arm up to block the blow. That should have been enough, but Rifkind hadn't recovered from the scattering of her will in Engelit's common room.

The force of the stick traveled down her arm, her spine, and to her knees, which buckled from the shock. More embarrassed than hurt, Rifkind tried to get her hands on the stick. The angle was bad. He drew back for another swing.

His wife screamed and ran, forcing him to choose between a standing fight and a chase. He chose the chase. Rifkind lunged for his leg as he surged past. It wasn't graceful or proud, but she brought him down and got control of the stick.

"The Bright Goddess says, honor your wife!" Rifkind snarled, raising the stick on him as he had raised it on her.

Any sense of triumph was short-lived. The wife-beater had friends who weren't afraid to come to his defense.

There were a few faces that Rifkind remembered from Engelit's; they'd figured out what had happened in the tavern and had an extra measure of ire in their snarls. Rifkind found herself using the stick as a defensive weapon, whirling it wide to keep the Epigots at a distance.

Behind her and beside her, Cho and Tyrokon came to her aid . . . with steel.

They were surrounded, outnumbered five to one, but Rifkind believed they could bash their way free, with a little help. Assurin and Tein were trained to defend their riders—a training that built on the stallions' instinct to defend what was theirs. Banin, though untrained, had that instinct and a tighter bond to excite it. Rifkind couldn't have driven him off, even if she could have spared the concentration necessary.

The war-horses didn't know—couldn't learn—the meaning of restraint. A strong rider might have pulled his war-horse back from a killing frenzy, but Assurin, Tein, and Banin had no riders and were wreaking havoc.

"Try not to hurt them," Rifkind shouted. "Just drive them back."

One of the boyos fell back against Rifkind, pushing her closer to the ring of angry men. She had no choice but to use the stick with offensive force, ramming the stout wood into the nearest gut, then smashing an end against a vulnerable nose. When blood sprayed from that second strike, Rifkind braced for a surge, but none came. Instead, the mob retreated one pace, then two, then it broke apart and ran.

The war-horses pranced a perimeter around their riders. They trumpeted victory, almost drowning out the energetic clanging sounds coming from the west side.

The palisade doors that had been closed since Vendle had gone his separate way opened, revealing a dusty blue cohort with swords drawn.

"Bloody Bright!" Rifkind swore as she threw down the stick.

In her mind, she could see a bad situation getting worse, much worse. There were bodies in the street, five that she could see; two of those smelled of death. They could claim self-defense, and hope they'd be believed, they could fight, or they could flee.

The cohort was on foot, the war-horses were within easy mounting distance. Finding Tyrokon on her right, Rifkind asked, "Stay or go?"

Tyrokon answered, without hesitation, "Go!" He whistled for Assurin.

Rifkind touched Banin's mind as she spun around quickly. "The woman—? The one who started all this?"

The last thing they needed was a battered woman riding double with them, but Rifkind wouldn't leave her behind—if she could find her.

The damned victim was nowhere to be seen. There wasn't time to look for her . . . or retrieve the damned camel. There was barely enough time to get mounted.

"Move it!" Rifkind shouted at her son, who stood with his back to her, arms hanging limp at his sides. "Cho! *Domhnall!*"

The boy didn't budge. Banin nuzzled Rifkind's arm. Why was she shouting when he was waiting, ready.

Rifkind grabbed the reins, found the stirrup, and swung up to the saddle. "Cho! Snap out of it!"

He didn't.

Tein was in reach. Rifkind caught the bay's reins and kneed Banin in Cho's direction. She gave her son a swat on the shoulder. He turned slowly, all the time in the world.

"What's the matter with you?"

Cho didn't answer, not directly, but from her perch in Banin's saddle, Rifkind could see that her son's sword had been thoroughly blooded. He wasn't the first warrior to freeze after making a kill; still, he'd picked an uncommonly inconvenient time to succumb. Rifkind struck him again, hard enough to make him sway.

"Mount up!" Rifkind thrust Tein's reins square in front of Cho's face. *"Now!"*

Stiff, but finally moving, Cho sheathed his sword and clambered into the saddle.

The dusky-blue cohort blocked the northern end of Epigos's street, so Rifkind reined Banin tight and made a southern run for freedom. The cohort was on their heels for a few strides, until the war-horses got their haunches under them. Their breed was renowned for its endurance and spirit, not its speed, but they were faster than men on foot, much faster in a sprint.

Sure as the Bright Moon watched from the heaven above, the council of Epigos had horses at its command, big Wet-lands horses and Asheeran jacks. They could order a pursuit, if it suited them. Rifkind kept Banin and the other two running south, then east of south until the animals were lathered.

Their water skins were with the camel and the Bright One knew where it was . . . probably in the hands of the Asheeran squatters or the town cohort. Either way, it wasn't with them and they could only wait out their sweat and thirst.

"Keep an eye out for rising dust," Rifkind advised.

Obligingly, Tyrokon stood in his stirrups. "I don't think we were followed."

"Can't be sure."

Cho was imitating a sack of grain thrown over a war-horse's back. Rifkind repeated her earlier question: "What's the matter with you?"

No answer.

"He's dead. You killed him . . . or he would've killed you. Make an end of it."

Cho blinked. He'd heard her, but he wasn't coming out of himself. Of all the complications Rifkind could have imagined, Cho freezing was the least probable—not Cho who won the Gathering's red staff whenever he contested for it.

"What did you expect?" she demanded.

Tyrokon, ever the peacemaker, tried to break the tension. "We need water, water and food."

That worked for Rifkind. "Give the war-horses their heads. If there's water out here, they'll scent it out. Look for trees. Where there're trees, there's water."

She was half certain the boyos would recognize a tree when they saw one for the first time.

"And food?"

"We'll have to forage. The Wet-lands are richer, thank the Bright One for that. You can hunt, can't you?" Rifkind asked her son. "You can do that?"

Cho's head dipped.

They pressed on, slower than before, eyes on the horizon looking for signs of pursuit or water. Tyrokon was probably right about the pursuit. Had they stayed, there'd likely have been a price to pay for the brawl and the killing, and the debt would still be there, if they returned to Epigos, but out on the greening grasslands between the sparse Asheeran steppes and the Wet-lands' cultivated fields, there was no one to care what they'd done in town.

The war-horses pricked up late in the afternoon and brought their riders to a water pool not long after sunset. Rifkind surveyed the ground.

"We'll camp there," she decided, pointing to the highest of the nearby hills. "If it suits you," she said to Cho, "you can linger here with your bow. Something edible's sure to pay a visit during the night."

"Shouldn't we keep moving?" Tyrokon asked.

"We're close enough to the Wet-lands. Lightstorms won't bother us and the nights here are cloudy as often as not. We're daylight folk from now on."

CHO HADN'T AGREED TO HUNT meat, just then, the thought of *killing* blanked his mind. And he hadn't agreed to wait alone beside the pool, but as soon as he was alone, some of his tension eased. As it did, he staggered into the tall grass—so different in smell and texture from the stubby, tough grasses of the Asheera—doubled over and emptied his gut. It had been the better part of a day since he'd eaten *stew*; there wasn't much left in his stomach beside hot juices that burnt his throat and sent him to the water, which was cool, if not sparkling clear.

Bloody Bright, he thought and then, because he was, indeed, alone, he said it aloud: "Bloody damn Bright!"

He couldn't get the image of a dying man off his eyes, couldn't get the feel of his sword sliding home between a pair of ribs off his right arm. The dark eyes of a stranger had glistened with tears that would never be shed, then faded to death. If Cho relaxed even a muscle, he returned to that moment, face-to-face with a man old enough to be his father and armed with a knife that was no match for a good sword.

"He was coming for me!"

One moment, they had been walking toward the wide track down the middle of Epigos. The next, some crazy woman was clinging to Rifkind. And the moment after that, they were surrounded. It was Rifkind's fault; it had to be. She'd done something—

She'd done what a healer was expected to do. She'd never even drawn her sword.

Shame on top of death guilt was more than Cho's shaky gut could bear. He made another dash for the grass.

"I'm strong!" he insisted, desperately, from his knees.

What he could not admit from his tongue to his ears was the confusion—the mix of sheer rage and utter humiliation—that went with the knowledge that Rifkind, his *mother*, had witnessed his weakness. He could bear Tyrokon. He'd seen Tyrokon in agony, Tyrokon writhing on the ground after a bad fall. They had no secrets, he and Tyrokon, but Rifkind had seen him in a frozen panic.

And then she'd left him alone to confront his memories. She was wise; Cho had to give her that. He *was* grateful for the privacy. In his heart of hearts, he was grateful, but in the places that ached, he seethed.

8

Their tent was with the camel, wherever it had gotten to, along with spare clothes, their cooking utensils, and the big water skins that had kept them going near the Death Wastes. Fortunately, the plains near Epigos were enjoying mild weather and there were ways to cook meat that didn't involve pots or spits.

"We'll do all right," Rifkind assured Tyrokon as they both scavenged fuel for a small fire. "I didn't like what I was seeing there in Epigos even before the mob broke loose."

"I was a fool to believe in Vendle's promises."

"Everyone's a fool, sooner or later."

Tyrokon's eyes were haunted, not as badly as Cho's, but sobered by the world beyond his father's wisdom.

"We'll decide what to do next in the morning," she said as gently as she could, "after we've had a chance to sleep and dream."

Not long after full dark, Cho returned empty-handed from the water pool. Rifkind was disappointed, but not entirely surprised. Knowing there was nothing she could say that would not make a bad situation worse, she ignored his silence.

They ate what little they'd had stashed in saddle packs and pouches, envying the war-horses who were having a good feed on the tender grasses of a Wet-lands spring. Then, because there was little to say and no inclination to say it, they bedded down.

Rifkind dreamt of Ejord Overnmont. His lips moved though she couldn't read the words he formed. He turned away and faded. In the dream, Rifkind pursued him all the way to the gray stone walls of Chatelgard, the Overnmont fortress high in the Glascardy mountains. The great iron-strapped doors were closed tight and all a dreamer's magical resources could not get her inside.

Rifkind awoke, exhausted by her fruitless dreams, in the cold hour before dawn. Quiet as an ant, she unwound from her blankets and sought refuge in meditation a hundred yards or so from the camp. The Bright One had gone to rest; Vitivar, Her rival, rode high in the heavens—not a good time for Rifkind to ascend into her *tal* to cleanse away the residues of her dreams. Rifkind absorbed herself in simpler, practical questions: What would she do next, where, and with whom? When she had her answers, she began redistributing the gear they'd brought out of Epigos and, doing so, awakened Tyrokon.

"What are you doing?"

"Separating out everything I won't need and you might."

"Might what?"

Tyrokon, never at his best in moments between dreams and thoughts, had the presence of mind to put an elbow into Cho's back. Cho came awake with a start. He rolled to his feet, a knife in his hand. Rifkind was impressed.

"What's the cause?" the rusty-haired boyo demanded, not yet ready to sheathe the knife.

"She's leaving."

Cho's expression froze. He didn't need to ask another question, not aloud.

"It's simple enough," Rifkind said. "Epigos didn't work. There's no place for you there"—she looked at Tyrokon—"there's no running away, either.

You, Hamarach, and Izakon are going to have to solve Asheeran problems in the Asheera. If you ride south and east from here, you'll come to clans you know. You'll get to Hamarach before Vendle can poison the well with caravaneer lies."

Neither boyo spoke.

"Oh, come now—south and east. You *were* paying attention?"

"Bloody Bright—" Cho began, until Tyrokon cut him off with the question:

"Why aren't you coming with us?"

"I promised your father I'd ride with you to Epigos and take its measure on your behalf. That's done. It didn't go as you hoped and it's time to move on. I've had another destination all along—Glascardy."

"Glascardy," Cho repeated. "Overnmont land. My father's land."

Rifkind growled, "We settled that. Don't start it up again."

After a long heartbeat, Cho finally sheathed his knife.

"Maybe I can find a place in Glascardy," Tyrokon said.

"If you thought Epigos was different—Glascardy's all rock and mountains. The mountain-folk homes are made of stone—"

"Caves."

"No, cut and carved stone. You belong under open sky, Asheeran sky."

"I've left the Asheera."

"Vendle will find Hamarach. The Bright One knows what he'll say, but it won't be the truth, won't be anything to your favor. You need to get there first with the truth."

"What's the truth? I was wrong to trust Vendle. I failed; there's the truth. Doesn't matter what I tell my father or what Vendle does. The truth doesn't change. I'd sooner ride with you to Glascardy and hope for something better than return to my father with my tail between my legs. Glascardy can't be worse than Epigos."

It could, but there was no way to convince Tyrokon of that, and then Cho entered the conversation.

"By what you've said about the Overnmonts, there's always a place for a man who knows his steel."

Rifkind blinked. She couldn't answer that without disparaging Tyrokon, so he did it for her.

"I'd be no good as a fighting man, but they'd have horses, wouldn't they? I could always take care of their horses."

A chief's son with a shovel and a steaming wheelbarrow? Rifkind shook her head. "South and east—"

"No, we're coming with you to Glascardy," Cho said firmly, drawing a stare from both Tyrokon and Rifkind.

"No."

"You can't stop us."

"I said *no*. Go back into the Asheera. Glascardy is mine. I was headed there before Hamarach asked me to change my direction. Glascardy is far from here. Two months' journey, maybe more."

"We'll follow you."

"Don't be foolish. You don't know the way—the way of the land or of the people."

"Is it my fault that I don't know the ways of my father's people? What are you going to do? Kill us to keep us from following you?"

"Of course not."

"Then it's settled: We ride for Glascardy, with you or behind. I can track you, you know I can."

Rifkind rose from her knees. It came to her, from that part of her mind where dreams and intuition dwelt, that she should have foreseen this. "There is much you don't know about the Wet-lands," she warned.

"Then teach us. Two months is a long time." When Rifkind didn't immediately answer, Cho added, "You *owe* me a chance to see my father's life."

Wearily Rifkind began the familiar refrain: "Ejord Overnmont is—"

"Somebody was and that somebody was not born in the Asheera!"

"All right. All right, we'll ride for Glascardy . . . together. But you do as I say."

"Done," Cho decreed with a rare show of enthusiasm.

With no tent and few provisions, their camp was easy to break. Come early afternoon, they crossed the road that connected Epigos with the Wet-lands' interior, or exterior, for the Wet-lands—as Rifkind had explained in a map she drew from memory in the mud surrounding a mid-morning water pool—were a nutshell around the Asheera. They were as thick as ten days' ride in some place, considerably thinner in most, and pierced by roads that put the Epigos roads to shame.

"When will we travel such roads?" Tyrokon asked.

"Not until the end. We can go faster through the grass."

She did not add that throughout most of Daria—as the Wet-landers called the greater land beneath their countries, provinces, and cities— Asheerans were scarcely real. Children were sent to bed with warnings— *Be good or the Asheerans will carry you off.* In Darian eyes, Asheeran men were demons and a woman like herself was not a healer but a witch, always feared and sometimes persecuted.

If Rifkind had thought a recitation of the risks would have discouraged the boyos, she'd have recited herself hoarse. Instead, she rode in long silences until the sun was nearing the horizon.

With the prospect of exploring the Wet-lands filling his mind, Cho managed to shrug off the death guilt he'd carried out of Epigos. While Rifkind and Tyrokon tended the camp, he took his bow, went hunting. He came back just before sundown with a winter-scrawny coney, a gray-feathered bird, and excitement sparkling in his eyes.

"I've seen your stone tents!"

"You stayed clear?" Rifkind asked, giving a closer look at the bird slung over her son's shoulder. She wasn't a great authority on domestic fowl, but it didn't look as though Cho had raided a farmer's coop.

"Clear of what?"

"The people, the stock. Every man's a clan here. Everything costs money, if you didn't grasp that yesterday."

"There wasn't anything to raid. The stone tent was empty."

"The people were inside—"

"No, it was abandoned. No one, nothing. The ground around it was open and muddy, but there weren't any tracks. No one had come or gone in a good while."

Cho had a tracker's eye and the wit to interpret what he saw, but he'd have to have gotten close, too close, to see that the mud was untrampled.

"We don't want more trouble, Cho. If we come to homesteads, we'll pass wide. Hospitality's not sacred here."

Tyrokon spoke up, "How far? I'd like to see a stone tent."

"Not far . . . if we ride."

"Don't be foolish."

They weren't children; she couldn't command them with an adult voice. They weren't her apprentices and she wasn't a chief whose word was law, so Rifkind watched them go. They asked her to ride with them and Banin was eager to go. She picked up the coney instead and gutted it with vengeance.

The meat was on a withy spit and the boys had been gone long enough for Rifkind to seethe with a mixture of anger and worry before Banin's head went up and he called a greeting.

Tyrokon sprang down from Assurin's back, a large undecipherable object in his hand. "Look what we found!"

"Didn't I tell you to stay away?"

"It was abandoned, Rifkind. No one had lived there for a year or more; animals had denned in the corners. This belonged to no one."

He held out what became a cook pot once she saw it correctly. A pot would be useful as they journeyed to Glascardy. She'd have taken it herself, if she'd ridden with them, if she'd agreed that the homestead was abandoned.

"It's not that the Wet-lands are more dangerous than the Asheera, they're different. What you've known all your lives won't help you."

Cho had a retort for that: "You survived."

"I was lucky."

"The great Rifkind . . . relying on luck?"

Before Rifkind needed to respond to that provoking question, Tyrokon asked, "Why would anyone have abandoned their home and left most of their belongings behind?"

That was an easier question to answer. "Plague. Vendle said it scours the land every winter."

"What about their healers?"

"No healers. They pray to their gods—Mohandru was their favorite when I left and growing stronger. He's the *weeping* god and his priests have the hearts of the poor and the ears of the lords. The only healing is what the gods will and what the women can provide with their herbs. Healing—true healing—is witchcraft here and witchcraft's forbidden. Oh, the lords and priests tolerate a bit of healing, a bit of witchcraft mixed with the herbs, but nothing too much, nothing that would diminish Mohandru's gifts."

Not surprisingly, Tyrokon's jaw hung open and Cho asked, "What kind of god is that?"

"A god who weeps and suffers for his worshippers and expects his worshippers to weep and suffer for him."

"I wouldn't worship such a god!"

"You wouldn't have to. I can think of a dozen other gods, including the Bright One. She's worshipped here, but only by girls and young women before they're married. There's a god of nothing but storms and war—Brel. Mohandru's a new god, a risen god, they call him: an avatar who once walked the world as a man. The plague will have worked in Mohandru's favor. A god who rewards suffering always does well when life gets hard."

Tyrokon found his voice. "Why?"

"Because when the suffering's done and death's come, a new life awaits, a perfect life."

"They don't die?"

"They die, all right. Their new life is *beyond* this life, another land that can only be reached through death. The more someone suffers, the better their new life will be . . . but it's all perfect."

"That makes no sense," Cho declared.

"It does, if you're born to it, I guess."

"If I'd been born to it," Tyrokon said thoughtfully, "I'd never have walked, would I?"

"But you'd be rewarded for your suffering. Your life *beyond* would be perfect beyond compare. The peasants and the poor worship Mohandru because he promises that their next life will be better because of the hardships they endure. The lords worship Mohandru because it gives them an excuse."

Cho asked, "Does Ejord Overnmont worship this Mohandru?"

"The Overnmonts didn't put much stock in gods, or they wouldn't have befriended me. I suppose if Ejord worships any god, he worships Brel—during the war he made the sacrifices all the soldiers did. But with lords, even with Ejord, I was never sure how much was pure worship, how much was show. A lord has to believe in himself, just like Hamarach."

Tyrokon came quickly to his father's defense. "He worships the Bright One."

"He honors Her. It's not quite the same," Rifkind replied quickly and immediately began to wonder if she weren't guilty of the precision of logic. Did she truly worship the goddess whose mark she bore on her cheek or did she merely honor the beliefs of others?

With her thoughts pulled in private directions, the conversation failed for want of answers to the boyos' endless questions and the little camp was quiet while meat sizzled on the spit.

9

The Asheera turned green each spring but the green of an Asheeran spring could not compare to the many shades and textures of green—grasses, bushes, and trees—that surrounded Rifkind and the boyos as they made their way north to northwest around the roughly circular continent. It was the season of abundance, of birth and—for hunters—of easy kills.

"I've thought it through," Cho said one evening when he returned to the camp with his bow over one shoulder and the day's kill over the other. "I've decided why Wet-lands prey is always born in pairs. That way there's one for the mother to raise and another for the wolves."

"And for us," Tyrokon observed.

He held out a hand for the kill. Tyrokon had become the middle man: He didn't hunt with Cho and he didn't challenge Rifkind's mastery of the cook-fire, so he'd become their butcher. He arranged the carcass on the ground before flaying it. Rifkind called him off before he'd made the first cut.

"Where did you find this one?" she asked her son.

Cho rolled his eyes. "Where I've found all the others: grazing in the grass."

"Not near a homestead?"

"You said, stay away, so I've stayed away. Why?"

"This one isn't a fawn, it's a calf, a cow calf. *Cows* don't roam free. They're homestead beasts. There're people around here."

"Were," Cho corrected. "There was a place but it was dead—empty— like all the others. The *cow* was loose and free."

Rifkind rubbed her forehead, as if the soothing gesture could touch her mind. They'd come upon a half-dozen or more homesteads—more, when she counted the ones only Cho the hunter had seen—and not one of them had been occupied. By the looks of things, there were simply no people left in the borderland.

She'd thought the plague the worst thing imaginable when it had burnt through the clans ten years' past. Fighting it with every healing trick she knew or could imagine had taken Rifkind and her sister healers to new depths of exhaustion. She'd lost more clansmen in a single winter than she'd lost in all the years before or since, but the healers together had beaten it. They'd learned its names and its hiding places and learned, too, that they could not wait until the disease appeared.

When plague emerged, which it did each winter as the clans came to their hard-weather ground, a healer did what she could for the suffering. Her greater energy went into laying hands on the healthy, because among the apparently healthy, there would always be a few whose bodies harbored the illness and who would spread it, if a healer did not call it out.

In her head, Rifkind should have known that it had to be worse in the Wet-lands. No amount of herbs or compassion could substitute for a healer's goddess-given skill. She reconsidered the dreams that drew her toward Glascardy. Yes, she'd considered the possibility that her old friends might have died, but her mind's eye had not seen them dead of the plague, pocked and wasted, with blood oozing through their skin like sweat.

"Are you all right?" Tyrokon asked.

Rifkind shook the grotesque images away. "We need to travel faster. There's enough meat here for three days, maybe four, and the Bright One's full-face. We can ride into the night. You haven't forgotten how?"

The boyos exchanged glances.

"The sooner we get there," Cho agreed as Tyrokon made the first cut.

When they'd fed like wolves, Rifkind left the camp for her nightly med-

itation. With her newly sharpened understanding of the plague's devasta-
tion, there was an extra urgency in her devotions but no response from her
goddess.

Banin surprised her with a soft nuzzle against her neck. His concerns—
Tired? Edgy? Need to run?—weighed against Rifkind's thoughts. She
scratched the endlessly itchy places where his horns erupted. The trek had
matured her war-horse. He took himself more seriously and paid closer attention to her desires, her moods. He'd put on muscle and his neck had
filled out; he'd be testing himself against Assurin and Tein before long.

"I'll have to start thinking of you as a stallion," she said, grateful to be
thinking of anything other than plague.

The dark-gray war-horse, shimmering steel in the moonlight, tossed his
head and pranced in place, wanting his rider, wanting to run, reminding her
that there was a time for fruitless prayer and a time for freedom.

Seizing a fistful of mane, Rifkind vaulted easily to his back. She pressed
a leg against his flank, a hand against his neck, and a vision of the northeast
horizon where Cho had killed the calf into his mind.

Moonlight had absorbed all the greens and browns from the landscape.
What it left was shrouded in shades of black and silver. Sharp, regular an-
gles betrayed the homestead and the hands of those who'd built it.

The fence that separated the yard from the grassland was intact, but the
gate was open, the house door, also, skewed on one hinge. A pair of windows gaped; the shutters that could have covered them leaned against the
dark wall as no homesteader would have left them.

Cho had the truth of the place, then: dead empty.

Rifkind eased to the ground. She gave Banin leave to nibble the grass
near his hooves, but enjoined him from wandering. Someone had made a
good start with a part-sod house and sturdy outbuildings. A half-dressed
scarecrow, looking no worse for the winter, stood guard over a plowed garden that still showed its furrows. Rifkind looked for the plow and found it
propped inside a three-sided shed. Beyond the plow stood a wagon, nothing fancy, but large enough to have brought the homesteader and carried
him away again, if he'd had a mind to leave.

Righting the door, Rifkind stepped into the house. She waited for her
eyes to separate the details—a table, a hearth, a churn, bowls, and other

signs of Darian life—from the darkness. A steep-sided box lay beside the hearth—no, not a box, not merely a box, but a rocking cradle, empty, of course. In the farthest corner, a roped-together bed spilled its mattress onto the beaten earth floor.

Cloth, her mind said. *Cloth and wadding* . . . but there was more that her eyes discerned, that her mind would not put names to . . . and she a healer who could put a name to injury and disease. Cloth there was, and wadding, also *bone* and *gristle.* That roundish lump—that was *skull* with *scalp* and *hair* still attached. And beside it, an *arm,* a *hand.*

Rifkind had walked the aftermath of battlefields. She'd seen the damage steel could do in the hands of a kill-or-be-killed soldier, but this was worse. This turned her stomach.

What had this family done to merit the rending of their bodies? What manner of man would wreak such damage on those who could not have been a threat to anyone?

Then it came to her, in a wave of relief: no man. Plague had come to this house to slay the farmer and his kin in their beds and animals had followed, and animals could not be held accountable for mistaking man for meat.

This is what comes of exalting a god who weeps and makes a virtue of suffering. Better a god that's deaf to one that weeps—

Her thoughts snagged: A deaf god, or a deaf goddess?

How can You let these things happen? Rifkind demanded, opening her mind to the moonlight. *You and all the others. What good are You?*

I've gathered the young women and taught them Your ways. I've sent them to You for blessing and sent them back to their clans. I heal, I teach, I bend my will to You . . . and to my clan, my chief. And this *is what I find. If I lived a hundred years and trained a thousand healers, I could not prevent this. Why ask me to teach and heal, if this is what remains?*

Unstrung, like the bones before her, Rifkind sank to her knees and covered her eyes.

I've reached the end, she thought for herself. *No more teaching. No more healing. I've gone back to the sword, but the sword is a young man's life and I feel old all over. Even my dreams are tired old things: remembered faces I'm more than a little afraid to see again.*

Turn around or forge ahead, it makes no difference.

I'm made of memories and habits, nothing more. I used up the parts that were me years ago. I gave myself to the Bright One, but now I've nothing left to give. Cho does not need me. Tyrokon may think he does, but he doesn't. Without me, they'd return home. Without my emptiness, I would have peace—

"I did not ask you."

A voice—a woman's voice speaking a language Rifkind had not expected to hear again, the words of her birth clan—came from behind. It raised the hairs on the healer's neck but did not quite paralyze her. With deliberate care, Rifkind lowered her hands. She knelt in the shadow her back created. Around her the light was silvery and brilliant.

"Forgive me," Rifkind began, because it seemed wise, after so many years of silence, to begin with an apology.

"There is nothing to forgive." The voice was rich and resonant, more like a man's, though indisputably a woman's.

"I did not mean to disturb You."

Laughter, like the tinkling of bells and a deep gong brought together in harmony. "I believe that you did."

"May I stand? May I face You?"

"Why not? You have before."

I'm older now, wiser—I hope.

The light shone from the goddess's face and hid any mortal features that might have lurked there. Within and behind the light draperies of deeper silver shimmered in pale patterns that generally matched the cuts of Rifkind's own garments. Her boots were sable; Her long, braided hair was the same shade. Her hands were bright silver, like a fresh-minted consha. This was not the goddess Rifkind remembered from their earlier encounters, who had been more like a living statue carved in a Darian style, yet she did not doubt for a heartbeat that she stood before her goddess.

Memory, after all, was a tricky thing.

"How may I serve You?"

"As you wish. Or not at all."

"Not at all? What have I done wrong?" The possibilities were endless and crowded Rifkind's skull to bursting. "I have lived to honor You. If I have failed, it was not for want of trying."

More laughter. "Very trying."

"Tell me what to do, and I will do it."

"Rifkind—*child*—your life is your own. It is not for me to tell you what to do. That time is passed."

"Passed?"

A sense of dread filled Rifkind. She'd seen too much death in battle and as a healer to truly fear it, but she did not want to die.

"You had a destiny, yes: The last in a long chain of destinies that returned Leskaya's Heart—"

The Heart was the great ruby Rifkind had inherited from her mother. It had fired the duel between herself and the dark sorcerer, An-Soren, and been consumed when he died.

"Each link in that chain lived only long enough to pass the Heart to the next destiny. Each link passed with grace and gratitude. None survived, until you. It was not—*anticipated*. The destruction of the Heart changed your destiny in ways unforeseen."

It was hard to tell with the light, but it seemed that the Bright One's shoulders rose, then fell.

"I was supposed to *die*?"

"Gods can bestow a destiny, but destiny—fate—is the greater power. Yours was misjudged. You went on . . . went on to raise the Landmother. That was two great destinies bound to a single soul. Destiny is death, Rifkind. The destined soul burns bright and fast. It consumes itself, yet you survived even the Landmother."

Rifkind struggled to understand her goddess's words. "Do I still have a destiny?"

"None that I would claim. None that any god would claim. You're free, Rifkind, free as no soul has been since souls began."

"Free? Is that what You've come to tell me, that I have no destiny? That I'm free to die?"

The light rippled. "You've been free since the Landmother subsided. Everything you've done has been your will alone. If you choose to die, then die you will."

"I did not *choose* to become Your Mistress of Healers."

"You most certainly did. *I* did not ask it of you."

"After Domhnall died and I followed the path You laid before me. I returned to the Asheera and became what I was meant to be: Your healer, Your Mistress of Healers."

"You took the easy way."

"I did not." Rifkind bristled. "I could have done anything; instead, I followed the path You laid before me when You granted me Your silver crescent. All I've asked for is a smile in the moonlight, a sign that what I've done pleases You. I've *begged* for a glimpse of Your majesty and now—now You tell me I've taken the easy way. Why now? Why tell me that now?"

"Because if you choose to die, you will die. That is what it means to be beyond destiny, beyond two destinies. Even gods have conscience, Rifkind, and I do not choose to have you on mine. You are a great healer, a great Mistress of Healers, but the easy path has weakened you to the point of death. Seize your life for yourself, Rifkind. Don't hide behind me."

"Hide? Hide! Who's been hiding? Every night! Every night since I returned to the Asheera!"

A SHAFT OF VAPORY LIGHT bent from the moon to the abandoned homestead Cho had dutifully ignored while hunting their supper.

"Do we go down there?" Tyrokon asked from Assurin's saddle.

The boyos had gone for their war-horses moments after Rifkind left. Cho had guessed her destination. When they crested the final rise, the homestead had been dark, quiet, and Banin was too busy cropping grass to notice their arrival. They'd been on their way down when the light shaft had suddenly appeared.

"Bloody Bright, no," Cho replied.

The light radiating from the homestead's door and windows, through the cracks in its walls and roof, brightened until there was color in the night before it faded to shades of silvery gray again. As the light dimmed, they could hear Rifkind shouting, though they couldn't distinguish her words.

"Do you think—?"

"Don't know. Don't want to find out."

10

Rifkind understood irony.

She could find humor in the demolition of cherished notions, provided hers were not the notions being demolished. Awakened from a sound sleep and asked about freedom, she would have answered, without hesitation, that freedom was a precious gift. Given a moment to rub her eyes and gather her wits, she might have agreed that destiny was a burden and freedom from destiny—any destiny—was good for the mortal soul . . . except when hers was the soul that had been freed from its burden.

All those years, Rifkind thought with a vehemence that brought Banin's head up. *How* dare *She? How dare She leave me in ignorance? All those times I sat before the rising moon . . . waiting for some sign that She approved of what I did. She* knew *and wanted nothing to do with me. A reward. She called it. I'd fulfilled my destiny and* freedom *was my reward! What freedom? My goddess abandoned me . . . turned Her back on me . . . let me pour my life into Her service when She no longer cared whether I lived or died!*

That, of course, was a lie.

The Bright One had ridden down a shaft of moonlight precisely because the goddess had feared Rifkind was losing faith with life itself; but the goddess had been wrong—which said something about a goddess's power.

Rifkind was far too stubborn to have ever thought of cutting short her life.

She didn't want me on Her conscience. I only have Her *word. Why should I trust Her word now, after all these years?*

The road that the Asheerans followed was bare earth, studded with rocks and pocked with the muddy remnants of earlier rain showers. Banin picked his way carefully, avoiding water whenever he could, even if that meant breaking the rhythm of his stride.

Rifkind should have been paying attention—would have been paying attention if she hadn't been so intent on nursing her goddess grudges—when Banin stretched his stride over a puddle and caught a rock instead. The rock shifted beneath his hoof and he stumbled, not badly enough to hurt himself, but enough to send Rifkind lurching forward in the saddle.

Mind yourself! Rifkind thought, with the edge she'd honed while thinking about the goddess.

Her thoughts packed a punch, which landed hard in Banin's mind. The war-horse shoved back and threw his rider out of his mind. He nearly threw her off his back at the same time. Rifkind's hand dropped to the pommel, her seething reverie shattered. Immediately, she stroked his neck, hoping to reassure him—to apologize—with a gentle touch.

Banin was having none of her. His head dropped and, squealing protest, he pulled away from her hand as much as any animal under saddle could escape its rider.

Sweet, Bright Mother—the invocation came reflexively to Rifkind, and without a whiff of irony—*What have I done?*

She was out of the saddle in a heartbeat, standing in the mud where Banin could see her. His eyes were distant, not familiar or welcoming. The war-horse had sealed himself behind a wall of instinct: another unexpected accomplishment. His wall was a flimsy thing compared to the defenses a healer mounted to protect herself. Rifkind could have blown through it . . . and managed only to pile stupidity on top of foolishness.

"I'm sorry," she said in the ordinary way, rubbing down his long nose.

"What's the problem? Is he lamed?"

Tyrokon's voice on Rifkind's right side. She hadn't heard him ride up, as ride up he must have done. For days now, he and Cho had been riding in her wake. That was how sour she'd become: not even Tyrokon was comfortable beside her.

Rifkind scratched the hairy whorl between Banin's horns as she straightened. He didn't pull away, but neither did his wall come down. Perhaps what had been thrown up by instinct was more than his animal intelligence could undo.

"No."

"What happened?"

I was a fool. I've been a fool since my goddess appeared before me to tell me that I was free. I should have told you right then, you and Cho both. I pushed you away, and now I've done the same with Banin. I'm sorry—

The confession was there for the speaking, at least until Rifkind swallowed it. In lieu of confession she offered a lie that was not utter falsehood, merely misdirection:

"He doesn't like the mud."

"We could go upland."

They could. For the last several days they'd been riding the flanks of increasingly impressive hills—the foothills of Daria's white-capped western mountains, Glascardy's mountains where Rifkind hoped to find Ejord Overnmont. Rifkind didn't know what the boyos thought of mountains; conversation didn't get that far (she had a better idea of their opinion of rain, but that was from overhearing the complaints they made to each other). Rifkind hadn't said anything about the mountains, but she studied them hourly. If just one of the distant mountaintops would match her memories, Rifkind would know where to turn and what paths to take through terrain that was not as forgiving as the wide-open Asheera.

"You said we'd have to turn upland eventually."

Rifkind nodded, facing up to another example of the obstinacy that had confined her since she walked away from her goddess. "Eventually," Rifkind sighed and let go of her stubborn anger. Inhaling, she felt naked and well aware that shedding a habit, especially one she had been nurturing with every waking breath for a month, was not so easily done.

"After what happened in Epigos, I haven't wanted to put us in a place where we'd be crossing paths with a lot of Wet-landers—"

"Epigos was Vendle's fault. We won't have those problems in the lands where your friend is chief."

Rifkind let Tyrokon's logic stand without correction. She hadn't let up stroking Banin's nose and his resistance was weakening. When she shifted her attention to the itchy place between his horns, he rested his chin on her shoulder. All was forgiven.

"See, he wants to get to the real Wet-lands, too. What are they called? Glass-something?"

"Glascardy," Rifkind replied as Banin nibbled her braids. "I'm not sure— I think we've come far enough and when we cross the hills we'll find ourselves in Glascardy . . . in Irdel, at least, the marcher holding. Or maybe not. Glascardy might lie farther down the coast."

"Marcher?"

Rifkind sighed again and began to explain the stricter sense of boundaries that prevailed in Daria and the shifty loyalties of men whose lands lay between one province and the next.

Cho, who'd hung back, deigned to join them.

"We're going to cross the hills!" Tyrokon announced.

"Why?" Cho asked, with an eye toward his mother. "Why now?"

"Because it's time." Rifkind studied the sun. "There's half an afternoon's light left. We could be in the forest before twilight."

Without hesitation, the boyos supported her decision. Rifkind mounted Banin and guided him into the grass. Tyrokon stayed close, asking questions, and Cho stayed with them, silent but listening as Rifkind answered. By dusk they were, as promised, riding uphill among the trees. Rifkind spotted a clearing where the spring grass had grown up enough to satisfy the war-horses for the night.

They had meat left over from Cho's last hunt and, though he was eager to test his skills in a new environment, he didn't argue when Rifkind suggested that night was no time to start exploring. Building a fire had rarely been easier with an abundance of tinder and wood underfoot. Stars appeared in the sky above the clearing, but there were no horizons other than the trees, which quickly became indistinguishable in the darkness.

"It's as if we're surrounded by a tent, but not inside it," Tyrokon said when they were divvying up the watches.

She took the first watch and waited until she could hear the boyos' steady breathing before turning her back to the fire.

Her mind was like a limb that had been bound too long in one position and ached to be set free. Rifkind had feasted on her own discomfort, using it to fuel her anger, but now she resolved to relax, to rise into her *tal* for her own sake.

The urge to tell her goddess that she was no longer talking to her goddess, however illogical, was a strong wind at Rifkind's back that she could resist only when she buried her face behind her hands and began, softly, to laugh at her predicament and, heartbeats later, at herself.

What would I have done differently? Rifkind asked herself when her laughter had burnt itself out. The answer was: *Nothing.* From the night she'd received her silver crescent, through her battle with the emperor's sorcerer, An-Soren, and the raising of the Landmother, there was nothing Rifkind would change. She'd wanted her goddess's blessing when she went to Cho's father and when she left him, but blessing or no blessing, she'd done what she wanted. The same held true when she returned to the Asheera. She'd have straightened Tyrokon's legs with the Bright One's approval or without it. She'd sought approval when she began training healers, but the lack of it hadn't slowed her down.

Do you hear me? I no longer seek Your approval. I haven't had it since before my son was born, and I haven't done too badly without it. If I tell You what I have done, it is to satisfy myself, not You. From this moment on, I intend to live my life as pleases me, and only me.

An owl hooted from the trees and it seemed that moonlight bent around Rifkind, swaddling her front and back. The owl hooted a second time and the illusion of being wrapped in moonlight, if illusion it was, faded. Rifkind moved her fingers and toes, breaking meditation's stillness. She returned to fire and when the moon cleared the top of the trees she awakened Cho, who'd drawn the second watch. He surrendered his blankets. Rifkind slept, undisturbed by dreams, until the sky had brightened to dawn.

In the mid-afternoon, they came to a fast-moving stream too wide to jump in a single bound. The boyos, who'd been deeply impressed by their first brook, stood on the banks in silent awe. Then Rifkind spotted swift, dark shapes surging upstream. Kicking off her boots and knotting up her breeches, she waded into the knee-deep water. Years had passed since Ejord had shown her how bears batted fish out of a stream and how a quick-moving man could do the same.

She needed three tries before she whacked one onto the bank.

"That's a start toward supper," she shouted and challenged them to help her catch the rest.

Looking doubtful, Tyrokon shed his boots. Rifkind showed him where to stand with his feet straddling the deepest channel and he clasped his hands together in a credible imitation of a bear's paw. He thwacked at the fish with more enthusiasm than success.

"Your turn." Rifkind looked at her son.

Cho shook his head.

"It's fun," Tyrokon added.

The sideways movement of Cho's head continued.

Fun was beneath his dignity.

He got his bow and arrows from Tein's saddle. Rifkind warned him that the water would play tricks with his aim and he shattered a few arrows against the smooth rocks of the stream bed before he believed her. He took the stream's measure, then, and put an arrow through one of the brown-and-silver fish. Tyrokon, whose legs had numbed quickly in the cold water, waded in to grab the arrow and after that it was a contest between Cho's bow and Rifkind's bare hands.

Rifkind gave up when Cho was three fish ahead. They had ten alto-gether, more than enough for supper and breakfast the next morning.

"Is it all this easy?" Cho wanted to know when they broke camp. "More water than all the sheep can drink, fish, nuts you can beat down from a tree?"

"Sometimes, yes," Rifkind replied after a moment's thought. "Wet-landers live in houses, not tents; and there are so many more of them. They can't pick up and move to the next well. Whatever you're used to, when it's gone, life gets hard."

Tyrokon asked, "This water, it could disappear?"

Rifkind said it could and that when drought struck the Wet-lands, crops failed and people starved, which drew her into a discourse on farming, as best she understood it, that had both boyos shaking their heads in disbelief.

They took their time traversing the forest—three days to reach the hill crests, another three to descend to the lowlands where they found a road wide enough for three riders abreast and the land was divided by waist-high walls of black and gray stone.

For the boyos, what they saw was wonder enough. For Rifkind, what was missing was more significant. In good years, the Darians fallowed half their fields, but looking across the landscape there were many more than half gone to seed.

The first inn they came to was a sad affair with gaping holes in its thatched roof and pigs rooting in the stable yard. Rifkind hailed the innkeeper in trade and got a blank stare for her efforts. She dusted off her long-unused Glascard dialect and asked where they were, how many days' ride to Chatelgard, and in which direction? She got answers: in Irdel, at the Earl's Inn on the Irdel Road, ten days out of Glascardy—with good weather—and a good ways farther on the Mountain Road to Chatelgard—for those fool enough to go there.

Rifkind thanked him with a seta and retreated to the road.

"I thought you said the inns were open to everyone," Cho said with a trace of his old insolence, which had been absent since he'd bested his mother at fishing.

"They were." Rifkind twisted in the saddle to see if they were being followed. "When I was here last, before you were born."

"What did he say about Glascardy and Chatelgard," Tyrokon asked. "I heard the names, but if that was trade, it went right by me."

"Nothing much. Nothing good and not trade, either. He wasn't the innkeeper; an innkeeper would have known trade. We're on the right road, headed in the right direction. We'll leave it at that until we're closer to Glascardy."

11

It wasn't all desolation in the Earl of Irdel's domain. Here and there, the Asheerans rode past communities that seemed to prosper in the plague's wake. Rifkind made a point of calling out a greeting in the Glascard dialect whenever they passed a farmer working his fields. She taught the boyos the same greeting, though no matter which of them lifted voice and hand, their greetings were rarely returned and never warmly. So Rifkind kept them on the Irdel Road, avoiding the hamlets and villages, hoping for a decent inn where she could catch a rumor or two.

She got her wish on their third day of road travel when they rounded a curve and beheld an inn with a fresh layer of whitewash on its walls. Though it was mid-afternoon of a perfect spring day and early to call it quits, Rifkind did just that, fishing out a trio of setas for the yard boy who was patently awed by the war-horses.

"Leave them in the paddock, there," she advised, pointing to an empty square off the stables. "They'll take you apart if you try to put them in a stall."

The boy, who hadn't seemed to blink since Rifkind approached him, took the collected reins as if they were poisonous serpents. Cho's Tein leaned forward to get a sniff of the youngster and gingerly the boy touched the bay's nose. Tein snorted, scaring the boy out of a year's growth, no doubt, but war-horses would have been too dangerous to keep if their temperaments weren't fundamentally gentle.

A mature man in a cap and apron—the innkeeper by the look of him—hustled through the doorway.

"Asheerans! Glory be to Mohandru, we don't see many of your kind around here." He spoke a clean variety of trade and had the wit to sound surprised, not hostile in the face of three strangers, each armed with a sword and knives. "What brings you to the Barking Goose?"

Rifkind held out her hand in the Darian manner. "The hope of a good meal, a clean bed and bedding, if it's to be had."

The innkeeper avoided her hand. "That's what you call a witch's mark on your cheek? It's been years since I've seen an Asheeran witch."

"Witch," the Wet-lands word for healer, and not a simple translation, either. In lands that harbored the priests of a score of gods, *witch* was the odd woman out, tolerated at best, always at risk for persecution. Narrowing her eyes, Rifkind studied the innkeeper and decided he was one of the tolerant ones. She tried to place him, but it was no use—she'd ridden at the head of an army. Several thousand men had had the opportunity to memorize her face while to her they'd simply been "the men."

"I'm called Rifkind," she said, switching into the Glascard dialect. "The tall one is Cho. The other's Tyrokon. It's their first journey out of the Asheera."

The innkeeper scratched the stubble on his chin. It didn't take healer's empathy to guess his thoughts: He recognized her name. "Rifkind, eh? I knew of a witch named Rifkind once. You don't look like her, though; and she'd be older now."

She was almost used to it, this stubborn refusal to connect her with her past. "It's a common name where I come from," she conceded with a lie; she'd never met another Rifkind. The smells from the inn's kitchen had reached her. There was a good meal waiting inside and no point in spoiling it with an argument. "You have a room with bed and bedding?"

"A nice one," the innkeeper agreed. "Fresh bedding, too, for a consha."

Rifkind produced the coins and offered her hand a second time. The innkeeper hesitated before taking it, but shook it firmly when he did.

The innkeeper led the Asheerans into his common room where the walls and ceiling were dark enough to require candlelight in the afternoon. Two long tables with benches beside them filled the center of the room. Small, square tables lined the walls. A handful of men in rustic clothes sat at one of the long tables, tossing dice. They looked up when the Asheerans entered and saw nothing that held their attention.

A man and woman sat at one of the small tables with eyes only for each other. Two young women sat at an empty table. The inn's wenches, by the look of them and attentive once the keeper caught their eyes. There was only one other man in the room, a rangy fellow sitting at the table Rifkind would have claimed for herself, the one with a clear view of all the doors.

In lieu of that table, she staked out the unoccupied end of the second long table.

"Any chance of bread right now?"

The innkeeper nodded. He relayed Rifkind's request to the wenches, then excused himself to tell his wife they had three more for supper.

"This isn't a good place to sit," Tyrokon advised the instant they were alone. He used the clan dialect.

Cho agreed. "If we can't sit where that solitary man is sitting, we need to sit where we can see him."

"*I* can see him," Rifkind hissed. "If we *all* can see him, he knows we're watching. Use trade," she added, in that language. "We have nothing to hide."

The boyos each gave her dark looks but sat down without further argument. A wench brought to their table a platter with loaf of bread and a crock of butter with a stubby knife rising out of it. Rifkind broke the bread and smeared a heel with the butter. The first taste flooded her mind with memories.

She encouraged the boyos to sample the Wet-lands staple, confident that the golden spread would lighten their mood, which it did.

They traded easy conversation about their war-horses while Rifkind kept a very discreet eye on the solitary man who was keeping an equally discreet eye on her. His clothes were clean and unremarkable, his hair was brown beneath a loose-fitting cap, but his face was weathered and, overall, she judged him old enough to have seen a share of the Overnmont battles. He didn't carry a sword, at least not on his left side, but there was a knife rising out of his boot and another hidden in his sleeve—unless Rifkind had lost her ability to spot hidden steel.

Another man might have been lost in his thoughts and no cause for concern, but the rangy man had an aura to him that even the boyos had sensed.

The Asheerans had just about polished off the bread and butter when the solitaire rose. He snagged Rifkind's eye and came directly to their table, seating himself opposite Rifkind, beside Tyrokon. His left arm stretched across the table.

Without benefit of introduction or pretense of friendship he asked, in fluid trade, "What draws a witch all the way to Irdel?"

"Dreams," Rifkind replied evenly. She shot glances at the boyos: This was her challenge, not theirs.

"Best keep them to yourself. People around here have had their fill of empty dreams. It'll fall hard on a witch who betrays them."

Without warning, the man brought his right hand up from his lap. Rifkind rose ever-so-slightly into her *tal* and appraised it with a healer's eye. The hand had been crushed long ago. Two of the fingers had been amputated, the other two curled toward the palm like bird claws, and the thumb, discolored by recent bruises and nicks, stuck out at an awkward angle.

"I can take the pain," she said, "but it's been too long for anything more. Battle wound?"

The man shrugged. "Did I say there was pain?"

"You don't have to. I see it." That was only the truth: black lines like spiderwebs wound around the man's hand. They twitched to the rhythm of his heart. "May I?"

Another shrug and Rifkind took the hand firmly between her own. She rose into her *tal*. The injury opened to her mind like a flower, surrendering its secrets without a fight. The pain of a dozen years fairly shouted its name, begging for release. It yielded to her command, but the bones were fused. Like the bones of Tyrokon's legs, they knew only the shape they had and could not be coaxed into another. She descended and opened her eyes.

"I know the name of your pain and of the man who held the shield, but I do not know yours."

"Wilts."

"I am called Rifkind. Beside you sits Tyrokon; the other one calls himself Cho. We're bound for the mountains beyond Glascardy, for Chatelgard itself. Do you know the place?"

Before answering, Wilts stole a glance at Cho and cranked his eyebrows, but if he had a question, he kept it to himself. "I've been there," he said. "It's not the place it was, but nothing is, is it? There's no love lost these days between Irdel and Glascardy. Lord Ejord Overnmont doesn't have the weight of his ancestors and Lord Ohlmer Ballard doesn't feel the pull."

Rifkind's heart leapt. By mentioning Ejord's name Wilts had eased more than a few knots out of her neck. Still, the implication, that Irdel no longer swore fealty to Glascardy was not good news and Ohlmer wasn't a name Rifkind associated with Ballards who'd ruled Irdel from their hold in Gryphonage castle almost as long as the Overnmonts had ruled from Chatelgard.

"Who's this Lord Ohlmer? A son of old Lord Ballard? A nephew?"

"Ballards are all gone, save for a few women—taken by the plague. Ohlmer took a daughter for himself and made himself Lord Ohlmer Ballard. The daughter died giving birth to the heir."

"Duke," Rifkind mused. Duke was the Overnmont title. The Ballards had been earls. "The road is open?" she asked cautiously. "There's no ban between here and there?"

Wilts shrugged. "So long as Lord Ohlmer collects his tolls, he doesn't care where you're bound. There's those who'd take his share, but he's got swords for them."

"I thank you for the information. It's good to know what lies ahead."

"And I thank you, witch, for what you've given me."

Wilts unwound from the bench and left the inn.

"He insulted you, he insulted Lord Ejord," Cho said, "and you didn't challenge him."

"There'll be time enough for challenges after we know all sides of the story."

"What's to know?"

"The plague has scoured these lands. It wiped out the Ballards, apparently. I need to know what it's done to the rest of Glascardy."

"You think it might have crippled Lord Ejord?" Tyrokon asked. "Maybe that's why you've had dreams."

"I don't know. I won't know until we've come to Chatelgard and I've seen what's to be seen with my own eyes."

That satisfied Tyrokon, who called for another bread loaf, but Cho settled into a sulk for reasons Rifkind did not trouble to guess.

The bread came with another crock of butter and dinner followed not long after. The kitchen aromas delivered their promises with a stew that was as flavorful as it was meaty. The innkeeper kept their mugs filled with dark, home-brewed ale, the best they'd had so far. Cho liked the Wet-lands brew and drank until his cheeks were flushed. Rifkind considered a warning, but the boyo's sulk hadn't lifted and she wasn't in the mood for a squabble.

The dicers ate quickly and dispersed. They were all replaced by an assortment of workmen, who by their familiarity with the wenches, customarily took their supper under the inn's roof. A minstrel with a battered harp appeared and took a seat by the hearth where he livened the room with a tolerable voice and a collection of common songs Rifkind had forgotten.

The dicers came back to set up a game at the next table. Rifkind caught Cho's eye, knowing beyond doubt what her son was thinking. In silence, they exchanged warnings that Cho pointedly ignored before joining them. Tyrokon, looking torn, stayed with Rifkind.

"Watch him," she said finally and got up from the table. She approached the innkeeper. "What are the chances of hiring a bath?"

The innkeeper grinned and named a price that was too high by half but worth every seta when Rifkind eased herself into the steaming tub in a private chamber behind the kitchen hearth. Water was precious in the Asheera, but firewood was even more so. No one would think of wasting it on a *bath*, but precious was different in the Wet-lands. Rifkind savored every luxurious moment and managed not to waste a thought on her sulking son until the water was less than tepid.

Emerging from the chamber, she surprised one of the scullions and asked if there wasn't a back stairway to the guest rooms. The girl stared as if Rifkind with her dripping hair, her foreign clothes, her knives, sword, and silver crescent was a legend come to life, then pointed a trembling finger at a closed door opposite the hearth.

Rifkind should have asked for a candle. The stairs were pitch dark and she stubbed the toes of both feet navigating the narrow, angled steps, but she found their promised room. Some time later, she heard the door open and wrapped a hand around the knife she'd hidden beneath her downy pillow.

"Who goes?"

The answer came back in Tyrokon's voice: "Us. Just us."

"There's a bar beside the doorjamb. Drop it in the brackets, for safety's sake—"

That required explanation and demonstration. Rifkind was wide awake again by the time she crawled back into bed—alone. As she'd expected, the boyos weren't tempted by a feather mattress. They'd learn.

There was a hot breakfast of porridge, eggs, sausage, and bread with jam and cheese waiting for them in the morning—for additional coin, of course, but worth every seta.

"I begin to see the wisdom of money," Tyrokon when they'd reclaimed the war-horses and were on the road again. "No chief could *give* away so much food."

"And getting money is no challenge," Cho added. "Their games are easy to learn and there's always someone willing to make a side bet."

Side bets? Her son was making side bets and well enough that he wasn't getting raked over? Rifkind kept her astonishment to herself. The strategies of gambling on gamblers weren't really that different from the strategies of winning the red staff at a clan Gathering, and Cho had proved himself a master of those.

Cho had watched her. "No warnings?" he asked with an edge. "No words to the wise?"

Rifkind shook her head. "If I had any—which I don't; I don't gamble—I'd be wasting my breath."

For a moment it looked as if Cho might launch into a tantrum, then he leaned back and laughed. Rifkind laughed with him and judged that her son just might be growing out of the quarrelsome boyo years into real manhood.

By late morning, the road had wound into heavy forest. Cho wanted to string his bow and hunt up their supper. Rifkind persuaded him to wait a while longer and was still pleased that he was being sensible, when the trees to their right erupted with men bent on havoc.

It happened so quickly Rifkind couldn't count the enemy.

She dropped Banin's reins, drew her sword from its scabbard across her back, and collected a knife from its sheath for an offhand weapon. Someone was shooting arrows.

By the Bright Moon's light, how Rifkind hated arrows, especially when the archers positioned themselves high in the trees.

Banin squealed and crimson rage flooded Rifkind's mind: He'd been struck high on the right-side haunch. Not a killing wound, nor even a maiming one, but enough to make her see red as well.

Rifkind chopped her sword into a brigand's neck. He went down and wouldn't rise again.

She used the knife to slash open the arm of a man who'd dared reach for her leg. Banin spun, favoring his right, and using his horns by instinct to clear a space for fighting.

But still the arrows came—not many and not telling, not yet. Nearby, the boyos shouted and fought. Rifkind couldn't spare a glance for their conditions, though she'd heard another war-horse squeal.

Damn their Wet-lands eyes for going after the war-horses!

She plunged her sword into a brigand's chest and jerked it free.

Three down—at least three—and nothing changed. There were as many of them grappling with her as before and, from the quietest place at the back of her mind, the thought arose that her luck might have finally run out.

Rifkind quenched that thought and rallied, picking her targets and ignoring the pain when a brigand got close enough to graze her thigh with his knife.

Then the chaos doubled. A brigand went down—an arrow protruding from his back.

Damn fool archers, shooting their own men!

But, no—*that* arrow had come from the road behind.

Another brigand had the same thought—his last; Rifkind brought her sword down through his neck. One more stood just out of reach. She kneed Banin and raised her sword, but the brigand ran first.

They were all running, all the brigands, running back to the forest and a mounted cohort was chasing them.

One . . . three . . . she counted five, no, seven mounted men with chain armor glinting on their shoulders racing the brigands for the trees. And another four remaining on the road. Three held bows with arrows nocked and pointed *her* way. The last wore a mail coif and carried his sword left-handed. They locked eyes. He wasn't advancing but she didn't dare turn away to check on the boyos.

"Cho? Tyrokon?" she called without looking. "Either of you hurt?"

"A scratch," from Tyrokon and "Nothing," from Cho.

"Stand your ground," she commanded them. "We're not out of this yet."

Screams came from the trees. The Asheerans had been spared one disaster. The question in Rifkind's mind was, had they tumbled into another? She stared hard at the coif.

"Wilts?"

"Aye, witch," he replied in Glascard dialect and, grateful as she was for the rescue, Rifkind didn't feel particularly safe. "I told you there were those who'd take Lord Ballard's share."

"You did."

"You'd be dead now, but for us."

"The odds were against us," Rifkind agreed.

"And still are. You'll come with us, won't you? Lord Ballard will want to meet the witch who rides his roads."

"What's he saying?" one of the boyos hissed.

"That we've been invited to meet Lord Ballard. Put up your swords, we're not going to fight our way out of this."

12

"No wounded. No prisoners," an out-of-breath boyo with flushed cheeks reported to Wilts when the cohort reformed. "A handful, no more, got away. We didn't give chase; your orders, sir."

"Lord Ballard's dogs will hunt them down soon enough."

"Yes, sir."

Rifkind observed the exchange, building her opinion of Lord Ohlmer Ballard who was likely to cast a shadow across the near future. She already knew he wasn't from the old-blood nobility and he hadn't given an oath to Irdel's traditional overlord. Now she added discipline to his qualities, the sort of discipline with ranks and honors that Ejord had maintained when he led the Glascard army. Together they hinted at an able warlord and trouble on Ejord's flanks.

"Witch, can you ride to Gryphonage?" Wilts asked, pointing his claw-like right hand at her blood-soaked thigh.

He knew her name, yet refused to use it—not a good sign. Rifkind decided not to mention that a healer didn't need to rise into her *tal* to heal her own wounds.

Banin was another matter. The arrow hadn't struck anything vital, but the young war-horse had never suffered an injury. Every few moments his head snaked past his rider's knee. A jack horse couldn't have hurt himself, but Banin had horns. He was a worse danger to himself—and his rider— than the arrow had been.

"Slowly," Rifkind said to Wilts, "and when we come to a stream, I'd like to wash my war-horse's wound and take a closer look at the boyo. He says it's just a scratch, but you know how boyos are."

Banin took another swipe at his haunch. Rifkind grabbed a horn before it connected with her sore thigh. She put the thought *Enough of that!* into his mind.

"There's a stream not far from here, once we leave this road."

While Wilts was waiting for his men to emerge from the forest, Rifkind laid a hand on her wound and sealed it with a sturdy scab. Barring major distractions, she'd be good as new by the time they got wherever they were going.

Wilts gave the order to move out and Rifkind found herself and the boyos at the center of a grim and well-equipped escort. They were safe from another brigand attack, but whether they were safe from their escort was another question.

An hour down the Irdel Road they came to another road—little more than a rutted, muddy track—that led, apparently, to Gryphonage. Banin took exception to the muddy track. His antics—and Wilts's disapproval— were almost enough to make the healer wish for a good steel bit for his bridle. In the end, she had to dismount and lead him onto the track.

You shame me, she put into Banin's mind. Usually that was enough to put the war-horse on his best behavior, but not when every stride pulled a bloody hole in his haunch.

Rifkind could have sealed it as she'd sealed her own wound, but she *knew* her wound was clean. She couldn't be sure about Banin's until she'd given it a healer's examination.

She'd need to do the same with Tyrokon. The boyo was pale and thin lipped. He cradled his "scratched" forearm against his torso and rode with Assurin's reins in his left hand.

When they came to the promised stream, Rifkind issued orders. Tyrokon obeyed, dismounting awkwardly and adamantly refusing assistance.

He said he'd stand through Rifkind's examination, but, claiming her own comfort, she sat him down in easy reach of freshwater and peeled back a blood-slimed sleeve.

"You've been bleeding the whole time," she chided him. "You're lucky you haven't bled to death." The boyo's response was lost in a gasp as Rifkind cleaned the wound with a stream-dampened cloth.

Tryokon's "scratch" had severed an artery. With one hand firmly on the boyo's wrist, she ascended into her *tal*. Expertly, but without the gentleness she could bring to her craft, Rifkind bound the vessels together. Once she'd assured herself that blood flowed properly, she drew the edges of the wound together and sealed them before descending into ordinary perception.

"Thank you," the boyo said softly.

"Next time, *tell* me when you're bleeding!"

He grimaced through a promise and stayed put, collecting his strength as Rifkind took a critical look at her war-horse's injury. Were Banin a man, she would have quieted his mind with dreamless sleep before probing the wound, but a man would have been stretched out on the ground, not standing on four legs. Banin whickered plaintively when she began calling the foreign bits to the surface. Rifkind spared a thought to calm him, then went back to work.

Tyrokon had lost more blood, but his healing had been simple in comparison. Sword cuts were always easy compared to arrows.

The sun had moved while she'd stood beside her war-horse and so had half of their escort.

"I sent them ahead, to tell Lord Ballard that we're coming," Wilts explained. "Can he be ridden?"

Rifkind nodded. She'd have given all the gold in her purse for something to eat. Two healings in an afternoon left her weak in the knees and queasy. The Barking Goose's hearty breakfast was a distant memory and a quick glance in Wilts's direction indicated that she'd find no sympathy there.

Beyond the stream the castle track wound into hills of fallow fields, pastures and sprouted winter grain. A pleasant scene and a distinct change from the neglected farms the Asheerans had passed along their way. Rifkind, whose Darian eye had been educated by the pragmatic Overnmonts, saw past the green prosperity. Having seized the Ballard lands by the bedsheets, Lord Ballard was enforcing his rights: The peasants were working his lands before they worked their own. An opinion made more credible when the peasants they passed offered token greetings and kept their left hands hidden.

The old Darian emperor had been doomed, according to Ejord, from the moment ordinary folk began making left-hand wardsigns against evil whenever he or his minions went by. Ejord's own father had fallen to the same peasant judgment. Rifkind did not hold much hope for Lord Ohlmer Ballard. She'd have refused his hospitality, if that had been possible, which—even with the reduction in their escort—it wasn't.

Wilts was a taciturn man who didn't talk to his own men, much less make casual conversation with strangers. The men spoke softly when they talked among themselves and when one man dared to whistle a song to break the monotony, his melody was quickly stifled by silence.

Shadows lengthened with no sign of a castle, or inn, on the horizon. Rifkind was ready to eat leather, but didn't complain. It was her healing— her healing of Banin—that had cost the party an hour or more of traveling time. Still, when they'd agreed to meet the new lord Ballard, she'd expected his castle to be nearby and believed that Wilts had conferred with his lord before setting out in pursuit of them. Neither assumption seemed to be correct.

There's no point to speculating, Rifkind chided herself. *We'll ride until we get there, then face what's there to be faced. There's no need to borrow trouble.*

Around sunset, they came to a hamlet not nearly large enough to support an inn. Wilts hailed the only man in sight—a farmer leading a mule— and for a moment Rifkind hoped they'd be imposing themselves on the peasants' hospitality. No such luck. Wilts commandeered a pole-lantern, nothing more. The sun set not long after they left the hamlet, leaving a half-waxed Bright Moon to light their way.

They rode well into the night, making up the time they'd lost to Rifkind's healings and then some before Wilts called a halt. Under orders, his men shared their rations. Everyone bedded down hungry, but none was hungrier than Rifkind who dreamt of food and awoke in a foul mood.

Around noon they came to a better road. The track had been a shortcut but, more important, the new road took them past a decent-looking inn where Wilts, without prodding, stopped for a meal and a day's provisions, both of which improved Rifkind's humor.

Once again, they rode well into the night before Wilts let them make a camp. The morning brought clouds and a fine rain that cut visibility and muffled sound. All day they rode as if they were trapped in another man's dream. Then, not long before sunset, the air cleared. They rounded a curve and there was Gryphonage.

The least castle was impressive to Asheeran eyes, but a castle like Gryphonage—or the Overnmonts' Chatelgard—was meant to impress the most jaded Darian. It stood on the highest land on the far side of a pleasant valley. Farmland edged the valley's stream: fields at the bottom, then pastures and orchards, and finally the forests from which the party emerged.

The castle itself was built from tan stone, with at least four towers and a curtain wall between them. Banners fluttered from the towers. Rifkind couldn't see them clearly, but she knew they'd be yellow with a green gryphon crest—unless the new lord Ballard had chosen some other device to proclaim his power. Some earlier Ballard lord had thrown up a double ring of earthworks around the castle. They were grass-covered now, and good grazing for flocks and herds, but they'd serve their purpose if anyone dreamt of ousting a Ballard from his seat.

Every castle of any size had its village and Gryphonage was no exception. Its village looked prosperous, at least from a distance. The road stayed on the north side of the valley; Rifkind never got close enough to see a face. The largest building in the village, and the only one built from the castle's tan stone, was the temple that flew the bicolored blue banner of Mohandru to the exclusion of all other gods.

Asheerans worshipped one god—one goddess—to the exclusion of all others, but it disturbed Rifkind to think that, with the coming of the plague, Mohandru had achieved such dominance in Darian hearts.

The sun had set by the time Wilts led them through the offset earthworks entrances. They came to the last obstacle, a drawbridge across the inmost ditch. The bridge had been lowered for their arrival and the portcullis raised to admit the riders into a smallish courtyard where yawning men held torches high and tall young man with golden hair and a taste for luxurious clothing hailed them from the top of the keep steps.

Lord Ballard's son, Rifkind thought, wrongly as it turned out. The young man was Lord Ballard himself, no more than half Wilts's age.

"Welcome to Gryphonage," the young lord shouted. "Dismount and make yourselves comfortable. Our hospitality awaits in the hall."

He was all smiles as he came down the steps. His trade was excellent. Whatever he'd been before becoming Lord Ballard, he hadn't been a thug or peasant.

A woman remained in the doorway he'd abandoned. Though the light could have been better, Rifkind judged her to be a year or two younger than the lord. Wilts had said a Ballard daughter had died giving birth to an heir. Either there was a younger daughter in the wings, or the new Lord Ballard had found himself a pliant bed warmer.

Rifkind's feet had barely touched the ground when Lord Ballard embraced her, arm in arm, cheek to cheek, right side, then left side. Even dire enemies embraced in Daria. Public embraces were part of the culture, especially here in the west. Rifkind played her part, gratified that Lord Ballard considered her a peer.

When Lord Ballard had released her, they both turned to Cho and Tyrokon. Rifkind introduced them as "Cho and Tyrokon, men of my clan," and immediately wondered what instinct had kept her from saying more.

No embraces between the boyos and the lord. A nod sufficed as it did with the men who'd been their escort. Grooms appeared to take their animals. They looked askance at the war-horses.

"Do you have a fenced field?" she asked. "They've never been within walls and I won't vouchsafe the life of any man or beast if they feel themselves imprisoned."

Lord Ballard thought a moment then said to the grooms, in the Glascard dialect, "Take them outside to the breeding paddock. See that grain's brought down."

The boyos wouldn't have understood a word of that, so Rifkind said to them, in trade: "Follow these men. When you've seen to the war-horses, come back to the hall."

The grooms led, the boyos and the war-horses followed. Banin whickered, but behaved well enough as Tyrokon led him away from his rider.

"Will you come inside? The fires are banked and the cook's abed, but I ordered plates of cold meat when we saw your torches."

Lord Ballard swept his arm toward the stairs, every inch a generous lord, as if he felt the need to flatter her, as if he hadn't known the invitation Wilts had put to her was one she couldn't gracefully—or safely— refuse. There was mystery in the air: Rifkind had questions without answers and questions she hadn't the wit, yet, to ask. Rifkind didn't know what she was getting into when she followed the young lord into his keep. She acknowledged the bed warmer, whose name was Irstia, with a smile; a courtesan's life was as mysterious to Rifkind's as hers would surely have been to the girl.

The girl blushed and turned away, giving Rifkind sight of a scrawny lad with hectic cheeks and a drippy nose. A village runt, she thought, then recanted. There'd be no sickly lads in the castle, not at this hour, not this close to the lord. Then it came to her: *the heir.*

Perhaps that was the nut of it: Wilts was old enough to have given his oath to the old lord Ballard. Maybe this sickly lad was what remained of his loyalty and the legitimate Ballard line. A loyal man might bring a witch to heal a sickly heir . . . or to get rid of him altogether?

They climbed the stairs to the great hall. There were candelabrum on a table opposite the hearth, casting golden light on a most welcome sight: a pyramid of small loaves, ewers, and cloth-covered platters. Servants hustled, lighting more candles and whisking the cloths from the plates.

Lord Ballard said, "Make yourselves a meal," and Rifkind, along with Wilts and his men, did. In due course, Cho and Tyrokon arrived, looking awed and wary. They were unprepared for a lord's hospitality, but they'd learned their lessons since Epigos and did nothing that they hadn't seen a native do first.

The trestle tables from dinner had been dismantled and propped against the walls, but there were benches available. Rifkind was among the first to sit, once she'd harvested a meal. The boyos joined her.

Tyrokon spoke first, in trade. "The war-horses are settled. There was a small house—"

"A shed, most likely," Rifkind corrected.

"Within the fence with them. We put their tack and our gear in the shed. They won't let strangers near it; it's as good as standing guard."

"Is this what Chatelgard looks like?" Cho asked before Rifkind could respond to Tyrokon.

"Similar, but smaller, quite a bit smaller. Chatelgard's carved out of a mountain."

Cho sucked air.

"Why?" he asked and Rifkind, seeing that they were being left to themselves while Lord Ballard conferred with Wilts, explained a little about fortifications and intimidation in a land where people didn't just head out in a general direction across the steppe but stuck to roads and rivers when they moved.

Lord Ballard came over before Rifkind got to the finer points of siege warfare.

"Will your young men bed down in the lower hall?" he asked.

Rifkind's first instinct was to say no and keep them close, though that could easily be interrupted as distrust. True, she *didn't* trust Lord Ballard, but there was no sense in blaring that about like a trumpet salute. "They'd be pleased to," she said with a smile. "And me with them."

"We have a room set up for you here in Augemon's tower. My late wife's ancestors built it three hundred years ago."

Secure on the bench, Rifkind rose into her *tal*. If Lord Ballard was hiding something—like an ambush or some other trickery—she should have been able to detect the deception, if not the content.

There was nothing. Either he was sincere . . . or very good at lying.

"Then I shall be honored to sleep there, and the boyos can bed down with your men."

The men, including Cho and Tyrokon, made one last visit to the food table then left Rifkind alone in the great hall with Lord Ballard. A yawning girl arrived and was told to escort their honored guest to Augemon's tower and remain with her throughout the night. Rifkind had seen more enthusiasm on the faces of men about to start a forced march. She tried to set the girl at ease with a simple question:

"What's your name?"

The girl shook so badly the flame in the lamp she carried flickered.

"There's no reason to be afraid of me. I swear to you, I'm not the witch you seem to think I am."

"Tess," the girl admitted, and, "I'm not afraid," which was a bald-faced lie.

They climbed a spiral stairway to a landing about six feet square. There were two doors, each a few feet from the diagonally opposite corners.

Rifkind couldn't help but notice that both doors were fitted with iron brackets and could be barred from the outside.

"Are these the rooms where your lord's guests usually stay?"

Without answering, Tess went straight to the door on the right that opened into a chamber that was somewhat larger than the landing. It held a four-posted bedstead high enough to require a step stool and hung with richly embroidered curtains. The floor was covered with a patterned carpet—an Asheeran carpet, unless the Wet-landers had taken to knotting their own. An impressive chair with tasseled cushions and a washstand with a bowl above and cabinet below completed the furnishings. There was no hearth but a wrought-iron brazier stood in a sandbox beneath a shuttered window. Allowing for the door brackets, it was a room fit for an honored guest.

Tess set the lamp on the washstand and opened the brazier, where embers glowed among the ashes.

"No need—not for me. I've slept within curtains before; I'll be downright warm by morning. I don't see a trundle, but the bed's more than wide enough for both of us." The girl blanched. Rifkind was about to insist that she was harmless, but that was an argument she wouldn't win. "As you wish," she said with a sigh. "Fire the brazier." She dragged the topmost layers of blankets from the bed and heaped them on the chair. "Stay warm. I'm for bed and sleep."

Rifkind threw her cloak across the bed, replacing one layer of blankets and unbuckled her sword rig. Tess flattened against the nearest wall. She was tempted to chastise the girl who'd been charged with her hospitality, then thought better of it. The years had smoothed the rough edges of her memories. In a distant way she remembered how her presence—her existence—as a sword-wielding woman, not to mention her complicated status had unnerved many of the Wet-landers she'd encountered, especially the women.

"I swear I won't harm you."

"I got my knife," Tess shot back.

Rifkind merely shook her head.

After pulling off her boots, Rifkind undid her belt with its many attachments and loosened the laces of her outer tunic and pulled it over her head. Even by generous standards, it was rank and ratty, though nowhere near as rank or ratty as her trousers, which were stiff with dried blood and scarred by a hole where the brigand's knife had found her leg. Rifkind had left her caves with spare clothing, even with lengths of silk thread and a bone needle . . . all of which remained in Epigos with the benighted camel.

Folding the garments with more care than they deserved, Rifkind said, "Tomorrow, I'm going to need to launder and repair my clothes, which means I'll need to *borrow* clothes. Can you arrange that?"

Tess's pointed chin went up and down slowly.

Rifkind divested herself of the knives she wore strapped to her forearms and the little dagger sheathed to her right calf. Then, clad only in her linen and the knives she never surrendered, climbed the bedstead stool.

"You're *sure* you don't want half the bed?"

The chin moved side to side.

"Until the morning, then; may the Bright One watch us while we sleep." She pulled the cords that held back the curtain and sealed herself in darkness. The feather mattresses—there had to be at least three—were almost too soft, too comfortable, but Rifkind persevered.

IT WASN'T THE SNORING THAT bothered Cho. He'd grown up in a tent surrounded by as many as twenty people: *silence* was more apt to keep him awake. It wasn't the stone walls, the thick stone columns, or the certainty that the room where he was expected to sleep had been dug into the ground. At least he didn't think he'd been undone by a *hole*. He could have conquered a little fear like that.

No, Cho was awake, as he'd been awake for the past two nights, because he couldn't get the brigand skirmish out of his head. The moment he closed his eyes they were back on the road, pelted by arrows, and in very real danger of losing their lives until Lord Ballard's men rode to their rescue.

Across the hall, lit by the light of a shielded candle, a few of the castle's men were engaged in a soft, but agitated, conversation. The words were meaningless to Cho, though he thought he'd heard sounds that might have been his name, the name he'd taken for himself. It would have been easier to know if the men were talking about him if they'd used the name Rifkind had given him.

Domhnall was a Wet-lands name and more distinct in any language than Cho.

Cho, who wasn't quite ready to think of himself as Domhnall, could see himself in chain-armor tunic, with a close-fitting helmet covering his hair, and greaves bound around his shins. He could hear himself rustling metallically as he strode. Lord Ballard's men were big men—a few were even bigger than him, a first in his lifetime.

Sedition rose in Cho's mind; he beat it down. He'd have no thought disparaging his friend, Tyrokon, nor his chief . . . but *if* his mother had birthed him in the Wet-lands? Bloody damn Bright, he'd still be a half-breed, but no two of Lord Ballard's men looked half so similar as any two Asheerans.

And *if* Rifkind had returned to Chatelgard . . . *if* she'd turned to Lord Ejord Overnmont as she'd turned to Hamarach?

Something very like a groan escaped Cho's mouth. Hamarach had treated him well, better than well. Cho loved him as a son loves a father. And Tyrokon had been his friend from the first stirring of memory. He didn't want to imagine his life without them.

But Cho couldn't sleep, either, and as the hours of night wore on, his imagination explored the unthinkable.

13

Rifkind awoke suddenly. Her nerves jangled with the sense that something was wrong and her mind needed several moments to recall that she had voluntarily ensconced herself in a curtained bed in Augemon's tower of Gryphonage. As quickly as she placed herself in her physical surroundings, Rifkind placed the lunar seat of her goddess in the heavens and knew that she had overslept by half a morning.

Sparing a thought to invoke her goddess—not quite habit, but short of prayer, as well—Rifkind spread the curtains and blinked into the light.

"You're awake," a voice announced the obvious.

Rifkind blinked again and saw the girl—Teas? Thessa? Tess? Yes, *Tess* sitting beside an open window, a heap of brown cloth in her lap, a somewhat tidier mass of green cloth at her feet.

Pointing at the green cloth, Rifkind asked, "Is that for me?" and received an affirmative nod.

Barefoot and chilled, she shook the cloth out, expecting two garments, finding one: a modest dress suitable for a much larger woman.

"Irstia gifted it to you herself."

Then there was no way for Rifkind to avoid bagging herself in yards of cloth. One did not refuse the largesse of the woman who was sleeping with the castle's lord, no matter her age or origin. Fumbling with the cloth, Rifkind located the hem, the sleeves, and the all-important neck hole. She flipped the hem over her head and hauled cloth for the sleeves. At least a foot of green cloth piled up on the floor. The sleeves fell a handspan or more below Rifkind's fingertips.

"Did the lady send a belt?"

Tess answered with a stare, so Rifkind looked for the clothes she'd discarded. She spotted the belt, but the rest of her clothes were gone.

"You took my clothes for laundering?"

A shrug in addition to the stare. "Dili said there'd be no point. The suede was cracked and the cloth would fall apart in the tubs."

Rifkind sighed. She couldn't fault the judgment. Her garments, especially her slashed and blood-soaked trousers probably had been beyond redemption.

Ejord hadn't cared whether his second wore Asheeran trousers or Wetlands dresses, and she'd conveniently forgotten how much it mattered to most Darians. She fastened her belt around her waist and pushed up her trailing sleeves before hiking armfuls of green cloth past the leather. The cloth itself was lambswool and softer than anything Asheeran women spun or wove. It smelled faintly of lavender and summer flowers—a true and valued gift, even if Rifkind would rather have her suede trousers.

"Does your cook lay out breakfast in the hall, or are we on our own to visit the kitchen?"

An attentive servant wouldn't have needed to be asked.

"Kitchen."

"Will you show me the way?"

Tess balled up the brown cloth in her lap—mending, no doubt: The fate of Wet-lands women no matter their station was bound to a short, steel needle.

They went down stairs that were steeper than Rifkind recalled. She was no authority on castle-building, but anyone with eyes could see that Gryphonage was a patchwork structure, full of mortared-up windows and jagged lines where new wall met old wall.

When they reached the bottom of Augemon's tower, Rifkind expected that they'd be headed out to the yard—kitchens, with their ovens and hearths, were fire-prone places that usually stood apart from a castle, even a stone-built castle—but Tess led the way along a partly enclosed gallery and then to the spiral stairs of a tower considerably larger than the one they'd left.

"Breakfast?" Rifkind suggested. "The kitchen?"

"Lord Ballard sent word you were to see him on waking."

And the lord's word was law, no matter the state of a healer's stomach. Rifkind grabbed a double handful of skirt and started climbing. When they'd passed two doors and the end of the stairway was in sight, Tess tapped on a door and stepped aside. With dark thoughts about servants, Rifkind lifted the latch.

She took the room in quickly. Lord Ballard stood in front of a dark wood table looking anxious. He was dressed for hunting in drab wools and suede but the room itself was a scholar's chamber. A dozen large, leather-bound books sat sharing shelves with glass and metal objects whose functions Rifkind could not begin to guess. A clutter of parchment covered the table, all of them rolled up, some of them sealed with blots of inky wax. Two chests, each with a lock as big as Rifkind's fist and two uncomfortable-looking chairs, both on the near side of the table, completed the room's furnishings.

Lord Ballard did not invite Rifkind to sit. She had the distinct feeling that, though the room was in his castle, nothing in it belonged to him.

"You've come to Irdel at a most fortuitous time," the lord said, ending Rifkind's inspection.

Rifkind asked a preemptive question: "Your son?"

Tension drained from the lord's face. "Yes. Yes. Wilts said you were a healing witch. Garris was born a weakling, but lately— I tell him he must conquer his weaknesses. He seems willing, but this winter, he took a cough. No matter what we do, it gets worse. I've sought advice. None of it is good, but I refuse to give up hope."

Garris, that was a name Rifkind remembered: The old lord Ballard had been a Garris. Like Asheeran clans, Darian families held on to their names. If the hectic-cheeked boy she'd seen in the entry was Garris, then Lord Ballard had reason to be worried, whether he was a loving father or widower with a tenuous claim to his late wife's property.

"I will be glad to examine your boy," Rifkind assured him. "When I glimpsed him last night, I noticed a flush in his cheeks. At the least, he has a lingering fever."

"Garris was born with a caul over his face," Lord Ballard explained. Darian physicians attributed much mystery to the membranes that occasionally covered a newborn's face. Rifkind had never understood why. In the Asheera, it was simply removed and buried with the afterbirth.

"When his mother died, the midwives said he'd follow. I've *fought* to keep him alive."

I'll wager you have, Rifkind thought, but children didn't choose their parents. "I'll do what I can for him."

As she had in the hall, Rifkind rose slightly into her *tal*. Lord Ballard did not have the aura of a cruel man, but what was more interesting was the fleeting sense that they were not alone in the room.

Rifkind narrowed her perception, but it was too late. Whatever it was—if it had been anything at all—was gone.

"We will reward you well."

"A good meal is all I need," Rifkind countered quickly.

Lord Ballard opened his arms, "My table is yours and more. I would be honored if you would remain with us awhile. I have some interest in other ways. There is much we could discuss."

Conversation wasn't the only thing on Lord Ballard's mind. Rifkind found his carnal interest more amusing than threatening. "I can stay for your son, then I'm bound for Chatelgard—"

"And Lord Overnmont," Lord Ballard finished for her. "Yes, yes. Wilts mentioned that. You'll find yourself more welcome here, dear lady. Lord Overnmont's closed his lands to magic, all magic, but especially witchcraft—even the likes of yours."

"Ejord?" Rifkind sputtered, unable to contain her astonishment.

"You speak familiarly of the Overnmont lord, but you do not know him."

"Know him? I'm *Rifkind*. I rode beside him when we put his father on the Imperial Throne."

Scowling deeply, Lord Ballard shook his head. "Be careful, dear lady. Perhaps Rifkind is a common name where you come from, but Rifkind—the Rifkind who rode with the Overnmonts—is dead. She went all the way around, north to east, after Lord Humphry Overnmont took the Imperial Throne, to a place called the Felmargue, a place that is no more.

"Emperor Humphry, he went mad with power once it fell to him. I was young, but I remember how fearful my family became. Then he went north to east as well, to Felmargue, in search of ultimate power . . . of new gods . . . or so it was said. Rifkind met him there, as if it were ordained, and terrible forces were unleashed.

"They died there, Rifkind and the emperor together and the new gods with them . . . but, before there could be any rejoicing, the plagues broke loose."

Rifkind absorbed Lord Ballard's words in silence. She'd almost become accustomed to Wet-landers refusing to recognize her for what she'd been, but this was the first she'd heard of her death. Except for her death, though, Lord Ballard's version of events in the Felmargue was not so different from her own memory. Blaming the plagues on the Felmargue aftermath was an intriguing addition.

Lord Ballard's assertion could be true. When the battle was over and the land had been reformed, everything had seemed fresh and promising. Rifkind had been confident what had been gained far outweighed what had been lost. She'd left at the earliest opportunity . . . she who knew how long a disease could simmer.

That, however, was for a moonlight meditation. The problem of the moment was the moment. Rifkind had no token that would verify her identity to a doubter.

"Rifkind *is* a common name," she lied. "I saw no harm in trading on a sister's deeds and reputation."

Wet-lands lords expected obedience—submission, when push came to shove—and Lord Ballard, whatever he had been before, had mastered his lordly lessons. His scowl lightened and became a stern nod.

"You'd do well to think on my invitation," he advised. "Irdel keeps an open mind where magic's concerned. We've lost too many souls to quibble about who wants to live here. Our laws are simple and just; abide by them and it makes no difference if you're a freedman breaking land or a sorcerer."

Having seen the damage one overpowerful sorcerer could do before she vanquished him, Rifkind could have questioned Lord Ballard's wisdom— could have, but didn't. Her plans hadn't changed. She'd leave for Glascardy and Chatelgard as soon as he'd done her best for the boy . . . though, she did have questions now she hadn't had an hour ago.

Rifkind stayed in the scholarly chamber awhile, listening to Lord Ballard extol the virtues of the domain he'd made his own. To hear him talk, for all their horror, the plagues had brought some good to the western quarter of Daria. There was clear land for the taking, now that there were so many fewer families to farm it; noble families like the Ballards had to protect the common folk around them, not merely collect tithes and taxes from them. There was opportunity for anyone with the wit to seize it.

The growling of Rifkind's stomach finally put an end to Lord Ballard's persuasions. She made her way to the kitchen for bread and leftover sausage. Then Tess reappeared to lead her through the castle maze to what she called the Strong Tower.

"New tower" could have been just as appropriate. Rifkind could fairly smell the mortar curing between the squared-off stone. There were arrow slits every few steps along the spiral stairs and, by the way the shadows fell, a good-sized porch atop the tower for archers and cauldrons. For all his talk about nobles protecting the commoners, Lord Ballard was clearly protecting himself first . . . from Ejord Overnmont?

The possibility existed. As lords went, Ejord had been talking about noble restraint and responsibility long before the plagues, but Rifkind couldn't imagine any lord of any stature letting a fief like Irdel go without a fight.

As before, Tess knocked on a landing door and left Rifkind to enter a surprisingly bright room where a little boy lay on a daybed listening to his tutor recite passages from a leather-bound history of western Daria. The boy brightened when he saw her.

"You're the witch!" he said in trade, which was often, for children of the nobility, their first language; they learned the language of the people they ruled later, if at all.

Rifkind tested him by replying in Glascard, "I prefer 'healer.' Wouldn't you rather a healer than a witch?"

While the tutor closed his book and scurried from the room—gone to report to someone, no doubt—the boy scowled and thought hard, but not about language. "A healer would be wiser," he answered in pitch-perfect Glascard, "but a witch is mysterious and more powerful, isn't she?"

Rifkind couldn't stop a smile. She recalled another sickly boy with out-sized wisdom. Like Tyrokon, Garris had charm and knew how to use it, especially on adults. Tyrokon, despite his withered legs, had been a healthy child. With or without a healer, his life had never been in danger. Garris, though, wouldn't last the summer without her help.

She sat beside him on the daybed. "I'm going to touch you. You may feel warmth or tingling—"

"I know," Garris said with a nod, his blue eyes huge in a weary face. "I'm not a *child*. I'm eight years old. I know all about witchcraft and sorcery."

Rifkind apologized for her mistake. Children were adamant about such things and, after Lord Ballard's refusal to see her for the age she was, she understood Garris's frustration. He was tiny for his age; she'd guessed him for four, five at the most. As for his claims about witchcraft and sorcery, she'd ask a few questions *after* she'd dealt with his lungs.

It hadn't taken more than the lightest touch, the slightest rise into her *tal*, to find the source of the boy's symptoms. His lungs were rotten and had been for some time. If she called out the disease, there'd be nothing left and he'd die beneath her hands. There were other ways to heal.

"Close your eyes," she said to Garris and brushed her palm lightly over his lids.

He slumped onto his pillows and she got to work, creating little castles of health amid the battleground of Garris's lungs. He wouldn't notice any improvement when she awakened him, but in a day or so, when she healed him again, she'd enlarge the castles' domains and keep on enlarging them until she could safely call the disease out.

Garris had expected a miracle. As soon as she awakened him, he pulled himself up from the pillows and succumbed to a coughing fit. Rifkind tried to soothe him, but he fended her off with pathetically weak punches.

"You *lied*!" he sputtered between coughs. "I'm not better."

"I didn't say you would be." She got a hand on his chest and the spasms subsided. "You know how weak your lungs are. I've barely begun to heal them. I'll come back—"

"When?"

"The day after tomorrow."

He scowled.

"Tomorrow, then—if you rest and eat a good supper."

"And then I'll be healed?"

Rifkind shook her head. "It will take time. Two weeks, maybe three."

"But I'll be better. You swear? I'm going to be lord of Gryphonage one day; when you swear to me, you have to tell the truth. Not like Illabin."

"No oaths. I'll do what I can, you'll do what you're told, and in three weeks, we'll see where we stand. Who's Illabin? Your tutor?"

"He's a witch, too, a sorcerer-witch. Father brought him here. He *swore* and made me drink awful things, dead things, and steaming things. He said I'd be riding a horse and practicing with a sword, but here I am, sitting in my room, listening to Fezzle read about dead people."

Lord Ballard had said he welcomed sorcerers. A father might try anything to bring health to a son as important as Garris.

"What did your father do to Illabin when he failed?" Rifkind asked, thinking of herself.

"Nothing!" Garris said with enough vehemence that he started coughing again. "I'm not supposed to *exert* myself," he said when Rifkind had again eased the spasm with a touch. "He couldn't do *that*. He couldn't do anything."

"But your father sent him away?"

Garris shook his head. Blond hair fell over his forehead: a practiced gesture, if ever Rifkind had seen one. She'd watched Tyrokon when charm had been his only weapon.

"He still comes and stays in the Strong Tower, but *I* don't see him. *I* don't talk to him. He lied."

The boy's cheeks were red as roses. Rifkind put her hand on his shoulder, melted his resistance, and pushed him back to the pillows. "I won't lie to you," she said. It was the same promise she'd given Tyrokon. "Sleep. Eat. Let your body follow where I lead it and in three weeks, we'll see."

His eyelids fluttered, then closed. Rifkind held her palm over his narrow chest. There was so much damage, she couldn't be sure that anything she did wouldn't simply push him closer to a final breath.

Illabin, she thought on her way out of the room. A name to put with the fleeting presence in the Strong Tower chamber? If so, then he was a sorcerer, not a pretender like so many. An-Soren had been a sorcerer; she'd killed him. But Domhnall had been a sorcerer, too. They came in every temperament and none of them were healers.

Tess had disappeared, leaving Rifkind to find her way through Gryphonage alone. The rising scents of the day's hot meal brought Rifkind back to the kitchen where she sated herself with a bowl of curds and whey. From the kitchen she could see that the outer gate was open and, recalling that Lord Ballard had consigned the war-horses to an outside stable, cast her thoughts in search of Banin.

She found him easily and absorbed his awareness. Banin liked the grain he'd been given, didn't like the fence that kept him from the *better* grass on the far side, and wasn't alone. Tein and Assurin were with him. They'd been *groomed*. Banin itched with jealousy.

Rifkind picked a winter apple out of the larder and went to find him. She wouldn't have been surprised to find both boyos with their war-horses or neither. The sight of Tyrokon alone, dragging a brush across Assurin's flanks, piqued her curiosity.

"Where's Cho?" she asked as Banin ate his first apple.

"Gone to play games with the cohort."

"Games? Dice again?"

"No. Weapons . . . the sword. To listen to the men talk, all they do is practice and fight, fight and practice. Cho couldn't resist. I watched awhile. It's not my style, but Cho . . ." Tyrokon's voice trailed and he swiped the brush with enough force to bring Assurin's head up.

"My son's built for the Darian style," Rifkind conceded. "If they put him in a mail shirt—"

"They already have. He's been dreaming of this, his father's world."

"His father was a sorcerer who didn't know the first thing about swords!"

Tyrokon cracked a smile that faded fast. "It doesn't matter who his father was or wasn't. In his heart, Cho thinks he's come home."

"And you?"

"The inns were bad enough: *walls, floors, ceilings.*" They'd been speaking the clan dialect, where there were no words for such things. "Last night, the ceiling was so low, I could reach up and touch it and the walls . . . I'd shut my eyes and feel them closing in around me."

"Let me tell you something about castle walls: They may be thick, but they're not as solid as they look. I've been in castles where there were whole rooms carved into the walls and secret passageways! Every lord who lives in a castle fears getting trapped inside it, so he builds himself secret ways to get around and get out."

Tyrokon's eyebrows lifted, but his despair went deeper than walls or dreams. There was a gap between him and Cho now, and nothing Rifkind might say would close it. She tried changing the subject altogether.

"Do I seem old enough to you?"

"Old enough how?"

"It's happened again. When I tried to tell Lord Ballard that I'd ridden with the Overnmonts, he wouldn't believe me. Says I'm not old enough—"

Before Rifkind could finish, she heard a familiar voice call her name. Tess with her skirt up in one arm, running down the road from the castle.

"Rifkind! Rifkind! Come quick! Garris's coughing *blood*!"

14

Garris was gray beneath his blond hair, except for the flecks of blood clinging to his lips and chin. Even his eyes were gray when he opened them
briefly. He fought for every breath and was losing the fight.

"I rested," he whispered hoarsely, a breath for each word. "I kept my
word."

Rifkind laid her palms on him, one at his forehead, the other at his
chest, and rose into her *tal*. She didn't know what was keeping him alive.
His little body was wasted. The time had come for mercy, for untying the
strands that bound the soul to flesh, yet she resisted that simple act, which
she had performed countless times before, and not merely because Garris's
father was in the room.

"I'll keep mine."

It wasn't easy. Pregnant women joked about eating for two. A healer, la-
boring at the limit of her ability, went deeper than that. Rifkind breathed
for Garris. She kept his heart beating, his blood flowing. Where his body
could be slowed to within a hair's breadth of death, she slowed it. Where it
could not be slowed, she kept it moving.

And she did all that with instinct while the greater power of her mind sought a sort of high ground from which she could begin the healing. When she had found that, and secured it, she opened her eyes.

The sun was gone. Light came from four stout candles impaled on iron spikes and set at the corners of the daybed. Lord Ballard sat opposite Rifkind. He had a knife in his hand and an inscrutable expression on his face.

"Is he—?"

Rifkind shook her head. Her neck was stiff as wood; she hadn't moved in hours. It took conscious effort to bend her fingers one at a time and lift her right hand from Garris's chest. She didn't try to move her left hand. She was still mostly in her *tal* and needed the contact to assure herself that her healing—what little she'd done so far—held.

"Food," she said to Ohlmer Ballard, forgoing his title and any other niceties. "Bread, cheese, sausage. Whatever you've got, cut up and brought here, in easy reach."

"You can't be serious. He can't—"

"For *me*," Rifkind snarled. She was in her *tal*; her words had power.

Ballard rocked back on his stool and leaned forward again. They locked stares.

"My will is all that's keeping your boy alive, and my will is like a fire that needs feeding."

Ballard gave the orders. Rifkind realized they were alone in the room and that the knife she could see wasn't the only weapon arrayed against her if she failed. But she wouldn't fail, not when she had gone this deep.

A boy not much older than Garris appeared with a pewter tray of boiled eggs chopped into quarters.

"Margary apologizes—" the boy began.

Rifkind didn't care. She grabbed a yellow-and-white morsel, wolfed it down, then grabbed another and another.

"Does he have a chance?" Ballard asked when the tray was half empty. "Can you heal him?"

"Ask me again in the morning," she replied and laid her hand once again on Garris's chest.

Morning came and Rifkind dared a descent from her *tal*. The tray beside her had gone from pewter to wood, from eggs to breadcrumbs, which she harvested with a moistened fingertip. She had no memory of eating the loaf.

Ballard still sat on the opposite side of the bed. His eyes were bloodshot and his face was rough with beard stubble. He'd put the knife away, at least.

Morning, yes, but not the morning after a single night.

"How long?"

"Three nights, and the days in between!"

Rifkind really hadn't felt the aches in her back and legs until she heard those words. Her hands were numb to the elbow.

"The only part of you that's moved is your right hand, eating us out of hearth and home."

And she had a hunger that went to her bones.

"He's alive," she said simply.

"I know that. I've held a mirror to his nostrils. But will he live? Will he open his eyes again?"

Rifkind nodded. "Soon," she said, but then Garris's heartbeat fluttered and she rose into her *tal* for another battle.

She had never fought so hard for a life. It went against everything she taught her apprentices. Death was not always the enemy and staying up in one's *tal* for days at a time put the healer at risk. The line between self and patient faded.

Metaphor became reality and Rifkind found herself confronting a horde of hairy serpents with jagged fangs but no eyes. She fought them with a sword made of flame and though she cut down hundreds, thousands surged around her.

"Rifkind! Rifkind!"

A serpent coiled around her wrist . . . no, it was a hand, pulling Rifkind down from her *tal*. She looked at a stranger's face in an unfamiliar room.

"Rifkind, you have to stop, rest."

Not a stranger: Tyrokon, and not an unfamiliar room, but Garris's room in Gryphonage. She looked down. Her hand was free. The boy's color was good. He was breathing regularly and with no help from her. She tried to move her hands, but couldn't find them. Her fingers began to tremble.

"I— I—" she groped for simple words without finding them.

Tyrokon grasped her wrists. He pushed her back in the chair she hadn't left for—how long? He folded her arms.

"I remember you talking to the girls. 'You can't do it all,' you'd say. 'Set their healing in motion, then let them finish it themselves."

With effort, Rifkind managed a nod.

"You were doing it all for Garris."

She had the will to argue with the boyo, but not the strength. "Tired."

"Lord Ballard's brought down another bed. You can sleep there—"

"Can't."

"I'll take your place. I know what to look for. If anything changes, I'll wake you up."

Liar, Rifkind thought. If she let herself sleep, she'd sink so deep that the end of the world wouldn't awaken her. The longer she stayed down from her *tal,* the more inevitable that deep sleep became.

Garris's fate was in his own hands.

Rifkind needed several tries to find the arms of her chair and when she tried to lever herself upright, her legs buckled. She'd have pitched forward, if Tyrokon hadn't been there to steady her. He steered her toward an empty daybed. She never remembered reaching it.

When Rifkind awoke after a two-day, dead-to-the-world sleep, a full week had passed since Tess had come running down from Gryphonage. The first thing she looked for was Tyrokon, who was nowhere to be seen, and Garris's bed was empty. She stormed down the spiral stairs in a rage only to be brought up short in the kitchen yard by the sight of Garris riding bareback on a placid pony. Tyrokon, who held the pony's reins, broke into a face-splitting grin and led the pony over for inspection.

A stranger's eye would have noted that Garris was painfully thin, with spindly bones and hollow cheeks, but Rifkind was hardly a stranger. She saw what wasn't there: the flush and the fever. She heard a boy who could prattle on, thought after thought, without succumbing to a blood-speckled cough.

Word that Rifkind was awake spread through the castle. Lord Ballard appeared with a dozen of his men. He spoke of miracles and rich rewards, both of which Rifkind rejected. She'd worked too hard to believe in miracles and rewards meant little.

Besides, Tyrokon had admitted that this was only Garris's second foray into fresh air and sunshine. The healing Rifkind had set in motion hadn't finished its course. Garris tired quickly—was tiring right before her eyes.

She resisted the temptation to lay hands on him then and there. Tyrokon had been correct when he'd recited her own words at her: Let them finish their healing themselves. For all that, she'd been too lost in a healer's obsession to listen to him. But that didn't stop her from sending the boy back to his room or from telling his father—

"It's too soon for celebrating. Go to the temple and give thanks, if you want, but wait a week, or, better yet, wait two weeks, before we start telling ourselves that what's done cannot be undone."

Lord Ballard back-stepped. He didn't like to be crossed, that was clear from his face, but he wasn't fool enough to challenge the healer who'd saved his son.

"Two weeks," he repeated, as if the words burnt his tongue. "Two weeks." He turned to his men. "That will give us time to summon the cream of Irdel for a festival. They can renew their oaths to me and to my son."

One and all, Lord Ballard's men agreed that Lord Ballard had had a good idea. He turned back to Rifkind.

"You'll stay, of course, for the two weeks and the celebration."

Rifkind, who needed more than two days' sleep to complete her own recovery, agreed without hesitation.

She might have objected to remaining at Gryphonage if she'd had foreknowledge of the weather. Rain started falling that evening and by the following morning it was clear that Irdel was in the grip of one of the rainy spells for which the west was justly infamous. Rain came sideways in the wind, pounding the north and west walls, though, now and again, the winds would shift and the southwest corners of the castle took the beating.

Weather didn't stop Lord Ballard's messengers from their circuits through his domain, proclaiming Garris's restoration along with an invitation—a command—to attend a celebration of that auspicious event. Calls went out for provisions as well and a steady trickle of carts made their way to the Gryphonage gates. The village temple, where the formal celebration would take place before the castle feast, got a refurbishing that saw the Ballard yellow-and-green gryphon banners fluttering from every peak and corner.

Rifkind avoided most of the fuss by overseeing Garris's recovery. Tyrokon joined her. Hamarach's eldest son was every child's ideal of an elder brother: worldly wise, patient, and just a bit of a rogue when necessary.

The pair conspired against Rifkind, to her great amusement, smuggling the boy down to the paddock where Tyrokon put him on Assurin's back. From the tower window, she watched as the war-horse, with Tyrokon at his head, plodded politely in endless circles.

Or course, seeing Assurin from a distance meant seeing Banin and Tein the same way. She'd made amends to Banin by visiting him each morning. She plied him with apples from the kitchen and took him out for gallops up and down the Gryphonage valley to remind him of what it meant to be ridden. His neck had filled out on Darian grass; there was no mistaking him for a colt anymore, or mistaking his pique over the attention Assurin was getting from the little rider with *apples* in his pockets.

Rifkind enjoyed a private laugh at her companion's expense then noticed that the third war-horse of the trio had scarcely moved the entire time she'd been watching the paddock. Tein had pressed himself against that portion of the fence that brought him closest to the castle. His head stretched closer still—

Waiting for a rider who now preferred heavy chain mail?

It dawned on Rifkind that, though she saw Cho several times a day, at meals and among the Gryphonage cohort, she hadn't seen him with Tyrokon, much less with Tein. He was probably the only person in the valley who hadn't congratulated her for healing Garris.

Like a veteran reluctantly belting on his sword, Rifkind left Garris's room in search of her son.

She found him outside the armory pounding grommets into a piece of armor-weight leather. Another man spotted her coming first and gave Cho a nudge. They were too far apart, still, for Rifkind to see Cho's face, but the vigor with which he laid the hammer and leather aside hinted strongly that she'd made a mistake.

If their eyes hadn't snagged, Rifkind would have walked away. But they had, so she stopped at distance where, if they kept their voices low, their conversation would not be overheard.

"What brings you down from your tower?" Cho began.

"I wanted to see how you were doing."

"A little late for that, don't you think?"

"Do we have to argue?"

"Your call."

They stared past each other until Rifkind said, "I saw Tein today. He looked lonely."

Cho glowered down at her. "I thought you didn't want to argue?"

Rifkind decided to try again. "You seem to have found a place here."

That got her a shrug. "I have a lot to learn. They've been practicing their style since they could lift a sword."

"You learn quickly."

"How would you know? You don't think about me from one day to the next. You don't know the first thing about me. You don't know the first thing about being a mother. You like children, all right, so long as they're sickly and not yours when the day is done. I'd have to be lying in the dust with my leg in pieces before you'd see me—and even then, it would be as a healer's challenge, not a son."

"You'd rather have been born with withered legs or rotten lungs? That's what you're saying? You're strong, Cho, strong and healthy. You've never *needed* a healer."

Cho retreated. His head bobbed, as if he were nodding agreement with voices only he could hear. "Forget it," he snarled. "Just leave me alone. That shouldn't be hard to do."

He stalked away and Rifkind had no idea how to call him back or if she even should.

RIFKIND SAW CHO IN the days that followed, but he did not see her. Once, and once only, she tried talking to Tyrokon and realized, in the nick of time, that she risked losing him, too, if she persisted. She poured her interest into Lord Ballard's son—

Maybe Cho *was* right.

Two weeks to the day after she'd awakened from healing Garris, Lord Ballard held a celebration in the boy's honor. It was not as heavily attended as Rifkind had expected. Apparently there were men in Irdel who did not feel compelled to answer their lord's summons or renew their oaths. The implications of that were for another day.

The celebration was for Garris who rode his pony at the head of procession winding down from Gryphonage to the village temple. Rifkind walked behind him, beside a herald who carried the gryphon banner.

The Gryphonage temple was dedicated to Mohandru, the Weeping God, but as the only temple in the valley, it contained side chapels for Daria's many other gods, including a niche for the Bright Moon in Her Darian aspect as the goddess of unmarried women.

Weeping Mohandru was not Rifkind's favorite deity and his priests had, in the past, struck her as austere, fleshless men dangerously devoid of humor and compassion. Considering what Daria had endured since her last visit, she was prepared for a hefty dose of Mohandrist abnegation before Garris received his blessing. She was pleasantly surprised, then, when the blessing priest proved to be a short, jovial sort who obviously enjoyed a frequent good meal.

He greeted them one and all with a smile too broad to be anything but genuine. When he proclaimed to the assembly that nothing pleased Mohandru more than the sight of Garris riding a pony, Rifkind was inclined to believe him and to believe that there was hope for the Mohandrists in general.

The priest—his name was Heft, which seemed very appropriate—accompanied them back to the castle's great hall where oath-giving was the next order of the day before the feast could begin. When all the nobles had bent their knees, Lord Ballard called Rifkind to the high table. He loudly credited her with his son's health, and gave two gifts: a golden ring and a fist-sized purse. After appropriate gratitude, Rifkind retreated to an empty seat at one of the long side tables. The ring was too large for any finger but her thumb and the precise contents of the purse would remain a mystery until she was alone.

The platters of food laid out on the banquet tables had been noticeably diminished during the oath-giving, but the page assigned to Lord Ballard's honored guest piled a high plate for her pleasure and, more importantly, brought her a goblet of snow-chilled wine. Her neighbors at the table introduced themselves. Rifkind parroted their names and forgot them almost immediately. Fortunately none of them wanted to get friendly with a foreign witch.

Halfway through the cold, spiced beef, Lord Ballard clapped his hands to summon his musicians. They entered with a fanfare that became a lively dance. Rifkind did not dance. During her first Wet-lands sojourn, she'd been taught that gentle art by Ejord's formidable aunt and the process had been sheer torture. One of the Ballard knights invited her to join him in the intricate, meaningless patterns. She demurred and, though it was cheating, rose into her *tal* just enough to surround herself with a pall of disinterest.

Cho and Tyrokon did dance—not well, of course, but with enthusiasm. Tyrokon played it safe, keeping to the herd of boyos who practiced their moves behind the tables and did not venture near the flirting young ladies, Rifkind's sullen maid, Tess, among them. Cho didn't let ignorance deter him. He approached the prettiest maidens and laughed at himself when he missed a step. Watching him with a mother's eye, Rifkind guessed her son was more than halfway drunk . . . and happier than she'd ever seen him.

She took a long swallow from her own goblet and, propping her chin on her elbows, allowed herself the thought that she'd gotten at least one thing right since riding away from Hamarach's tents.

She was enjoying that thought when a cold tingle shot down her spine. Instantly she stiffened. The chill hadn't been a draft come down from the ceiling, hadn't been anything physical at all. Someone with a potent *tal* and the ability to rise into it had cast his consciousness at her—

His? Could she be sure that chill had emanated from a man's *tal*?

Rifkind had only instinct to rely upon, but instinct was certain. There was a man in Lord Ballard's hall who was, as Wet-landers named them, a witch . . . or a sorcerer . . . or possibly a priest?

Heft, the jovial Mohandrist was between the tables, dancing with his flock. He was scarcely better at the patterns than Cho and, by the russet glow of his cheeks, at least as deep into his wine cup. If he was the source, then he was better at doing two incompatible things simultaneously than anyone Rifkind had ever met.

The only name that floated to the surface of Rifkind's mental inquiry was her old, and vanquished, nemesis An-Soren. There had been a man who routinely used *tal* powers to spy on everyone. And, powerful as he'd been, An-Soren had learned the art of insignificance. He could hide in a crowd when he'd chosen.

Rifkind glanced from face to face, seeking a strong *tal* while trying not to draw attention to herself. Finding nothing among the faces, she looked into the shadows, which were numerous and inky in any room as large as the great hall and lit only by a hearth and a hundred or more candles.

There—in the archway niche beneath the spiral stairs.

For a heartbeat Rifkind had something, then it was gone. Deciding to investigate, she swung her legs over the bench where she'd been sitting and made her way along the edge of the hall, but by the time she got to the niche it was utterly empty. She touched the stones. Sometimes a presence lingered; not this time.

It's my imagination, Rifkind chided herself. *I'm tired. I've drunk too much wine myself and tomorrow we're leaving—finally—for Chatelgard.*

Looking through the dancers and across the hall, she spotted her page laying her goblet across her plate in preparation for removing it to the kitchen. She could hardly blame the lad, not when she'd been shedding indifference, though she would have liked to finish the wine.

What she wanted now was a few hours to collect her thoughts before getting a night's sleep and an early start on the morrow's journey. Glancing at the boyos, Rifkind knew an early start wasn't likely. If the pair were ready at dawn, when she wanted to leave, it would only be because they hadn't yet collapsed from their carousing.

Rifkind made her way to the head table, instead, where Lord Ballard presided over the festivities without being a part of them. She reminded him that she and the boyos were leaving in the morning and thanked him for his hospitality, in the event that their paths did not cross again. The lord accepted her thanks while assuring her that he'd be at the gate to wish her a good journey. Then she retired to her tower chamber.

Tess was missing, still dancing, no doubt, and oblivious to her duties. Rifkind shed her dress and folded it carefully. She wouldn't be needing it again; she'd imposed upon the castle seamstresses and acquired a new pair of riding breeches for the trek to Chatelgard. The suede wasn't as soft as she would have liked—she'd probably be healing chafes in awkward places in a day's time—but anything was better than riding in a full-circle skirt.

She left the door unbarred for Tess's eventual return, and tucked Lord Ballard's purse—a generous assortment of silver coins—under the girl's pillow. A girl could dower herself with that purse and, for all her sullenness, Rifkind bore Tess no ill will. She left the night lamp burning and climbed into her bed, pulling the draperies down behind her.

Minutes later, or hours, perhaps, Rifkind awoke from a dream about Ejord.

"Tess?"

"My lady?" the girl replied. "Is there—is there something you need?" No mistaking the lack of enthusiasm in her voice or the thickening of wine.

"No, I was just making sure. Did you bolt the door?"

Rifkind listened to metal scraping against metal.

"I'll dress myself in the morning. If you hear me, just roll over and go back to sleep."

"Yes, my lady." Rifkind heard the sound of bedcovers being turned back and the distinct jingle of coins in a pouch. "Thank you, my lady."

Rifkind punched up her pillow and smiled to herself. She was back asleep before another thought crossed her mind . . . and rudely awakened by something heavy and insistent pounding on the bolted door.

"In the name of Lord Ballard, Duke of Irdel, open this door!"

Tess screamed while, in pitch-dark confusion, Rifkind wrestled with the bed curtains. The pounding continued. The heavy door jounced on its hinges.

"What shall we do?" Tess asked between screams and sobs.

"We open the door," Rifkind said calmly as her feet found the floor. Thoughts of poisoning and injury swirled in her mind. A healer was required. She could imagine no other reasons for the commotion. "Stand back while I throw the bolt."

She'd scarcely drawn the bolt back when the door bucked open. Men with torches shouldered into the chamber. Men with drawn swords surrounded her.

"Rifkind, witch of the Asheera, you are commanded to come with us."

"There is no need for weapons," she protested. "I'll dress quickly—"

A man with neither torch nor sword in his hand stepped behind her, seized her right wrist and then her left. He bound them tightly behind her.

Rifkind was too startled to struggle effectively. "What is the meaning of this?"

"You're to be held on suspicion of witchcraft."

"That's nonsense! What I've done, I've done with the lord's permis—"

Rifkind's chief accuser, the man who held the sword that pointed into the hollow of her neck, lowered his weapon and clouted her hard across the jaw.

"You'll be quiet," he snarled. "Now, bring her along."

The man who'd tied Rifkind's wrists gave her a shove in the back. Rifkind held herself any man's equal when there was steel in her hand but she was at an insurmountable disadvantage in the center of a ring of armed men. Barefoot and clad only in her linen, she went where she was propelled, stumbling on the stairs and picking up splinters from the rough-wood planking.

"I demand to see Lord Ballard—"

"Oh, you'll see him, all right. You'll see him in judgment."

They brought her down to the great hall, which was dark and empty, then up another column of spiral steps to the topmost room. One of the torchbearers opened the door toward himself while another man bruised her ribs shoving her across the threshold. By the time Rifkind caught her breath, the door had slammed shut and a bar, rather than a simple bolt, had been dropped across it.

The world had turned upside down so quickly, Rifkind could scarcely think. Never in her life had she been bound in any way, nor deprived of her freedom. She fought panic with every heartbeat and crashed around the black room, tripping over chests, battering herself against stone walls until she stumbled into a long-disused hearth.

Sinking to her knees, Rifkind went to work rasping the coarse, hairy rope around her wrists against the corner stones. She ground until her shoulders burned and her wrists bled from fiber abrasion, but the rope held. She took a deep breath and ascended into her *tal* to restore herself— mindful that she was borrowing exhaustion, yet risking it anyway.

The hearthstones had been carefully worked, smoothed and rounded off. They were worthless when it came to rasping through rope. Twice more Rifkind worked herself to the brink of agony, twice more she restored herself, then the well was empty and she fell forward into oblivion.

15

A very bright light—the sun—shone on Cho's face and a ratty piece of leather lay in his mouth where his tongue should have been. The world swam in odd shades of gold, green, and purple when he opened his eyes and, thinking instantly of a lightstorm, he shut them tight again. Then he remembered the wine he'd drunk the previous night, goblets of which he'd lost count, and remembered where he'd drunk them: in the great hall of Gryphonage . . . Lord Ballard's castle . . . in the Wet-lands . . . where he'd come with his mother.

Bloody, bloody Bright One—

Gryphonage never had needed, and never would need, to worry about a lightstorm, but Rifkind had come to him and Tyrokon yesterday, telling them to be ready to leave for Chatelgard.

Cho could fairly see her standing at his feet, chest-high woman that she was, her black eyes shining like jet, her lips pressed together until they all but disappeared, oozing disapproval like sweat. He opened his eyes a second time, averting his head from the sunlight, half-expecting to see *her* looming over him in real life as she had in his imagination.

But there was only air and the sound of men snoring off a drunk.

Oh, bloody Bright—

If he'd been able, Cho would have crawled back into mindless sleep. If he'd been able, which he wasn't. He was awake, with all the demands that morning made on an abused body. He sat, he knelt, he used both hands to lever himself up from the horsehair pallet where he'd passed the smaller part of night, the larger part of morning.

The lower hall fell off to his left; he barely caught his balance. The effort made his head throb, but it cleared his mind, too, and the spinning, falling sensations ceased. He made his way to the pissoir where the stench was enough to knock him back a step. Gathering strength, he held his breath until that pressure, at least, was relieved.

Stepping out of the alcove, Cho took note that he wasn't the worst off. Barely a third of the pallets had been rolled up against the walls—and no telling how many of them had never been *unrolled*. The rest of Gryphonage's cohort lay sprawled with arms or legs trailing onto the floor and still in the clothes they'd worn to the lord's feast, as Cho himself was still wearing yesterday's clothes.

Not Tyrokon. The chief's son slept tidily on his side, his arms crooked beneath his head and his blanket draped across his shoulders as if his mothers had slipped by to tuck him in.

Cho nudged his friend with his foot.

"*Shh-shhsh,*" he cautioned as Tyrokon rolled and opened his eyes. "We're in deep now."

"Wha—?" Tyrokon warded sunlight with a raised arm.

Then it must have struck him: Sunlight meant they were late for meeting Rifkind. He threw back his blanket, reached for his breeches.

"How're you feeling?" Cho asked.

"Better than you look. Better than I'm going to feel when we find her."

They went to the kitchen yard where Rifkind had told them to meet her. She wasn't there. An old woman sat on a bench plucking a freshly killed chicken. In his fractured Glascard, Cho asked if she'd seen Rifkind.

"Rifkind! Rifkind!" He traced a semicircle on his cheek.

"The witch?" she replied and shook her head.

Tyrokon wanted to visit the room where Rifkind had been staying. "Could be she's still asleep herself."

Cho wanted to find Lord Ballard, the major domo, or one of the other castle officers. "We can say we've been looking for her."

They compromised and went up to the great hall where someone in authority could usually be found.

They found Delan, the castle armorer, sitting in a patch of sunlight, mending chain. Like the old woman, he hadn't seen the witch but he, at least, spoke trade and offered to take them up to Lord Ballard's privy chamber.

"The lord'll know who's gone through the gate, e'en if he didn't see it himself."

The Ballard lord sat at a small table, eating breakfast and surrounded by advisers. By the bobbing of heads and the pointing of fingers, the men weren't in agreement. They fell silent as soon as they caught sight of Delan and his guests. Not that it would have mattered. Though the men of Gryphonage seemed to all understand the trade tongue, they spoke their own language among themselves. Cho had picked up some of local phrases, most of them having to do with swords and sparring, gambling and women; Tyrokon hadn't gotten that far. They could have stood between the lord and his advisers and not guessed a word of their argument.

Lord Ballard looked up from his plate of eggs and sausage, the mere sight of which turned Cho's stomach. "I was expecting you two," he said in trade.

Those words, on top of the eggs, made Cho's head swim. He touched Tyrokon lightly. Tyrokon was Hamarach's son; he had a way with words Cho could only envy.

Tyrokon nodded slightly before saying, "We're looking for Rifkind, my lord. We were supposed to meet her—supposed to leave. And we haven't been able to find her."

"Ah! You've missed her," Lord Ballard said lightly.

"Missed her?" Tyrokon asked after exchanging a worried glance with Cho.

"Dawn she said and dawn she meant. When you weren't there, she mounted her horned stallion and rode off saying you could catch up or stay behind. If you ride hard, you might catch her before sundown. Or stay. I can always find room for a man with a strong sword arm."

Cho was tempted, by the goddess, he was tempted. He was outraged that Rifkind would ride off without him or Tyrokon . . . and she complained about *his* temper. Then colder thoughts took control: If his mother wanted to be rid of him, well, she'd get her damn wish, but not before he'd had words with her one more time.

Tyrokon didn't seem to know what to say next. Cho stepped into the void. "We appreciate your offer, Lord Ballard, and we'll be back to take it, but first we've got to catch that witch."

Lord Ballard smiled. "Very well. Stop by the kitchen and gather what you need before you leave."

The last thing Cho needed just then was food. He thanked the lord again and thanked Delan, as well. Wet-landers were fussy about such things and he needed to be attentive to them, if he was going to make Gryphonage his home. They left the chamber without need of Delan's guidance.

"I can't believe it," Tyrokon said in clan language while they descended.

"I can. She's been looking for a way to leave us behind since we left Epigos."

"No—"

"Yes. She never intended to bring us to Chatelgard. She's a witch, just as they say. You can't trust her."

Tyrokon shut up, which was just as well; Cho was in no mood to hear anyone defend his impossible mother. "We've got to stop in the lower hall."

"Why?" Tyrokon countered. "What's down there? I'm wearing everything I brought into this place, so are you."

"My sword—"

"With the war-horses."

"My *new* sword."

Tyrokon sucked air. "A club with edges."

"Maybe—but the weapon you need if you're up against a man in a chain. Put enough behind it, and it can bust the links."

"If you say so. From what I've seen, there're plenty of gaps in a chain mail shirt, plenty of places to thrust sharp steel."

Cho didn't argue. When push came to shove, Tyrokon didn't have the legs or the brawn to stand toe-to-toe with a Wet-lands man-at-arms; his only hope lay in the lighter Asheeran sword. Cho wanted his new weapon. He'd have liked to have the mail shirt that went with it, but the lord didn't give away mail as readily as he gave away swords. He belted the heavy sword against his hip and led the way to the yard.

The iron-strapped gate was open. Once through it, they had a clear view of the paddock where, just as the lord had promised, there was no sign of gray Banin.

The left-behind war-horses were agitated. Heads bobbing, they trotted along the paddock fence, their sweated coats glistening. When they caught sight of their riders, they came to the gate making all the noises war-horses could make. Tyrokon set about calming Assurin with strokes and soft words, but Cho's bitter curiosity got the better of him. With Tein, butting his shoulder at every step, he marched to the shed where they'd stowed their tack and personal gear.

"Damn her!" he snarled from the doorway. "She took Tein's saddle!"

"No."

"See for yourself."

Tyrokon came and saw. There was Assurin's saddle—a gift from Hamarach—thrown over a log with Rifkind's battered old saddle, the same one she'd sat in when she first visited the Wet-lands, in front of it, and no sign of Cho's trophy saddle.

"I don't believe it."

"Believe it," Cho shot back. "There's nothing she won't stoop to."

He wanted to swing the old saddle over his head and hurl it into the woods beyond the paddock, but that would leave him riding bareback and there was no reason to punish Tein for Rifkind's sins. Still, he needed to lash out. His hands curled into fists and his head throbbed like there'd be no tomorrow. For the sake of his headache, Cho struggled to flank his raging anger, then Tyrokon thumped him on the arm and he damn near let fly.

"Something's not right," Tyrokon insisted.

"Yeah, my exalted mother's a thief and a coward."

"No. Banin's halter's still hanging there."

"So? She took my bridle as well as my saddle—" but that assertion, however satisfying, was not, as Tyrokon had already said, right.

Rifkind didn't use a bridle with Banin. Bloody Bright, there were times when she should have, but she'd let the young war-horse bolt before she'd admit she couldn't control him with her mind. Moreover, neither of their two bridles was missing and, now that Cho gave a closer study to the clutter, all three of the saddle packs were heaped together in the corner. He was racking his mind for an explanation when Tyrokon stated the obvious—

"She's still here."

"Why would Lord Ballard say she'd left?"

Tyrokon answered with a question of his own: "Why would he go through the trouble of taking Banin out of the paddock to make us believe she had? It must have taken three men, at least, and three more to keep Assurin and Tein out of it."

Cho's mind raced. "Not stolen—*hidden*. Hidden to make us think the worst."

"Not the worst. The worst would be they got her locked up some place . . ."

They looked at each other.

"Why?" Tyrokon asked.

Cho shook his head. "Everything was honor and smiles yesterday. I didn't hear anything Lord Ballard said, but he gave her a purse and a ring."

"Then it can't be Lord Ballard. Maybe that Wilts fellow. I didn't see him this morning."

"We can go back to Lord Ballard tell him that there's a dastard under his wing."

They were at the foot of the castle hill when a young woman came running down to meet them. She had the pale yellow hair that Cho had never seen in the Asheera and which alternately fascinated and repelled him. Last night it had attracted him and he'd flirted with this very girl, squiring her through a clumsy rendition of some inscrutable dance. This morning, with more important things on his mind and a lingering headache, the streaming hair had the look of death and disease.

He fervently hoped she had some other destination in mind, but hope failed and she cut him and Tyrokon off.

Reaching past the headache, Cho tried to remember the girl's name—Bess, Pess, Tess, or something like that. When he'd been flirting, and nearly drunk, it hadn't mattered that she didn't speak trade and he hadn't learned enough Glascard to carry on a civil conversation. Now words tumbled out of her, all meaningless gabble, except for one: "Rifkind."

"Can you make sense of what she's saying?" Tyrokon asked.

Cho shook his head. "She's talking about Rifkind, I think."

"Me, too—"

But before Tyrokon could say more, the girl had grabbed Cho's hand in one of hers and with the other begun to point at the part of the castle the men called the Winter Tower. Cho freed himself and the girl turned frantic, repeating the healer's name and jabbing the air as if her fingers were weapons.

"Rifkind's up there in that tower," Cho said.

"That's not where she's been. Something's seriously wrong, Cho."

Cho agreed. He started up the hill and was astonished when the girl seized his arm to hold him back. He snarled a curse at her, because oaths were oaths regardless of their language. She let go as though he'd gone steaming hot and Cho got back to walking. She called after him, one phrase repeatedly, one phrase of which Cho didn't understand a single word.

Finding Lord Ballard was as simple as passing through the castle gate. Dressed in riding leathers, the Duke of Irdel stood beside a massive Wetlands horse, parceling out orders. His five-man escort had already mounted. To a man, they fell silent at the sight of the two Asheerans.

"A word," Cho began in trade and the stares grew sharper.

A few of the standing men exchanged words Cho wouldn't have understood even if he'd been able to hear them. Lord Ballard stepped away from his horse, but not before he'd glanced at his escort that didn't require translation. Until that moment, Cho's instincts hadn't let go of blaming his mother; suddenly they did and he felt naked. Tyrokon closed in, and that felt better, but they were still two against more than twenty.

"How may I help you?" Lord Ballard asked, his smile a telling contrast to the look he'd shot at his escort. "I was just leaving myself. We're going in the opposite direction. I can have someone ride with you, if you don't know the way to the Irdel Road."

"We— that is, I—" Cho stammered. "My mother's war-horse is gone, but not her saddle. We— I think— if you were told she left—"

Lord Ballard picked one word out of Cho's confusion: "Mother?"

Cho flinched. Rifkind hadn't explicitly told him to keep quiet about their mother-son relationship, but she hadn't volunteered it to anyone since they'd left the Barking Goose, and he'd been more than comfortable to leave it unacknowledged.

He ignored the lord's question, saying, in as firm a voice as he could muster, "I think she's still here, in your castle."

Lord Ballard's eyes drifted rightward, a sure sign that he was thinking fast, then he broke into a grin. "I warned her it wouldn't work—that you two were too clever. The witch has agreed to stay with Garris while I'm away, but she wanted you to continue on to Glascardy."

Lie . . . lie . . . lie! Cho could imagine Rifkind agreeing to stay with the boy. But send him and Tyrokon on to Chatelgard? Even if they'd known the way, there wasn't a chance that she'd let her son meet the man who was— who should have been—his father without her there to control everything.

Lord Ballard barked Glascard orders and a few names into the clutch of standing men. "My men will take you to see her. You can settle this amongst yourselves. Go or stay, as you wish, but I must be going."

He mounted and gave the signal for the other riders to follow him out the gate. The standing men reformed around Cho and Tyrokon.

"You'll come with us," a man said—his name was Ricose and Cho had sparred with him on the practice ground. They'd joked about the advantages of thrusting weapons versus slashing ones, but there wasn't a hint of humor in the man's eyes now. When Cho hesitated, Ricose's hand dropped to the sword at his hip.

"What's going on?" Tyrokon demanded.

"We're being taken prisoner. I'm right, aren't I, Ricose?"

Ricose frowned. "You'd have been wiser before to mount up and ride out. You'd be wisest now to come quietly. You won't have long to wait. The lord will be back from Merrinen in a day or two."

Cho didn't know what to believe, whom to trust. Everything had happened too quickly for his wine-fogged mind to untangle, but one thing was certain: He and Tyrokon didn't stand a chance against twenty-odd Wetlanders with mail shirts and swords. They accepted their escort into the castle and along corridors and stairways he'd never traveled before. They came to a heavy door with a heavier bar and the biggest metal lock Cho had ever seen. Ricose had the key, two men raised the bar, a third opened the door, and the boyos stepped into darkness.

16

Cho waited until there was only silence on the far side of the heavy door, then he powered his shoulder against the wood. It gave a fraction before coming up hard against iron hinges and the thigh-thick bar.

"I do not *understand*!" he shouted and hit the door again, bruising his shoulder while gaining nothing.

"Wet-landers can lie while they're smiling," Tyrokon replied calmly from the depths of utter darkness. "We saw it in Vendle, in Epigos, and now on the face of Lord Ballard. They're none of them to be trusted."

"Right," Cho snarled before slamming the door a third time. "But, *why*? Why put us in here? Why put Rifkind wherever he's put her? Why treat us like honored guests one day and lock us up the next?"

"We'd know, if we could have followed him."

Cho growled and took a running start at the door.

"We're not getting out that way."

In his mind, Cho saw the planks, the metal lock, the heavy bar, and knew Tyrokon was right. They were caught in a stone-walled box with no hope of escape. He couldn't see the walls, but with each breath he was sure they were closing in around him. His choices were simple: fight or lose himself to panic, so he fought, hurling himself at the door.

A hand touched his arm. "That won't help."

"I've got to do something. Standing here . . . I can feel the walls squeezing the life out of me—bloody Bright!" Cho put his fist against the wood. Pain—the mixed pain of foolishness and split knuckles—shot up his arm. "I'll go mad."

"If you've got to hit something, hit the walls."

"A lot of good that'll do, when I can't budge the door."

"Rifkind said Wet-lands walls aren't as solid as they seem. There'll be a hollow spot and a passage behind it."

"Rifkind said *what*? Bloody Bright—you've got to be joking."

Cho made a fist, cocked it, then relaxed. The only sound was Tyrokon tapping, tapping, tapping on the wall. As usual, Rifkind had gotten in his way.

"A hollow?" Cho sighed in defeat.

"A hollow sound—a *different* sound."

So, Cho tapped, starting with the stone around the door, then moving high and low, outward toward his right, counter to Tyrokon. He'd cleared one corner and was approaching the second when, to his astonishment, he heard a *different* sound.

He called Tyrokon over.

"A lot of good it's going to do us," Cho complained when they'd tapped out an archway shape that rose no higher than his thigh. "Stone's still stone."

But Tyrokon was busy, tapping, scratching, thumping and making other noises against the stone, ignoring anything Cho had to say. "Found it! Tell me if anything moves when I turn this stone."

Incredibly, Cho heard something *ping* on the far side of the archway. He got his hands around the roughest stones and pulled. The archway swung on concealed hinges. It was a door, faced with stone, and beyond, air with a musty odor.

"Let's go," Tyrokon said.

"Me first," Cho insisted, asserting his claim to protection. The squat arch opened to landing, a wide spot at the top of a flight of narrow stairs made more treacherous by the utter lack of light. He had to descend to make room for Tyrokon. "Go slow," he advised. "These steps aren't much wider than my foot."

Tyrokon, smaller and wirier, squeezed more easily through the arch. Cho resumed his descent.

"Wait up. There's got to be a way to close this behind us."

"Bloody Bright!" Cho's panic returned. "You'll seal us in here!"

"Not likely . . . whoever made this was thinking about escape, just like us."

Cho could only stand, both arms braced against the narrow passage walls, while Tyrokon went back to his tapping. After an eternity, stone scraped stone and Tyrokon was ready.

They came to other landings where Tyrokon found other stone latches, none of which he manipulated.

"We could wind up in Lord Ballard's chamber! Best we make our way to the very bottom. I smell water, don't you?"

Cho didn't smell anything except his own sweat and fear, not that he'd admit it.

Somewhere between the third and fourth landing his heel slipped and he went down three steps at once before catching his balance.

"You all right?"

Cho forced out a single word: "Fine."

Step by dark step, Cho's panic peaked and ebbed. A man couldn't maintain a burning fear for long, not when the walls *didn't* move. And then they came to a landing that wasn't a landing but a dogleg to a man-high arch. Cho reached out and was glad of the caution: Flat wood met his hand at half an arm's length.

"What is it?"

Cho ran his hands over the wood. "A barrel, a stack of them. We're out of the passage," he whispered, "and into the next place"—he took a deep breath—"a small room, I think, with lots of barrels. My guess: There's another way in, and if you came through it, you wouldn't see this passageway for the barrels."

"Rifkind said as much." Tyrokon tried to squeeze past, but Cho caught his arm.

"No telling what's ahead; I'm still first."

Debris covered the floor. Cho bent down to examine it with his fingertip. *Leaves*, he concluded after remembering the brown-gold shapes littering the roadside. Rifkind said they fell from the trees before winter, though how *leaves* came to lie on a Gryphonage floor was beyond imagining.

They agreed on an exploration strategy: Cho went right, Tyrokon went left, slowly, quietly . . . until Tyrokon let out a yelp followed by a wooden crack and, a heartbeat later, the *plonk* of something hitting water.

"Ty?"

"All right. Almost found the water the hard way."

They came together beside a hole in the floor large enough to swallow a man feet first. There were iron mounts a handspan high circling the hole. Tyrokon had tripped over one and, sprawling flat over the hole instead of stepping into it, spared himself from disaster.

"I don't think this room gets visited much," Cho said, weighing the leaves and the exposed well in his mind.

"That's good."

"Only if there's another way out. Back to finding a door—but check the floor first."

Taking his own advice, Cho groped his way to the wall he'd been exploring. He'd cleared a corner and gone another six or seven feet when the wall suddenly stopped. He eased into the emptiness, smelled fresh air, and felt thorns with his outstretched hands.

"I've found it!"

By the time Tyrokon joined him, Cho had untangled his way through a break of nasty, but far from fatal, thornbushes. By the light of a half-phase Bright Moon, the boyos looked up Gryphonage's outer wall to a solitary guard leaning on the battlement. There was little risk that the guard could hear a whispered conversation, but Cho took no chances and gave Tyrokon a shove back into darkness.

"We've got our way out. Just keep low and quiet as we cross the ditch, then circle around, get the war-horses, and—"

Tyrokon interrupted: "Rifkind," he said. "We're no closer to her than we were locked in that room . . . farther, in a way—we were both in towers."

Cho sighed. He hadn't forgotten his mother. "Yeah."

The third way into the storage room wasn't hard to find. The heavy wooden door would have been impossible to open, had it been closed and the heavy timber propped beside it dropped into the iron brackets, but the door stood open and the boyos set their feet on a spiral stairway that led toward light that seemed noontime bright. The light proved to come from the night lamp on the far side of a malodorous drapery covering the wall of a pissoir, the very pissoir that stood at the far end of the lower hall where they'd slept each night since arriving at Gryphonage.

Cho's heart skipped in gratitude: the niche was empty and a cautious glance past the doorjamb revealed double rows of men sleeping on their pallets beneath the light of two additional night lamps, one just outside the pissoir, the other at the hall's far end, where the swords were stored.

"Walk slow," he whispered to Tyrokon. "Like it's any other night and you've woken up full of wine, but keep walking until you get to the stairs. Don't stop . . . and don't speed up, either, if anyone hails you. Wait on the stairs; I'll be right behind you."

Tyrokon nodded and strode out of the pissoir, following instructions, except when he paused to stretch and yawn.

Cho began his walk when Tyrokon entered the dim light of the second lamp. He didn't pause, or stretch, or yawn, but turned left where Tyrokon had turned right and oh-so-carefully helped himself to two, then three, of Lord Ballard's swords. Despite Cho's efforts, the scabbard rings clinked when he straightened and he froze, expecting the worst.

He could see Tyrokon waiting on stairs and watched his friend descend a step. As if he had the *tal* of a healer, Cho willed Tyrokon to remain where he was and, by the Bright One's grace, Tyrokon stood still. Then, after the longest moments of his life had passed with no untoward activity in the hall, Cho tiptoed to the stairs.

Tyrokon greeted him with a hissed, "Bloody Bright!"

Cho didn't answer, just jutted his chin and thrust the swords at his friend. Tyrokon understood and took the topmost one. He buckled it over his hips, then took the third sword and held it while Cho did the same.

"Now," he whispered, "let's find that damned tower where they've locked up my mother."

He ascended the spiral in dimly lit silence. The great hall, like the lower hall beneath it, served as a dormitory for much of the Gryphonage household and, as with the lower hall, it was quiet. Cho struck off for the spiral in the far corner of the hall, only to be tugged back. With hand signals, Tyrokon indicated a different spiral. Cho scowled—he didn't know which

stairway connected to which tower and intended an orderly search, farthest to nearest, but Tyrokon was determined and, rather than risk attention, Cho followed his friend's lead.

"That girl pointed at the tower they call the Winter Tower," Tyrokon
whispered when they were within a stairway coil. "That's *this* tower. I explored them all while you were sparring."

Cho drew breath for an argument, then let it out with a sigh. He followed Tyrokon as the passage widened into a dark landing and stopped behind him when a brightening spiral warned that there was a lamp, at least,
on the next landing.

They drew their stolen swords, leaving the third sword on the dark
landing, and with Cho in the lead, ascended into the light.

The girl might have been telling the truth: Two men guarded a barred
door. Two men who should have been flogged. By the way they were
slumped against the walls, both men had dropped straight down into a
snoring sleep.

Cho flexed his fingers against the wire-wrapped hilt of his sword. The
only way to be sure the Wet-landers wouldn't rouse and raise an alarm was
to slay them, but even as he weighed a slash across their throats against a
thrust through their unarmored hearts, he knew he couldn't do either, not
as they slept.

Luck stayed with them until they had their hands on the wooden bar,
then a gust of doubt swirled through Cho's mind. All his certainties shook.
He lost the thread of everything—his name, his skills, his reason for standing in front of a barred door—everything except a terrible, irresistible exhaustion. He'd let go of the bar and was sinking to his knees when the
unseen wind reversed itself.

"Cho? Cho, Tyrokon—is that you?"

Cho shuddered and the drowse vanished. He recognized Rifkind's voice
and knew with cold certainty how the guards had wound up on the floor.
Before Cho could decide whether to be grateful or enraged, Tyrokon answered her question:

"It is. We've come for you."

"Quick then, unbar the door."

That was Rifkind all the way: giving orders without a word of concern
or gratitude, but Cho got his hands under the hinge end and lifted. As soon

as the door was cleared, she came out looking worse for the wear in a pale, shapeless gown and her arms bound behind her back. Tyrokon, who was closer, took care of the rope around her wrists. When she brought her hands around, they were dark with fresh and clotted blood.

"I'm all right," she assured them. "Are you?"

They both nodded, though Cho couldn't get past the sight of his mother's bloody hands.

"A bit of help here?" she snapped a moment or two later.

For the second time Cho shook himself out of a drowse. Tyrokon and Rifkind had seized one of the guards and were dragging him into the room that had been Rifkind's prison. She had done something to them, then, the way healers could when a man was in great pain . . . or obeying orders. Swallowing hard, Cho grabbed the second guard under the shoulders and dragged him across the threshold.

"Will they die?" he asked.

Rifkind hesitated before saying, "They'll have the world's own headache. Get the lamp, would you? Which one of them has the smaller feet?"

"Feet?" Cho asked, while Tyrokon got the lamp.

"I assume you've found a way out. I don't see you carrying my clothes and I can hardly ride like this, so let's see which one has the smaller feet, because it's his clothes, his boots I'll be wearing."

She wasted no time, once she'd made her choice, stripping the unlucky man down to his drawers.

"There's a problem," Cho admitted, once she'd started to dress. "Banin's gone. Lord Ballard told us you'd ridden away—that's what started everything. Banin's not with Tein and Assurin. He could be dead—"

"He's not—I'd know—and he's not far, either. We'll find him once I've gotten my bearings." She cinched a belt twice around her waist. Her wrists glistened in the lamp light but weren't slowing her down. "Let's go."

They restored the bar to its brackets, confining the guards in the event—which Cho judged unlikely—that the pair awoke before the Asheerans had made good their escape. Rifkind welcomed the sword they'd left on the landing below—not that she'd needed it. She'd armed herself with the guard's weapon that she'd taken along with his clothes.

But she did say thank you, which stuck in Cho's mind as a measure of what he needed to do to get her attention.

Rifkind was impressed, too, to hear of their explorations and discoveries.

"I was just heeding your words," Tyrokon explained. "You said the walls were hollow."

The healer's eyebrows rose. Cho wondered if you could call someone a liar when their words were honest by accident. By then they were descending the spiral stairs to the great hall. No one had to tell Rifkind when to be quiet; the woman was silence incarnate when she chose to be and she chose silence all the way to the musty storeroom where the wall passage had ended and the bramble-hidden arch opened to freedom.

"A postern, and left open," Rifkind mused before explaining that it was a rare Wet-lands stronghold that didn't have a secret exit hidden along its walls. "Ballard's not so careless; he doesn't know—no one's told him. He's been here nine years, at least, and he doesn't know the castle. He summons his lords, and they don't all come. There are pieces here I can't quite fit together."

"What's to fit together?" Tyrokon asked. "He locked you up and said you'd left, then he did the same to us. The man's a schemer and not to be trusted."

Rifkind agreed. "True enough, but there's a greater pattern just beyond my grasp."

"Well, leave it there," Cho snapped, lest the two of them get caught in some abstract discussion while Maudin's guards patrolled the ramparts. "We're dead meat if we aren't far from this valley by dawn."

Clouds had blown in since the boyos had found the postern gate. The Bright One's light was banked and a goodly wind raked the trees, providing cover for such small noises as the three made creeping around the castle. Cho picked the deepest shadows for their path to the paddock where they'd last seen Assurin and Tein and he expected Rifkind to carp. She didn't, just bent low and scuttled between them.

The paddock was as the boyos had last seen it with two irritable warhorses guarding the shed where their gear sat untouched and intact. They'd be leaving Gryphonage almost the same way they'd come to it.

"They took my saddle when they took Banin," Cho explained when they were in the shed. "Left yours behind—"

"And a good thing, too. There're twenty gold destinsi beneath the horn . . . and I was afraid we were going to have to make the run to Chatelgard with nothing to our names." Moving blind, she fingered the saddle and they all heard the soft *ssh-clink* of coins before she threw the saddle over Tein's back. "Now, give me a moment to find Banin—"

She stood stock-still a moment and Cho found himself thinking of the charcoal war-horse; and thinking that he was getting another taste of his mother's *tal* applied to something other than healing. He was sure of it when he felt a returning sensation, quite unlike anything he'd ever known before, of a heavy head, a full belly, and *four* feet on the ground.

"That way," Rifkind said as the sensation faded. "And lucky for us, it's where we're headed."

17

The clouds that had covered the Asheerans' escape from Gryphonage soon thickened and leaked. Drizzle came first, then with wind-driven down-pours that dropped the temperature like a stone. They'd been through worse coming off the steppes, but that was when they'd had cloaks to keep them dry. With nothing but tunics and trousers, they were quickly soaked to the skin, shivering, and miserable.

Rifkind suffered most. She'd gone a day and night without food, which was hard for any healer, and doubly hard for a healer who'd squandered her resources in futile attempts to free herself. Her wrists ached where she'd chafed them raw. She longed to heal herself, but didn't dare. Willpower alone kept her upright in the saddle. Any attempt to rise into her *tal* would have sent her into the mud.

Pride kept Rifkind from speaking up. Another person—a person who hadn't been face-to-face with her goddess—might have called the storm a godsend. It covered their tracks as quickly as they were made and all but guaranteed that Lord Ballard's hunting dogs would be unable hunt them down. The storm slowed the Asheerans, too. Rifkind wished they were farther along when, despite the weather, hints of dawn brightened the eastern horizon.

"Are we going to push on until the war-horses founder?" Cho asked irritably.

How long had he been waiting for her signal to stop while she'd been loathe to admit her weakness? "We have to get off the road first—"

"The war-horses won't like that. They don't like trees."

There was no need to tell her that, not with Banin's tree-suspicion pressed against her thoughts. With no rider urging them forward, the three war-horses had reached their own conclusions and stood side by side with their heads hanging low.

"In this light, this weather, this is as good a place as any to get under the trees," Rifkind said. The words were scarcely out of her mouth when she felt light-headed.

Tyrokon's question, "Are we tucking in until it's dark again?" seemed to arise from the end of an echoing well.

Rifkind started to say no, getting to Glascardy was more important than staying hidden. They had a grace period. Lord Ballard had gone who-knew-where. Until he got back there was a chance—maybe a good chance—that no one from Gryphonage would come after them.

The words got tangled in her mouth and, suddenly, she was slipping sideways. Mud cushioned her fall. The war-horses retreated in their determination not to step on a fallen rider. She was quite by herself and flat on her back when, amid a confusion of footsteps, Tyrokon declared:

"You're hurt!" in a voice full of astonishment.

Rifkind hugged her hand, saying nothing. She got one foot under her, but her strength was gone. The best she could do was sit.

Cho asked, "Can you walk?"

"Give me a moment."

Tyrokon wanted to know, "What happened?"

"No food. No sleep—"

"No difference," Cho snapped. "Can you sit astride? I can lift you up and lead Banin."

Rifkind would crawl before she accepted that sort of help, and she very nearly did, falling onto her arms before she found the balance and strength to stand.

"Right or left?" Tyrokon asked and, because she was facing right, Rifkind chose that direction.

With a death grip on the saddle girth she led the boyos into the Irdel woods.

The world had brightened to shades of gray when she came to place where dark rock thrust out of the forest floor. Tufts of grass would sustain the war-horses, but do nothing for a rider's hunger. Still, the rock provided shelter from the rain that continued to fall and a thick carpet of rust-colored needles beneath a stand of evergreens promised tinder for a fire.

A rabbit bolted from beneath the evergreens. Cho cursed Wilts for taking his bow weeks ago and himself for not thinking to steal one from the weapon rack in the lower hall when he'd had the chance. He could set snares, but knowing nothing about the way game moved across the land, he doubted he could catch them a meal.

His Darian sword was a weapon for killing men, not hunting game, still, he went off with it in his hand, promising to return with something that could be roasted over a fire.

Rifkind meant to stay awake, to tend Banin and get the fire started, as she usually did, with a bit of magic drawn from her *tal*. She didn't remember sitting down, much less falling asleep, and came awake with a yelp when Tyrokon shook her shoulder.

"It's not much," he said, offering her a skewer of meat that might have begun the day as half a scrawny rabbit.

Overall, Rifkind felt better for the rest, and better still after biting into the meat.

"How far to the Overnmonts?" Cho asked from the far side of a fire that sizzled in a lingering rain.

"What was it, two days from the Irdel Road to Gryphonage? Beyond that, I'd guess a few days to the border, a few more days to Isinglas, and a week from there to Chatelgard."

"Too far. We've got nothing. We won't make it unless we can resupply ourselves."

Tyrokon added, "If we dare. Lord Ballard's sure to be looking for us."

"He's not at Gryphonage," Rifkind reminded them. "We don't know what his men will do when they find we're gone. Let's hope they don't make a move without their lord's say-so. In the meantime, we ride hard for the Irdel Road. Remember, we passed villages. They weren't much, but we've got gold. You can get anything here, if you've got enough gold. We should be safe once we get to Glascardy. I don't think Ballard will pursue us into Glascardy."

"I bet you didn't think he'd lock you in a tower, either," Cho muttered and Rifkind couldn't disagree with him.

"What good is gold?" Tyrokon asked, ignoring the silence between mother and son. "We're different. Our skin, our hair, our eyes—anywhere we go, people will know what we are, which is almost the same as knowing *who* we are. One good look and someone's going to run straight back to Gryphonage."

Rifkind couldn't argue with that logic, either. "It's a risk we'll have to take. Cho's right: We're not getting to Chatelgard with what we've got. The weather's moving on toward summer, but the nights are cold, and so is the rain. We need cloaks. Cho needs a bow, and I need a pair of boots that fit. We either buy what we can with our gold or we go outlaw to take what we need—and then Ballard *will* have a good reason to hunt us down." She finished the meat and used her sense of the Bright One to measure the amount of sunlight left behind the clouds. "Sweet Mother—the day's half gone! Scuttle the fire. We've got to move."

And move they did. Pursuit never materialized, but neither did opportunities to spend their gold. There weren't many villages on the road to Gryphonage and those they passed were all flying green-gryphon banners. Rifkind didn't want to take the chance of entering them. The war-horses did fine on the lush spring grass, but the Asheerans were reduced to acorn mash when Cho's snares came up empty.

"Spending your gold isn't going to be easy when we can't trust anyone," Cho said when, after two lean days, their track merged with the Irdel Road.

Then their luck turned. Around mid-afternoon they met a Luccan peddler coming the other way with his mule team and cart. He wouldn't make change for Rifkind's destinsi and he didn't have a bow, but he was willing to sell them some food and had a stock of mantles and a pair of ladies' shoes that didn't threaten to fall off Rifkind's feet. They weren't worth a fraction of the destinsi Rifkind surrendered for them. Never again would she forget to stash some silver and copper with her gold.

The peddler guessed they were running from something and offered his assessment of the road ahead of them: "You'll meet a few o' Lord Ballard's patrols as you get closer to the Albinet, but they're not looking for anything particular, not yet, anyway. An' when you come to the Wayside, take the east fork. It's longer, but I know the ferryman. Hanno's his name. Tell him you made a trade with Jancinto and he'll take you to the other side, no questions asked."

"Do we go east?" Cho asked after they'd separated from the peddler.

Tyrokon answered first: "He reminded me of Vendle. I don't trust him. I'd sooner go any way but east."

"We'll see," Rifkind temporized. "I've never met a peddler who didn't have some reason for steering clear of a lord's men."

The Asheerans were out of step with the Irdel inns, which were generally a day's journey apart. They made camp beneath a magnificent sunset. They ate the peddler's sausage and beans, setting aside half for the next day and were on the road early the next morning and abreast of another inn before noon. It wasn't the Wayside and it wasn't the Barking Goose—that inn had been behind them when they'd joined the Irdel Road—but it was quiet and the innkeeper had leftover stew in his pot that he was willing to sell.

Like the peddler, he was eager to possess one of Rifkind's destinsi, reluctant to commit to a precise exchange rate. Rifkind bargained hard to get them a sack filled with loaves, cheese, and lengths of smoked sausage sufficient for a week's journeying and, for Cho, a short bow plus ten arrows left in lieu of room rent by a huntsman who'd never come back to redeem it. The trade still leaned heavily in the landlord's favor, but Rifkind was satisfied and drank to the innkeeper's health.

Cho frowned when Rifkind offered him the bow that was a foot shorter than an Asheeran bow and made of wood alone rather than the painstaking layers of horn, sinew, and wood favored by clan bowyers.

"You were eager enough to lay hands on Wet-lands steel," Rifkind chided the boyo and, when he didn't rise to the bait, announced that she'd keep the bow for herself.

"You're no archer," he snarled.

"And neither are you, without a bow."

Cho snatched the weapon, strung it, and spent an uneventful afternoon in the saddle with a bow once again slung across his back. They ate well that night. Come morning, they were four days out of Gryphonage, without a hint of pursuit or ambush. At noon they reached the Wayside Inn where Rifkind dared ask the best way into Glascardy.

"The Albinet River's broad and swift this time of year," the innkeeper replied. "You won't be riding those horned horses across. There's a ferry straight ahead and another, if you follow the east fork. It's a narrower passage there, but treacherous, too—and I don't mean just the water."

So, to Tyrokon's relief, they continued straight ahead, away from the peddler's advice.

Rifkind had seen the Albinet before, many times while she rode with the Overnmont army. She'd seen the ocean, too, and raised the Landmother in a marsh that touched every horizon. As big water went, the Albinet was middling wide, middling swift, and the flat-bottom ferry waiting at the river's edge, just another part of a day's journeying.

The war-horses had a different opinion. All three of them planted their hooves on the last bit of road and with white, rolling eyes, refused to take another step. The boyos weren't much better. Their jaws dropped and they exchanged rebellious glances.

"It's called a river," Rifkind snapped, "and we want to be across it—into Glascardy—before sunset, so close your mouths and follow me."

Rifkind pressed her heels into Banin's flanks and her imperatives into his mind. He pranced in place a moment then, tossing and snorting at every stride, approached the ferry, leaving the boyos to master their misgivings.

The ferryman came out to greet her. He proved to be a Glascard from the far side who'd been hoping for a last fare to take across the river and wasn't fazed by the prospect of gold-skinned Asheerans or horned war-horses. Old enough to inspire confidence on the river, he was too young to have fought in the war, and didn't seem to recognize Rifkind's name when she mentioned it. The name Ejord Overnmont brought a different reaction:

"I've seen him myself. There's not a holding or hamlet he hasn't visited, taking oaths and handing down justice."

"So, Ejord Overnmont's lord of Glascardy, and a good lord, too?" Rifkind asked.

"He's a man, like the rest of us—" the ferryman began, but before he could elaborate, a war-horse squealed in anger. Rifkind and the ferryman turned in time to see Tein rear up and Cho lose his seat.

"Bloody Bright—" Rifkind swore, softly repeating the words that Cho shouted as he tumbled to the gravel separating the dock from the road.

Asheerans did *not* fall off their war-horses. They were plunked into a saddle before they could walk and kept their seat as if there was glue on their backsides. Rifkind doubted that Cho had ever fallen, though he did it well, tucking himself into a ball and rolling as he struck the gravel. It was unlikely that he'd damaged anything more delicate than his pride, but she dismounted anyway and went to check on him while Tyrokon heeled Assurin around to chase Tein who'd bolted in the opposite direction.

Cho waved Rifkind aside. "He's never done that."

"How many times have you told Tein one thing with the bit and reins and another with your mind?"

"I'm no healer." He stared at his hand, which had borne the brunt of his landing and a gravel imprint.

"All that means is *you're* deaf, not him. Think about it: Banin and Tein aren't different; we are. Men and healers."

HIS MOTHER MIGHT as well have struck Cho a blow in the stomach, though, for once, the shock to his thoughts was joy: Tein *heard* him!

Tyrokon was a friend, but Tein was a piece of his soul. He confided everything to his war-horse, and Tein had heard.

For a heartbeat, Cho considered his mother, who'd never seen fit to share the wondrous secret and who *heard* her war-horse; and for another heartbeat he recalled that *she* was unfair and the world was *unfair*. But, for once, joy was stronger than rancor.

He heard Rifkind ask, "How's the hand?"

"Fine. Sore, but fine."

She held out her hand to help him up. Cho refused the offer and was standing on his own when Tyrokon returned, leading Tein. With thoughts alone, he greeted his war-horse.

The bay head swung around, dark eyes met his: proof enough that Tein had *heard* . . . and that Cho was deaf.

"Good," Rifkind interrupted. "Now, lead him onto the ferry and use his trust to keep him calm."

Cho took the reins and, supremely conscious of all the eyes on his back, led Tein to the wide plank stretched between the solid shore and the shifting ferry. The wood gave a little beneath Cho's weight, sparking all his fears. Tein snorted and pulled back.

Rifkind barked, "Cho!"

He mastered himself and Tein followed meekly up the plank, onto the wobbly thing called a ferry. They stood together, nose to nose, while first Tyrokon, then Rifkind led their war-horses aboard. The ferryman lifted the plank away and—damn his eyes!—leapt onto the ferry, setting it into motion that went straight to Cho's gut.

Gritting his teeth and stiffening his knees, Cho held on to his balance and his breakfast even when the river grabbed the ferry, pulled it away from the bank.

"Not long," he whispered, thinking the ferry would shoot across the river, but no, the water pulled the ferry parallel to the bank and the ferryman with his oar made precious little forward progress.

When they were equally far from both banks, the ferryman seemed to lose his grip on the oar. They spun completely around and Cho was sure they were doomed to a watery death. Tein squealed and beat his front hooves against the ground that wasn't ground—

"Cho!" Rifkind shouted. "Calm him!"

Cho reached deeper into himself than he'd ever reached before. He found the calm he felt when he faced a new opponent in the red-staff arena and wrapped it around him. He told himself he was the best, because that was what he told himself when he fought for the red staff, and was still repeating the words in his mind when the ferry bumped up against the Glascardy bank.

18

The deeper they rode into Glascardy, the more Rifkind remembered and the more she noticed what had changed. Great swaths of springtime wildflowers brightened the fields on either side of their road. Beautiful, yes, but most of those fields should have been sown with grain that was beautiful in its own right because grain kept people alive.

Not that the Glascards they encountered were starving. Living Glascards had plowed and planted enough land to feed themselves and their neighbors and their livestock to a rosy-cheeked glow . . . for now, at least, until next winter when the plague was likely to return.

The Asheerans had slept under the stars since crossing the Albinet, in part because lengthening days meant warmer nights and in part because Rifkind had chosen not to mingle overmuch with the Glascards until she and the boyos came safe to Chatelgard. The folk they'd encountered on the Isinglas Road weren't hostile, but they were wary of strangers, cocking their fingers in ward signs and spitting in the dirt once the war-horses had passed.

They've always been like this, Rifkind reassured herself when they'd overtaken a farmer and his cart only to hear the by now expected expectoration in their wake. *Ejord used to say that a man's not really a Glascard unless his grandfather was born here.*

But she took no chances. She'd broken two of her gold destini into conshas and setas at the first Glascard inn they'd encountered. They bought food from the farmers they passed, paying too high a price every time, and supplemented their bread and cheese with whatever Cho could bring down with a bow he loudly and frequently decried as inferior to the one he'd lost to Wilts.

For the six days since crossing the Albinet, they'd been blessed with bright, cloudless skies, but their luck was running out. A coastal wind had blown up and mountains of gray-bottomed clouds were crowding in.

"Will it rain?" Tyrokon asked.

The boyos couldn't predict west-country weather worth a damn.

"Not before sunset, and then, with those clouds, we're likely to see a day or two of soggy weather."

Neither boyo liked being wet to the skin—nor did Rifkind, for that matter—but Cho was the one who complained about it before it happened.

"What about an inn? . . . If it's going to rain all night . . ."

Rifkind was no more eager to get drenched as she slept than they were and agreed that they'd take shelter at the next inn. As inns went, the next one was far from the largest or most prosperous. It hung a signboard that had something to do with a ram. There were words beneath the painted ram, but Rifkind's flair for language did not extend to reading.

A boy of about nine or ten came out to greet them. He took one look at the war-horses and ran back inside.

"Let's hope that's not an omen," Rifkind mused as the cloud overhead leaked a pair of raindrops onto her head.

The innkeeper appeared on the porch, wrapped in a heavy apron and wiping his hands on a pale towel.

"By Mohandru's tears!" he swore in the Glascard dialect, then switched smoothly to trade: "Asheerans! Ah, but you're a long way from home. It was just yesterday that I heard of Asheerans on the Isinglas Road and didn't believe a word."

Rifkind would have preferred a different god and was not pleased to think that word of their presence was preceding them, still, raindrops were falling thicker and the air echoed with middling thunder.

"We want a room for the night, supper and breakfast tomorrow, and a paddock for our war-horses," she replied in flawless Glascard. "We'll pay any fair price in good coin."

The innkeeper was plainly surprised that an Asheeran might speak his native language, but he recovered quickly, naming a price that was high, but not unspeakably so. Rifkind dismounted and the boyos did the same. The keeper gave his boy a shove toward the war-horses. Once again the boy turned and ran into the inn.

"No matter," Rifkind assured him and, receiving directions, led the boyos and the war-horses to an empty paddock behind the stable.

With thunder thickening around them, the Asheerans stowed their gear in such shelter as the paddock afforded. Rifkind hadn't asked for grain and there was none within the paddock, but there was a goodly growth of grass. She bade Banin to take care of himself and raced for the porch. Cho beat her, but she beat the downpour and only Tyrokon got drenched.

The innkeeper fed them well on roasted fowl and winter squash—one of the best meals they'd had since leaving the cook fires of Tyrokon's mothers behind. A traveling bard offered to entertain for a seta a song. Rifkind paid for a few songs from the war years. When they were sung, she herded the boyos upstairs to a room that was cramped and musty, but still better than rain-soaked mud.

Rifkind dreamt of Chatelgard—an imposing place in any season and virtually impregnable, but not a particularly practical seat for Glascardy's ruling family. Winter sealed the narrow trails four months out of the year and spring wasn't much better. Meltwater and rain loosened whole slabs of the mountainside, isolating the fortress until laborers could repair the narrow trails . . . the narrow trails . . .

Rifkind sat upright. A river ferry had nearly unstrung her son. What would he do when he found himself with sheer mountain on one side and sheer nothing on the other? There was no answer in the quiet room and no sense borrowing tomorrow's trouble today. She resettled onto the pillow and willed herself into a dreamless sleep that lasted until after the room had brightened with dawn.

Throwing open the shutters, Rifkind surveyed the sky from east to west. Yesterday's clouds still mounded up in the east, hiding the risen sun, but the rain had stopped and the west, the usual source of Glascardy's weather, was clear. She awakened the boyos and led them downstairs where the aroma of sizzling sausage was thick in the air.

The common room bustled with wenches, folk whom Rifkind recognized from the previous evening, and strangers, one of whom caught her eye across the banister. He hadn't been around for supper or the bard's entertainment, and he wasn't one of Ballard's men, but as sure as Rifkind stood gaping on the stairs, she knew him.

And he knew her. He rose from his stool, eyes locked on hers.

The not-quite-stranger was a respectable sort with dark, clubbed hair and a trimmed beard, both liberally salted with gray. Rifkind guessed him to be somewhat older than herself, but still in his prime. He wore dyed-wool garments in blue and burgundy that fit him well. There was a sword on his hip—nothing fancy, but the scabbard leather had the sheen of frequent use about it as did his boots, which could have served equally well for stirrups or striding.

She'd known scores of men who fit his description, though they'd be old men now. She'd have known this man when he was twenty years younger, but try as she might to erase the years from his face, Rifkind couldn't match him to a memory. Then he swiped his felted hat from his head and held it over his heart.

"My lady Rifkind—can it be you?" he asked in Glascard.

The voice sliced through the clutter in her mind. "Anderly? Anderly Werth?"

"The same!" he said, breaking into a grin. "Brel's sword—what brings you to Glascardy?"

Rifkind descended the remaining stairs. "I'm looking for old friends and today I've found one."

Anderly had been one of the youngest warriors who'd answered the call of old Lord Humphry Overnmont to bring down a corrupt and tired empire. He'd been the son of a petty lord who held barely enough land to put armor on his heir and his heir on a horse. By the time they'd parted company, Anderly had risen far beyond his father in a feudal hierarchy that was always more flexible in practice than in theory. When the fighting had ended and Humphry had claimed the imperial crown, Anderly could have stayed in the capital, but—like Ejord—he'd preferred Glascardy to power and politics.

"Sit with us," Anderly said, and the men he'd been with moved swiftly to shuttle extra chairs to their table.

Rifkind introduced Cho as her son and Tyrokon as her clan chief's son before switching to the trade tongue to say—"They speak trade, but they haven't had time yet to learn more than a few words of Glascard."

Anderly nodded; his men did too, but with less enthusiasm. They were a common sort, good men, no doubt, but younger men who saw the crescent and saw a witch as well as a foreigner. Anderly eased their minds with a call for another pitcher of beer. Rifkind had never acquired a taste for beer before sunset and called for cider for herself and the boyos. When everyone had a brimful mug, she raised a toast to years well spent then got down to the serious business of exchanging stories with a man she was inclined to trust.

Her own story was as obvious as it was simple: She was alive, she was in Glascardy, she had a half-blood son and a chief who trusted her with his son, she was on her way to visit an old friend. She covered it in a few moments, leaving out any mention of Irdel and Ohlmer Ballard, then listened to Anderly give a similarly quick accounting of the good and the bad in Glascardy, and especially the plague.

"The last two winters have been easy, compared to what came before. Some say that's because there's so few left to die. Myself, I'm up to meet with Lord Overnmont—Ejord, you remember—to ask for relief from my rents and the right to open my lands to lordless men."

Rifkind latched on to the words that were most important to her ears. "You're headed for Chatelgard?"

"Chatelgard? No. Lord Overnmont's not at Chatelgard, not at this time of year. I'm headed for Raval and the quarter-day session."

Raval was an Overnmont holding toward the coast, the exact opposite direction of Isinglas and Chatelgard. Had Anderly not crossed her path this very morning, she and the boyos would have found themselves high in the mountains pounding on the locked door of an empty fortress. Yet, it was like the Ejord she remembered to take the four-times-a-year sessions to his people rather than have them climb the treacherous road to Chatelgard.

All in all, the news was reassuring and good.

The wench arrived with mugs, pitchers, and a loaf of brown bread pierced with a meaningful knife.

Rifkind had expected Anderly to suggest that they travel together, but Anderly had the manners of a soldier through and through. When food appeared in front of him, he ate until it was gone, without rest, without conversation. It was the antithesis of an Asheeran meal where a clan and its guests could effortlessly stretch a meal from sundown to midnight.

When there wasn't a crumb left on any plate or knife, Anderly announced that it was time to be on the road to Raval. He made the offer Rifkind had expected earlier, an offer she accepted gladly. An hour later they were on the road, a company of twelve, counting the Asheerans, riding at a road-eating walk. Away from ears she didn't trust, Rifkind resolved to share their Irdel misadventures, beginning with a question:

"What do you know of Lord Ohlmer Ballard, who's calling himself Duke of Irdel?"

Anderly shook his head. "He's what we call a new man—one who rises up like smoke to take another's place. I've heard said his father was a stabler on one of the outlying Ballard estates; and I've heard that he's the natural son of a priest that the old Ballard took pity on. What I know is that when word came that plague had swallowed the Ballards down to their last daughter, Lord Overnmont sent a man of his own picking to wed her. But she was taken when he got there—by Lord Ohlmer. We call him Ballardskin, because it took a woman to make him a lord.

"This new lord Ballard sent him back with word that Irdel was done making oaths and taking orders. We took council at the next quarter day. Lord Overnmont, he asked if we were ready to make war on Irdel, to take their oath by force and set a man of our own in Gryphonage. Truth to tell, my lady, we'd be hard pressed to raise an army these days and not against Gryphonage. There's a place that's proof against siege. Time will come, we said. Maybe next year or the year after that, Lord Overnmont will raise the question again and we'll have the men."

"But—except for the oath—you hear nothing ill of Ohlmer?"

"Nothing that comes to me, nothing that can't be said of any man, including Lord Overnmont, including myself, for that matter, if you listen to my tenants. There's too much work to be done and not enough hands to do it. You think there's ten households in a hamlet, then come spring, you're down to eight—one lost to plague and the other just packed off. I need the right to take lordless men, like the ones who take mine, if I'm to see the work done. That's what I need, and that's what I'm going to say to Lord Overnmont. Lordless men or he's got to give me relief."

Where there was money, Rifkind mused, two thoughts were never far from a man's mind: what he owed and what was owed to him.

With Anderly, there was a third thought: magic. According to him, sorcerers—he was careful to avoid the word "witch"—had been springing up like mushrooms after a summer storm. Three had tried to set themselves up on his land just in the previous year. He'd seized their property and run them off, despite their pleas and threats.

"Begging your pardon, but there's no place for that kind among law-abiding folk. They all say they do only good—healing and weather wards and charms against the plague—but there's not one of them who wouldn't claim all the power An-Soren once held and use it the same black way. It's getting worse. Five years ago, sorcerers were rare as hen's teeth, now they're everywhere.

"Our priests say it's all a sign of the gods' displeasure and tell us to dig deeper for our offerings. A tithe isn't enough; they ask for an eighth—an eighth! They talk from both sides of their mouths! Mohandru's the god who cares for the suffering, they say. Well, there's suffering enough with the tithe. If priests can't entreat their god for one in ten, then it's time for new priests . . . or new gods.

"We need relief."

Rifkind nodded. In the end, Anderly's third thought was just a variation on the other two, and all so deeply rooted in his mind that he scarcely knew how quickly he returned to them. In lulls—when good manners led to polite questions—she told Anderly what had happened in Irdel, leaving nothing out. He displayed proper outrage at their imprisonment and admiration for their escape, but nothing except his own situation held Anderly's attention for long.

By late afternoon Rifkind was regretting her eager decision to travel with him, then she recalled that things were not so very different in the

money-less Asheera. A man with a favor to ask of his chief might spend
weeks working up the courage and words to make his request. Even her
own apprentices were apt to sink into intense silences before asking a favor.

Rifkind listened as Anderly refined his arguments and marveled at how
much she had mellowed.

They would have reached Raval by sunset of their second day's riding,
or so Anderly predicted, until the road brought them to a washed-out
bridge over a rocky, white-water stream. The local lord had assigned men
to repair the span they called Millers Bridge, but it would be midsummer
before their work was finished.

The workmen had rigged a rope-drawn raft to serve as a ferry for themselves, but it was nowise sturdy enough for horses, even one at a time.

Rifkind would have forded the stream at the first stretch of calm water,
but Anderly insisted on a roundabout detour to another bridge, a half-day's
ride upstream. When Rifkind chided him gently, he prickled, saying, "I've
lost too many men to things I could not control to risk them crossing
Millers Stream when it's in raging flood. There's time yet to the quarter
day and I'd sooner face Lord Overnmont safe than sorry."

Rifkind bowed her head and followed. The bridge at Grayway was solid
and the Red Boar Inn, which she remembered from years past, stood on
the far side. Anderly bent her ear over supper with another full-length
recital of the case he planned to make to Ejord, but not even that could
spoil the meal. She had a quiet room to herself with a freshly aired bed and
was surprised when she lay wide-awake all night, imagining, rather than
dreaming, Ejord's face.

The next morning Banin caught her restlessness and chafed at the
leisurely pace Anderly set. The morning was long, the afternoon longer still
until, at last, they crested a hill to look down on Raval—a small castle compared to Gryphonage or Chatelgard, with but a single tower in the corner
of a fortified square. There was a village, too, that looked to hold a dozen or
more families. A red-and-gold pennant flew from the tallest tower of the
castle signaling that the Duke of Glascardy was in residence.

After months of journeying, Rifkind would have set her heels against
Banin's flanks and approached the castle at a canter, if not a full gallop.
Anderly, who had grown quieter as the day progressed, preferred a digni-
fied walk that, if nothing else, gave the castle ample notice of their arrival.

The gates were open and a welcoming party some two dozen strong formed to greet them. They were all men—which was to be expected for the quarter-day session. Like Anderly, the lords of Glascardy rarely traveled with their families.

Rifkind strained her eyes looking for Ejord and found him beneath a head of hair that was no longer as fiery bright as it once had been.

He'd spotted her by then and though there was a smile on his lips there was only emptiness in his eyes.

19

In all her dreams and daydreams, Rifkind had not prepared for the possibility that Ejord Overnmont would not be pleased to see her. She became a stranger in her own body, catching her thigh on the saddle as she dismounted. She had to remind herself to breathe.

Bright Mother! What have I done? Why have I come?

Ejord greeted Anderly Werth who, bless his oblivion, seemed unaware than anything was wrong. Then Ejord was moving toward her with his arms open, a strained smile fixed on his lips, and that dreadful emptiness in his eyes. Rifkind stepped into his embrace.

Her friend was headblind, a peculiar condition that made him proof against all manner of magical deception, and proof against a healer's empathy as well. She could grasp no insight into his mood as he bent stiff arms around her, scarcely touching her at all. And she tried, by all that she'd ever held holy, Rifkind tried.

"You've changed even less than I might have expected," he said in Glascard.

"Less?" Rifkind mumbled.

Ejord hadn't heard the question, or ignored it. "Jenny will be glad to see you." He looked over his shoulder to the men who'd followed him. "Go. Find her and tell her who's here."

Someone took off at a run.

Rifkind had not trekked all the way from the Asheera to see Ejord's younger half-sister. Jenny was good-hearted and clever and, most important, had always been easy to talk to. Jenny would tell her what was wrong and whether she should leave at once.

Only a heartbeat's time had slipped away, yet it was long enough for Rifkind to be startled when Ejord asked, "Who are the young men?"

"My son," she answered, switching to trade for the boyos' benefit. "Domhnall—we call him Cho. Don't ask me why. And my clan chief's son, Tyrokon."

"Cho," Ejord repeated. "Tyrokon." He embraced them each in turn and more warmly than he'd greeted Rifkind, which confirmed Rifkind's worst suspicion: that her friend's coldness was directed at her, personally and specifically.

"Come inside," Ejord said, sticking to trade for the boyos' sake. "The kitchen will find something for you to eat. They've been feeding extra mouths all day. I'm sure you're hungry."

Anderly Werth separated further from his men, one of whom continued to hold the reins of his horse and would see to its stabling. They were good men who knew what was expected of them. Two of them held out their hands for the Asheerans' reins, though they'd never led, much less stabled, war-horses before.

Rifkind saw an arrow of opportunity. "I'm afraid these three aren't the gentlemen that Turin was. They've never been confined and I wouldn't want to try them now. Do you have a paddock we can turn them into?"

Ejord nodded and said, "Take them to the orchard," to one of his men. He seemed relieved that she wouldn't be following him to the kitchen. Then again, she was a bit relieved herself to gather the boyos and the war-horses and follow a man of perhaps thirty winters through the hodgepodge of tents already set up outside the castle walls.

They did not talk, not a single word to the Overnmont man or among themselves until they were alone in a fenced apple orchard.

"What's wrong?" Tyrokon asked before he undid the girth of Assurin's saddle.

"I don't know."

"He wasn't expecting you," Cho surmised. "I didn't see anything except surprise. He'd probably forgotten about you . . . thought you were dead or something."

Rifkind was desperate enough to take Cho's suggestions seriously. Could Ejord have forgotten her? Could she have appeared as a ghost . . . an unwelcome ghost: *You've changed even less than I might have expected.* What might Ejord have expected?

And, though she'd given fleeting thought to mounting up and riding away posthaste, Rifkind realized she'd have to have her answers, however painful.

"He's not in league with Lord Ballard?" Tyrokon asked, raising a possibility Rifkind refused to consider.

"No. No, it's personal, that much I'm sure of. I'll find out. I'll ask and be done with it."

"What about the other men? What about us? Should we be extra careful?"

"Be as you'd be around your father, if he weren't your father."

"And stick to our own language?"

"No, stick to trade."

There was a two-wheeled handcart propped against one of the apple trees. It had seen better days, but it would serve to haul their gear up the hill. Banin protested that he was being left alone with horn-snatching *trees,* which in his mind were dark creatures in constant, menacing motion. Rifkind gave him a good scratch and all the assurance that there was nothing to worry about, which she didn't feel for herself.

With Cho and Tyrokon pulling the cart, they were nearing the tents when a young woman came running toward them. Even without the red hair flying free behind her, Rifkind would have known Jenny simply by her exuberance. The breath she'd been holding since her eyes met Ejord's escaped and she raced forward. They clasped hands and spun around like children.

"Rifkind! Rifkind! I've hoped and hoped but I never truly believed I'd see you again! And your sons!"

"One of them," Rifkind corrected, in trade and parceling out their names before introducing Jenny as "The lady Gwenifera."

"Oh, bother that!" Jenny continued in trade. "Jenny's the name my mother gave me and nothing my father gave me afterward will change it." Jenny grasped the boyos' hands, one each in right and left.

Jenny hadn't changed, not in personality and scarcely in looks. Her hair was nearly as thick as it had been the day she and Rifkind had gone their separate ways from the Felmargue. Her skin retained its radiance.

Before she could stop herself Rifkind blurted out, "The years have scarcely touched you!"

"What did you expect?" Jenny answered just as quickly, then cocked her head and laughed. "Mohandru weeps—you haven't figured it out, and you a healer!"

"Figured what out?"

"The Well! The Well of the Black Flame. We used its magic to shape the food that fed us all. We had no choice; we'd have starved otherwise, but fools that we were! Domhnall was immortal because he used the Well to create the food he ate. The immortality was in the food. We didn't eat enough to become immortal, but even the little we ate has made a difference . . . and more so for you. You worked in the Well chamber. You were up to your elbows in it. You haven't changed, Rifkind, truly you haven't changed at all. How could *you*, of all people, not notice?"

Rifkind rubbed her cheek where her silver was rooted. "I was busy," she said after a moment. "It wasn't important."

"Oh, Rifkind—you must tell me everything." Jenny swept Rifkind into an embrace. "Everything you've done that kept you from realizing the truth."

Embarrassed that she truly hadn't noticed, Rifkind freed herself. So much now made sense, but she never had paid attention to her appearance. Mirrors were rare in the Asheera; she'd never owned one nor sought one out and Hamarach was not a man for compliments.

Jenny took Rifkind's hand again. "What a fool I am! You've been traveling—for months, if you've traveled a day—and here I am pestering you for stories when I should be leading you to a glass of cool cider and a comfortable chair."

Rifkind dug in her heels. "First, I must know this—am I welcome here?"

"Welcome? Unexpected, but a thousand times welcome."

"No . . . truly. I looked into Ejord's eyes as he greeted me and what I saw there was not welcome."

"Nonsense. This is *my* home, mine and Jevan's. My brother holds the sessions. He hears the pleas and makes the judgments, but he's our guest when he's here, and so are you."

"I am not mistaken," Rifkind insisted. "Ejord smiled, but on his lips only. There is something and I cannot guess what it is." She recalled his expression. "Not so much anger as disappointment and sadness."

Jenny sighed. "As a guess—Alysse, his wife—"

"That was an old story before you and I left for the Felmargue. He needed a lady, and I was never suited . . . our love wasn't suited. We were always more like brother and sister. Besides, it's been over twenty years—"

"She died," Jenny said, stopping Rifkind cold. "She died last winter, just past solstice. Of the plague. She insisted on nursing the sick . . . you would have liked her: she was sensible, wise. And she wouldn't retreat up to Chatelgard while ordinary folk were sickening and dying. Stubborn! The word for 'stubborn' was Alysse when it came a lady's obligations. They had some fearsome rows and Alysse won them all. She did good, much good, and we all came to believe she was one of the untouchables—the ones whom the plague would not take. You know about our plague, our annual visitor?"

"It breached the Asheera and returns each winter," Rifkind said. She could already see where Jenny's story was headed and saw no purpose to adding that she and her sister-healers had been able to hold the plague at bay.

"We were wrong about Alysse. She had Reyna, their eldest daughter, with her, bringing food and clean bedding to the sick, when she took sick herself. They made it back to Pascel, outside of Isinglas, where they were wintering.

"There's one plague, but two deaths. The lucky ones die quickly; Alysse withered for weeks. There was nothing anyone could do. Nothing. But Ejord—he told me afterward—went out in the snow when the moon was high and bright. He *prayed* to your goddess—and you know how Ejord feels about gods and prayer! He called your name."

"I didn't—" Rifkind began, but she did. Her dreams of Ejord mouthing words she couldn't hear had begun around the solstice. "If I had left immediately and traveled hard, it still would have taken more than weeks."

"He knows that . . . in his head. In his heart . . . Being Lord of Glascardy is not what it was—you know that, if you've had your eyes open. Trials only brought them closer together. He's been like a ghost since she died. Poor Reyna and her sisters: it's been as if they've lost both their parents. I wasn't sure he'd come here for the sessions. He mourns her, and when he saw you, he must have thought of her dying. But you can cheer him, I know you can."

Grief was not a healer's malady. It did not have a name she could call from her *tal*. Time was its only balm, and not always then. Rifkind doubted she could ease Ejord's pain. She had failed him, innocently perhaps, but failed him all the same, though there was no explaining that to Jenny.

The red-haired woman was full of plans, starting with supper. It was difficult, if not impossible, to resist her enthusiasm.

"People have been arriving for the sessions all week, so there's a crowd. No avoiding that, but afterward, when Hevigern starts singing, we can slip away to the garden, Jevan and I, you and Ejord, then we can leave you to talk. He'll tell you. You two were always like that. Sometimes I thought you didn't need words at all."

And sometimes they hadn't. When the subject had been rebellion and tactics they had been separate pieces of a single mind, which had been a very good thing because neither of them had been raised to lead a Wetlands army. They were amid the tents then and word had spread that Rifkind—*that* Rifkind—had come to Raval. There was a generation of men who had changed to remember, another generation to meet for the first time, and a litany of those whom time had claimed.

Beyond the Glascards, the boyos stood with the handcart. They nodded when Rifkind introduced them, but they weren't drawn into the circle around her where conversation was, at any rate, going on in rapid-fire Glascard. Sensing their isolation and frustration, Rifkind pulled Jenny close.

"I'm not going anywhere for a while. Can you show the boyos where to stow our gear and point them toward food?"

Jenny was on the move in a heartbeat.

AFTER A LIFETIME OF WAITING, Cho had finally seen his dream. He'd met Ejord Overnmont, shaken his hand, and been sent to take care of the warhorses and saddles because the Overnmont lord had taken one look at Rifkind and gone cold.

It was that obvious and nothing the red-haired woman did could change it.

"Come along," she said, talking to him and Tyrokon as if they were children when she couldn't be much older herself. "There's bread and cider on a table outside the kitchen—"

Cho cut her off, "Just tell us where the kitchen is. We'll find it ourselves after we've cleaned the leather."

"The stable boys—" she began, then blinked. "The stables are there—with the thatched roof. Anyone you see can point you to the tack room. See that square building with the black roof? That's the kitchen and there's a table set outside it for guests. If you need anything else, ask for me or Lord Jevan. Supper will be in the forecourt. You'll hear a gong, then just follow everyone else."

Cho nodded. He'd forgotten her name and didn't ask her to repeat it. Tein would fly before he'd ask anyone for anything now that his mother had muddied the water . . . again.

"She's pretty," Tyrokon said when they were alone in the cluttered shed where a dozen saddles already sat on boxes and barrels. Contrary to Rifkind's command, he hadn't offered his opinion in trade.

"Not with that hair!" Cho continued in the clan's dialect. "They're all so pale, these Wet-lands women. They've got spots on their faces. Their eyes are watery and yellow-y hair's bad enough, but sunset hair—"

"Lord Overnmont's hair must have been that color once," Tyrokon jibed. "And yours is half red."

Cho ground his teeth. Rifkind had never described Lord Ejord. She wasn't much for describing anything and Cho wouldn't ask. But Tyrokon had a point: Rifkind's hair was Asheeran black; Ejord Overnmont's hair could have been fiery; and his hair was the color of brown rust.

She lied about so many things.

Tyrokon interrupted Cho's spiraling thoughts. "Hand me one of the saddles. I've cleared a space for them . . . unless you're serious about wanting to oil them down right away."

Cho muttered and tossed Banin's saddle into Tyrokon's arms. He knew what he didn't want to do, including oil the leather. What he wanted to do was murkier. He tossed Tein's saddle and was reaching for Assurin's when he felt a tug on his tunic.

His nerves were raw—that's what Cho told himself a moment later when he found himself confronting a waist-high girl-child with one fist cocked. Bloody Bright! At least he hadn't let loose on her and she didn't seem to notice any danger.

"Be you Rifkind's son or other one?" the child asked in awkward trade.

"Her son," Cho admitted. "That's Tyrokon in the corner."

The child nodded in that solemn way children have when they've solved some great mystery. Then, quick as a bug, she jabbed Cho's hand with a pointed finger and said something totally incomprehensible before folding her arms across her narrow chest.

"Well, you're for sure a disappointment to her!" Tyrokon laughed in the clan's language.

Cho had turned and was preparing a choice retort when a fourth voice was heard from the shed's doorway. It prattled in Glascard and came from a woman—not the red-haired woman by its tone. Cho couldn't tell more than that; she was silhouetted by the sun. The child took a backward step, the woman, a forward one.

The woman was another redhead, but there the resemblance ended. She was, in some undefinable way, younger. The pale features that seemed so unhealthy on others were, on her . . . entrancing.

"Please forgive my sister for whatever she's done and said. Lysse is fearless and has no manners." The older sister looked down at the younger. "A terrible combination. Apologize to our guests." The words were severe, but the tone wasn't.

The girl giggled something Glascard.

"We're not rustics, Lysse. Say it so they can understand."

Lysse said, "Sorry," and took off running.

"She's a terror. I'll see to it that she doesn't bother you again. Is there anything that you need? Father says—"

"Your name?" Cho asked before he could stop himself.

"Alareyna. Lady Alareyana Overnmont, if we're being formal. The family calls me Reyna; you can call me Reyna, too. From all Father's said about Lady Rifkind, we're almost family."

"You can call me Cho—"

Tyrokon cleared his throat loudly.

"And he's Tyrokon."

"Cho. Tyrokon," Rayna repeated, getting the accents right. "A pleasure. You're coming to supper, aren't you? There are so many guests, I'm sure we can find a place to sit together and get to know each other better."

"We'll be there," Cho promised.

Her eyes were blue, like the sky and not at all watery.

Then she was gone, skirt and hair flying as she chased after her fearless sister.

"Close your mouth," Tyrokon suggested.

Cho seized Assurin's saddle and threw it much harder than necessary.

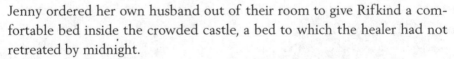

20

Jenny ordered her own husband out of their room to give Rifkind a comfortable bed inside the crowded castle, a bed to which the healer had not retreated by midnight.

Earlier, supper had been a haphazard affair of too-small tables and too many servants. Formal order had been utterly breached with lords and commoners crowded against each other in the quest for a chunk of bread and bowl of surprisingly tasty stew. By accident and deliberate navigation, Rifkind had gotten within arm's length of Ejord several times, only to have the crowd close in between them. She did not believe her failure to have a private conversation was at all coincidence and had camped out on an overturned barrel all evening, in easy distance of Ejord's camp tent, waiting for an opportunity to clear the air.

The sessions wouldn't begin until the next day when everyone would get a fair chance to air their grievance to Glascardy's lord, but that hadn't kept a steady procession of men and a few women away from Ejord's tent. Through the lamp-lit canvas, Rifkind had watched their silhouettes: Ejord seated behind a folding table while one petitioner after another tried, with varying degrees of dignity, to prejudice their judge.

Hamarach suffered the same assault, though among the clans, every day was a session day and Hamarach would never have been subjected to the procession that Ejord endured. Rifkind sympathized with her old friend and had begun to question her intentions. It was one thing not to go to sleep on an estrangement, but another to be the last person to bend a tired ear.

A stout fellow in the rich, colorful garb of a merchant followed a rail-thin commoner into the tent. When he came out, there was no one waiting to take his place. Rifkind made her decision from need, not wisdom. She approached the young man standing guard outside the tent.

"Ask your lord if he will see me?" She didn't bother to identify herself.

The guard went inside where he and Ejord shared a conversation that did not carry beyond the canvas. When he returned, he held the canvas back, allowing Rifkind to enter.

"I'm late," Rifkind said as their eyes met. "I could have gotten here sooner, but not soon enough. I am sorry. From the depths of my heart, I am sorry."

Ejord took a motionless moment to absorb her words. "Jenny," was the first thing he said. "I don't know why I told her, any more than I know what made me start praying. I've never believed in gods. Our lives are determined by fate and destiny. My Alysse's destiny—"

His voice caught on his late wife's name and Rifkind measured his grief, which was considerable and raw despite the passing of nearly six months.

"I'm sorry. You were well-matched."

Ejord stared silently.

"I could have saved her, if I'd been here. We have faced the plague in the Asheera. We cannot banish it entirely, but we have learned a few of its secrets. I had no idea you were still being ravaged."

"Less than before. We, too, have uncovered secrets. We know about bedding and clothes. We burn everything that's touched the plague-struck. Alysse was distributing new linen when—" As before, Ejord's voice faded when his thoughts turned toward his deceased wife.

Rifkind was wary where it came to grief. Before she was Cho's age, she'd lost all her family and she'd lost Cho's father before they truly knew one another. Since then, she'd hoarded her love and, though she'd been intimate with death, she was mostly untouched by grief. Ejord Overnmont was one of a handful of souls she cared about. Digging deep into memory, she found the advice she'd swallowed while learning the healer's craft.

"She lives in you. She'll never know joy again, if you don't allow yourself to know it."

Ejord gave her to glower of a man who'd nearly drowned in compassion.

"You *will* heal," she said with a bit of edge on her voice. "It's heal or wither away. You don't have any control over it."

He exhaled a bitter laugh. "My goal is numbness. If I feel nothing, I remember nothing. If I remember nothing, I feel nothing."

"Does it work?"

"Until it doesn't. Something happens, some small thing, and the whole weight crashes down on me. Or worse, the weight doesn't crash right away. I'm surrounded by what life has become; she's not there in my every thought . . . until I *do* remember. I can bear the weight of losing her, but the shame of forgetting her, for even a moment, that I cannot bear."

Rifkind chose not to argue with him. "I would not add to your sense of shame."

"It's hardly your fault. For three years we were rarely out of shouting distance and Alysse was a name, a face from the old emperor's court, and no more fondly remembered. Then you were gone from my life and Alysse fulfilled it. Now she's gone . . . and you're back. But if you tell me this was your plan, I would not believe you."

"Dreams," Rifkind said without warning. "I began having dreams . . . and I had done all that I could do in the Asheera."

"You've left for good?" Ejord asked guardedly.

Rifkind shrugged. "I told Tyrokon's father that I'd be back, but I don't think he believed me."

They stared at each other, feeling the lateness of the hour and the passage of years.

"It *is* good to see you again. I'd wonder what you were doing . . . usually when the weather was bad and I'd think of you with only a tent for shelter." Ejord smiled, his first genuine smile of their reacquaintance.

"You care too much for your walls. A good tent does not suck the warmth from you the way Chatelgard's walls did every winter."

He offered Rifkind a cup of wine. She asked the names of his daughters, though she knew them, and much more, already from Jenny. Ejord wanted to know about the journey. He'd heard of Epigos and, surprisingly, of the huge lightstorm over the Death Wastes.

"The priests say without it the plague would fade . . . and so would sorcery and, for once, I agree with them. There's been a regular explosion of sorcerers along with the plague."

Rifkind nodded. She was about to bring up Irdel and Ohlmer Ballard, but yawned instead. "There's time?" she said, more question than statement.

"After the sessions," Ejord agreed. "Brel's fist, I thought there'd be two dozen cases at most. My steward tells me there're forty . . . and not everyone's arrived who's expected."

They parted on quiet, but good terms, with a gesture that was more than a handshake, less than an embrace, and entirely satisfying, at least for Rifkind.

The camp had retired for the night. She didn't pass one guard who was awake outside his lord's tent, or find one who was awake at the castle's closed gate. There'd be no climbing the tower to the room Jenny had so carefully prepared.

The night was warm, the grass was soft and there was plenty of it just beyond the gate. Rifkind slept well but was first at the kitchen when the drudges set out piles of day-old bread for the early risers. Jenny berated her soundly for ignoring hospitality, but was relieved to learn that she and Ejord were talking to each other again.

Ladies had a simple choice in the upper reaches of Darian society—which was where Rifkind found herself when she consorted with the Overnmonts. They could sit about, gossiping and stitching on impossibly tedious embroideries, or they could tie up their sleeves and work beside the commoners. Rifkind *could* thread a needle, but she didn't enjoy bending thread one whit, so she stood behind the trestle table, ladling porridge when it became available to everyone who appeared with a bowl or cup.

And appear they did. Ejord had complained that forty cases awaited him, but no one came to the sessions alone and everyone who lived in the village seemed to have been drawn up Raval hill by the promise of a free breakfast. The sun was high and Rifkind had emptied two large kettles before the crowd thinned.

She'd fed Tyrokon who'd told her that Cho was breaking fast with the family. He'd winked as he spoke, which pricked Rifkind's curiosity. She found Jenny and asked if there was anything she should know about her son's behavior.

"Nothing . . . you've taught him well, but he and Reyna have snagged eyes."

"Sweet Mother."

Jenny's brows pulled together. "You don't trust him with her honor?"

"He grew up convinced that Ejord was his father, which would make them half-sibs, like you and Ejord."

Jenny was reassured, but Rifkind went searching for her son and spotted him—and Ejord's daughter—in the orchard fussing over Tein. The pair weren't alone; a passel of younger children were with them—a mixture of Ejord's and Jenny's offspring, Rifkind guessed. Knowing Cho, any intervention would only lead to temptation. She circled the hill to the tent courtyard where Ejord sat in the sun with the Glascardy coronet on his head.

The whole idea of the quarter-day sessions was justice rendered before witnesses, so there were benches where folk could sit or stand. The better-born had chairs and servants holding sunshades. Rifkind settled again for the grass. She listened to two farmers argue over the ownership of the calf of a cow that had gotten cozy with the wrong bull; and the complaint of a merchant who wanted to pay his tax on his costs rather than on the price he charged to his customers. But when two squires squared off over mill rights that involved competing maps and seal-fringed charters dating back to Ejord's grandfather, Rifkind got bored and left.

Ejord wasn't the only one holding court. A cohort of merchants and peddlers had set up their stalls around the castle and along the road from the village. Rifkind could have bought anything from a steaming mincemeat pasty to a length of southern silk embroidered all over with animals that had never been born. There were entertainers as well—jugglers, a pair of acrobats, a woman who ate fire, and a puppeteer. Tyrokon sat with the children in front of the puppeteer, clearly enthralled by the mayhem and the crude humor that required no words to understand. Cho wasn't with them.

Rifkind's son and Reyna showed up for supper, after the sessions had shut down for the night. Reyna sat beside her father, as befitted the Overnmont heir. Cho sat with Rifkind and Tyrokon, at a cloth-covered table well to one side.

"It's looking like you finally believe Ejord Overnmont's not your father."

Cho didn't meet her eyes. He just knifed another mouthful of chicken in a dark, sweet sauce

"She'll need to make a good marriage: someone the Glascards will accept as their lord and someone who's hard enough to keep the Ohlmer Ballards of the world on the far side of Glascardy's borders. There won't be room for love."

Cho recoiled with indignation and, aware that another word would be a word too many, Rifkind said nothing more. While village musicians struck up their drums, flute, and seven-string harp, she retreated to the castle and the comfortable sleep she'd missed the night before.

The second day of the sessions was much like the first. The Glascards whose cases had been settled headed home, replaced by late arrivals. Ejord could have refused to hear these new complaints, but that wasn't his way. The castle kitchen, which hadn't planned for an extra day of endless appetites, turned noticeably less cheerful.

A mid-morning rain that looked to have staying power finished what the kitchen had started. The sessions field dissolved into a quagmire. Merchants who'd been hoping for final sales watched their prospective patrons strike their tents and hurriedly packed up their wares to follow them away from Raval castle. By late afternoon, when Ejord pressed the great seal of Glascardy in a blot of wax to seal the last charter of the sessions, only Anderly Werth remained, still trying to get relief from his taxes.

Rifkind was with Jenny, surveying the damage done to a small bridge between the village and the castle when a frantic workman raced up and dropped to his knees.

"There's been an accident," he said, doffing his cap and wringing it ruthlessly in his hands.

"The children!" Jenny gasped.

The worker shook his head. "Emmel. He slipped and fell beneath the wagon. He's bad, my lady. There's bone sticking out."

Any other day, Emmel was as good as dead, but on this day Jenny could glance to her right and see someone who might be able to save him.

Rifkind dipped her chin and the women set off behind the workman. Rounding the castle hill, they came in sight of a tight-knit cohort moving toward them.

"Priests," Jenny whispered, laying a hand on Rifkind's arm. "I thought they'd gone. Best to be careful, Rifkind."

And priests it was, the dozen or more of them who'd stood witness throughout the session and now stood between Rifkind and her patient. She shook off Jenny's hand and kept walking.

"I went through this with Ejord *and* his father," Rifkind groused, "back when we were fighting the emperor. I don't dispute the existence of witch-craft and they don't consider me a witch. They've known where I've been since the sessions started. If they had an ax to grind with me, I've been available."

Of course, there'd been no talk of healing then and Rifkind wasn't fool enough to think that their appearance, massed together and grim-faced, was coincidence.

They were province priests who stood high in their various hierarchies, with all the fine cloth and talismans their positions implied. At the rear of the pack, Rifkind caught sight of pearl-gray robes, the hallmark of a priest-ess of the Bright Moon in Daria, but her attention fixed on the man in front. He was tall and thin, black-haired beneath a conical headdress and clad in the white-streaked blue robes of Mohandru. The irregular white streaks symbolized the Weeping God's tears, though they reminded Rifkind of decay and disease.

The Mohandrist was flanked by two lesser priests of his order. All three of them carried bleached-wood staffs topped with silver-wrapped crystals. Rifkind didn't have to rise far into her *tal* to feel the power arrayed against her. Taking a deep breath, she stepped sideways into the soggy grass, as if to let the priestly cohort pass, as if she could avoid a confrontation.

The Mohandrist and the priests behind him matched her stride.

"Turn back," he said, planting his staff and rising higher into his *tal*.

For anyone with the *tal* to see it, the crystals began to glow.

There had been times in Rifkind's life when she would have responded with manifestations of her own. In her early days, when she'd worn the dark ruby called Leskaya's Heart on a gold chain around her neck, she

could have called down enough power to flatten the chief Mohandrist and
each of his friends. Leskaya's Heart was long gone, consumed in her duel
with An-Soren, and little as she liked the Weeping God, Rifkind wasn't
about to slay his priests out of hand.

"A man has been hurt. I don't know if I can heal him, but I mean to try."

"Turn back," the priest repeated. "This witchcraft you call 'healing' is an
affront to the gods. We forbid it."

Rifkind replied, "I do nothing without my goddess's blessing," and rose
into her *tal* just enough to give the priests a sense of her power. The silver
in her cheek grew warm.

"Blasphemy!" the Mohandrist snarled, fingering his staff like a swords-
man with itchy fingers. "Anathema!"

The cohort behind him began a chorus of whispered prayer to their patron deities.

"A man is dying. Let me try to save him."

"If his time has come, we pray for him. We *weep* for him as he passes
into the next life. May his judgment be swift and gentle. May he awaken in
the place beyond care."

"May he awaken in his own bed! Let me pass—"

"Witch!" a priest called from the center of the cohort. The others nodded and prayed harder, like a swarm of angry bees.

"We went through this twenty years ago! I'm a healer, a priestess of the
Bright Moon. I can't speak for witchcraft, except to say I don't practice
it . . . and the hierarch of your order agreed with me."

Jenny's hand fell on her arm again, urging retreat.

"We have a different hierarch now. He sees witchcraft with clearer
eyes," the Mohandrist said, a cold smile flickering across his lips. "We no
longer make exceptions. Interfere with the gods' will, and you will be held
accountable, no matter whom you claim for a friend."

Rifkind caught herself gauging the priests' power and caught herself a
second time before she did anything rash. The Mohandrist clearly had faith
in his threat as well as his god and Jenny's hand was trembling. But Rifkind
couldn't retreat quietly.

"How do you hold a man who pulls another man out of a flood, or a
mother who rescues her child from a burning tent?"

"They use only the wits and strength naturally given to mankind. You consort with demons disguised as gods."

Rifkind ignored the slur. "A man will *die*."

"Better death than demons."

"Rifkind," Jenny added softly. "You've tried."

"Tried's not good enough." But she wasn't going to duel with the ranking priests of Glascardy. "His death will be on your conscience."

"Death is the gods' will fulfilled."

Rifkind turned to the workman, who'd witnessed it all and said nothing. "I'm sorry. I would help Emmel, if I could, but these—*these* won't allow it. I'm sorry."

She turned and walked away through the grass. Jenny called after her, but she was in no mood for friendship.

IT HAD TAKEN SOME CAREFUL maneuvering—and he owed Tyrokon a major favor—but Cho had detached himself and Reyna from her younger sisters and cousins. He suggested that they walk to the orchard and was heartened when she said yes without hesitation.

Getting to know a stranger wasn't something Cho had practiced the way he'd practiced with his sword. Strangers, especially beautiful young women, weren't common in the Asheera where everyone in the clan knew everyone else from the moment of birth and even the Gatherings brought the same people together season after season.

Fortunately for Cho, Reyna's education had been quite different. She explained that as the lord of Glascardy's eldest child—a daughter, true, but destined to be Glascardy's lady—she'd been taught to begin conversations with questions about a stranger's background. Did Cho have brothers or sisters? How hard had it been to train his war-horse? What did he and Tyrokon do when they weren't training their war-horses or watching over a flock of sheep? What was it like to live in a land without houses or castles? Why did Asheerans speak the trade language? How did Asheerans know where to dig their wells?

Cho answered the easy questions about himself and Tein, he explained that what Reyna called the trade language was the language of prayer, common to all the clans, each of which had its own guarded language. But he had no idea about the wells. So far as he knew, the wells had always been there, as reliable as sunrise.

"A stream is natural," Reyna countered, "but *wells* do not simply appear. Somebody had to dig them."

"Not our wells," Cho insisted and, having decided that this getting to know a stranger was a lot like sparring with a practice sword, began asking questions himself.

21

Rifkind fumed. She climbed to the castle parapet, wedged herself into one of the gaps, and reacquainted herself with all the reasons she disliked priests. Her mood had only hardened when Jenny emerged through the trapdoor.

It wasn't her friend Rifkind saw, but all things Darian. She gave Jenny a scowl that meant, *To hell with your gods and your priests. You deserve one another.*

Jenny paused, then climbed the last few steps. "They're gone."

"They've *left*," Rifkind corrected. "They're never *gone*."

"Emmel lives. They've taken him down to the village. His family stands beside him. They beg for you to come. Whatever they have, they say, is yours."

"You know better than that."

Jenny's eyebrows rose. "I know there's no predicting you when you're angry. I can do what I learned from you in the Felmargue, but I can't *heal*, and Emmel needs healing."

"After those priests, I'd imagine he needs a miracle."

"Shall I tell that to his family?"

Rifkind answered by extracting herself from the parapet. "No, you'll take me to his home."

The injured man lay on the table in the front room of a narrow, dark house, surrounded by family and neighbors. The air was thick with odors from the incenses the priests had thrown at a wound they couldn't begin to tend. Rifkind cursed them silently for making her task more difficult.

An old woman approached holding two gold coins in her outstretched hand.

Would witchcraft—real or imagined—be so feared in the Wet-lands if its practitioners were not also renowned for their greed?

Rifkind waved the woman away and took her first good look at the erupting fracture. "Boil water," she said to Jenny who had followed her into the house, then added all the other items she expected to need, from a pair of ax handles to splint the leg and a silk-threaded needle, because now that Emmel's wound had been dusted with incense there was no way she could draw the edges together. Emmel's women went for the water while Jenny left the house for the castle and a silk-threaded needle.

"I need room," Rifkind told those who remained crowded around the table.

Reluctantly, they retreated and Rifkind rose into her *tal*. Her anger vanished, it was just another distraction she couldn't afford as she contemplated the ruin of Emmel's left leg. She would have preferred to attack the shattered bone first, but the wound still bled and the priests' incense was exuding a myriad of poisons. Oblivious to the women who'd retrieved the simplest of her requirements, Rifkind stanched a leaky vein even as she extracted the name of the first poison and called it out of the wound.

She was aligning the bone chips when a force beyond reckoning brought Rifkind down from her *tal*. She scarcely knew her name and made no sense of the confusion around her until three men lifted Emmel from the table.

"You can't—" Rifkind tried to stop them but was stopped herself by a hand circling her forearm.

"Come on! We've— We're *attacked*!"

"Jenny, I'm not finished." Rifkind surged toward her patient and was again thwarted. "He'll *die*."

"We'll all die. The roof's afire!"

Jenny tugged and Rifkind, still protesting like a drunkard, lurched toward the door. Her senses cleared. She smelled the smoke before they reached the single street that fronted all the village houses.

"What's happening?"

"The gods know. An attack. Mounted men, they fired the roofs on their way to the castle."

Jenny pointed beyond the village. Rifkind followed her friend's finger to the castle where riders—at least a score of them—swarmed and smoke rose from the outbuildings.

"Who? Why?" Jenny murmured as her hand fell.

Something jostled Rifkind from behind. She turned and saw Emmel stretched gracelessly in the dirt on the far side of the street. Already he'd gone gray and waxy. All her efforts had been wasted. The man was dying before her eyes and there was nothing she could do about it.

Fire was a fact of life in Daria's close-built villages, even if it arose more often from accident than attack. Amid the smoke, village families formed human chains to shuttle out what they could from their homes before the flames ate down from the thatch. Emmel had been forgotten, and so had she and Jenny.

"We've got to get to the castle," Rifkind decided now that she was the one who had her wits about her and Jenny seemed frozen to the ground.

The red-haired woman shuddered when Rifkind touched her. "My children!" she shouted and began to run.

Rifkind did all she could to stay with her friend as they raced to the castle. No Asheeran was a stranger to a lightning raid made by one clan upon another, but such things were rare in the Wet-lands and almost unheard of against a castle with its walls, its men-at-arms, and its gate which, on this fine early summer evening, had stood wide open.

Whoever they were—and they carried no banner to proclaim their allegiance—the mounted raiders had planned their outrage carefully. Four of them remained at the open gate while their comrades swarmed the castle courtyard. Jenny was determined to get past them, but Rifkind had seen their swords and mail.

"You won't get past," she shouted and hauled her friend forcibly off the road.

"Where are the men?" Jenny screamed. "Jevan! Jevan! Ejord!"

The calls were pointless. Raval castle had been taken completely un-awares and Rifkind with it. She had her knives—Rifkind always had her knives—and a good three yards of skirt to trip her up.

The raiders noticed them and their clothes, which weren't the drab, shapeless garments of common women. They exchanged words among themselves, words Rifkind couldn't hear, then stared in an unmistakably predatory way. It didn't take a healer's empathy to guess what was on their minds.

Rifkind bent down, pretending to fuss with her boot laces, but palming two of her knives instead and whispering to Jenny, "Stay low. If they charge, drop to the ground. You can't outrun a horse and they can't grab you if you're flat on your stomach. The horses will avoid you."

"Rifkind—?"

"They're after women. It's in their eyes."

"My daughters!"

Jenny got one stride toward the gate, but no more. Rifkind stuck her leg out to trip her friend for fair. "Stay down," she snarled and braced herself for the two raiders bearing down on them at a canter.

Neither man drew his sword. The one on her right leaned out of his sad-dle, arm extended. The other split close to the left, as a herder might block the escape of a skittish sheep.

Rifkind repeated her advice, "Stay down."

A very good rider could swing far enough from his saddle to scoop up an object from the ground, but not a rider in heavy mail and not a woman-sized object that put up a kicking, slashing fight. Rifkind, though, was bet-ter at giving advice than taking it. With the blades of her knives concealed against her forearms she stood stock-still as the raiders closed.

Their mail came down to their elbows and covered their thighs. Leather armor protected their forearms and lower legs. The one reaching for her had taken off his gauntlet, which gave her one small target. Otherwise, there were the horses' flanks.

Asheerans and Darians alike held it dishonorable to attack a man's mount. Rifkind, who gave away every physical advantage when she fought, had never been picky about honor. Drawing a last breath, she waited until a heavy arm fell around her shoulder, then exploded with a war cry that came from within her *tal*, with feet, elbows, and her knives.

The horses weren't battle-hardened. Rifkind's magic-laced war cry alone might have spooked them. As the animals squealed and veered, the raider reaching for Jenny had a choice: abandon his attempt to seize a woman or fall out of the saddle; neither one left him in control of his horse, which bolted.

Rifkind's raider had a better seat, a better mount. He held one of her braids in his fist when she slashed her knife along his horse's shoulder. The animal reared and for a heartbeat they were all three connected—raider, Rifkind, and horse—then they came apart.

The raider, realizing he couldn't hold his prey, delivered a chain-mail backhand to Rifkind's silvered cheek. With her vision partly lost to blinding pain, Rifkind fell on her back, but clung to consciousness and watched the horse's hooves come down perilously close to Jenny's head.

She looked up to see the glint in her raider's eyes shift from abduction to murder. He reached across his body for his sword.

Rifkind still held the knife she'd used to score the horse. She had less than a heartbeat to change her grip on its hilt and hurl it at the raider's narrowed eyes. Her aim was off; the blade merely grazed his temple, but it made him flinch and that was enough. Rifkind rolled out of harm's way as the horse cantered past. She meant to roll up on her knees, but the damned skirt tangled and she lost precious time freeing herself.

She had one knife left and two incensed raiders closing in on her. Again she held her ground, shifting the knife to her throwing hand and intending to run straight at the first horse to get within five paces. She hoped to spook it and create confusion between the two raiders.

Before Rifkind made her choice of which horse to rush, someone blew a trumpet.

The raider who'd backhanded her held his course, but the other one reined his horse for the road. This time Rifkind had an extra moment to check her aim—the raider's left eye.

The blade flew home and the raider went instantly limp. The sword fell first, the raider followed. The panicked horse raced after its companion.

By then, the raider cohort had cleared the gate. Rifkind counted two bright-colored skirts furling around a raider's saddle. There might have been more; she couldn't see the far side of the cohort as it galloped past.

Overnmont men raced out of the castle. They got off a few arrows, none of which struck a target, before the raiders were out of range.

Rifkind offered Jenny a hand up out of the grass and together they ran to the castle gate.

The courtyard was chaos with folk down everywhere, most of them ser vants who'd gotten in the way. Flames licked up from a half-dozen or more small fires. Jenny's first thought was her family, Rifkind's was for the wounded, and the women were separated.

Rifkind was taking quick stock of the casualties when Jenny shrieked. Thinking Jevan had gone down, Rifkind raced to the sound, but it wasn't dark-haired Jevan who lay in the dirt but Ejord himself with a blood-soaked tunic and deep gouge against his collar bone.

He's gone, Rifkind thought. No matter how many times a healer faced death, its sting was sharper on a familiar face. *That's too much blood and the cut goes too deep.*

Mindless of anyone around her, Rifkind knelt. She placed a hand on the intact side of Ejord's neck and, against expectation, found that his flesh still held life. Reflexively, Rifkind reached for the Bright Moon and found her just below the evening horizon.

Sweet Mother, help me. Strengthen me!

She had depleted her healing strength in the futile healing of Emmel. Healing Ejord—if Rifkind could, which was by no means certain—would drain her to the bone. Like Garris in Gryphonage, Ejord would need the essence of life itself. But this wasn't a castle nursery. This was a killing ground.

You never know what's waiting—

And she didn't, except for one certainty: Ejord would die if she didn't give everything in her power.

Healing an Overnmont was a tricky task. The family was headblind—immune to the subtler forms of magic that affected the mind. An Overn-mont could be slain by magic, if it had a physical manifestation and he could be healed by it. But there was no quieting his mind or holding a tide of awareness at bay until a healing was complete. Ejord might awaken—it was unlikely, but it could happen and it could be fatal to them both.

"Rifkind!"

Tyrokon's voice caught her on the verge a healing trance. The Bright One had not abandoned her! The boyo had been watching her all those years while she healed him. He knew how to support a healer, knew better than Jenny.

"Help me. Hold him. Keep him still," she commanded and, seeing him move toward her, slipped into the trance.

Years of experience, not planning, guided Rifkind. Within her *tal,* she was everywhere at once: stanching blood, drawing the tiniest bits of flesh back into their proper pattern, and always keeping a firm grasp on Ejord's essence, binding it to his flesh with her own will.

She couldn't spare the thought to count the number of times he nearly slipped away. Each time she pulled him back until everything was restored—not to health, she didn't have the strength for that, but given time and the will to survive, he'd recover. He'd even move his arm and his fingers again, though his sword-wielding days were over.

Sighing and trembling, Rifkind sat back on her heels. Hours had passed. The Bright Moon had moved past mid-heaven. Someone had set oil lamps beside her, as if she needed light to work her healing magic. At first she couldn't see past them and thought she'd been left alone, then, as her eyes adjusted, she made out Tyrokon . . . Jenny . . . and a handful of others, each of them with grim frowns on their faces.

"He'll live. With good care, he's going to live a long time—"

"Cho and Reyna are missing," Jenny said.

Tyrokon added, "That's what I wanted to tell you."

Rifkind heard the words and understood their meanings, but she'd drained herself so completely in healing Ejord that she felt nothing.

"We searched everywhere, looking for everyone," Jenny explained. "Four are missing: Lysse—Ejord's youngest, one of my young ladies, and Cho and Reyna. The other girls say Reyna went off toward the orchard with Cho earlier in the afternoon and that they hadn't come back. We hoped they saw the attack and hid themselves, but they should have come back by now."

"I went down to the orchard as soon as I could," Tyrokon continued, "and couldn't find a trace of them."

"Who were they?" Rifkind asked.

One of the castle veterans stepped forward. "Irdel men."

"Irdel?"

A chill shot down Rifkind's spine. The Irdel border wasn't that far away, if the raiders had come from the borderland. She didn't think it was likely that any border lordling could have mounted a score of raiders. No, that number came from a larger castle. From Gryphonage? And if it had come all that distance from Gryphonage, then it had left there before she got to Raval.

"You're sure they came from Irdel?"

Jenny nodded. "So it would seem. We brought down three of them, including the one you slew keeping me safe. Tyrokon says he recognizes one of them from the lower hall at Gryphonage."

Rifkind looked at Tyrokon.

"I didn't know his name; Cho would, when we find him. They sparred a lot. He had a sword scar across the bridge of his nose. I'd know it anywhere. The other ones I'm not so sure of, but I think they're Ballard's men, too."

Her suspicions were confirmed then. She remembered the moment when the raiders had charged toward her and Jenny. She'd assumed the men had rape on their minds, but could they have recognized her with her Asheeran braids and goddess-marked cheek?

"Ejord's steward's gone out to chase down the rest of the lords for council . . ." Jenny gave her brother a long pensive look, reminding Rifkind of the trouble that would likely follow if she couldn't keep Ejord alive. "Jevan and Lord Werth gave chase as soon as they could get mounted. The great gods know what's happened to them . . . They don't know who they're chasing."

"But why the children? Why take children?"

"Not children," Jenny corrected. *"Daughters."*

Before Rifkind asked another foolish question, her mind cleared enough to understand why Lord Ballard, or any lord, might target the Overnmont daughters. Whoever married them would be in a good position to claim Glascardy when Ejord died. And though Ejord had spoken of finding good men for his daughters and Glascardy, too, custom was harsh in western Daria: a single man who took a girl's maidenhead became her husband. It was supposed to protect the girls from rape but often it was the logic behind abduction.

Rifkind looked down at Ejord who was rested somewhere between sleep and unconsciousness. She wished she could touch his mind to keep him there. He'd be wild when he learned what had happened to his daughters.

Shouldn't a mother whose son had disappeared be as enraged as a father who'd lost his daughters?

Rifkind got one foot under her and tried to stand, but the twin goads of guilt and shame weren't enough to overcome exhaustion.

You never know what's waiting—

She clenched her teeth and tried again, this time successfully. "I'll find him," she vowed, but her leg nearly buckled with her first step.

"When light comes, we'll all look," Jenny said calmly. She released Tyrokon and put an arm around Rifkind to steady her. "It's too dark now, even for you and the Bright Moon. I'll find you something to eat and put you to bed."

Rifkind resisted her friend's guidance. "I've got to stay here." She pointed at Ejord. "If he wakes. You Overnmonts—damned difficult to heal."

"We'll take him to his bed—"

"No!" Rifkind shook free and very nearly toppled to the ground. "He can't be moved, not for a day, at least. My healing barely holds him together; it needs time to strengthen."

The two women stared at each other. Jenny blinked first. She gave orders to rig a canopy over Glascardy's lord and sent women to the kitchen for whatever food could be found in the middle of the night. The women came back with cold stew and stale bread, both of which Rifkind wolfed down without hesitation.

"Now, *rest*," Jenny said, pointing to a pile of blankets. "I'll keep watch. If Ejord so much as twitches, I'll waken you."

Rifkind muttered an objection, but in taking the edge off her hunger she'd left her arms, legs, and even her eyelids too heavy to lift. She was asleep as soon as she was horizontal and stayed that way until Jenny roused her.

"Someone's coming up the road. The guard's gone out to meet him. It might be Cho. Whoever it is, he's hurt."

The sky above the castle had lightened to lavender—meaning Rifkind had gotten only a few hours of sleep, not nearly enough to restore her, not nearly enough for another major healing.

"How's Ejord?" she asked, while climbing to her feet.

"Hasn't moved. I'd have wakened—"

The rest of Jenny's assurances were lost as the gate guard shouted, "It's him. Come quick, my ladies. It's the healer's boy and he's reeling."

22

Cho came through the castle gates draped between two guards. To a jaundiced eye, he gave every impression of a man several hours into a roaring drunk . . . until the trio came out of shadow and light fell on the bloody smear covering the left side of Cho's face. Rifkind, whose eye had been particularly jaundiced, reached the boyo a half step behind Jenny who had somehow come up with a length of damp linen.

"It's not as bad as it looks," the red-haired woman announced.

Cho deflected Jenny's help with an awkward swing of his arm. "By the Bright One, it wasn't my fault." He looked at Rifkind as he spoke. His tone was both defiant and defensive. "They came outta the trees. 'Cross the stream."

"He's had his bell rung," Jenny decided, moving in for another swipe with the linen.

Cho tried ducking under Jenny's cloth—a bad move on his part. He'd have collapsed without the guards. "Four of 'em. Couldn't take them."

"Let's get him seated," Rifkind suggested.

"Wasn't my fault," the boyo insisted when the guards sat him down on an overturned crate.

Rifkind wasn't interested in excuses or explanations. She held up her forefinger. "How many?"

"One . . . two . . . no, one. Bloody Bright! I had one, I know I did. Everything's jumbled." Cho reached up to rub his forehead; Rifkind stopped him. "They got her," he said when their eyes met. "He was lifting her up when I got blindsided."

"Hold still."

A healer could be gentle only when she was strong. This close to exhaustion, all Rifkind had was brute force. Her son flinched when she pressed her palm above his gashed forehead and heaved herself into her *tal*. She felt the angry swelling within the boyo's skull and gave thanks that it was, overall, a small bruise, unlikely to worsen or cause lasting harm.

"Wasn't my fault," Cho repeated when she lowered her hand.

Rifkind grasped Cho's chin and forced eye contact. "No one's saying it was. We were all attacked. The village . . . the castle. There had to be a plan. Reyna's not the only one carried off. One of her sisters was taken, too, and a tiring girl. Lord Ejord was nearly slain." She turned the boyo's head toward the very pale, very still man.

Rifkind's redirection affected Jenny who was not satisfied with the servants' efforts in erecting a shelter above her half-brother. Gathering the guards who'd helped Cho into the castle, she gave orders and left Rifkind alone with her son—which, Rifkind mused, might have been her purpose from the start.

Some women had an instinct for whom should talk to whom, when and where. A good many of the healers Rifkind had taught possessed that instinct, which she lacked utterly.

She and Cho stared at each other until Cho broke the silence.

"It wasn't my fault. Even if I'd had a sword . . . there were four of them. Mounted, armed, and armored."

"Did you recognize them?"

The boyo blinked in surprise and set his wound to oozing. "No. Who would I recognize?"

"Irdel men. I slew one outside the gate. Tyrokon said he recognized him or one of the others from the lower hall at Gryphonage, but dead men often resemble one another."

"You slew one?"

Rifkind started to answer then realized that Cho did not want to hear how she, hampered by a skirt and armed with a boot knife, had slain a raider when he'd failed to protect Reyna. "Jevan and Lord Anderly went out with all the men the castle could spare. We'll know more when they get back." Having dispensed her comfort, she turned to more important considerations. "You seem to be talking better already. Can you stand? Walk?"

Cho needed only a heartbeat to slip into a sulk. "I'm bleeding. I was down and out and I'm still seeing double. Aren't you going to heal me?"

"There was an accident, a broken leg with the bone protruding; you'd gone off with Reyna before it happened. Before I'd finished— sweet Mother . . ." Rifkind recoiled from the memory of Emmel lying on the village street. "Then Ejord. He took a cut to the neck that should have killed him. I'm not a well, Cho; I can't raise water every time. Scalp wounds bleed, but they won't kill you and neither will that bump on your head. You'll heal fine on your own."

The castle men had the canvas arranged to Jenny's satisfaction. Now she was fluffing out a pillow.

"No!" Rifkind shouted. "You *can't* move him!" She turned back to Cho. "They're not used to our ways. They don't know what to do. They're head-blind, all the Overnmonts. I can't empty their minds; I can barely keep them under while I'm healing them. You can help. You can watch while I try to get some rest."

Cho's nostrils flared like an angry war-horse's. "Find Tyrokon," he said and walked away.

Rifkind didn't bother calling after him. She'd have been angry, too, in his place, but only if she'd also been too stubborn to recognize a healer's responsibilities. She looked around for Tyrokon without finding him.

"You there," she called to a boy of about twelve who stood watching her from a distance. "I've a chore for you. Find Tyrokon for me."

Instead of running off the boy approached cautiously. "I'm not castle-folk, my lady. I don't know who your Tyrokon is, nor where to find him."

A village boy then, which brought the fires and Emmel back to mind. "How does it go for you? How many were hurt?"

"Only a few, my lady, when the raiders came a-thunder down the castle road and there wasn't hardly enough room to get out of their way."

"Badly?"

The boy shook his head. "None . . . except . . ." He twitched from one foot to the other. "Except Emmel."

Rifkind felt the familiar pang of failure and relief at the same time. "Was he kin to you?"

Another shake of ragged brown hair. "My father's the wheelwright," he said, as if that should explain everything.

Another time and Rifkind might have asked another question. Just then she was far too weary. "Can you find a castle boy and ask him to find Tyrokon, he's Asheeran, like me . . . with a limp?"

The boy cocked his head. "The lord going to live?" he asked with a child's directness.

Rifkind answered the same way. "If he lives until sundown then, yes, I expect Lord Overnmont to survive. Now, go find Tyrokon or find someone who can."

She had no idea how long he was gone, though it couldn't have been too long—the shadows hadn't changed appreciably. Exhaustion had gotten the better of her and she was dozing when a hand fell lightly on her shoulder.

"It's chaos in the kitchen," Tyrokon said, "but I found some meat that hadn't turned."

He offered Rifkind a plate. She was beyond hunger, which, for a healer, was far gone, indeed. Tyrokon chided her and she picked up a morsel. It had no taste and lay heavily in her stomach, but with Tyrokon watching her, she ate until the plate was clear, then laid a hand on Ejord's forehead. His skin was slightly warm—the best she could hope for under the circumstances. *Rest*, she thought; she hadn't the strength for a *tal* command, even if it could have penetrated the Overnmont headblindness. *Stay still.*

"Watch him," she said to Tyrokon. "Rouse me if he moves. Put a hot coal in my hand, if that's what it takes."

Tyrokon swore and Rifkind leaned against the nearest wall.

The next thing she knew she was lashing out with her fists and connecting with bone. She opened her eyes on Tyrokon who sat back on his heels, rubbing the jaw she'd clouted. Ejord lay exactly as he'd been before, save that the shadows had moved around him. A bell clanged in the background—loud, but nothing she couldn't have slept through.

"There had better be a good reason for waking me."

"Riders, a good number of them. The lookout spotted them coming out of the forest. It's too far to tell if it's the raiders come back for another try, or the castle's own men. The lookout says there's more coming in than rode out. The lady's rung the bell to call the villagers, just in case, and all-arm the men."

Raval's courtyard teemed with frantic villagers and men whose anxious glances said they were all too aware of their reduced numbers as they buckled on their swords.

"At least they won't take us by surprise."

Jenny's red hair was a beacon in the chaos. She was arguing with a robust old man. They were both pointing at the gate, which was wide open.

"I'll see what I can learn. You stay here. Nobody so much as *touches* Ejord, understand?"

Tyrokon nodded.

As Rifkind crossed the courtyard she spotted her son shaking himself into a chain-mail shirt. He'd found himself as a Wet-lands warrior. She shouldn't have been surprised, but she was.

"Rifkind!" Jenny hailed her. "Tell Somers that we've got to keep the gate open till the last moment."

"Let them scatter in the fields," the old warrior countered. "They'll survive. It's not the village these men want, it's the rest of Lord Overnmont's daughters!"

"Do we know it's the raiders come back?" Rifkind asked.

"They've come out of the forest," Jenny replied confidently. "And there at least twenty of them. We sent out fifteen."

Rifkind would have preferred a more precise identification. "Seems like we've already got most of the villagers inside."

"Not the men," Jenny said quickly. "They're down in the village getting things set back to rights. They know to come when the all-arm bell rings. If there is to be a fight, we'll need every man."

Somers shook his head. "If it's them, there won't be a fight. They'll set a siege with demands. The fewer extra mouths we've got, the better . . . and the better chance of getting word to our own men."

They were both right. Rifkind was spared the need to choose a side when the lookout shouted down, "There's a gray horse in the lead."

Jevan rode a raw-boned gray so pale it was almost white. Jenny was relieved; Somers saw a trick.

"Could be anyone riding that horse," he grumbled.

But it was Jevan, Anderly, all their men, and a few more besides. They intercepted the village men, sent them back to their repairs and came through the gate at a trot. Man and horse alike were sweated and weary. Jevan took the water his wife offered and spilled it over his head.

"Did you find them?" Jenny demanded—not a question Rifkind would have wasted time asking. The men were tired, but none was wounded and, more significantly, there wasn't a young lady to be seen riding behind her rescuer.

Jevan and Anderly both shook their heads. That was the only thing they did together. Among the Glascardy nobles, Anderly Werth held the higher rank and intended to make his report, never mind that Ejord was in no condition to hear it and Jenny, the only other Overnmont around, was Jevan's wife.

Despite one man interrupting the other, the tale that emerged was a simple one. The men had followed the road toward the Grayway Bridge that Rifkind and the Werthers had crossed a few days earlier. They'd hoped to catch up with the raiders, or with other Glascards on their way home from the quarter-day session who should, by the great gods, have noticed a party of raiders coming or going.

But it seemed that every Glascard had made haste getting away from Raval. The few peasants Jevan and Anderly had encountered swore they'd seen no one riding past their fields and the only nobleman they'd caught up with—who happened to be Anderly's brother-in-law—swore on a chest of relics that no raiders would have gotten past him and his men. To emphasize his loyalty, Lord Stantin had split his own escort, accounting for the eight additional men standing in the Raval forecourt.

"They must have crossed at Millers Bridge," Jevan said.

"Millers Bridge is out," Anderly countered.

"There's a ford not a quarter-mile from the bridge. And a track nearby. The pig men and charcoalers were the only ones who used it, but since Irdel's broken loose, smugglers have been running it clear down to the Albinet."

Anderly wasn't persuaded. "A track's no match for a road." He continued the tale. "When we got to the Red Boar and they hadn't seen them, we figured we'd gotten ahead of them and went into the forest expecting to flush them out, but we couldn't find them—"

"They're halfway to the Albinet by now. Into Irdel, if they rode hard. We should have taken the track from the start, like I said," Jevan's voice rose.

Anderly blinked but didn't apologize. "There's nothing to be done but muster as many as we can and take an army into Irdel."

Rifkind seized a momentary lull in the conversation. "If you're going into Irdel, you're going to Gryphonage."

Every man who'd ridden into the forecourt gave her his full attention.

"Gryphonage!" Jevan exclaimed. "We need to be certain before we take Glascardy to war with Irdel."

"My boyos recognized one of the men we killed. We *know* something turned. We were honored guests one moment and prisoners the next, then we escaped. Ballard wasn't there. I counted on confusion to keep them from pursuing us, and I thought I'd counted right, but it seems not."

"How did they know to look for you here?" Jenny asked. "Didn't you tell them you were going to Isinglas and Chatelgard?"

"I told them I was going to meet Ejord. They must have known I'd find him here; it's not as if the quarter-day sessions are exactly a secret."

Anderly Werth spoke up. "They came after Lord Overnmont," he said reasonably. "Lord Overnmont and his daughters. Two of them."

"He's a widower now, and I healed his son."

"Who else but Ballardskin?" Old Somers added his voice to the chorus. "Where else but Gryphonage? Your proof will be nine months in the making!"

And the men were into it, saying nothing new but saying it loudly and widening the gap between Anderly's men and Raval men in the courtyard.

"Rifkind!" Tyrokon's shout brought quiet. "He's *moving*!"

Rifkind had to run to reach Ejord first. His eyes weren't open and, so far, it was his left arm that moved, not his seriously damaged, scarcely healed right side. Rifkind put a hand on his forehead, willing him back to unconsciousness and accomplishing the exact opposite.

"Don't you *dare* try to move and undo all that I've tried to do for you!" she snapped as their eyes met.

Ejord first words were unintelligible.

"You're alive, be grateful for that. You took a sword between your neck and shoulder that should have killed you on the spot—and *will* kill you yet if you so much as twitch that right arm. If you weren't a headblind fool, I'd have put you away for two nights' running."

"Who?"

"Who's dead? You lost five good men, another ten injured—none as bad as you. Who attacked us? We don't completely know, but it's likely they were Irdel men, probably from Gryphonage. Jevan and Anderly went after them. They've just come back empty-handed and arguing about where the sun rises."

Both Jevan and Anderly wanted to argue that, too; Rifkind silenced both of them with a single glower.

"What else?"

Rifkind shook her head. "Nothing else. Nothing that can't wait until you're healed up."

"How long?"

"A few days, a week until you can sit and stand, but"—Rifkind met her friend's eyes—"it was bad, Ejord. You're left-handed now."

Despite her warnings, Ejord struggled to survey the damage for himself. Rifkind put her palm on his chest and held him down.

"Reyna?"

Rifkind wouldn't lie but she could slice the truth exceedingly thin: "Not here. They fired the village. Some families have lost everything."

Jenny threaded through the crowd, her apron looped over her arm and bulging with an unseen burden. "I've got berries here," she said to Rifkind. "Berries and nuts, for his strength, right?"

"You remember well," Rifkind agreed.

Food was fuel. If Ejord was awake, then he needed to eat. Rifkind propped him up carefully on rolled-up blankets, then let Jenny take her place.

"Our lord needs to know the truth," Anderly hissed into Rifkind's ear. "We need to know what he would have us do."

Rifkind had no intention of replying. Ejord couldn't have heard his oath-man's words and he'd fall asleep quickly enough. That was the way of a healing man: a little food, a lot of sleep. But Ejord *had* seen Anderly bend down and, despite the intervening years, he knew Rifkind as well as anyone. He caught Jenny's wrist in his left hand and held it tight enough to restrain her and challenge Rifkind.

"Reyna?" he repeated.

Jenny turned to Rifkind with desperation in her eyes. Before Rifkind could respond, Anderly leapt into the silence.

"Taken, my lord, along with Lysse and a castle girl. With your permission, my lord, I'll lead the men we have into Irdel immediately and send a hue-and-cry throughout Glascardy for men to join us at the foot of Gryphonage."

Ejord shuddered with shock, but he managed to whisper, "Do it."

Rifkind couldn't believe what she'd heard. "There are two hundred men, at least, quartered at Gryphonage. If you took every man here you wouldn't have enough to storm Gryphonage! They'll come out of that castle and wipe you out."

"We'll besiege it," Anderly countered. "Ballardskin's men won't fight. They don't love their lord. With your permission, my lord, I'll offer amnesty to any man who renews his oath to Glascardy. We'll double our number as we march; I swear it, my lord. They'll come out of Gryphonage, for sure, but not to fight. Ballardskin doesn't hold them."

"I was *there*," Rifkind reminded them all. "Your Ballardskin's men didn't hesitate to obey their lord when he told them to lock me up."

But Rifkind fought a losing battle.

"I should have done this long ago," Ejord said to her alone when Jevan and Anderly were bickering again.

"With all of Glascardy behind you."

"There isn't time. We'll have to hope Werth's right."

Rifkind's opinion of that rumbled deep in her throat. "Fools. All of you, utter fools."

Ejord grasped her arm as he'd grasped Jenny's. "Go with them," he pleaded. "She'll need healing."

"Not as much as you need it now," Rifkind snapped, not adding that if they were right about Ohlmer Ballard and his intentions, then Reyna wasn't going to need healing half as much as she'd need a midwife.

"Jenny can take care of me—" Rifkind opened her mouth to object, but Ejord pressed on. "Don't try to tell me otherwise; I *know* how you work and your part's done. All that's left is for me to lie here, making a pig of myself until my flesh is knit. Jenny can feed me . . . and Werth can seal up a castle with Raval's help, but you're the one I'd have waiting for my daughters, if I can't be there myself."

He was right, of course, at least about Jenny's ability to do what needed doing, and Rifkind couldn't refuse a direct request. She made a few more half-hearted attempts to sway the men to caution, all to no avail. Anderly's escort with Lord Stantin's additions, plus every man Raval castle could spare would ride out in the morning. Ejord's household, those who hadn't already ridden out with his steward, would fan out across Glascardy, rallying men to join Anderly's siege.

Rifkind, at Ejord's insistence, would ride with Jevan and Anderly.

Oaths were sworn on it and Rifkind was left alone with a friend who could barely keep his eyes open.

"You'll keep them in line."

Rifkind snorted. "I'm no priest; I don't trade in miracles."

"It's my fault. I should have gone after Irdel the moment Ohlmer Aksel refused to renew the Ballard oaths. I never should have let him bed that girl. But I didn't want to risk the lives. I should have found a good, young man for my daughter and raised him up beside me, but I thought of her as a child and didn't want her to become a woman too soon."

Ejord's eyelids fluttered and closed. Rifkind pressed her palms against his temples. She rose into her *tal* and gave him what little strength she'd been able to draw into herself, then, after charging a kitchen boy to sit beside him, went to make her own preparations for the ride to Gryphonage.

CHO KNOCKED LIGHTLY ON THE open door to the chamber where Rifkind was sitting cross-legged on a high bed, taking stitches in a padded surcoat that was undoubtedly too big for her.

"I expected to see you wearing mail," she said when she looked up.

"I wouldn't ask Tein to carry me and a mail shirt, too. You don't object?"

"Object to what? Consideration for Tein's back?"

"That I'm riding with you to Gryphonage."

Rifkind stuck her needle in the surcoat and set it aside. "Would it matter if I did? How's the head?"

"You were right. It scabbed up by itself and I'm not seeing double any-more. I'm ready to ride."

"Do you have any idea of the dangers we face?"

"I've listened. I know how badly outnumbered we'll be, but—"

"And I know why you'd find a way to ride with us no matter what I said. The siege isn't the half of it. We'll be lucky if Jevan and Anderly haven't come to blows before we leave Glascardy."

"You'll keep them in line."

Rifkind laughed, short and bitter. "You vastly overestimate my talent when it comes to reining in a Darian lord. They're each loyal to Ejord—loyal to a fault—but not to each other. Jevan's an outsider—not born here and married to his lord's bastard sister. He's got no clout of his own—you should be able to understand that."

Cho had heard all that from Reyna, but had not expected his mother—who was so tight with both Jenny and Ejord—to speak so bluntly.

"Anderly's willing to carry Glascardy's banner and rescue his lord's daughter, all while bringing a recalcitrant province back into the fold, but don't for one moment think that's *all* that's on his mind. He's got a son about your age. At the end of the day, his ambitions aren't much different than Lord Ohlmer's, save he'll have Ejord's blessing."

Cho's heart had skipped a beat. This was not the conversation he'd an-ticipated. "Why are you telling me this?"

"Because you're smitten and someone needs to tell you that even if you stormed Gryphonage yourself and came out with Reyna's pretty little hand on your arm, the girl's not yours to keep."

She had come uncannily close to the secret scenes he hadn't shared with anyone, not even Tyrokon. "Lord Ejord wouldn't—"

"He most certainly will—and if you do, in fact, care for Reyna, you'll bend over backward to get out of her way."

"But—"

Rifkind scowled as she shook her head. "Believe me in this. Reyna's an Overnmont. She'll marry for Glascardy, not love. Get out of her way, Cho. Stay out of her way. Let her do what she has to do."

23

Two score of riders departed Raval castle just after dawn the next day. As late as midnight Jevan and Anderly had been arguing the merits of following the road down to the Grayway Bridge and beyond to the Albinet—longer, but faster—against those of following the track the raiders themselves must have taken through the forest. In the end, Anderly agreed that the forest route was best even though there was a chance—remote, but real—that they'd catch up with the raiders or at least learn something of their intentions from the trail they left.

Hearing the two men agree on something lulled Rifkind into thinking that the two halves of the party might set aside their conflicting loyalties and work together. The Bright One knew it would take cooperation and luck to set siege lines around Gryphonage and hold them until reinforcements arrived . . . led, she hoped, by Ejord Overnmont.

He'd been stronger when she'd roused him, not long before the party left Raval. His fingers had tingled and he'd wiggled his thumb, both signs that her healing efforts had taken root. Rifkind had pressed her palms against Ejord's temples again, risen into her *tal*, and, once more, given him all that she had to give.

She dozed in Banin's saddle as Jevan led them single-file along the forest track and when she wasn't dozing, she nibbled from a sack of fruits, nuts, and cheese morsels that Jenny had thoughtfully prepared for her.

"Keep him quiet as long as you can," Rifkind had told Jenny out of Ejord's hearing. "Whatever he wants to do, tell him he can't do it for at least a week. If he won't listen . . . well, you've got herbs, don't you?"

Jenny had nodded hesitantly. "Will that be safe . . . after your healing?"

"Safer than having him think he can chase after us before he's ready."

A week before he's ready to come after us, Rifkind told herself as she swayed, eyes closed, in the saddle. *Two weeks, then, to show Ballardskin—* she caught herself using the Glascard nickname. It never paid to belittle your enemy, especially when you were taking the battle to his heart. *Two week to show Lord Ballard that Glascardy won't stand for an abduction. A week for Ejord to heal and for his stewards to muster sufficient men. A week until he can bring them into Glascardy. Two weeks. That's all we need.*

They rode as hard as good horsemanship would allow and camped where twilight found them. A few of the men set snares for whatever might wander close during the night. Not that they'd go hungry. Every rider was packing enough food for four days, six at a stretch. After that, they'd be on their own in Irdel. Jevan and Anderly had money. Rifkind had the remains of her stash. Food was sure to be expensive for Overnmont loyalists on the far side of the Albinet.

For the moment she had the crumbs of Jenny's feast and the mash of meat and vegetables Tyrokon seared over a small fire.

The forest was quiet and not likely to spawn an attack before dawn. Anderly and Jevan sent a man around with straws for a minimal watch. Four men had drawn the short straws before the Asheerans took their turn. One of the Werthers came up with dice. That lured the boyos, but not Rifkind, who curled up against Banin's saddle.

Clouds moved in during the night. By morning a light rain was filtering down through the trees. The sun came out by early afternoon. The temperature rose, but the air remained thick. Gnats by the thousands swarmed each rider, each animal. The only sounds were the animals' tails swishing futilely and riders slapping their cheeks and necks.

Between the heat and the gnats and the runnels of sweat running down her back, Rifkind didn't twig to the sound of rushing water until it peeked through the trees.

"That's a *ford*?" Cho demanded. He'd picked up the word from the Glascards—he was picking up enough words to make himself understood in that language—but clearly he'd imagined something different, something calmer than the froth and rocks of Millers Stream.

Anderly had already spurred his reluctant horse into the churning water. His men followed, then Jevan and the Ravalmen—which was all well and good for men mounted on animals that were, on average, several hands taller than the three war-horses.

"We're going to get wet," Rifkind said to the boyos who had, surely, come to the same conclusion.

"Soaked" was closer to the truth. All three war-horses balked at the stream's edge, forcing their riders to dismount and wade into the water, reins in hand, to lead them across. Rifkind went first and was doing fine until she stepped off a rock and found herself at the current's mercy. Fortunately she had wrapped Banin's reins around her wrist. The war-horse didn't panic, the leather held, and she clambered back to shallower water.

"That's it," she sputtered, putting one foot into the stirrup and hauling her dripping self into the saddle. "I can't swim, but you can."

Banin begged to differ, but Rifkind goaded him forward. He squealed when he lost his footing, then instinct took over. His legs worked the water and they moved steadily toward the opposite bank. The boyos had an easier time of it with Banin on solid ground, shaking himself from nose to tail like a dog.

RAIN THAT DAY AND TWO days later didn't completely wash out the Irdelmen's trail. A score of men with prisoners cut a swath through the forest. On the third day they found a length of torn blue cloth tied to a bush. Only a few inches were visible from horseback, but Cho was the tracker he claimed to be and spotted the tatter.

He bounded down from Tein's saddle to unknot the cloth. "Reyna! Cloth from her dress. She's leaving us signs. Telling us where they're taking her."

No one doubted that the cloth had come from the resourceful girl's hem, but if she were trying to leave messages for her rescuers, that was the only one they found.

Two days later, they came to the Albinet—to Hanno's ferry, which the Luccan peddler had recommended and Rifkind had decided against. Hanno admitted he ferried smugglers across the river but swore he hadn't seen the Irdelmen and their prisoners until Anderly put the tip of his sword against his throat. Then he admitted they'd come through five days earlier: twenty-four men and three women, one of them no more than a child. The women hadn't said anything. They'd looked frightened and weary, but otherwise unharmed.

"Did they say where they were going?" Anderly demanded, wiggling his sword.

Hanno swore again. "They followed the track, that's all I know."

"They're bound for Gryphonage," Jevan interrupted. "They're there by now and we're wasting time."

Hanno had the sense not to ask them for fares. He was worn out by the time he got them all across, but he was alive, free to offer his services to the next smuggler and that, Jevan and Anderly agreed, was sufficient payment.

The track split in two on the Irdel side. One branch went straight north, the other veered easterly. Gryphonage lay to the northeast between the tracks. Jevan wanted to follow the northern track, which was all the reason Anderly needed to prefer the other one.

Rifkind decided it was a convenient time to remove a stone from her boot. She was relacing it when Cho cast his shadow in front of her.

"I think they're both wrong."

Rifkind looked up, asking silent questions.

"I found something."

Remembering his success with Reyna's hem, she followed him a short distance up the northern branch. Cho pointed at the grass that, to her, looked exactly like every other clump of weedy grass growing beside the rutted track.

"No," her son insisted. "*Look* at it. Look at how it's broken. And here—"

He knelt down and passed his hand above grass that was indeed flat to the ground. "See? *That* takes weight. That's what I noticed first, but here's the proof—" He led her farther from the track to a patch of dirt where even Rifkind could see the distinctive curves of hoofprints upon hoofprints.

"Our raiders," she surmised.

Cho grinned as he nodded and lost about five years from his face.

"Couldn't they have stopped to rest—or argue—just as we're doing?"

"Yeah, but they don't come back to the track. See?" He pointed at a trail of scuffed dirt leading deeper into the forest. "The ground's higher, harder; it doesn't hold their hoofprints, but see the broken branches . . . and—" Cho ran ahead to a dying shrub, plucked something from its branches, and came running back. "Look here." He twirled a tiny bit of woolen fiber between his thumb and forefinger. It wasn't blue and it was too small to have been a deliberate discard, but that didn't diminish Cho's excitement. "They're going *south*."

"You could see *that* all the way from here?"

Cho's scowl returned. "You think I put it there and pretended to find it?"

"No—I'm amazed, that's all, at what you see."

"You'll tell Jevan and Anderly to come this way if we're going to find Reyna?"

Rifkind brought the two men and a handful of others to see the hoofprints. They listened politely as Cho explained what he saw in the scene and passed his bit of wool fluff between them.

Jevan spoke first, and spoke to Rifkind, not her son: "Do you believe him?"

Rifkind nodded without hesitation, then hedged by saying, "Someone stood their horses here and headed out for the south, not the north or east."

"There's nothing south of here," Anderly complained.

"Merrinen." Jevan corrected. "Keep going in that direction and you're sure to cross the Merrinen Road."

"Merrinen's been abandoned for years—since the plague first struck. The land was never much good . . . too boggy. When hard times came, those who survived packed up and went back to where they were from. It's gone wild since then."

"What better place to hide an abducted bride?"

"Gryphonage." Anderly fairly spat the word out. "They came from Gryphonage and that's where they return. Mark me: There's nothing along the Merrinen Road. The boyo doesn't know what he's talking about."

The boyo in question tensed and clenched a fist. Rifkind grasped his forearm and squeezed it. He didn't relax, but he didn't do anything foolish, either, which was more than could be said for Anderly and Jevan. The uneasy alliance between the lords of Werth and Raval reached its breaking point when Anderly made a snide allusion to the way Jevan's nobility stemmed from his marriage to Ejord Overnmont's bastard sister. Though Jevan had surely heard such remarks before, he retaliated this time.

"At least we all know where *my* loyalty lies."

Anderly's hand dropped to his sword hilt. "Unsay that!"

Rifkind swore under her breath and did what no man would have dared: She strode between the glowering men. "Enough of this! When Ejord charged us with besieging Gryphonage it was with the belief that his daughters had been taken there. It's the daughters that matter, not the siege."

She'd fought beside Anderly Werth, laughed and drunk wine with him. She thought she could bring him around, and quickly discovered that she'd thought wrong.

"Run up to Merrinen, if you like," Anderly snarled. "A few marks in the dirt. The boyo could have made them himself or you with your witchcraft. I gave my lord my word: We're going to Gryphonage. If we fail to bottle them in . . . may the gods hold judgment upon your souls. Mount up!" He shouted to the men who would follow him to the road where their horses were waiting.

Of the two score Glascards who'd ridden out of Raval castle, nearly thirty went with Anderly, and some of them were Ravalmen.

"I'm sorry," Rifkind said to Jevan when they and their stalwarts were left alone. "I thought he would listen. I didn't count on pushing him over the edge."

Jevan shrugged his shoulders. "It was bound to happen . . . and a fair warning of what's to come. I would have been happy with a little farm somewhere out of the way, but my lord—and my wife—wouldn't have it that way.

They've tried to make me over in their image but in the eyes of Werth and the rest, I'll always reek of the Felmargue. We can still catch up with him . . . I've eaten enough crow in the past twenty years to have gotten a taste for it."

"No!" Cho interrupted. "The raiders went south."

"If they did, then they've got us outnumbered. Rifkind, isn't there something you can do to be sure?"

In her youth, Rifkind had put much store in scrying the past and the future. She still carried five crystal stones for the purpose, but it had been years since she'd used them. "Nothing that I'd trust more than my son's tracking."

Jevan looked up at the cloudless, sunless, pearl-gray sky. "Let's get started. I think there's enough light left to catch the Merrinen Road before sundown."

Cho and Tyrokon rode at the front of the short column. Rifkind urged Banin forward to ride between them. Cho was in constant motion, looking right, left, up, and down with each of Tein's strides, but his face was a thin-lipped mask. Rifkind said nothing, confident that silence would suck the words out of him eventually.

"What if I'm wrong?" he asked as he caught a branch and stripped it of leaves.

"Men will die . . . at Gryphonage or right here with us. Maybe Jevan or me or you or Tyrokon. So you'd better be right. Are you? Are we following the raiders?"

"Yes. We're far behind, but we're following them."

They reached what remained of the Merrinen Road as the sun slipped below the treetops. Their track had become a road, an overgrown, abandoned road. As Anderly Werth had promised, Merrinen was empty land. But not completely empty. Even their least observant man could see that the scrub growth covering the road had been recently trampled.

"If memory serves," Jevan said without dismounting, "there were four settlements—you couldn't call them proper villages—up the Merrinen Road. We should be able to move fast enough to reach the first by nightfall."

His memory might have been right about the settlements, but he was wrong about the pace they'd be able to keep. They hadn't gone a mile before the road turned to mud.

"Dikes must've burst," one of their men said. He had a cousin who'd lived—and died—in the Merrinen villages and knew something of the constant battle the villagers had waged with dikes and drains against their boggy land. "It's only going to get worse," he added.

Worse arrived in swarms of mosquitoes and gnats. The cousin said the air would clear an hour or so after dusk, but no one had the stomach for continuing the journey through a cloud of insects. They made their camp in the middle of the road—the highest, driest patch of ground in easy reach.

"Get a green wood fire going," the cousin suggested. "The smoke'll thin them out a bit."

A greater challenge would have been finding seasoned wood for a smokeless fire. Breathing smoke was scarcely better than swatting bugs, but they all did it while the animals stood nose to rump and lashed their tails relentlessly.

The buzzing and stinging did abate when full darkness descended over the camp. The Bright Moon was up, Vitivar, too, but both were hidden behind thick clouds. Such light as they had beyond their sulky fire came from heat lightning in the distance. The way things had been going, Rifkind expected as she bedded down, to wake up drenched. Instead she was called awake at dawn, when the insects swarmed again.

They reached the first of the Merrinen settlements around midday. "Abandoned" was too kind a word for the handful of walls and charred timbers that could have been home for no more than a few families. The men they were pursuing had thought the same. Their tracks continued on without interruption.

Mid-afternoon saw the winds pick up and the clouds turn black. Wetlands storms wouldn't destroy a man's mind the way an Asheeran lightstorm could, but when the sky began to crackle and boom, the party sought shelter in the forest undergrowth.

"It won't last," Rifkind assured the boyos as the clouds unloaded torrents of rain and, in the greater measure of things, the storm lasted no more than an hour, though it had seemed endless while it raged overhead.

Huddled amid bushes that provided the illusion, rather than the substance, of shelter, they'd smelled lightning when it struck close and been rocked on their heels by deafening claps of thunder. Most of the men had passed the storm on their knees, praying their hearts out.

They were lucky, considering how panic had spread among the animals, that the tether lines had held but there was no question of continuing their journey. Everything they'd carried or worn was soaked through and even the war-horses weren't fit for riding. Rifkind reached into her *tal* to kindle a fire while the boyos and a pair of Glascards went hunting.

A magnificent red-and-gold sunset found them wearing almost dry clothes and waiting impatiently as a small deer roasted on an improvised spit. Like wolves, they ate heartily, not knowing what the next day might bring or when they'd have time for the luxury of fresh-roasted venison.

Before bedding down for the night, they moved their camp to higher ground. The hunters had been stopped by a stream that was already out of its banks from the storm and Glascards knew that a storm like the one they'd endured brought a second wave of danger in the form of floods that might occur hours or days after the downpour.

Rifkind and Tyrokon both drew short straws for the overnight watches. Cho offered to swap.

Rifkind surrendered her straw with a grin. "I'll never refuse a full night's sleep."

"SHE STOOD UP FOR YOU," Tyrokon said, not for the first time in the whispered conversation he and Cho were having.

"She said it would be my fault if anyone dies."

"My father leads the clansmen when they raid. Is it his fault when a man dies?"

"No," Cho answered quickly, then changed his mind. "Yes."

Tyrokon, wisely, said nothing more. Cho wrestled silently with the possibility that Rifkind had, at long last, treated him as a man. Something had definitely changed when the two Glascards, Lord Jevan and Lord Werth had split the party, but not in any way that he'd hoped for.

Cho's consolation was his confidence that they were getting closer to Reyna. But for the thunderstorm, he was sure they would have come to whatever place where the raiders held her prisoner and he wasn't responsible for the storm.

He'd never been so scared as he'd been when that storm had lashed them. He'd curled up on his knees, closed his eyes, held his hands over his ears, and caught himself screaming in sheer, mindless terror. When he'd mustered the strength to open his eyes at the storm's height he'd made out his mother's silhouette through the sheeting rain. She'd been hunched over on the ground with her head tucked against her knees.

The mighty *Rifkind* cowering with the rest of them.

No, Cho had nothing to be ashamed of and in the morning they'd continue their journey. The trail was gone now, washed away by the storm, but Jevan and Bron, whose cousin had lived and died in these woods, said that they were on the only road through Merrinen.

I'm coming, Cho thought to the red-haired beauty in his mind. *I'll find you. I'll make you safe again.*

The forest was quiet. The infernal buzzing and stinging insects had mostly quieted for the night and the *drip-drip-drip* of rainwater off branches and leaves had abated. Their comrades snored lightly but not Rifkind; even in sleep, Rifkind was contained and controlled.

The animals stirred occasionally. The boyos scarcely looked up when their hooves snapped a twig, but when wood snapped at a greater distance, it caught their attention.

Cho jabbed an elbow into Tyrokon's ribs. "Did you hear?" he whispered softly.

Tyrokon's silhouetted profile bobbed up and down. "What next?"

"Another sound," Cho replied.

They both laid hands on their weapons and held their breath. Cho willed his vision to penetrate the darkness. One of their animals whickered, an innocent sound that brought Cho to his feet.

It's nothing, he argued with himself, then he saw the light hovering right where they'd heard the sound. It was tiny, a brilliant fist of cool, white light. Definitely not a torch or flame.

Cho squinted hard.

Was it steady and round? Vague and flickering? Was it larger than he'd first guessed?

Yes, larger—*growing* larger. And as it grew, it became less regular in shape, less uniform in brilliance. It had eyes, it had a face and streaming hair. Streaming *sunset-colored* hair and a slender figure revealed by her gown, which flowed behind her as she ran through the trees.

"It's her!" Cho shouted, rousing the camp. "Reyna!"

The light-bathed figure froze. Her features were so clear, so familiar, as if she were merely an arm's length away. Then her eyes widened. She turned and ran.

"Come back! Reyna, come back! We're your friends. We're here to rescue you!"

Cho felt Tyrokon's hand on his arm. He shook free of restraint and gave chase.

24

Rifkind was on her feet with bare steel in each hand before she was fully awake.

The first words she heard came in Tyrokon's voice: "Wait for me!"

The other men of their party were shaking off their dreams as well and eagerly leaving camp in pursuit of Tyrokon who was pursuing—what?

Jevan rushed past. Rifkind shouted his name and snagged his tunic.

"What's going on?"

"The daughters. We've got to catch the daughters. See them, there, where the light moves—"

Rifkind looked and saw darkness. "What light?" she demanded, but she'd gotten all she was going to get. Short of slashing Jevan's arm with her knives or tripping him and breaking an ankle or two, there was no way she could keep him from charging after the others. Suddenly alone in the camp, she strained her eyes to see what the men had seen and saw nothing.

They've lost their minds, she thought as she sheathed her knives, and was struck by a counter-thought. The Bright Moon was below the horizon; the red moon ruled the sky. Vitivar's power had been broken ages ago, but there was always someone looking to reassemble the shards. They'd never succeed, but when the Bright Moon was resting, then mischief could claim an advantage.

"Bloody Bright," she swore, entirely without irony. She loosened the war-horses from the tether line. *Guard the camp,* she pressed into Banin's mind. She'd never made such a request of him or any other war-horse. They weren't watch animals though they did have an instinct to defend their herd . . . if, with a few pointed thoughts, she could persuade Banin that a collection of saddles and traveling gear was a herd.

She couldn't spare more than a few thoughts. Already the sounds of men chasing whatever it was that they chased were fading.

Sword? she asked herself. If sorcery was involved, a sword wasn't likely to be much use, but she'd feel better with steel riding between her shoulders. After shrugging into her sword rig, Rifkind rose slightly into her *tal* where she could perceive light all around her—life light, the faint shadow-light of the forest itself, the dull glow of lesser life, and the bright white souls of her companions.

Rifkind moved at speed, guided by the wounded branches the men had left in their wake. She came to the swollen stream—a blacker-than-black gash in the night. The men had made their way across. Reluctantly, Rifkind waded after them. She stumbled and emerged soaked to the bone. There'd be a reckoning, she vowed as she paused just long enough to empty her boots.

She'd gone a mile—a thousand strides, more or less—before she began to gain ground. They were no longer chasing something but were bunched together and moving constantly. Dancing? Fighting? Rifkind slowed down and fingered the loop that held her sword in its sheath.

There was light around the men now, real light as opposed to soul light, and, once she was close enough, she didn't at all like what it revealed. The men were split into two groups. One appeared to be fighting within itself, the other was fighting a creature like nothing Rifkind had seen before.

Take a man and cross him with a tree two times his height, then transform his flesh into shimmering smoke—that was what Jevan and three other men fought and were not vanquishing.

A fifth man lay on the ground, his body shrouded in the peculiar darkness that enveloped a fresh corpse when viewed from within a healer's *tal*.

How? Rifkind wondered. How could something as insubstantial as smoke kill a man?

She got her answer when the creature lashed out with one of its long, gnarled limbs and a man went flying. He wasn't dead when he struck the ground, but he didn't get up, either. She told herself that if the creature were substantial enough to lift a man off his feet, then it was substantial enough to feel the bite of her sword; and, even as she held the thought in her mind, she recalled the power of wind and rain.

Rifkind unslung her sword and invoked her goddess. She was two strides short of the fight when the second brawl spat out a body— Tyrokon's body—which groaned and slowly levered its face out of the muddy leaves.

"Rifkind! Bloody Bright! It's Cho. He's gone mad. He thinks—he thinks *that* is Reyna—"

"And didn't you all."

"Not once it turned on us. He's fighting us to stop us from fighting it."

"Hold him."

Tyrokon grimaced, then added a warning: "It's not alive. Bron put an arrow right through it where its heart should have been."

Rifkind was disappointed, but not surprised. "Try not to hurt him," she said before returning her attention to the smoke-and-light creature.

"Stand down!" she shouted to the men fighting the creature and rose completely into her *tal.*

From that vantage the creature had a face: dead-black eyes and a mouth that was little more than a round, black hole. It had heard her shout and saw her if not for what she was—an Asheeran healer with a sword—then for something different.

It flailed its arms, knocking Jevan and its other attackers to the ground, then it roared. The men cowered from the unearthly sound. Rifkind took the sword hilt in both hands and came on guard behind the weapon. She drew her strength out of her *tal* as a spinner drew yarn from a distaff and sent it winding around her blade.

The creature lashed out with an overconfident swipe of what passed for its right arm and fist. Rifkind swiveled her wrists and lopped off a forearm's length of its substance, which vanished before it hit the ground.

She settled quickly behind steel again, waiting for the creature's next move. Its maw widened and turned red. It let out a noxious roar that passed on either side of Rifkind's upright sword.

It grew back its arm.

It struck again, a more tightly focused blow. Rifkind met it with the sword for the second time and with the same result: The limb vanished as it fell and regrew moments later.

The creature responded with a flurry of attacks from the right and left. Rifkind used her *tal* to see and meet each attack. The sword sang in her hands, but the final result was the same: She was unharmed and so was the creature. Her defense was solid and she could fight from within her *tal* indefinitely, but if she wanted to defeat the creature, she was going to have to dig deeper and take risks she hadn't taken since she'd raised the Landmother in the Felmargue.

Most people could be taught to harness the strength inherent in their *tal* but Rifkind had never known anyone else who had her ability to reach beyond her own *tal* into the raw strength of the elements. The danger was that she'd overreach, as she had done in the Felmargue, and awaken a power she couldn't control.

When the creature launched a spate of ferocious attacks, Rifkind decided she had to take the risk. Retreating a pace, she extended her awareness into the earth and summoned its strength.

Her nerves burned with power they were never meant to contain. Her senses sharpened to the edge of agony: She'd get one chance to break the creature before she would have to release what she'd summoned.

The creature roared when Rifkind charged. She thought her ears would melt from the assault, but her discipline held and she brought her sword through a series of swirling cuts that shredded the creature's limbs into flaming motes, which, after they disappeared, did not reappear.

Before the creature could react to its maiming, she swung her sword on the diagonal, slicing through its torso from what would have been its left shoulder to its right flank. It released its *tal* with a lightning-like flash and a blast of wind that propelled Rifkind backward.

She lost her concentration when she collided with a tree and, in that moment, released what she had drawn out of the earth.

Cursing herself and the world in general, Rifkind scrambled into something that resembled a decent defense. She needn't have bothered. The creature was gone and so was the light that had flowed from its body. Rifkind drew several ragged breaths before noticing that the second brawl—the brawl between her son and his companions—still raged.

She snapped the first branch she touched and ignited it with a touch from her *tal*.

"Cho!" she shouted with a lingering trace of the earth's power in her voice.

The Glascards stood down leaving Cho on his hands and knees. He raised his head to look at her. His nose was bloody and his face was dark with bruises, but his eyes were his own.

"It's over," Rifkind said and sheathed her sword.

He shook his head. "Reyna was here. I *saw* her."

"You saw what the creature wanted you to see—it lured you with your desires." And Rifkind had seen nothing. "It was female," she decided, though she hadn't been aware of its sex when she'd vanquished it.

Nearby, Jevan called out, "Who's here? Give out your name and whether you're hurt."

Nine men answered after that, leaving Bron, the Glascard with a Merrinen cousin, and Tyrokon unaccounted for.

Jevan appeared at Rifkind's side with a length of deadwood, which he ignited from her branch. "Fan out. We're not leaving anyone behind."

The men rallied to the light, gathering branches, and lightning them as Jevan had done. In the expanded light, they saw Tyrokon on his knees, holding his ribs.

"You got me good," he said when Cho offered a hand up.

A man named Samnet called out that he'd found Bron's body; the creature had slashed his throat. Another Glascard declared that he'd found a cave that reeked of death and was afraid to explore farther on his own. Rifkind saw no reason to explore the cave. Though the men didn't agree about what they'd seen, they were unanimous about the need to check out the cave. Rifkind demurred and was conducting a leaf-by-leaf examination of the spot where the creature had last stood when she heard her name shouted.

"Come quick! We've found one that's still alive."

Thinking that they'd found another luminous creature, Rifkind unsheathed her sword as she ran to the cave, but she quickly understood that it wasn't monsters they were talking about but men. The cave mouth was littered with bones: weathered bones and bones with bits of gristle still attached.

Most of the bones appeared to come from animals, but there were a good many human skulls and several fresh ones. The creature she'd vanquished had been a man-eater as well as a tempter . . . temptress, and it appeared that the Irdel raiders had run afoul of it, too.

Rifkind shouldered her way through the men; she froze when she beheld the man they expected her to heal. He was alive, but barely. His left arm was gone at the elbow, his right leg at the knee; the wounds were sealed with a blobs of glistening darkness. A similar blob covered much of his abdomen and a portion of his scalp.

"He's unconscious," Tyrokon told her unnecessarily.

He's half-eaten! Rifkind wanted to shout, but the sight had left her nauseated and speechless.

"One of the Irdelmen," Jevan said, "or I miss my guess. Got more than he bargained for. Too bad we can't question him. You'll—you'll *release* him?"

Rifkind got past her nausea. She knelt beside the man and laid her hand on his brow, being careful not to touch what the creature had left behind, and rose into her *tal*. There was no way she could heal him. It wasn't the missing limbs, the creature's gooey extrusion did an exemplary job of stanching blood and blocking infection. She could have sealed the stumps, but the creature had already devoured most of the man's liver and shredded his intestines.

He was less a man than an animate corpse. It was more punishment than any man deserved, even one who'd kidnapped a friend's daughter.

Within the pall of unconsciousness, the man—his name was Grenner— was mad with fear. She calmed him, blocked the pain, and slowly awakened him.

"Mohandru . . . Mohandru . . . sweet tears of Mohandru . . . ," he babbled, then his eyes opened. He saw, he remembered, and began to tremble.

"We've killed the creature who tormented you," Rifkind told him. It was impossible to be certain, but he might have been one of the men she'd faced outside Raval castle. "What were you doing on the Merrinen Road that it captured you and your friends?"

"Friends . . . friends . . ."

Grenner moaned and started to slip away. Rifkind restrained him with a touch from her *tal*. "What of the girls. Were the girls with you?"

"One . . . the youngest." Grenner's eyelids fluttered. "We split them. Two for my lord, one for the spire. Promised. Told to wait. Only two . . . only two to the spire . . . with the girl. It came after dark . . . the wraith—"

It was one thing to speak a language, another to know precisely what each word meant. In Rifkind's mind, the Glascard word "wraith" conjured a ghost, the husk of a departed spirit. Ghosts were weak and pitiable; they didn't fight with the strength of several men or consume men as a spider consumed flies.

Rifkind wanted clarification, "Wraith?"

"From the spire . . . from the spire. Should've known when it killed Bish, Endle, and Larsignet. Dragged 'em off. Should've turned and run 'fore it was too late. Thought we could handle it."

Rifkind looked at the body parts, did the math. "If Grenner's the sole survivor," she said to Jevan, "then there might be more than one of these 'wraiths' in the forest."

"Brel's fist," Jevan swore anxiously. "Find out what the 'spire' is, and where it is, so we can avoid it."

Rifkind didn't need to ask; Grenner had heard Jevan and answered, "Ill-abin . . . the sorcerer . . . his place. My lord said . . . said yes. For a price . . . two daughters . . . one each—"

Jevan shouted, "Damn him! Damn Ballardskin!" and Grenner began to tremble again.

Rifkind nailed Jevan with a glower and reached deeper to calm Grenner. "Where is the spire?"

Grenner shook his head. "Don't know . . . guide waiting . . . only two, and the little girl. Told to wait."

"How long?"

"As long as it took. Too late. It came . . . the wraith . . . Mohandru! Mohandru! The wraith! One by one. Why me? Why? Why? *Why?*"

Grenner's eyes widened, then rolled back in his head. His back arched and his limbs, stumps and all, thrashed against the stone.

Rifkind turned to Jevan. "I don't think he can tell us much more. Is there anything else you want me to ask him?"

"Does he know where Lysse is? Is she still in this 'spire'?"

Rifkind shook her head, but roused Grenner and asked the questions.

"Brides . . . for my lord, for Illabin."

"Brel's fist! She's a *child*!"

Grenner looked at Jevan and the sight clearly terrified him. Whether it was his struggles or for some other reason, the wraith's extrusions were losing their effect. Grenner's wounds had begun to bleed again.

"It's over," Rifkind said, pressing her hand firmly on Grenner's forehead.

He calmed, then, moments later, stopped breathing altogether. Some of the Glascards, recognizing what Rifkind had done, drew Mohandrist signs in the air. They retreated when she stood up.

"They split the girls," Rifkind said to Jevan. "We didn't consider that."

"We weren't thinking sorcery, either," Jevan snarled. "Unnatural things. If—if that *thing*—if he turned our Lysse into that wraith—"

"Not likely. Look around. It's been laired here for quite a while—if it's the only one. Have any of you heard of Illabin?"

Heads shook, but only Jevan answered: "Lord Ejord won't let sorcerers set up in Glascardy. It's a law I'm happy to enforce. Ballardskin took the opposite view—because it *was* opposite, anything to say that Irdel wasn't part of Glascardy any longer."

"Ohlmer never mentioned the name when we were at Gryphonage, I'm sure of it. Probably didn't want to mention that he'd sold a piece of Irdel . . ." She paused. "For what? He didn't need sorcery to raid Raval. That was pure muscle and steel."

"He needed to know where and when," Jevan reminded her. "He knew you'd go straight to Ejord once you escaped."

"Straight to Chatelgard." Rifkind agreed, then her memory cleared. "Wait! The boy, Garris, he mentioned Illabin. Sweet Mother, what did he say? Something— Ballard brought Illabin to Gryphonage. He promised to heal the boy . . . and didn't. I pegged him for a charlatan and didn't ask more. Should've."

"You didn't know," Jevan said. "Now we do: Ballardskin's in league with a sorcerer. By all the gods, I wish we knew where this damned 'spire' is. Sounds like a tower to me, like Raval. We've got to send someone back to Raval. If the raiders split the girls, we've got *two* castles to besiege. You're confident Grenner didn't know more than he let on?"

"He didn't have the strength to lie." Not with her hand pressed against his forehead.

"Then there's nothing more we can do here. Tomorrow we'll see if we can find that 'spire.' Does anyone happen to remember the way back to our camp?"

Jevan tried to make light of a real problem and made himself seem younger than Cho or Tyrokon in the process. The Black Flame had done him no favor when it preserved his face nearly as it had been twenty years earlier.

Rifkind laughed. "I had no trouble following you here—you left a trail a child could follow. Reversing it shouldn't be a problem."

"What about him?" one of the Glascards pointed at Grenner's corpse.

"Carry it if you want. We'll bring Bron back with us. I'm not burying a good man in this lair of bones."

"SORRY IF WE hurt you," Tyrokon said to Cho as they trudged through the forest.

"Not your fault. If that's sorcery, I don't care if I never meet it again. What did you see?"

"Three women. I recognized Reyna . . . I think. I saw *something* and thought it was Reyna."

"I saw her so clear I could almost touch her."

Tyrokon waited a moment before saying, "If you'd known they'd split the captives and taken Reyna to Gryphonage, would you have gone with Anderly?"

Cho had a quick, honest answer for that question, but kept it to himself. "It's not as if we can fight sorcery. Look what happened to us. We'd have wound up like those raiders. Rifkind's the only one who can fight sorcery. We just get in her way. Wait and see, tomorrow she'll go off on her own."

"Off where? You're our tracker. We wouldn't be here at all except for you. She'll need you."

"Reyna—" Cho almost said the words on the top of his mind. "You'll see, she won't ask for anything," he said instead.

25

The camp was quiet, save for the sounds of tired men sleeping. Bron's body, wrapped in his cloak, awaited funeral rites before burial, rituals the men would perform without Rifkind's assistance. He'd been a Mohandrist, a believer in a better life that began after death. As a healer, Rifkind fought death, but when it came, that was the end. Thinking about the afterlife was a waste of time that could have been spent sleeping, if Rifkind had been able to sleep, but it was the afterlife or the problems Grenner had raised when he spoke of sorcery and a spire that kept her awake.

Jevan interrupted Rifkind's idle thoughts. "Still awake?" He offered a chunk of dried meat from his pack; he knew her well.

Rifkind accepted the offering.

"I've come for a favor."

"I'll do what I can, if I can."

"We need to find that 'spire.'"

"No question there." Rifkind tore off a mouthful and began chewing.

"So, I was remembering how, back in the Felmargue when Humphry's army was on our threshold, you went out alone one night to scout his camp. When you came back, you said Humphry was dead. You never said how he'd died but I always assumed you'd done it yourself . . . and that you weren't—weren't quite yourself when you did—"

Rifkind was grateful for the excuse chewing gave her to remain silent. She remembered the moment when she'd killed Humphry Overnmont as well as she remembered any moment of her life—and she hadn't, as Jevan put it, been herself.

"I remember that we argued—Jenny and I and everyone else—whether you'd made yourself invisible or whether you'd become an eagle. Invisible wouldn't help us now; we don't know where the spire is. But it's no secret an eagle on the wing can see its prey on the ground."

Rifkind swallowed a lump that was still more leather than meat. "That was a long time ago. I did things then that I couldn't begin to do now."

"That's not the way it works."

"I beg your pardon?"

"You were closer to the Black Flame Well than Jenny or me and we don't forget. Whatever you were, whatever you knew, it stays the same."

"Speak for yourself. I'd like to think I'm a little wiser now, a little less reckless."

"They're not the same thing. If you could become an eagle and fly over the forest—"

"It wasn't an eagle; it was a panther, a big, black panther we call the ger-cat. As a child, I dreamt of being a ger-cat. I made a dream come true, for a night. I wasn't much good at being a ger-cat with four legs and a tail. I wouldn't know what to do with wings."

"Wouldn't it be worth a try? I wouldn't ask, if I could do it myself. Jenny and I have a boy who's Lysse's age. I think of him."

Rifkind surrendered. "I scarcely know where to start."

"Start with a dream."

After saying that she would need to dream alone, Rifkind left the camp. She stumbled into a fallen tree trunk and, deciding that it would make as good a resting place as any other, settled in.

The hard part, as it turned out, wasn't dreaming herself into the semblance of an eagle; the hard part was recreating the Rifkind who'd believed she could do anything she wanted or needed to do and even that was only as difficult as leaping a bottomless chasm of caution and doubt.

Because I can—

And why not? She was Rifkind, Mistress of Healers, vanquisher of sorcerers. She argued with goddesses and had outlived not one, but *two* destinies. If anyone could fly, she could . . . and did.

The flying part proved easy, so long as she didn't think about it. The hawk—in the end she'd become a hawk because she knew hawks; the Asheera was home to hawks, not eagles—didn't think about flying any more than Rifkind thought about walking or riding. It rose above the trees in exhilarating spirals. It looked down and saw . . . very little.

The Asheeran hawk was a daylight hunter. She'd have been wiser to dream herself into an owl, but a lack of vision wasn't an insurmountable problem.

She was Rifkind in a hawk's body. She could rise into her *tal* and see the *tal* of every other living thing from background haze of the forest itself to the pinpricks of her Glascard companions and, in the distance, a shaft of light—a spire the same color as the dark moon Vitivar had been before it set.

The hawk wheeled and stroked its wings toward the light.

The stone-walled spire was less impressive than the warding light the sorcerer Illabin had thrown up around it. Before the plague had emptied the forest of its common folk, the squat tower had almost certainly been home to whichever second son of a second son Ejord had seen fit to install as the Lord of Merrinen.

It stood atop the best hill that the forest had to offer. In better times, Merrinen's farmers had chopped down a broad ring of trees spreading down from the hill's flanks. The forest was beginning to reclaim what it had lost, but cover was still sparse. There'd have been no way for Jevan to lead them unseen to the spire's gate.

Rifkind circled the spire, studying Illabin's warding with the vision her *tal* provided. The sorcerer had woven his tower's defense like a fishnet with a mesh tight enough to touch any man or woman who crossed it. With her *tal* vision, Rifkind might have been able to thread herself between the shimmering filaments. It would have been a close fit and she had no way of knowing what punishment the warding delivered. From its sheer size, she doubted it packed a fatal punch, but surely it would alert Illabin to any intruder . . . any *human*-sized intruder.

The warding mesh was easily wide enough to admit a stooping hawk. She spiraled upward until she was high enough to see the barest hint of lavender on the eastern horizon, then let the hawk do what came naturally to it.

Vision had never been so sharp as the moment when she targeted one diamond-shaped gap over all others. Wind had never echoed so loudly in her ears. Her heart had never beat so quickly as when she hurtled through the gap.

The stone wall loomed; the hawk veered sharply, beat its wings, and found a perch on the narrow ledge of an arrow-slit window.

While her hawk-self preened its feathers, Rifkind made herself small, hoping to disguise the power of her *tal*. She could have hidden herself altogether, but not while wearing a hawk's shape. It seemed wiser to remain a hawk, with the hawk's ability to escape and it was certainly easier for the hawk to pass through the narrow slit.

Hawks were not made for flying in narrow, enclosed spaces. Rifkind hopped up the stairs where—given the dreary similarity among Darian castles great and small—she expected to find private chambers and, hopefully, Ejord's youngest daughter. She hadn't thought through how she would get Lysse out of a locked chamber and didn't have to. The two doors at the top of the stairs stood open. The rooms beyond them were empty.

She hopped down the stairs until she was level with a row of arches cut into the upper reach of the hall. Someone was up early and giving orders in an imperious tone:

"Hurry up! I want to be gone by first light. Not that one! Have you half the sense the gods gave to ants?"

With a single flap of its wings, the hawk leapt to an arch sill from which Rifkind got her first look at Illabin. He was a young man—which, somehow, she hadn't expected—a bit heavy-set with wild brown hair partially restrained by a knot at the base of his neck. He wore ordinary clothes, ordinary, at least, for a wealthy man.

With her hawk's vision, Rifkind could count three rings on his left hand and four on his right. With her *tal* vision, she could see that each ring shimmered with its own light and Illabin's *tal*, which surrounded and rose an arm's length above his scalp, had an amber tinge. Color was not especially meaningful where *tal* was concerned, though Rifkind took note that Illabin's was similar to that of his warding and of the dark moon.

She'd have been in trouble if Illabin had looked up, but the sorcerer was the sort of man who'd rather shout orders than do anything for himself. He was fully occupied making life miserable for the servant trying to pack piles of garments and miscellany into three large boxes.

Rifkind wondered why the sorcerer was preparing to leave his tower— had he sensed her victory over his wraith? —until her hawk's vision caught a flicker of movement in a far corner. Not a mouse, but a girl absently braiding her strawberry blond hair. Rifkind cursed herself for not having probed the shadows with her *tal* vision, then realized that Lysse's *tal* had been hidden. A child with talent and a sense of despair could have disappeared into herself, but Lysse was a headblind Overnmont, which meant Illabin had meddled with her.

Images blurred on the border between Rifkind's outrage and the hawk's predatory instincts. The hawk spread its wings and had begun the powerful down sweep that would propel it into a talons-out flight to the sorcerer's eyes. For one heartbeat Rifkind believed in the hawk's instincts, then, because no hawk was large enough to kill a man, she willed it quiet.

In principle Rifkind had no objections to sorcery, even sorcery that drew its power from the dark moon. If he hadn't taken Lysse, Rifkind would have left Illabin alone, but he had taken Lysse and meddled with her, and that earned her enmity just as it demanded the child's rescue.

He's packing. He's leaving. Once he's gone, it'll just be the servant. Even if the servant's another creature like the wraith—

Rifkind had defeated one wraith, she was confident she could defeat another and rescue the girl. And then what? Follow Illabin down the road?

The road! There was only one road in Merrinen. If the sorcerer went any way but north, he'd be in forest until he came to the high mountains, so it was more likely that he'd travel north, deeper into Irdel, toward Gryphonage . . . and past the Glascard camp.

If we were careful, we could ambush him. He's only one sorcerer. There's a limit to what one sorcerer can do, even with seven rings on his fingers. He's taking his boxes. He won't be traveling fast, I can fly faster than he can travel—

But Rifkind would have to fly alone. Not even in her wildest leap of self-confidence could she imagine a feat of magic that would get Lysse out of the spire castle any faster than her child's legs would carry her and, however much she wanted to go after Illabin, the child came first. It wasn't an easy decision and before Rifkind was comfortable with it, the sorcerer himself made it moot.

The chests were packed, the servant had struggled off with the largest of them, and just when Illabin should have been walking out the door, he went into the shadows where Lysse still fussed with her hair. His back obscured Rifkind's view. When he turned, he had Lysse's hand in his own. The girl walked beside him like a well-trained dog. Illabin waited patiently until the servant had picked up the third chest, then guided his human possession from the hall.

Rifkind's hawk retreated from the archway sill. It returned to the arrow-slit window and launched itself into the air.

The sun had risen and shone directly on Illabin's warding. The mesh that had been so easy to see by dawnlight was barely visible. It would have been easier to see on the shadowed side of the tower, but that was the side where Illabin was making his final preparation.

Precious moments passed before Rifkind spotted a gap she was sure of, then one more moment slipped away as her hawk circled upward until it had climbed above human vision but not its own.

What luck, Rifkind thought as the hawk's eyes showed her a simple two-wheeled farmers' cart hitched behind a plug horse. *I'll out-fly it with ease.*

Lysse sat docilely amid the chests, once again playing with her hair. The servant handled the reins and whip, which he cracked twice to get the horse moving. Illabin sat beside the servant, rigid as a statue with his be-ringed hands carefully folded in his lap.

Rifkind waited just long enough to be sure that the cart was headed north then flew ahead of it. She followed the road, because the Glascard camp was nowhere near as obvious from above as Illabin's warded spire had been, and relaxed enough to marvel at the many-layered view of the forest her hawk's eyes provided.

The last thing she expected to see beneath her hawk's wings was Illabin's cart. Yet, there it was and, though the plug horse's head hung low and its hooves seemed to drag across the ground, it was quickly in front of her. Rifkind demanded more speed from the hawk. Its wings stroked deeper and it gained a mote or two, but it could not overtake the cart.

That can't be—

The hawk's wings faltered; it lost altitude and speed. The cart came to a curve and disappeared from sight. In her hawk's dream, Rifkind couldn't out-speed the cart and couldn't understand why. She endured a surge of panic for herself and for the Glascards in their roadside camp before realizing that she didn't have to fly. She could simply awaken.

"To the road!" Rifkind shouted once her thoughts had returned to the body she'd known all her life.

She ran from her resting place to the camp proper. Two men were digging Bron's grave—no easy task without a shovel. The rest lazed in the morning sun of what promised to be a scorching day.

"To the road!" she repeated. "The sorcerer's coming with Lysse. We can ambush him, if we hurry."

Any other man might have asked questions, but Jevan never hesitated. He seconded Rifkind's commands, dividing the men: six, including the boyos, on the far side of the road, one more as a lookout up the road, the rest with Rifkind and him on the near side. Their archers, including Cho, would hang back while swordsmen rushed the road, balking the horse, and bringing the cart to a stop.

Rifkind would deal with Illabin, how she didn't quite know, but as her imagination had never failed her in a fight, she wasn't worried.

"It worked, then. You became an eagle and flew to the spire," he said to Rifkind when everyone was in position.

She nodded. "A hawk. You were right, all it wanted was a dream."

"How long before he gets here?"

"I don't know. He left the spire in a cart. He had Lysse in the back, a servant driving, and the sorriest horse I've seen in a long time pulling it. I was sure I could fly faster—I don't know what got into me: I should have just woken myself out of the dream, but it turned out better that I didn't. I'd have told you that he wouldn't roll past for hours and I'd have been wrong. He's using sorcery, somehow, to spirit the horse along. When I looked down, it seemed as if it were just plodding, but it passed beneath me and I couldn't catch up."

"Man-eating wraiths and road-eating horses. That's serious sorcery."

"And, he's done something to Lysse."

Jevan's face hardened.

"I don't know what, but she's completely docile. She sat by herself, playing with her hair, until he came to fetch her. He hid her *tal*."

"What's that mean?"

"*Tal*'s your essence. It flows out of you from the moment you're born to the moment you die. When I heal, I use my *tal* to surround yours and quiet it while I work. You become unconscious, but another healer would still see your *tal* in its usual place. Lysse was conscious, but unaware, and I couldn't see her *tal*."

"Lord Ejord's right to ban them all from Glascardy."

"Priests, sorcerers, even healers, we all use *tal*, only we use it differently. I could do what Illabin's done—what he's done to Lysse, anyway. It's not sorcery that's bad, it's what a sorcerer does. The person, not the power."

Jeven was skeptical. In his mind, power couldn't be separated from the person wielding it and Rifkind, who was only half-convinced of her own argument, was unable to sway him.

The men grew restive, hunkered down in the forest scrub. Rifkind began to doubt what her hawk's eyes had shown her, then the lookout whistled and she vaulted into her *tal*. The men knew what was expected of them. They moved quickly, but not quickly enough. With a roar quite unlike anything they'd heard before, the whole forest quickened southward, toward Illabin's spire, then rebounded to the north. Leaves and twigs showered the Glascards who lost their composure and looked at one another rather than at the road.

Even Jevan forgot his purpose enough to ask blankly, "What was that?" while other men could be heard asking the same question.

Rifkind blinked, she shook her head as she descended from her *tal*. "Illabin. Sweet Mother knows how—"

"There're *tracks* in the mud!" a man shouted.

"But he's gone by so fast we couldn't see him."

They all followed her to the road where, plain as day, two straight lines had been carved into the drying mud.

"Find me a fresh hoofprint," Rifkind said to her son.

CHO KEPT HIS MOUTH SHUT as he strode up the road, but anger had come to a quick boil inside him. With the wheel tracks to guide him, any damn fool could have found a fresh hoofprint once he strode beyond the addled mud where the Glascards had ridden their animals the day before.

She insulted him. Demeaned his skills. Belittled him in the eyes of the men.

Lord Jevan was emphatically *not* the man that Lord Ejord Overnmont was. How could he be? He didn't look old enough to have grown children. Something to do with something he and his wife had eaten long ago. Something Rifkind had eaten, too, and the reason none of them looked their age.

Bloody Bright, Cho had always thought it was just another healer's trick . . . another sign that she wasn't interested in having a son, but she'd sworn she hadn't noticed. Sworn in front of everyone and everyone had laughed and joked at him—at *him*!—saying that if he weren't careful, he'd wind up older than his mother!

His cheeks had burnt then and they burnt now with the memory.

Cho looked down at the hoofprint. "Got one," he turned and shouted.

Rifkind started walking toward him. "Now find me another," as if finding one hadn't been humiliating enough.

"Right here," he shouted, without looking down.

"You're sure?"

Rifkind broke into a trot and Jevan behind her. Cho looked down quickly . . . looked down on perfectly unblemished mud where, by all that he knew of the stride of horses, there should have been another hoofprint.

"Not quite," he admitted.

That wind *had* been uncanny. After that wraith-thing, this whole forest was uncanny. But hadn't there been a moment—the memory of a moment—when he'd seen a dun horse pulling a cart with two men sitting on the bench?

If memory served, the horse had been walking . . . but a walking horse left prints that were separated by no more than a man's regular stride.

There were no hoofprints within that distance. There were no others to be seen. It was as if the walking horse had set down one hoof, and one hoof only, which was impossible.

Cho scrambled up the wheel tracks, just ahead of his mother. They went a good twenty yards before they found another pockmark in the drying mud.

"Bloody Bright," Cho swore softly. "The ground's soft. There've *got* to be other prints. I *saw* a nag; it didn't take twenty-yard strides. No horse takes twenty-yard strides."

He looked at Rifkind, expecting her to say something wise and unpleasant, but she was pale . . . pale and frightened.

Bloody Bright—*she* was frightened.

Cho looked down at the hoofprint.

"What do we do now?" Lord Jevan asked.

"We ride hard for Gryphonage and hope that we're not too late."

26

The Glascard party rode hard through steaming sunlight and thunderstorms that shook the trees but did nothing to break the oppressive heat wave. Pushing their animals to their limit, they completed their journey in three sweat-soaked days, which was, of course, three days longer than Illabin had taken.

Rifkind was ready to concede that Anderly was right when he said the lords of Irdel wouldn't fight for their lord. Their party wasn't invisible and if Anderly had set his lines, word that someone was besieging Gryphonage should have gotten out. They'd ridden with their weapons ready, but aside from peasant ward signs, no one had paid attention to their passage.

From their first glimpse of Gryphonage, they knew there was trouble. The castle and most of the hill on which it stood were hidden by a thick fog that reminded Rifkind of nothing so much as a cloud about to spawn a lightstorm.

"Where's Anderly and our men?" Rifkind asked, shielding her eyes from the afternoon sun that should have banished the fog long ago.

Jevan pointed first to the ragged line where the forest gave way to meadows and fields. "In there." Then he pointed at the fog-shrouded hill. "I don't like the looks of that. Do you think our sorcerer's got a hand in it?"

Rifkind nodded.

"He's a powerful one."

She nodded again.

They reined their animals off the road and hadn't gone far into the forest before they were hailed by friendly voices.

A bearded Glascard descended from the trees and greeted them with, "Decided there was nothing to be found up in Merrinen, eh? Decided to join the party?"

Jevan didn't rise to the bait. "How goes it?"

"Well enough. Dicey at first and the men were eyeing the chickens for fare, but the locals liked the look of Glascard coin when we told them we'd be glad to pay for our food. Makin' them rich, that's what we're doing. The castle knows we're here and don't much care. Look at it . . . well, not now, but the Ballard's castle's another Chatelgard. There's a well in there that's good in the worst summer an' enough food for years." He began walking, leading them along a deer path.

"So there's been no skirmishing? They haven't sent anyone out?"

"They sent out one man under a flag of truce when we first arrived. He met with Lord Anderly. Our lord didn't tell us what he said, except to send a man hightailing back to Glascardy with a message soon after. We've had reinforcements: twenty men from Bowsler with Lord Ivander. We're digging in."

Anderly was waiting for them when they reached a tree-shaded camp straddling a narrow brook. "Back from your wild-goose chase? The girls are all here."

"They are now," Rifkind countered and Anderly shrugged.

She swung down from Banin's saddle. It was unthinkable that an Asheeran wouldn't tend her own war-horse after a grueling ride, but Anderly was already walking toward a lean-to set up on the camp's fringe, Jevan was following him, and Rifkind didn't want to be left out. Banin shared an image of desolation. She scratched the whorl between his horns and handed his reins to Tyrokon.

Ivander saw them coming and met them at the lean-to. He was a tall and stout man who compensated for his baldness with a dark and extravagant mustache that descended in two finger-long braids from the sides of his jaw. By the lines on his face, he was old enough to have fought with Lord Humphry, but Rifkind didn't recognize the name and couldn't recall his face. He greeted Jevan with a comradely embrace and greeted her with a nervous nod.

Thinking he might have come to Gryphonage by way of Raval castle, she asked Ivander, "How is Lord Ejord?"

"Alive, so far as I know. I gathered up my men the same day I got the message that Ballardskin had stolen the girl. Can't stand for that, no matter what he says, what proof he offers."

"What proof?" Jevan asked and Anderly explained:

"Ballardskin send out a herald soon after he saw us. The herald offered a parchment with wedding lines, his and Reyna's, all signed and sealed by priests and witnesses. He told us to stand down before our rightful lord. He's bedded her, no doubt of that, but a marriage without her father's permission? Of course, Ballardskin thinks there's no need for permission. His men told him they'd slain Lord Ejord and, right there in the moment, I decided not to set him straight. I've told the men to speak of Lord Overnmont as though he'd died. Better the surprise when the Overnmont banner comes up the road."

Rifkind wouldn't have thought of lying to the herald and wasn't confident that the men could keep their tenses straight, not if they were trading daily for food with the locals, but otherwise she approved of what Anderly had done.

"What can you tell us about that fog surrounding the castle?" she asked. "When did it appear?"

Anderly began, "Three days ago—" and was interrupted by Ivander saying, "We'd arrived the evening before—"

Anderly tried again, "I'd posted guards along the road—" and Ivander interrupted again, "My men, fresh after a night's sleep."

Rifkind sighed silently. If Ejord were with them, he'd have been able to keep the rivalries on a short leash, but with him recuperating at Raval, men like Anderly and Ivander would rub elbows at every opportunity. It didn't help that she was a woman. She resigned herself to hearing one story told twice and at the same time.

Fortunately, it was a simple story.

Ivander had led his men up to Gryphonage the morning after Anderly arrived, allowing the Glascards to double their siege patrols. At noon, and with no one reporting movement on the road, a cart carrying two men had suddenly appeared—by magic—at the Gryphonage gate. The Glascards could do nothing to stop it from entering the castle, having positioned themselves beyond the range of the castle's archers, and their own archers were equally disadvantaged.

The rest of the afternoon passed without further incident and sentries were posted for the evening watch. Again, all was quiet—until midnight when a cloudless night filled with fog.

"And not a misty fog," Anderly explained.

"No, not at all misty," Ivander agreed. "More like smoke, smoke from a rotted fire."

A reeking smoke, then, that cooled the air. Anderly and Ivander were both awakened. They agreed they'd heard sounds within the smoke.

"Men," Ivander insisted. "We heard men marching."

Anderly disagreed, "Not men. Men walk. Those were sliding, dragging sounds. I thought of a snake, a snake as large as a man."

"Aye, and kept your men close."

Ivander had sent his men into the smoke and lost two of them. Lost in the truest sense. They did not return to camp and come dawn, when other men went searching for them, not a trace of either could be found. The smoke had retreated to the castle where it hung in faint tatters from the towers and battlements.

"Not like what you see now," Anderly said. "It's come down each night and each morning there's more of it left to be seen. Now you can't see the castle at all."

Ivander got the last word: "It's no natural thing, that's for sure. Ballardskin couldn't stand on his own so he's propped himself up with a sorcerer."

"A sorcerer by the name of Illabin," Rifkind said. "One of the men in the cart, the one sitting beside the driver. Lord Overnmont's daughter Lysse was in the back."

With neither help nor competition from Jevan, Rifkind told Anderly and Ivander, too, what had happened since the Raval party had split on the far side of the Albinet. She almost lost them when she described the wraith they'd fought.

"That's no wraith," Ivander insisted. "Wraiths are the same as ghosts."

Anderly couldn't let that go unchallenged. "Wraiths are the ghosts of men who died violently."

"It doesn't matter what we call it!" Rifkind snapped. "Wraith or not a wraith. What matters is that it enthralled our men, killed one, and ravaged the Irdelmen. Either it was native to the Merrinen forest—which I doubt— or Illabin summoned it and can summon another. I'm going to set wards around the camp."

"What about sentries?" Anderly asked, his first sensible question. "Can you ward a man? We've been without sentries since Lord Ivander's men were lost."

"After what we saw in Merrinen, I wouldn't send a man into harm's way. The wraith wasn't man-clever. It would attack anything it encountered, man or beast, us or them, including anyone trying to resupply Gryphonage."

"And if it's men we're hearing, not some midnight monstrosity?" Ivander asked.

"How much could they bring in at night, through the fog?" Anderly replied.

The two men rattled at each other but, in the end, neither wanted to risk his men. Jevan didn't enter the discussion. The discussion went on a while longer, covering the mundane issues of food and shelter for the new arrivals and the digging of another set of privies, within Rifkind's warding but farther from the lean-tos than the current set.

The camp was already aromatic and buzzing with flies.

Rifkind did her part. It had been years since she'd laid down a warding line, but like healing and swordplay, the skill stuck with her. She spent the rest of the afternoon shuttling between the stream—where she filled her water skin with running water and a dash of salt—and a roughly circular perimeter that included a nice flat space for the privy diggers. By the time she closed the circle, she was sweat-soaked and quietly envious of the men who'd shed their tunics.

There were some traditions that were too ingrained for even Rifkind to break. Instead, she hiked upstream of the camp and, after shedding her boots, belt, and weapons, soaked herself in a thigh-high pool.

She was damp but not dripping when she returned to the camp. Supper was bubbling on the hearth, courtesy of the hunters and scroungers, and cooking by itself because no one wanted to brave the flames' heat to tend it. She spotted the boyos sitting a bit apart from the Glascards.

"Join you?" she asked from a polite distance.

Tyrokon nodded enthusiastically. Cho, who'd been stretched out and drowsing, muttered something unintelligible as he sat up. Both of them had hacked off their heavy braids during the brutal ride from Merrinen to Gryphonage. Men would never wind them around their heads as women did whenever there was heavy work to be done. With their sallow coloring, they'd never pass for Darians but, without the braids, they weren't Asheerans either.

"So, what rumors have you heard?" Rifkind asked as she sat.

"We're to lie to the locals and tell them that Lord Ejord's dead," Cho replied.

Tyrokon's Glascard wasn't nearly good enough for rumor gathering.

"The cloud around Gryphonage isn't natural," Cho added.

"Does it remind you of anything?" Rifkind was genuinely curious if the boyos saw a lightstorm resemblance, or if that was something only she had noticed.

Both boyos shook their heads. "They say a cart with two men on the bench appeared all of a sudden at the castle gate. Sounded a lot like the cart we didn't stop or see."

"Illabin," Rifkind agreed. "I wondered what had set him packing. I was afraid it was us vanquishing his wraith, but now I think that Ohlmer had some way of telling the sorcerer that the Bowsler men had come to reinforce the siege."

"That's a *good* thing?" Cho snapped.

"I'd just as soon our sorcerer wasn't thinking about what or who had done in his wraith. The longer he goes without suspecting we've got some defense against his magic, the better."

"You're better than him, right?" Cho asked with something akin to concern in his voice.

"I'd like to think so. I'd like to not find out for sure."

"Someone's got to get Reyna and the other girls out."

Rifkind met her son's eyes and nodded.

Tyrokon, as always, spoke into the silence. "One of Anderly's men said that he'd married her—"

"*Raped* her!" Cho snarled back.

Rifkind swallowed her own sentiments and said, calmly, "I don't doubt that Ballard's got her hand on the marriage lines."

"Threatened her! Forced her."

Rifkind cut her son short with a simple question: "Can a man rape his wife?"

She noted with some pride that the boyos both recoiled from the idea. Hamarach had raised them well and set an admirable example, but Hamarach's right to rule stopped at the threshold of another man's tent and the situation was worse in Daria. "Women have a saying here, 'The only way out of a bad marriage is death.'"

"Even if her family disapproves?" Tyrokon asked.

"That depends. At home, your father's word is all the law there is within the clan, but the Wet-lands are filled with law. There's the old imperial law that says marriage is a contract between the heads of two families. And Mohandru's law, that says any oath of marriage, even one given in secret, is binding; but not everyone follows Mohandru and not all the gods agree with Mohandru's revelations. Then there's the custom of a place and ancient rights. Every lord keeps a man who knows nothing but law who, no matter the situation, can find a law that's broken or upheld.

"The question is, do you *want* a daughter back after she's been abducted? She's neither a widow nor a virgin. What bargains do you have to strike with the next man who takes her? Or, do you keep her at home—?"

"Stop it!" Cho snarled.

"Stop the truth? Impossible. Be glad you weren't born female. Reyna's lived with the risks all her life."

"When do we attack?"

"We don't. This is a *siege*, Cho. It isn't about rescuing a woman, it's about cutting a lord off from his roots and bringing him to heel. With a castle like Gryphonage that could take years. Reyna can bear him a passel of children before he throws down his sword . . . and he might win his point before it's over. It could happen; it has happened. Glascardy needs a lord more than it needs a *good* lord."

Cho gave his mother a look with edges and poison.

"Ask Jevan, if you won't believe me. Ask Anderly. Ask Ivander. Reyna's hope right now isn't that someone breaks down the gate, it's that Ballard dies. Death is the only way out."

Cho spat an oath and stormed out of the camp.

"He's smitten," Tyrokon said softly when he and Rifkind were alone.

"That was foolishness from the start. He should know better. He'd never have thought to marry your sisters."

"None of them has hair the color of the sunset."

Rifkind nodded and changed the subject. They talked as they had talked many times when Tyrokon had lain in her cave, waiting for his bones to harden. They saw Cho returning to the camp. He wouldn't come near them—near her—joining the inevitable dice game instead.

She felt sorry for her son; not as sorry as she felt for Reyna. The girl would need a convenient murder if she was to get her life back, and even then, it would be tarnished.

Her conversation with Tyrokon faltered, drowned out by an uproar of cicadas.

Rifkind tried to remember when she'd decided she would never marry. It was an old idea, perhaps the oldest in her head. Certainly older than her resolve to be a healer or to master the sword.

A man called out that supper was ready. Rifkind shook free of idle thoughts. Food was always more welcome and far more useful than introspection.

At sunset, she and Jevan joined Anderly and Ivander on the forest verge where, even as the cicadas made their racket and the clouds turned shades of amber, the fog surrounding Gryphonage could be seen creeping down the hill.

Ivander said, "It'll reach us by full dark."

Jevan asked about the castle village where the common folk were caught.

"They lock their doors—" Anderly began.

Ivander interrupted. "Them as have doors."

"They gather in the houses that have them and hold tight to their children."

A salt-and-water warding couldn't stretch around a whole village, but

Rifkind could have added something to the locks and chided herself silently for sitting around talking to Tyrokon when she could have been spreading safety. Heft, the village priest, wasn't a half-bad sort, not like the Mohandrist who'd challenged her at Raval.

It wasn't the fog that disturbed her, but what the fog might hide. A sorcerer who could animate the wraith they'd met in the Merrinen forest—a goodly distance from the tower where he lived—could wreak considerable havoc across a short patchwork of meadows and fields.

In the interlude between when the Bright Moon rose and when the fog engulfed the camp, Rifkind saw her handiwork shimmering with its own light. The men, of course, saw nothing. She told them where she'd drawn her line, though she needn't have; the fog stopped as if it had encountered the clearest, strongest glass. It climbed upward, hiding the moon and stars, covering the camp like a dome.

The men grinned and clapped one another on the back: Their witch had thwarted Ballardskin's sorcerer. Rifkind didn't join them. It remained to be seen if Illabin's consciousness was *in* the fog—if he'd know there was a clearing where it didn't penetrate and what he'd do afterward.

Beneath the fog, time passed slowly. The men gambled and dared to complain about the smoke from their fire, which could not escape the dome of Rifkind's warding.

The healer got the answer to her questions about Illabin's awareness about around midnight when a good many of the men had gone to sleep and she was drowsing. Ivander had described the sound as men marching; Anderly had compared it to a serpent's glide; Rifkind, when she first heard the sounds, judged them somewhere in between. She tightened her scabbard behind her shoulders and prodded Jevan.

"We're going to have company. Wake the men and tell them not to panic."

She might as well have told them to fly.

Ivander's men in the northern quarter of their none-too-large camp raised the alarm: Embers in the fog, man-high, and paired.

By the time Rifkind got to the front of the crowd, a yard or so within her warding line, the pair had become three pairs, the glowing eyes of things that might once have been men. They were dressed as men, but their features were both sunken and swollen. Their mouths gaped, their lips hung loose revealing their square, human teeth.

They shambled into Rifkind's warding then wailed and retreated when it touched and blackened their flesh. From a safer distance they flapped their arms like flightless birds.

"What—?" Jevan began only to lose his question when one of Ivander's men shouted, "Great Mohandru weeps! That's Jordie, my brother—him that was taken th' other night."

The men around him gasped and agreed while others who had not known poor Jordie simply gasped.

"Illabin's raising the dead," Rifkind whispered, half in awe. Not even An-Soren—her measure for powerful sorcerers—had managed to raise the dead.

And she'd had Leskaya's Heart to augment her own power when she'd battled him.

27

The walking dead departed a few hours after they'd arrived; the fog, at dawn. Men who had stayed anxiously awake all night watching Rifkind's warding, hoping it wouldn't fail, but expecting it to at any moment, let their breath out in heavy sighs. Those who weren't assigned to morning chores looked around for places to sleep.

"We won," Anderly said when he, Ivander, Jevan, and Rifkind met outside his lean-to.

As might be expected, Ivander had a correction to make. "We didn't lose. It's not the same thing. Those *things* didn't take anyone, but we didn't take down any of them."

"He's right," Rifkind said with a nod to the bearded man.

Jevan looked for compromise. "At least there's a way to protect ourselves."

Rifkind grimaced. "For now. The sun will bake the power out of my wards. I'll have to lay them again before sunset . . . and we have to hope Illabin doesn't figure out what we're doing or how to counter it."

"Can he do that?"

"Anything can be countered," Rifkind said before she called over one of Jevan's men and told him to return to the village for more salt.

She passed the morning by herself, sitting on a black granite boulder overlooking the stream. Anything *could* be countered, including Illabin's walking dead, if she could just imagine a way to do it.

Rifkind had never been called squeamish. She faced the deprivations of injury and disease without flinching, but she came up short when she tried to imagine how she might animate a corpse. The mere thought of reaching through her *tal* into dead flesh revolted her and she'd made little progress. Her humor worsened when she returned to the camp and learned that she had less than half the salt than she'd had the previous day.

"They get it from the castle in exchange for their labor," Jevan explained, speaking for the men who'd gone to the village. "When our men asked if no one could go to the coast where the saltworks are, the villagers laughed and said Ballardskin claimed all the works for himself three years ago.

"We can't break that man quickly enough: Without salt, these people are either starving or slaves."

"So, we've gotten all we're going to get?" Rifkind asked absently, her mind already churning toward alternate wards.

Jevan nodded. "The men say we were lucky to get this much. The Mohandrist priest offered the stock he kept for cleaning his altar. It cost twice as much for half the grains. He said his god would understand."

"Blood," Rifkind said abruptly. Blood was salt and liquid together. Blood was also the essence of life. It could raise a powerful warding, powerful and unpredictable. She didn't like using it, but she liked leaving the villagers unprotected even less.

One less night of clean, pure sea salt around the camp wouldn't make much difference. She was going to have to switch to blood anyway.

"Have the hunters gone out?" she asked, hoping they hadn't and she could tell them not to bleed their kills.

They had gone, but there was Cho, squatted up with the gamblers. He seemed almost eager when Rifkind asked him to get his bow and hunt a rabbit or squirrel.

"Don't bleed it out," she told him. "It's the blood I need for the camp's wards. Not a lot. A single squirrel will suffice."

Tyrokon went with him and once they were gone, Rifkind hiked to the village and the little cottage beside the temple. Heft listened with attentive suspicion as she told him what she planned to do with the salt.

"Witchcraft," he carped.

"Then you do it and make it godly protection. There's a sorcerer in Gryphonage. He's making the fog and, unless I miss my guess, he's raising the dead. That's *real* witchcraft for you."

The Mohandrist's eyes narrowed. It didn't take talent to become a priest of Mohandru, only a bit of ambition and a gift for memorization, but Heft didn't have the look of a fool. It seemed, as he pondered Rifkind's challenge, that he took his responsibilities seriously.

"What would I do?"

"You can bless water, can't you? Bless the salt as well. Mix them on your altar then paint them around, like I'm doing. Pray. You've got prayers for protection?"

"Yes . . . but no more salt."

"Pray harder," she suggested. "You and I, we both use salt for cleansing. What else cleanses? What would lay down a line of life that death couldn't cross?"

The priest thought a moment. "Wheat . . . the first grain of the harvest. I have some still from last season's harvest. Eggs. Raw eggs—they're life incarnate."

Rifkind's eyebrows shot up in surprise. Eggs would work and she'd never have thought of grain; Asheerans weren't harvesters. It wasn't a bad idea.

The priest mistook her expression. "Milk," he countered quickly. "I could heat a gruel of eggs, milk, and grain upon my altar. Would that protect us?"

"As well as anything I can do. If not, you can bake bread," Rifkind replied. She might try gruel herself . . . if the blood didn't work. She squinted and caught sight of Heft's *tal*—a small brightness hovering at eye level. "Don't forget to pray."

"You tell *me* to pray?"

"Belief makes all the difference," she said, especially for an ordinary man with an ordinary *tal*.

The Mohandrist peppered Rifkind with questions as they went from window to door and back again. He was well on his way to witchcraft by

the time she finished and she walked back to the camp feeling well satisfied with her subversion.

Cho had returned with a scrawny groundhog that Rifkind bled into a
bowl and diluted with two parts of water. Inspired by the priest's inven-
tiveness, she added a mug of the local ale and a raw egg. When the sky had
begun to redden, she inscribed a circle around the camp.

The fog crept into the forest after sunset, as it had every evening since
Illabin's arrival, but the walking dead never made their appearance, which
was, in many ways, far more nerve-wracking. Ivander proposed sending
men out to hunt the corpses but backed down when Rifkind assured him
that sending men across her warding line would dissolve it.

Rifkind said nothing about the village, but if she had been Illabin, and
she'd found her magic thwarted at its main target, she'd have shifted her
attention somewhere else, somewhere less prepared and more innocent.
She had prayed little enough lately, in part because she'd begun to make
peace with the idea that, without a destiny, she was beyond a goddess's car-
ing, but she prayed as the Bright Moon set for the safety of Mohandrists
and their priest.

At dawn, Rifkind saddled Banin—who needed the exercise—and cantered him over to the village. Her suspicions proved accurate. Illabin had
sent his corpses in a new direction. The salt-and-water wards had held, but
neither Rifkind nor Heft had thought to ward the sheds where the villagers
sheltered their animals. In a way, the carnage there—half the cows, two
pigs, and all of the mules—was more devastating than a loss of human life.

People came and went on their own; animals had to be purchased.

Heft blamed himself. "A line of life to protect life," he said, not once but
several times. "All life. What will become of them without the animals?"

Rifkind made free with Glascard largesse. "When Glascardy reclaims
Irdel, you'll see the animals replaced, two for one."

Ejord would chide her for her generosity, but he'd honor the promise . . . if he could. If he still lived. She'd hoped for word from Raval.

The silence from that quarter weighed on her as heavily as a lack of
sleep. Still, she rose into her *tal* and applied her healer's craft to the animals that could be saved. Heft, she noted, breathed not a word about
witchcraft.

"Protection's not enough," she decreed to the council of Jevan, Anderly, and Ivander when she returned to the Glascard camp. "We've got to take away Illabin's weapons."

She'd expected an argument; she would have argued against abandoning the wards and risking men's lives. The Glascards felt differently. To a man, they wanted to fight their enemy. That afternoon, after eating a hearty lunch, Rifkind traced a much smaller circle that protected their animals, their food, and little else. She offered to anoint each man with her concoction. Even the boyos refused.

"Don't forget, they're already dead," Ivander told his men and all the others. "There's no stopping them with an arm wound. Brel's fist, there may be no stopping them short of chopping them into little pieces like meat for the pot."

Rifkind might have said it differently, but she couldn't have said it better.

Sundown brought the fog into the Glascard camp. It reeked of dust and decay and brought a sneezing frenzy to more than one man. Between the campfire and light from the Bright Moon overhead, it was just possible to see a man at arm's length and know that he was living, not dead.

The Glascards, with Rifkind and the boyos among them, arranged themselves in a loose, outward-facing circle and had been told to hold that formation, lest the walking dead find a way to flank the camp and attack them from behind.

Soon enough paired specks glowing red appeared in the fog. The three walking dead had become five, and one of them dressed in armor, but that was still well within the Glascard strength.

Anderly's men stood in the quarter where the walkers first attacked. As Ivander had predicted, a wounding slash to arm or leg did nothing to slow a man who was already dead and a thrust through the heart served only to immobilize a weapon at a critical moment. It would take three or four men working together to surround a walker and winnow him down.

Anderly shouted for assistance. The fighting circle collapsed as the other men came to his aid. Rifkind saw no need to elbow her way into the fight. She hung back and watched as the man who'd claimed one of the walkers as his brother demanded the right to behead him.

Beheading was not enough to stop a walker's attack. Both arms had to be lopped completely off and his torso toppled and trampled before he would lie still.

Four of the five walkers went down quickly as the Glascards hacked through their enemies who, when all was said and done, had little skill with the weapons they carried. The fifth walker, the one protected by chain from the neck down and a plumed helmet from the neck up, wielded his sword like a champion.

Someone shouted, "It's old Lord Ballard himself!" and the Glascard ring fell back a step.

That was all the opportunity the thing that had been Lord Ballard needed. He struck quickly, wounding one of the unarmored Glascards in the thigh and very likely killing another with a thrust through the throat.

Anderly and Jevan urged their men forward, but it was Ivander, who had taken the time to buckle on his armor, who got square in front of the dead lord and met him stroke for stroke.

"I called you friend," Ivander roared after muscling away a particularly powerful attack, "and wept at your dying. Now I'll make you twice dead!"

There was nothing fancy about Ivander's sword work. He beat Ballard back a step at a time until the dead man was trapped against a tree, then Ivander made an all-out thrust, piercing the chain mail and impaling him to the trunk. Ballard's corpse slashed at Ivander's empty hand as he retreated, but failed to free itself.

"Take him, men! Beat his sword away, then pierce him good and rend him down."

Rifkind couldn't see who disarmed the lord who, in life, had been both loved and respected, but the deed was done. She turned away as the carnage began. Ivander did the same. His face glistened in the firelight.

"You're wounded."

Ivander drew back as if she'd struck him. "A scratch."

"From a dead man's weapon. If Illabin's got the power to raise the dead, then I'll wager he's got the wit to poison their blades."

"Magic. Sorcery," Ivander snarled, turning each word into a curse. "It's all the same. All witchcraft. The plague takes good men and leaves witchcraft behind."

"I'd just as soon it didn't take you. Let me see your hand."

Ivander glowered and made one of Mohandru's ward signs with his good hand before he extended the other one. Rifkind rose into her *tal* and confirmed her suspicions. The malice eating into Ivander's bleeding palm was neither poison nor disease, but a sacrilege of the two. Fortunately, it was also newly introduced and easy to uproot. Rifkind descended and released the old fighter's hand.

"That's all?" he asked probing the dark line across his palm.

She nodded. "You might have a scar; you've got skin that scars easily. But all your fingers should work as they did before. Come and tell me if they don't."

Ivander flexed his fingers with a baby's intense curiosity. "I felt nothing."

"I'm good at what I do, same as you," Rifkind told him with a laugh. "Now, I've got to look at Anderly's men."

She left Ivander staring at his hand.

As expected, one of Anderly's men was beyond help and the other already complained of aching cold spreading from his wound. Rifkind ordered him lie down where he stood and rose swiftly into her *tal* to tend him. The wound held the same blend of poison and disease, but deeply entrenched for a wound that was less than an hour old. Teasing it out, tendril by tendril, she became aware of movement at her back and sides and wished she'd thought to find Tyrokon before ascending. Asheerans knew to keep their distance from a working healer; Tyrokon would have kept the Glascards at arm's length.

But it was Tyrokon himself who hovered at Rifkind's elbow when she returned to ordinary perception.

"You better come see what's happening," he concluded, offering her a heel of bread and a hand up.

The men were gathered in a tight knot that split apart when Jevan spotted Rifkind and called her name. He looked healthy enough, as did the others. She needed another moment to realize that the problem was on the ground.

"Bloody Bright—"

An arm—a left forearm with hand attached but neither sleeve nor jewelry nor elbow—lay palm-up, twitching like a landed fish as the thumb beat against the ground. While Rifkind watched in disbelief, it flipped itself over and, using its fingers as legs, began dragging itself across the dirt . . . across the dirt in the direction of Gryphonage.

A few feet away, a man shouted, "It's opened its *eyes*!"

Piece by piece, Illabin's creations were trying to return home.

"What do we do?" Ivander asked. She'd risen considerably in the man's esteem.

"Sweet Mother, I don't know. Don't let them go wherever they're trying to go. Burn them, I guess—but handle them carefully . . . and stay out of the smoke."

The men liked the suggestion. They threw every stick of wood onto the campfire and when it blazed shoulder-high, they began tossing Illabin's handiwork into the flames. The ensorcelled flesh resisted the fire and where shape permitted, it writhed like a stuck snake. More than one piece had to be thrown in a second time.

When the flames did catch, the flesh burnt with a midden's stench.

The fog had retreated and the sun arisen before Ballard's last sinew had been reduced to char.

"Drench it with clear water," Rifkind suggested. "Drench, then smash the lumps and bury them deep."

The men liked that idea, too.

CHO HADN'T BEEN AFRAID OF the walking dead—they were nothing compared to the wraith they'd faced in the Merrinen forest—but the sight of animated body parts had come damnably close to unnerving him. So, naturally, when the sun finally rose, he volunteered to search nearby for whatever straggling flesh they might have missed.

In the shade of some briars several hundred yards from the Glascard camp, he found a foot making slow progress toward Gryphonage and stabbed it with his sword. A liquid too dark to be called blood seeped from the fresh wound, but the steel held and he lifted the appendage carefully.

The Glascards had built a second bonfire for the stragglers. Cho was halfway back when Tryokon let out a yelp. They'd started the hunt together then split up because there was a lot of ground to cover and because, once your gut had turned itself inside-out a few times, there really wasn't any need for two men stay close together as they chased body parts.

Tryokon's yelp hadn't been fear or pain, but it demanded investigation so, with his trophy balanced on his sword tip, Cho backtracked.

"Look!" Tryokon said, pointing at the grass. Just one word, repeated several times.

Cho parted the grass with his foot and it was a good thing his soul knew his stomach was empty as a widow's bowl, else he'd have lost it again.

It wasn't big and it probably wasn't dangerous—just a scrap of flesh that might have come from a man's arm or leg—a thick finger, and the whorl of an ear, stuck together and *working* together.

While Cho watched, the flesh contracted, bending just enough to brace the ear-whorl against dirt. Then the flesh flexed, projecting the finger forward. The finger found purchase, braced, the flesh released, and the whole gruesome chimera was the finger's length closer to Gryphonage.

"Like it has eyes," Cho murmured.

"How'er we going to kill something that doesn't know it's *dead*?"

Cho didn't have an answer, but he did have the curiosity he'd inherited from both his parents. He held his sword above the chimera. A slight shake and the foot was atop the flesh, the ear, and the finger. They shuddered—he almost thought he'd heard a thin wail—then tussled a bit. The ear came loose, then reattached itself to the wound Cho had made in the arch of the dismembered foot. The ragged edge where the foot had joined an ankle tightened around the scrap of flesh.

The new chimera—more than twice the size of what it had been, with a finger at one end and five toes at the other—stretched toward Gryphonage.

"Bloody Bright!" Tyrokon swore, a measure of his distress; Tyrokon almost never cursed. "Stop it! How? How could you?"

"I had to see if it would. I thought it would, but I had to see."

Cho poked his sword at the chimera, neither piercing it nor breaking it apart.

"Don't," Tyrokon warned. "Or you'll wind up no better than the sorcerer."

"I'm not—" Cho protested, then caught himself. What was Rifkind, if not a sorcerer? Or his father?

Now that he'd fallen in love with Reyna, Cho found it easier to accept that Ejord Overnmont was not his father, which left him on the verge of accepting his mother's tale of the Well of the Black Flame as truth. For a heartbeat, Cho could see himself making chimeras and worse, then he brought his sword down.

"That's yours," he said, flicking the overlong finger toward his friend before stabbing the foot through its ear.

Back in the camp, Cho pressed the chimera against a length of red-hot wood until it began to shrivel and char and the heat traveled up the sword to his palm.

"Enough!"

Cho leapt away from Rifkind's voice, nearly losing his sword and definitely losing the chimera, which crumbled into unrecognizable black bits. He hadn't heard her ease up against his right side.

"Let it go."

Rifkind had her wise face on and Cho could imagine that his mother was leaning against him with all the weight of her healer's magic, though he couldn't feel anything that would prove her interference.

"Why didn't you kill him when you had the chance?" he demanded, in hopes of saying something that would wipe the wisdom off her face.

It didn't work; she barely blinked before saying, "I didn't have the chance."

"He's got to be stopped."

"We have stopped him. We've seen his weapons. They're ugly and they're unnatural, but we've stopped them. Illabin's bottled up in Gryphonage. He's not getting out."

"What about everyone who's bottled up in there with him?" Cho meant not everyone, but Reyna. "What are we going to do to set them free?"

Something akin to worry flashed across Rifkind's face, but it was gone in a heartbeat. "We don't have the men. Maybe after Ejord gets here . . ." She shook her head. "Castles like Chatelgard or Gryphonage, they can't be taken by force; there just aren't enough men. You've got to circle them tight and wait them out."

"If this"—Cho jerked his sword tip toward the fire—"is what he's sending out, imagine what he's got inside!"

"Don't think about that," Rifkind suggested, but Cho couldn't do that. He couldn't get the image of Reyna surrounded by groping hands out of his mind.

28

After the Glascards finished scavenging for chimeras they settled in for what they hoped would be a quiet day. Rifkind was sound asleep when a shadow fell across her face. Her hand was on a knife hilt before her eyes were open.

Jevan took a backward step. "Company's coming," he said. "We thought you should know."

"And you drew the short straw for waking me?"

Jevan grinned and looked younger than usual. "Your son suggested tossing pebbles."

"Then I'm grateful for small blessings. Who's coming?"

Jevan couldn't answer that question. "The lookouts spotted a dust cloud. It could be anyone, including a peddler with his wagon, but after Raval, we're not taking chances. So far as we know, no messages have gotten out of Gryphonage, but—Brel's fist—they can raise the dead. Who knows whether they can get a message out? The village has no love for the castle. I don't think they'd have gone looking for anyone to break our siege, but all it takes is one."

Rifkind shrugged into her sword rig before following Jevan to the edge of the woods overlooking the road where half the Glascard strength had formed a cordon out of sight of the castle. By then the dust had become a trio of riders traveling at a hard pace. By any normal measure, the Glascards had nothing to worry about, but Ivander, standing a few feet from Rifkind, ordered his archers to nock their arrows.

The riders reined up. Words that didn't carry to the woods were exchanged and before the dust had settled, the men who'd formed the cordon were waving enthusiastically to their comrades in the woods.

"They're ours!" a man shouted. "Messengers from Lord Ejord!"

The archers stood down. Rifkind followed them and the others out of the woods. They met the riders halfway up the hill and surrounded them.

Rifkind listened while Anderly, Ivander, Jevan, and every other man peppered the newcomers with questions. In short order she learned their names: Balthus, the black-bearded spokesman of the three, Randel, who echoed everything Balthus said, and Galdric, a powerfully built warrior who said nothing at all.

She learned as well that her healing had held and Ejord had recovered without relapse. He was still weak—which was to be expected—and smart enough to know that he couldn't race cross-country into Irdel. Ejord was making a virtue out of necessity. He'd left Raval with the two hundred men who'd answered his call to arms and was traveling slowly, not straight for Gryphonage, but roundabout, visiting the towns and lesser lords of Irdel, offering them amnesty if they'd bend a knee and add their men to his.

"Should be four hundred or more," Balthus said confidently.

Rifkind glanced at the three commanders and saw the same expression of concern on all their faces. The little village of Gryphonage, with which they'd maintained friendly relations, couldn't withstand the needs of a four-hundred-man army.

Ivander echoed her thoughts when he asked, "Where's his baggage train?"

"Right beside him," Balthus replied. "All goes well, they'll be here in two days, three at the outside. We were sent to give you cheer . . . and warn Ballardskin. Lord Ejord said to tell Ballardskin that he can avoid a siege by letting the girls go and surrendering the castle."

"Will you go with us to the gate?" Galdric added, speaking for the first time.

The cloud around Gryphonage was visible from the hillside where the Glascards conversed, but a newcomer wouldn't realize what it meant. After a silent exchange with his fellow commanders, Anderly explained the situation.

"Ballardskin's sealed himself in with a sorcerer—a sorcerer who commands the dead. I'd think twice, were I you, before I rode into that cloud."

The messengers had their orders from Ejord Overnmont who outranked Anderly, Ivander, and Jevan combined. If Galdric had hesitated, Rifkind thought the other two might have been willing to reconsider, but Galdric was too much the warrior to be daunted by any sorcerer's cloud. He unfurled the red-and-gold Overnmont banner and declared his intention to ride alone, if necessary, though he was willing to wait until horses were brought up for the siege commanders.

They invited Rifkind to join them; she declined.

"Ballard's gone too far to surrender to the likes of any of us," she said and stayed on the hillside, watching as the horsemen cantered up the road, into the cloud, and out again.

"At least they all came safely out," she said to Cho and Tyrokon who'd been close but silent since she and Jevan had left the woods.

Along with the other Glascards who'd stayed on the hillside, she headed for the camp.

Cho stuck close. "When Lord Ejord gets here, then we'll attack. Four hundred men . . . that's got to be enough."

"It's too many—too many to feed, too many to keep clean. Think about it: When the clans gather, every clan brings its own food . . . and leaves its herds behind—"

"But this land's richer than the Asheera," Cho protested.

"Not that much richer and a siege takes months."

"Not a siege, an attack! I've heard the Glascards talk about them: battering rams, scaling ladders, *tunnels* to bring the walls down."

Cho never mentioned Reyna's name, but she was the fire in his eyes when he talked of attacking the castle.

"Look, Ejord's hoping that if he shows up with the lords and burgers of Irdel beside him, Ballard's going to realize that he can't succeed. First, because he didn't kill Glascardy's lord; second, because Irdel's abandoned him; and finally, with Ejord alive and Irdel supporting Ejord, Reyna's value—and the value of any child he can get on her—drops.

"And there's where it gets tricky; in the end, the girls are all Ballard has to bargain with. He could send one of them out in pieces, in hope of cracking Ejord's resolve . . . and, knowing Ejord, it might work."

"If Ballardskin *didn't* have Ejord's daughters . . . then what?"

"Then he has nothing to win or lose, and nothing to bargain with. He might surrender, but he might just stay behind his walls. They tell tales of a siege in the reign of Darius the Third that lasted five years and only ended because the castled lord had died . . . of natural causes. They were eating rats by then . . . and each other, if you believe the tales."

"Can't *you* do something?"

"Let's see what the sorcerer does without his corpses. It's not just a castle we're up against. It's a castle and a sorcerer."

The Asheerans entered the camp. The riders were already there and dismounted. Ivander boasted that he'd ridden right up to Gryphonage's iron-strapped door and demanded an audience with "the man calling himself Duke of Irdel."

"He's lucky he didn't get a bucket of boiling oil dumped on his head," Rifkind muttered.

"Who would have dumped it?" Cho asked.

Rifkind acknowledged a good question. The men she'd known for a short time would follow orders, just as the Glascards would, but they weren't inherently evil and they couldn't be happy about having a sorcerer hovering around their lord, especially one who relied on the risen dead.

Ivander had moved on to a litany of Ballardskin's faults, none of which was news to any of the Glascards, and many of which were physically impossible.

Rifkind had heard enough. She headed for the field where the three war-horses were pastured apart from their hornless cousins. When she touched Banin's mind, the gray war-horse looked up from his grazing and came at a trot. He wanted *apples* and *scratches* and his rider's presence. Rifkind couldn't provide the apples.

Cho and Tyrokon joined her for similar purposes. Cho had his bow and arrows. He headed to hunt and—according to Tyrokon—to be alone.

Rifkind asked if anything specific was bothering her son; Tyrokon professed not to know, which she suspected was less than the truth, but didn't challenge the boyo's stiff-lipped assertion.

The sun was noon-high and the day had once again heated up to summer's fullest intensity. Even the perpetual dice game had fallen into a lull as men who'd lived through a harrowing night caught up on their sleep. Cho wasn't the only hunter out looking for supper and he wasn't the first to return, though like the others, he was empty-handed. They'd wrung the easy prey out of the woods around Gryphonage. The canny animals had made themselves scarce. Dinner consisted of a grainy soup streaked with eggs and spotted with a few vegetables.

The men complained that the villagers had food and livestock that, since they wouldn't sell, should be taken by force. For a few moments, the Glascards teetered on the verge of pillage. Jevan and Anderly threw their weight against the idea but it took Ivander grabbing two of the would-be raiders by the collar and knocking them together to reconcile the men with the food in front of them.

Rifkind stayed out of the dispute. She didn't need to rise into her *tal* to sense that the men weren't really interested in food or villages; it was nightfall that had them spooked and fear of what might walk out of the fog. Once again they faced the dark without a ring of protection. With their swords drawn and their backs to an unlit bonfire, they waited as fog seeped through the trees.

One man heard something and attacked a sapling. Another man saw something and did the same.

"It would almost be easier if we *were* attacked," Jevan whispered to Rifkind after the second tree had been vanquished.

Rifkind grunted and regripped her sword. She was half into her *tal* and her wariness was wound as tight as it could go. She sensed nothing alive and moving that was larger than a swarm of mosquitoes and nothing at all that was dead and moving. Yet when leaves rustled, she was one of a half-dozen who leapt forward, steel at the ready.

Her nerves steadied when the Bright Moon rose, not because of any protection her goddess might have provided, but because she knew the night was half over. The second half of the night was as interminable as it was uneventful. A few of the men keeled over from the sheer strain of exhaustion atop anticipation.

Tyrokon was one of those who fell. His weak legs buckled beneath him. Rifkind told him to sit by the unlit bonfire. He wouldn't go, not until dawn signaled the fog's retreat and everyone stood down.

Anderly dropped an arm around Rifkind's shoulder. "So much for the sorcerer!" he said, echoing a sentiment the other men were expressing with back-slapping laughter.

Rifkind grinned. She was less confident that they'd run through Illabin's bag of tricks, but she'd learned a few things campaigning with the Overnmonts, including when to keep her doubts to herself.

Breakfast was the same as dinner, only cold and crusty. Rifkind dumped her bowl behind a bush. There were limits, even to a healer's prodigious appetite.

She returned to the camp in time to see Heft striding into the camp ahead of the village elders. The elders were in their everyday clothes: tattered at the hems, patched at the joints, and stained from hard use. The priest, though, was in his finest robes with a broad-brimmed hat that had to be treacherous on a breezy day and a blue velvet stole. For a moment Rifkind thought the god's tears had been stitched into the stole with dark silk, then she realized that the curving ovals were all that remained of giltwork that had been removed before the stole fell into the possession of a poor village priest.

But Heft wore it and the absurd hat proudly. He faced Rifkind as an equal.

"The sanctity of the village cemetery has been violated," he said as if reciting a seldom-used ritual. "We warded the village, as you suggested. We heard strange noises during the night, but we weren't invaded. Then, this morning, when the women went to the graves, as is their custom, they found the desecration. Dirt had been thrown up from the most recent graves, and"—Heft made teardrop-shaped ward signs with the fingers of both hands—"the *bodies* are gone."

Rifkind's heart sank. She berated herself for not anticipating Illabin's response and needed a moment to muster her thoughts. "How many graves?"

"Three. Three torn open and empty, but others are disturbed."

"Disturbed? How?"

They'd had an audience from the beginning: the village elders and a few of the Glascards. Now they had all the Glascards with Anderly, Ivander, and Jevan shouldering their way to the front. Heft waited for complete quiet before saying:

"The ground above the graves has risen. The turf has split apart and the ground is warm to the touch."

Rifkind pushed stray hairs off her forehead. She should have eaten breakfast, miserable as it was. "Show me."

The priest couldn't have looked happier if all his superiors had granted him their blessing. "At once. Follow me."

She did, and the elders, the lords, and half the camp, including both Cho and Tyrokon, followed her. They trooped down the hill, across the road, up another hill to an open clearing in the woods above the village.

The desecrated graves, with their rudely scattered clods of rich, brown dirt, were obvious from a distance. The disturbed graves were harder to spot amid the gently undulating ground, but Rifkind needed only to rise slightly into her *tal* to sense the wrongness.

She would have inspected them immediately, but there were customs to be observed: Thigh-high markers of dark granite, rough-shaped into cylinders and speckled with layers of lichen, defined the sacred ground. Heft led Rifkind around the perimeter to a pair that were a few handspans taller than the rest. He kissed his fingertips and transferred the kiss to the stones.

Out of respect for people, not gods, Rifkind did the same.

Her path took her past one of the empty graves. A shroud and other grave goods lay in disarray at the bottom of the shaft. There was a single dirt-caked boot standing amid the ground-level clods, which was reassuring in a macabre way: No *conscious* corpse would walk away from its grave with one shoe on, one shoe off.

And it had walked away. A broken-grass trail ran in a nearly straight line from the grave toward Gryphonage.

"We'll be fighting a half-shod ghoul tonight," Rifkind said to the lords who followed her.

Ivander replied, "We'll give him an extra whack for carelessness."

Jevan, Anderly, and even Rifkind chuckled, then remembered the location and sobered instantly.

Rifkind stepped around an undisturbed grave and knelt beside one that had heaved up. Rifkind felt a repulsion that ran deeper than fear emanating from the grave. *Warding,* she thought, and laid to deflect a strong *tal.*

"Stand back," she advised her audience. "All the way back: beyond the markers."

Closing her eyes, Rifkind placed her hands palms-down on the turf.

Icy cold wound up her arms, followed by fire, and a sense that she was being dragged by the elbows deep into the earth. Drawing on the same reserves she'd used to push back the patrons of Engelit's tavern in Epigos, she hurled her will against Illabin's warding. It held a moment, then shattered like green wood in a hot fire.

Bystanders yelped and Rifkind leaned heavily on the grave, catching her breath before probing the secrets the sorcerer had tried to conceal.

"What has the sorcerer done?" Heft asked from the entrance as soon as Rifkind sat back on her heels.

Rifkind shook her head. "I don't know. I can't describe it—it's like nothing I've felt before. There's something down there—"

"A corpse—"

She shook her head again. "Not a corpse. Not *just* a corpse. Not dead, not alive, not finished."

Ivander had an idea for that: "We'll dig it up and finish it ourselves."

"Maybe."

"What *maybe?*"

"Let me think," Rifkind demanded.

She was still partially in her *tal* and none of the men was tempted to disobey. For all the good that quiet did. Rifkind couldn't get her imagination completely around Illabin's sorcery, except to know that whatever he'd done in the village cemetery was incubating like a disease.

Rifkind walked the cemetery without disturbing Illabin's wards, counting four more upthrust graves. She turned to the priest. "Say your prayers. I'm going to burst Illabin's wards and then we're going to dig. We're going to burn what we find, no matter what it looks like or who it was."

Heft blanched but nodded. "All of them?"

"All but one." She strode to one of the warded graves. "We'll leave this one alone and see what hatches."

"Is that wise?" Anderly asked. "If we can destroy what he's made, shouldn't we go ahead and destroy it?"

"There are other cemeteries—"

"Brel's balls," Ivander swore, "there's a whole crypt at the castle. Five generations of Irdel lords, or more. That's where he got old Lord Ballard we fought the other night."

Rifkind's heart skipped a beat; she'd forgotten the crypt. "No," she said, to herself as much as Ivander. "Let him think we missed one. Let's see what he's conjured up. We'll learn more about the man we're fighting."

"He raises the dead," Ivander grumbled. "What more do we need to know?"

But he got out of the way as Heft came past muttering his prayers and flinging flecks of colored powder onto the graves. Rifkind never ceased to be amazed by what a priest carried within his loose-fitting robes.

The elders sent a runner back to the village for every shovel from every household. Anderly, Jevan, and Ivander debated whose men would do the digging and whose men would spend the night in the cemetery. Anderly and Jevan sent across the road for their men while Ivander went to tell his men to prepare for a harrowing night.

The old graves were the easy ones, filled with bones that no one remembered. The newer graves were a different matter. Heft's rituals couldn't cushion the shock of seeing what was never meant to be seen.

The elders, who had made themselves silent witnesses to extreme measures, quailed when the sagging shrouds were hauled out of the ground. Each of them broke ranks at least once, but returned, paler than before to stand behind the priest.

No one disputed the need for burning the village's dead; scarcely anyone said anything at all. The profanity and crude humor that was a soldier's stock in trade went unheard. Throughout the afternoon the loudest sounds came from Heft chanting the Mohandrist funeral rites again and again.

The sun had set and fog was creeping down from Gryphonage when the men put up their borrowed shovels. They still faced a long night of waiting in the camp for who knew what to emerge from that fog. Rifkind called the boyos aside before they left the cemetery. They were filthy with dirt and sweat and numb around the eyes.

"Make sure Ivander brings me some food," she said. "Meat, if the hunters had any luck."

Cho rolled his eyes, but Tyrokon nodded and promised.

29

The fog had begun to make its nightly seep away from Gryphonage when Ivander led his seven men to the cemetery. They all wore chain and carried newly made clubs in addition to their swords.

"Been thinking about the other night," Invader explained. "Swords are good for killing a living man but a hefty stick with a stone lashed to one end is just about right for knocking apart a bag of bones. If that's what we're up against—" His eyebrows rose, inviting Rifkind to offer her opinion of the night's likely enemy.

She declined.

Ivander's men hadn't brought food, but Tyrokon had: village bread and a beaker of soup that was still warm and mostly unspilt. It was the same soup they'd had the night before and for breakfast, too, freshened with wedges of some pale vegetable Rifkind had never tasted before. It was hard as wood and breathtakingly bitter. Her eyes watered as she chewed, but she got it down. She offered the empty beaker to Tyrokon who'd sat on the ground kneading his right leg like a baker.

"Everything all right?"

Tyrokon's hands jumped away from his leg. "Fine. I strained some muscles, that's all. Tripped going uphill. My own fault."

"I can take the pain—"

The boyo shook his head.

"Where's Cho, anyway? I asked him to bring my supper across."

"Guard duty with Jevan's men. After last night, they didn't ask me to draw straws. I guess that's what comes of falling down at your post."

"You weren't the only one."

"I'm not much for Darian fighting. I'm better off doing chores."

He was right, of course, but it grieved Rifkind to see her chief's son reduced to serving others. "You've got your sword. Stay here. Ivander'll be glad of another blade."

Tyrokon looked over his shoulder, toward the Glascard camp. Rifkind didn't have to rise into her *tal* to catch the unease that surrounded him or put a name to it: Cho. The lifelong friends were pulling apart, not consciously, but inevitably as Cho remade himself as a Darian warrior.

It was always harder on the one left behind.

"There's no telling what we're going to face tonight. I wouldn't say no to having you guard my back."

Tyrokon turned away.

"There's time enough for listening, if you need to talk."

The boyo shrugged. "No. No need. I'll stay if you want. One place or the other, it's all about the same."

Rifkind sensed a lie, but left it unchallenged.

Ivander's men had already gotten out their dice. They'd won and lost the same coins ten times, but that didn't dim their enthusiasm for the game that was any soldier's chief weapon against both boredom and fear.

"I see you've laid two fires," Ivander observed when Rifkind joined him.

"The smaller one's for us, while we wait. The other we kindle when we've got something to burn."

"You're thinking it will be more of the same?"

"I'd like to think we've seen all of Illabin's tricks, but he's clever, he's strong, and he's not going to give up. I can't guess why he started raising corpses—they weren't what attacked us in the Merrinen forest. We called that a wraith and it didn't have a body you could beat apart with swords or clubs. Maybe corpses are easier here where there are so many of them.

Take the corpses away and maybe he'll make a new wraith, or maybe something altogether different. I would."

"Never had much liking for the Ballardskin. Always thought there was something wrong about the way he showed up out of nowhere to marry the last Ballard daughter, but I never figured him for a sorcerer's cat's-paw."

"I healed his son. He seemed like a good father, for what that's worth. The boy said Illabin had tried to heal him. Things must have started there. Probably Ballard thought he was the one using the sorcerer. You never know. It usually starts out that way."

Ivander cocked his head slightly. Priest, magician, sorcerer, witch, and healer—they were words everyone used and none of them, none at all, had a precise meaning that excluded the others.

As if to emphasize that ambiguity, Heft came puffing up to the cemetery, still in his hand-me-down splendor, but without the ludicrous hat.

"I'm here to help."

"The villagers need your help," Rifkind suggested.

"I've warded all the crossings and told them to stay safe in their homes no matter what. They're good people; Mohandru will watch out for them. I've come to help you."

Ivander bristled. The warrior was no Mohandrist. Tonight, when he'd be facing the gods-knew-what, he'd added a large bronze fist of Brel to his armor. "We've got no need for weeping. If you can't wield a sword, go home."

He crowded the priest.

Heft tugged on his stole. Standing arrow-straight, his eyes were level with the bronze fist resting on Ivander's chest. He had to tilt his head back to meet the warrior's eyes. "I looked into the bowl of tears," he said with a remarkably steady voice, referring to the oracular device Mohandru was said to favor. "I saw myself here. It is my god's will; you won't chase me away."

"Let him stay." Rifkind laid a hand on Ivander's forearm. "He can tend the fire. It's time the smaller one was lit."

The first tendrils of fog had reached the marking stones surrounding the cemetery.

"I will do that," Heft agreed. "But, first, I must purify the grave."

Rifkind shook her head. "We do nothing that Illabin might sense from his lair."

"His name was Bernel. He died before I came to the village. His wife wrapped him in a shroud she wove herself. Their children and grandchildren still live above the mill. They are good people; he was a good man. I *will* purify his grave. Whatever unholiness rises from it tonight, it will not be Bernel."

Rifkind imagined herself in the little priest's position and stood aside. Heft entered the cemetery. He scattered his powders on the earth and within heartbeats Rifkind sensed a change in the air around them. She rose slightly into her *tal* and found a throbbing, like the slow beat of a giant heart.

Maybe Heft's purification had started it; maybe the priest had nothing to do with it. Either way, it had begun.

Descending, she said, "Light the fire," in a tone that allowed no disobedience.

The fire was lit, but Heft took no part in tending it. He stood outside the gate stones, his hands hidden in the folds of his robe, while Tyrokon fed sticks as needed into a fire that cast more shadow than light among the graves. An hour, at least, passed before the most subtle among Ivander's men picked up the throbbing.

"It's waking up," the man said and pocketed his winnings from the dice game.

By the time Heft started chanting, the dice game was history and only Ivander remained unaware of the drumbeat pulse. The man was probably as headblind as any Overnmont. Rifkind undid the thong that held her sword in the scabbard against her spine. It was a little move that would not have cost an eyeblink in battle, but with her heart beating in rhythm with Illabin's sorcery, an eyeblink was nothing to waste.

"Getting close, is it?" Ivander asked.

Rifkind nodded and used the question as her excuse to approach the grave. Inside the marker stones, the ground throbbed beneath her feet. She was crouching down for a closer inspection when the turf tore open and a hand thrust upward. It was lumpy, misshapen, and easily twice the size of her own hand, but with four fingers and an angled thumb, there was no denying that it was a hand.

Illabin's wraith in the Merrinen forest had been an insubstantial thing. The walking dead he'd sent against the Glascards and the villagers were fundamentally flesh and blood. But the hand rising out of Bernel's grave seemed to be made of earth itself, as the Landmother had been all those years ago. The size was wrong; the Landmother could have held the entire cemetery in Her palm, but the similarity left Rifkind gaping.

The hand thumped down, narrowly missing Rifkind's feet. She staggered backward and regained enough of her composure to bare her sword as Illabin's latest monster used its freed hand to lever itself out of the ground.

Rifkind took a swing at the monster's upper arm as it emerged. Her steel struck deep and stuck fast, like a boot in bottomless mud. She wrapped both hands around the hilt and barely wrenched it free.

The monster's shoulders were up by then and its head, which bore glowing yellow-green eyes but nothing that resembled a mouth or nose.

Ivander let loose with his war cry and charged into the cemetery with his great sword held high. He delivered a blow that went clean through the monster's neck. He retreated, clearly believing that he'd struck a fatal blow, but the monster's head remain firmly on its shoulders. The damp earth of the grave had yielded before Ivander's sword and reformed behind it.

Ivander swung again, an upward cut that would have sliced into the monster's vital organs—if the monster had been made of differentiated tissues. The great sword stuck in the monster's wound. Ivander tried to free it, but the blade was in too deep and the monster had risen far enough to free its other arm.

It backhanded Ivander across the midsection, lifting the burly man off his feet and hurling him across the cemetery. He landed hard with his arms and legs askew. For a heartbeat, Rifkind thought him dead. The Bowslermen had the same thought. Not one of them took a forward step.

The monster pulled the great sword from its torso and flung it aside, then it planted both hands on solid ground and clambered out of the grave. Standing straight it was half again as tall as Ivander, which left Rifkind swinging at its hips and abdomen.

Rifkind delivered a stroke that would have disemboweled an ox but had no noticeable effect on the monster. It swung its hand into the broken ground and came up with a fist the size of Rifkind's head. She dodged the blow by ducking low. Before the monster could check the momentum of its swing, Rifkind sliced through the narrows behind the oversized fist. Weight, more than steel, separated one from the other, but before she could congratulate herself, the monster dragged its stump arm through dirt and came up with another bulging fist.

She dodged another mighty swing. The monster wasn't slow, but it wasn't subtle, either. She could anticipate its moves even though she couldn't counter them . . . yet. From relative safety, she surveyed the cemetery.

Ivander had pulled in his splayed limbs. "After it!" he growled, raspy but still very much alive. "It's nothing but *clay!*"

Clay, Rifkind thought as Ivander's men weighed their options and decided it was wiser to attack a monster than disobey their lord.

The monster seized one of the attackers, shook him hard, and tossed him aside. If the shaking hadn't broken the man's neck, the headfirst landing did. The monster swung its fist and knocked down another Bowslerman. He lay moaning, half-in, half-out of one of the graves they'd dug up earlier. Two out of seven, not counting Ivander himself who continued to chivvy his men but hadn't risen from the ground.

They weren't winning this fight.

Clay, clay, clay. Rifkind tried it in all the languages of her mind.

Clay was mud; mud was dirt and water. Add more water and mud washed away.

Water. A stream wound between the castle and the village; it flowed past the bottom of the cemetery hill. A short walk away, if she could get the monster to follow her. If she could keep it in the water long enough—

Ivander's men had fallen back. The monster lurched to one side, tearing a huge foot that trailed roots and shredded cloth out of the dirt and planting it again.

Rifkind charged the monster, delivering a cut meant only to get its attention, and darted out of reach again. The thing proved it had a mouth somewhere when it roared loud enough to drive everyone back another step. But it lifted its other foot and took a step toward Rifkind.

One step and nowhere near as lengthy as it could have been. How many steps to the stream? A hundred? More? Certainly not less.

She charged again. The monster met her halfway with a sweeping fist.

Rifkind scooted under it and barely avoided an open grave. She strained a muscle keeping her balance; that would have been worthwhile if it had gotten the monster to take another step toward the stream, but the monster stayed where it was.

A Bowslerman imitated her attack, making a quick slash at the monster's flank before retreating. He got the monster moving again, albeit in the wrong direction.

Did she dare shout out a command: *Drive it to the stream?* Was Illabin's monster deaf and dumb as dirt? Or could it hear and understand? Could Illabin hear?

Rifkind was on the verge of deciding to take the risk when a new notion struck her: *Clay. Mud and water. Take away the water . . .* Bake *away the water and the clay became bricks as hard as stone.*

"Fire!" she shouted. "Take wood from the bonfire, kindle it, and bring it here. We're going to *bake* this abomination!"

Ivander's men hung back, seeming not to understand Rifkind's command, or simply refusing to obey, but Heft and Tyrokon got their feet under them.

While Rifkind kept up a steady flow of attacks and dodges, the pair followed her instructions. They swiped the monster with burning brands, igniting the bits of root and wood protruding from its unnatural hide.

The little flames weren't enough to do serious damage, but some part of the monster had been human once and retained enough humanity to dread fire. It flailed at itself and at the brands.

Tyrokon dodged, slipped, and fell. Rifkind called him out of the skirmish. He swore he was unharmed and reclaimed his brand, which had ignited the grass where it had lain.

Something about the burning grass evoked a panicked cry from Illabin's monster and before Rifkind could think to take advantage of it, Heft was drawing a pattern of fire around the monster. He left a gap that began on one side of the unlit bonfire and ended on the other.

The Bowslermen, at last, understood what Rifkind and the priest had in mind, or perhaps it was the laughter of their commander as he chortled, "A deer run. A ruddy damned deer run!"

Either way, they got their own brands and waved them from outside the priest's circle, driving the monster toward the gap. When the monster hesitated a few feet short of the gap, Rifkind threw aside her sword, grabbed a brand from the nearest Bowslerman and leapt over the burning grass. Recklessly within its reach, she battered the monster with flame and it, not grasping that Rifkind and her swirling fire was nothing it needed to fear, retreated into the gap, into the bonfire, which Heft quickly touched with his brand.

The monster lurched forward. Rifkind brandished fire to drive it back. In confusion and doom, it threw back its head and howled. The shrill sound made Rifkind's ears ache, but she held her ground, waiting for Illabin's monster to bake into a brick statue.

She was wrong about the statue. The monster didn't harden; it exploded, bit by bit, limb by limb, until its torso crashed into the fire and the wailing ceased.

"Well done!" Ivander shouted. He stood, barely, with his arms looped over the shoulders of two of his men. "Well done, indeed! To think of fire that way."

Not to be outdone, Heft offered his own interpretation: "We were blessed!"

Rifkind shook her head. "We got lucky." She retrieved her sword. "I had a lucky thought."

"Not luck," Heft countered. "A blessing. I prayed to Mohandru."

"Not to argue, but I didn't see a god's hand come down to help us just now."

"I was frightened. I didn't know what else to do, so I prayed that Mohandru inspire *you*."

"I'm done with gods, all gods," Rifkind told the priest. "And the gods are done with me."

She prodded a chunk of the monster's arm that lay in the flames with her sword. The mud and clay shattered into a dozen pieces. She'd thought of water, but water was too far. She'd thought of fire. It wasn't a great leap, a great inspiration. She hadn't turned to her own goddess and she certainly hadn't turned to Mohandru.

She hoped.

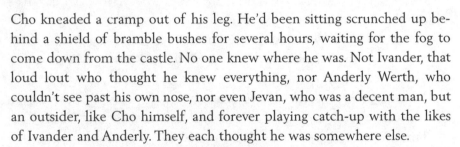

30

Cho kneaded a cramp out of his leg. He'd been sitting scrunched up behind a shield of bramble bushes for several hours, waiting for the fog to
come down from the castle. No one knew where he was. Not Ivander, that
loud lout who thought he knew everything, nor Anderly Werth, who
couldn't see past his own nose, nor even Jevan, who was a decent man, but
an outsider, like Cho himself, and forever playing catch-up with the likes
of Ivander and Anderly. They each thought he was somewhere else.

Cho imagined the looks on their faces when he strode into the camp
with Lord Ejord's daughters on his arms and that other girl trailing along
behind.

Rifkind said there was no hope. Their siege wasn't about rescuing the
kidnapped girls. It was too bad about Reyna, too bad about Lysse, but done
was done. Lord Ejord's daughters were ruined and bottling up Ballardskin
and the sorcerer in Gryphonage was the best revenge the Glascards could
achieve.

It was strange, sometimes. He would have thought his mother would
burn for the girls, but no one could be colder about a person's fate than

Rifkind. He couldn't imagine the expression on *her* face when he returned. He'd like to shock her, but in his heart of hearts, Cho feared Rifkind's expression wouldn't change at all.

She might take it out on Tyrokon. Tyrokon was the exception to no one knowing where Cho was. Tyrokon didn't know precisely where Cho had hidden himself, but Tyrokon knew what Cho had planned. He'd wanted to come along; Cho had seen that in his friend's eyes, but Cho's plan would have pushed Tyrokon beyond his physical limits. There was no place in it for a friend who couldn't race silently up a flight of stairs. There was a place for someone who'd lie to Rifkind.

If anyone had asked him—which, of course, they hadn't—Cho would have argued against leaving a grave unpurged. Whatever the sorcerer had done in the graveyard, if Rifkind could put a stop to it, that's what she should have done on the spot.

Coming back after dark to see what emerged was just about the dumbest idea Cho could imagine, though it fit nicely into his own plan for rescuing Reyna; he didn't have to worry about sorcery, if Rifkind had the sorcerer distracted.

The sun finally sank below the western cloud bank. The sky began to darken and the fog began its nightly creep. Cho envisioned the path he'd take down the slope to the stream, across the stream, and up the hill to the castle wall where he, Tyrokon, and Rifkind had made their escape.

Rifkind was certain that the postern gate would have been sealed; Tyrokon agreed. Cho had convinced himself it would be just as they'd left it. Nobody in Gryphonage would have guessed that the great witch Rifkind had been rescued the hard way by her son. No. They'd think she'd witched herself out of a locked room, and witched him and Tyrokon the same way.

Stars were twinkling before the fog reached Cho's brambles. He started along the path he'd marked in his mind, slowing down after he'd crossed the stream. Fog slicked the turf grasses that covered the castle hill, but they'd have been slippery even without the moisture. A man in chain armor would have had to crawl up the slope while the castle's defenders rained arrows around him.

Maybe Rifkind was right that Lord Ejord would need hundreds of men to successfully assault Gryphonage . . . which only made Cho's plan more ingenious.

When he got to the base of the wall, Cho was out of breath. Slumping against the wall, he caught the guards' conversation.

"—another one."

"Who?"

"Jarem."

"I saw Jarem this morning. He was as alive as you or me."

"Have you seen him since?"

"No, but I'll see him tomorrow. The spook's a strange one and—all right, what he did with old Lord Ballard, that wasn't right. But he's got no interest in the living . . . Well, except for the little girl. Poor thing."

"Better her than us."

"Red." A third voice added itself to the overheard conversation.

"Red," one of the original voices repeated solemnly.

"That was his own fault," the second voice, the voice that believed Illabin had no interest in the living, offered another excuse.

"Be damned. He asked a question!" the third voice snarled.

"Lord Ballard said—"

"Ballardskin!" the third voice shouted.

The next sound Cho heard might have been a fist hitting a man's jaw. The sound after that definitely was.

The first voice shouted, "Enough!" and silence followed.

Cho pounded a triumphant fist against the wall, then gave thanks to the Bright One for guiding him to just the right spot at just the right moment. If the worst happened, if the postern gate had been sealed, he'd still have something to take back to the camp, something to report to Lord Ejord when he arrived.

The walls of Gryphonage might be solid, but the men within them weren't.

He crept silently along the wall, easing behind the bushes that concealed the postern door. Suddenly, Cho's mind filled with his mother's voice and talk of "warding" and the power a sorcerer could plant in anything as trap for the next person who came along. If Illabin had learned of the postern, then he would have warded it and Cho would have needed a talent he didn't have to detect, much less disarm, the sorcerer's handiwork.

He doesn't know, Cho told himself, but the confidence he'd had in sunlight deserted him.

His nerve failed inches before his fingers would have touched the weathered door, if it remained as they had left it, off its hinges and propped against the doorway. Between the dark of night and the fog he couldn't see a foot in front of his face.

It's just a door!

Cho's hands hovered then dropped to his sides. Of all the deaths he could imagine, death by sorcery—stuck like a fly in a sorcerer's web—was the most horrific.

Bright One—

He caught himself on the verge of prayer. Asheerans believed in the goddess of the Bright Moon, but they didn't beg favors. At least the men didn't. Women were always praying for something. Tyrokon's mothers didn't let him do anything without a prayer. Even Rifkind prayed, though, with her, prayer was probably different. Men paid proper respect and gave thanks, as Cho had given thanks for what he'd overheard, but men took care of themselves. They faced their fears =

He took a deep breath, raised his arms and straightened them. His fingers touched wood. Nothing happened, nothing at all. The door *was* as they'd left it, no hinges, no warding. He lifted it gently aside and entered the small room filled with neglected barrels and windblown leaves.

With one hand tracing the interior wall and proper concern for the open well whose location in the floor Cho couldn't quite remember, the boyo made his way around the room.

He found the archway that connected to the hollow wall passage Tyrokon had found beyond their cell. They'd closed the cell's little door behind them and passed a half-dozen or more similar stone-plugged escape holes on their way down.

When he made his plan, Cho had rejected the hollow wall passage in no small part because the risks of opening the wrong knee-high door were too great. Cho'd hoped to find Reyna in the tower chamber where they'd found Rifkind, even though he knew—from Rifkind—that he'd be better off looking for Reyna in Ballardskin's bedchamber.

He'd had Tyrokon drill him on the castle pathways, which spiral stairways, which corridors led from one tower to the next. Just to be sure, he ran through them mentally one last time before approaching the third way out of the postern room.

Cho moved with confidence until his tracing hand touched an iron strike plate.

Bloody Bright!

He'd completely forgotten there was a second door, a door that could be locked and barred with heavy timber. It was too late to worry, the door was wide open, the way they'd found it the first time, and as for warding, well, if there'd been any, he'd be up to his armpits in sorcery.

Another miscalculation greeted Cho at the bottom of the stairway: It was hours earlier than it had been when they rescued Rifkind.

The stairway was, if not brightly lit, several shadows better than totally dark and, beyond the stairs, the men in the lower hall were wide awake, doing what men did in the evening. Notwithstanding the overheard parapet conversation, the men of Gryphonage wouldn't take kindly to a onetime prisoner walking into their midst.

There'd be no slipping into the pissoir at the top of the stairs or passing himself off as just another man whose bladder had awakened him from a sound sleep.

Cho considered waiting on the stairs for snores to replace the hum of conversation, but the odor wafting down from the pissoir was overwhelming. He retreated to the outer doorway.

Patience was not generally a warrior's virtue, but it was a hunter's skill and Cho had mastered it along with the bow. Tucked behind the bushes hiding the postern, he pared his mind down to a thoughtless awareness of sound and movement.

If the guards deviated from their routine march along the parapet, he'd notice. If something made a sound in the turf, he'd notice that, too.

When an inhuman roar pierced the fog, Cho more than noticed. He sprang to his feet, his hands on the hilt and scabbard of his sword. In doing so, he made more noise than he'd made since leaving Tyrokon. His heart filled with dread that he'd given himself away and he scarcely dared to breathe.

Fortunately, Cho wasn't alone in his astonishment. The parapet rang with footsteps and he dimly heard his trio of guards checking one another's perceptions.

Above and below, they waited—hoped—for the sound to be repeated. The first time wasn't enough, not when you'd let your mind go thought-

less. Cho needed to hear the sound again to know what had made it. Minutes passed, long minutes, eternal minutes. He thought the sound had
come from the cemetery, though fog had a way of playing tricks with
sound. He thought of the grave and Tyrokon, and of the wraith in Merrinen forest.

But Rifkind was in the cemetery. Rifkind who stood her ground against
mounted raiders and shimmering wraiths.

Cho shied away from the thought: *Would she save me?* But he knew, as
surely as he knew his name, that she'd save Tyrokon.

Finally, there was another sound, a wail that echoed with despair and
death. Rifkind had won again. Her son didn't doubt it for a heartbeat.

The guards on the parapet exchanged opinions. They'd noticed the roar
and the wail, but ignored any sound Cho had made leaping to his feet. He
took their inattention as a sign that it was time to head inside and make a
name for himself rescuing the Lord of Glascardy's daughters.

The stairs were new-moon dark. The pissoir was empty and the lower
hall was dark except for the night oil lamps at either end.

Beyond the pissoir, Cho heard no conversation, only snoring. He made a
point of hitching up his trousers as he left the pissoir.

His heart fell. Only about half the pallets were occupied; more significantly, two men stood in deep conversation beneath the light of the far-
end lamp.

Bloody Bright! he swore silently, which did not break masculine tradition because it was an oath, not a prayer.

The pair didn't seem to have noticed him. Weighing the risk of walking
the length of the hall to the other stairway against ducking back into the
pissoir, Cho chose to risk the walk. He kept his head down, his pace deliberate, and strode past the pair whose conversation was pitched too low for
overhearing.

Up the hollowed step of the spiral stairway to the great hall Cho went,
never breaking stride though he couldn't breathe and his lungs were on fire
by the time he completed the spiral.

The great hall was empty except for the dogs who wuffled as Cho entered their territory. What little light the hall held came from a single lamp.
Cho couldn't see the dogs and he couldn't see the walls, but Tyrokon had
given him good instructions for finding Rifkind's prison tower.

He walked confidently, as a Gryphonage man would walk—or would a Gryphonage man carry a torch?

Cho didn't want to take that risk.

Pale light filtered down from farther up the spiral. Cho took that as a good sign. He'd almost reached it when he was hailed from below.

"Who goes?"

"Ricose," Cho replied, that being the only Gryphonage name he could remember on short order.

It was the wrong name.

The man below started up the stairs.

Cho faced an instant decision: sword or knife? He went for his knife, thinking that—bad as it was—it was only one man, and a knife was quicker and quieter than a sword for a shadow kill.

"Stand down!" the man below shouted.

There was no way Cho could do that. He braced himself against the spiral's inner spine and prepared to strike blind.

But it wasn't one man, it was two, and at least one more hurried down to join the commotion.

Cho didn't know more than that. He was fighting for his life by then, and fighting with the wrong weapon. He planted the knife in flesh, evoking a shout more angered than pained and with his now-free hands grappled for the hilt of his sword, but the Gryphonage men were pounding on him.

Cho's left arm went cold . . . bone cold and he couldn't make his fingers do anything.

They're killing me, he thought. *I'm dying. Here. Now. I'm dead.*

Death was cold, like his arm, quiet, and dark. Endless dark deeper than a new-moon night.

He had a final sensation of falling, then nothing—nothing at all until he felt hard stone beneath him.

Death is not like this, Cho thought with absolute certainty . . . and he was right, because he wasn't dead.

He ached all over and he hurt in more places than he could count. He couldn't see . . . because his face was against stone and he could hardly open his eyes. He tried to rearrange himself and discovered that his arms had been bound tight behind his back. But his legs were free . . . stiff and sore, but free.

Laboriously, Cho knelt up. He banged his left arm in the process and learned whole new words for pain from a swath of injury that stretched from just above his wrist to just below his elbow. Irresistible tears flooded his cheeks. He clamped his teeth together to keep from crying out because with the pain had come memory of his last moments on the spiral stairway.

If he wasn't dead, then he was in prison . . . again. And he'd be damned to Vitivar before he let his captors hear him scream.

Fighting the pain took more strength than Cho had. He pitched forward and only with the greatest of efforts managed to land on his right side . . . his *good* side of the moment, though *good* meant only that he could bear the agony without fainting.

The sharpest pain receded. Cho levered himself to his knees again. His cell was dark, but an ordinary dark, not like the absolute dark of unconsciousness . . . or death.

There was light: a palm-wide, forearm-high window that cast a rectangle of light on a wall that was a few steps away . . . if he could stand or walk.

It took a while, but Cho did rise and did walk and did gaze through the narrow window at a narrow sliver of bright blue summer sky.

Afternoon, he thought. *The rest of the night. All morning.* Just as he'd known that he wasn't dead, Cho knew that he hadn't lost any more time out of his life, but a night and a morning were enough. Rifkind and Ivander would have come back from the graveyard. They'd have met with the others. His clever lies would have untangled. Tyrokon would have told the truth by now.

Cho didn't blame Tyrokon.

There were noises opposite the narrow window, where the door had to be.

I didn't even try the door, Cho thought as it opened.

"He's up," a man said in Glascard.

Other men entered the cell. They seized Cho by the shoulders, jostling his bound arms, his injured left arm.

Once again, he found new words for pain. He would have fallen if the men hadn't been there. He would have cried out, if he hadn't poured all his strength into being quiet.

Cho's mind slipped away for a moment.

There were stairs. He descended, his feet missing more often than not, but he had a warrior's heart and it hardened to the pain. When they reached the landing, Cho had his balance again and walked erect into the great hall of Gryphonage. The hall seemed bigger because it was empty, except for a pair of high-backed chairs and a knot of people at the far end. Cho, who had grown up in Hamarach's tent, understood that he was being brought before justice.

He would have expected that, if the pain had subsided soon enough to give him a moment to think clearly.

"I can walk," he told his escort.

They loosened their grip, but stayed close, as if there was anything a prisoner could do as he walked the length of that hall.

The knot dispersed. Two men went to the chairs. Lord Ohlmer Ballard sat in the larger chair, and immediately began drumming his fingers on the armrest. Not for a moment did he look straight ahead, but to one side. Cho followed the lord's gaze and found nothing, not even a door or a dog.

A man Cho didn't recognize sat to the lord's right. Seeing that man's wild brown hair Cho wished he could do something about the tendrils obscuring his vision. Before Cho had finished his regrets, the unfamiliar man swept his hand across his brow, giving Cho a better view of the four heavy rings on his right hand. Sorcerer's rings. The man with the wild brown hair was Illabin.

Cho spotted Wilts, who'd saved his life not so long ago; like Lord Ballard, Wilts wouldn't meet a prisoner's eyes.

Oddly, considering what had held them at Gryphonage in the first place and what had gotten Rifkind into trouble, there was no sign of the little boy, Garris. Maybe there was no place for the boy in his father's plans—in Illabin's plans—now that they had Lord Ejord's daughters.

They were there: Reyna on the lord's left, the younger one on the stranger's right. He hadn't recognized Reyna at first. Lord Ballard had put a white veil over her sunset hair and there was no expression to her face. She and her sister just stared straight ahead. He stared back, but she didn't see him.

Rifkind's words haunted Cho's memory: "There won't be anything left to rescue."

Bloody Bright, his mother was a colder woman than any man, but she'd spoken the truth.

If he'd had his bow, Cho would have killed just then, arrows for Ohlmer and Illabin, for what they'd done, and one for Reyna, for mercy.

Not that it mattered. He didn't have his bow, his sword, nor the least knife.

His escort laid hands on him again some five strides short of the chairs. Lord Ballard finally looked at him, but it was the sorcerer who spoke.

"You're the witch's son?" he said, in trade, so Cho could understand every word.

"My name is Domhnall."

The stranger thumbed a ring. "The witch's son?"

Cho wanted to say something clever, something heroic, even if it got him killed on the spot, but the best he could manage was a nod.

"She's with the men in the forest?"

Cho nodded again.

"Corporeal?"

That wasn't a word Cho had heard before. Illabin thumbed another ring. Thoughts that were not Cho's own thundered within his skull: *In the flesh. Tangibly. Mortally.*

"She's there," he said with difficulty.

"She sent you? How? What is she using? What power has she invoked? How did she get you into Gryphonage?"

"She didn't. I came myself. Through—" White light exploded. Bile surged in Cho's throat. He couldn't breathe, couldn't think. The pain in his arm was a scratch compared to the white light.

"How did she get you past my wards?" The question surrounded him, filled him.

"No—" Cho gagged. Hot liquid dribbled past his lips, down his leg. White became black, cold, tight and tightening. *A taste of your own death.* "Help."

Black became soot-stained grays and browns . . . the browns of the great hall's beams, the grays of its ceiling. Cho was on his back, numb and unable to move.

"The truth, boyo."

The truth was that his nose was broken, there was blood pooling in his ear, and he hadn't seen the punch coming. Hadn't seen it coming because there'd been nothing to see. He'd been struck by sorcery. He was as powerless as a mouse in the claws of a cat.

"The truth, or you'll die. How did she get you past my wards?"

The truth hadn't helped, so Cho lied. "She turned me into a bird and I flew in."

Once again Cho was flung back. This time his jaw took the punishment. His mouth filled; he'd bitten through his tongue.

"The truth!"

Before Cho could think of another answer, Lord Ballard interrupted. "He's a warrior, not a witch. He's not afraid of dying. Give him to me. I'll take him below. There are better ways to get the truth from a warrior."

31

"Riders coming," a man called, relaying a message from the road.

Rifkind looked up from sharpening her sword.

"Lord Overnmont?" another man asked, the very question that had formed in Rifkind's thoughts, though she had kept her thoughts to herself and was not responsible for the inquiry.

"No. From the castle."

Rifkind was on her feet in an instant. She sheathed the sword over her shoulder. It had been sharp enough when the day began. She'd been honing it for want of something better to do.

Tyrokon stood up, too. The boyo's face was full of the misery only the young could feel when they were still feeling things for the first time. His eyes snagged Rifkind's then drifted away.

She would forgive him . . . eventually, but not yet.

They'd spent the rest of the night in the cemetery, watching the stars shine. At dawn, they'd trooped back to the forest camp. Rifkind and Ivander had conferred with Jevan and Anderly, who'd had nothing to report. She hadn't spared a thought for her son. And why should she have? She had

Tyrokon's word that Jevan had wanted him for guard duty; she trusted Tyrokon. Then Jevan had asked, "Where's Cho?"

Where, indeed?

Not anywhere that he'd sworn to be. Not catching an uninterrupted night's sleep. Tyrokon had claimed ignorance until it had been clear to one and all that Cho was nowhere in the siege camp.

"He had a plan," the boyo had confessed. "He was going to sneak into the castle, through the postern gate. He was going to rescue her—Reyna—and her sisters before Lord Overnmont got here. He thought— He thought it would make him a man in your eyes."

Rifkind supposed that Tyrokon had had more to say. She didn't know for certain. Once the words were out of Tyrokon's mouth, she'd turned her back on the entire camp and marched off to the tree line where she'd stared at the near-perfect dome of fog concealing the Ballard castle.

Foolishness. Stupidity. Idiocy, she'd thought in the castle's direction. Hadn't she warned her son to put the girl out of his mind?

But he's in fallen love.

The thought came unbidden, in a soft, unfamiliar tone. Fallen in love. She'd stood there just behind the front line of the forest, pondering the phrase, coming to the awkward conclusion that, if falling in love was the source of Cho's supreme recklessness, then she had never succumbed to its delusions.

Love without its tumbling aspects, love that shone like a steady sun on those who stood in her sphere, that love Rifkind knew and that love surrounded her son, Tyrokon, Ejord, Jenny . . . yes, Jenny, and a handful of others.

They were hers, and she loved them.

In her mind's eye, Rifkind had seen her son crushed within Illabin's amber wards. No one did that to one of hers and survived. Alone and in silence, Rifkind had sworn vengeance.

She'd returned to the camp and found a whetstone, even though she'd known that steel wasn't the weapon she'd need against the sorcerer. The sweep of stone against metal had steadied her thoughts. She'd been sorting through the words she'd use to persuade Ejord of the necessity of an assault when the "Riders coming" call had come up and she'd gone again to the forest edge.

There were three of them, one in front, two behind. They all wore chain that glinted in the sun. The one on the right rear carried an inverted spear to which a length of bleached cloth had been tied. They dismounted, surrendered their weapons and horses, and waited at the roadblock until a half-dozen Glascard footmen arrived to escort them up the hill.

Rifkind kept a close eye on the leader who did everything with his left hand. Halfway up the slope, she confirmed her suspicions: The leader was Wilts, whose pain she'd taken in the Barking Goose, and he'd come to tell her that her son was dead.

Dead.

Rifkind drew a ragged breath during which she saw Cho as an infant, fresh from her womb. She let the breath go, taking the memory with it, leaving vengeance behind. She took another breath and saw her son as a toddler playing with Tyrokon outside Hamarach's tent, and she let that breath go, too. She took a third breath and a fourth until she had seen her son at all the stages of his short life. She exhaled them all until only vengeance remained.

Time had passed without Rifkind's notice, not much, but the slope from the road to the camp was empty. The men, all of them, clotted together near the lean-to. Rifkind put her shoulder between two Glascards and wormed her way to the front where Ivander, Anderly, and Jevan faced Wilts and his two-man escort.

Wilts was saying, "You can't expect me to take *your* word—" He fell silent when he saw Rifkind.

Ivander held a coiled parchment at his fingertips. He offered it to Rifkind. She took it and held it without unrolling it. There was no point. She didn't know top from bottom when it came to written messages. Apparently there were nearly as many ways of writing as there were of speaking but none of them had taken root in the Asheera and none of them yielded their secrets to a healer's empathy. Rifkind could recognize her name when she saw it, sometimes, but not always.

Rifkind caught Jevan's eye. Back in the Felmargue he'd been as ignorant of writing as she remained, but old Lord Humphry Overnmont had given his natural daughter a noblewoman's education and, beyond doubt, she'd shared it with her husband. Rifkind rose ever-so-slightly into her *tal* to plant an idea in his thoughts.

Whether he'd needed a healer's nudge or not, Jevan took the parchment from her fingertips. "Ballardskin wants us to do homage to him. He says now that Lord Ejord's dead and he's married to an Overnmont daughter—as he used to be married to a Ballard daughter—that he's our rightful lord. He offers mercy if we do it by sundown."

Nothing about her son. Nothing about dead men walking or giants climbing out of the ground.

But then, why should there be? That was sorcery and Ballardskin's message had nothing to do with sorcery. It was all about the social code that underlay every province of the old empire where every man except the emperor owed an oath to someone. If Ejord *had* died, then the Glascards *would* be owing their oaths to their deceased lord's daughter's husband, just as Wilts and the Irdelmen had owed it.

Idly, Rifkind wondered how Ohlmer was styling himself. Lord Ballard of Irdel and Glascardy? Or was it Lord Overnmont? Had he appropriated the Overnmont as he'd taken the Ballard?

"Lord Overnmont's coming," a Glascard in the ranks declared. "You'll see. Ballardskin's the one who'll be looking for mercy."

Wilts looked up. "So you say."

Rifkind had not descended from her *tal*. She looked at Wilts and saw a man torn between an honorable oath and the dishonored man he'd given it to. "So *I* say," she said.

Wilts met her stare with hollow eyes. "I've a separate message for you." He dug into his messenger's satchel and produced another piece of parchment, this one folded rather than rolled.

Dreading the embarrassment that was sure to follow, Rifkind accepted the parchment that was lumpy and heavier than she expected. She opened one crease, then another, aware that everyone was watching her and that the worst was yet to come.

And it did, though not as she expected. For a moment Rifkind thought the message had been written with rust-red ink, rather than black, then she realized there was no message, at least not a written one. Instead there was an object, not too long, gnarled yet slender . . . like a finger.

It fell away from the parchment as she opened the last fold and landed between her feet. She stared at it while Wilts said, "I'm to tell you, if you want him, you're to come and get him, else he'll come out like that, piece by piece."

Not *like* a finger, but an actual finger, a middle finger by the look of it. One of Cho's middle fingers. Her son's. And sliced off while he was still alive. She knew that; a healer always knew such things even when the flesh in question had bled out.

"Lord Overnmont will be here today," someone said, possibly Jevan; Rifkind couldn't be certain, the voice sounded as if it were coming from a great distance.

"We'll get him out."

No, that voice was Jevan's. Rifkind met his old-young eyes and shook her head.

"My message. My son. My destiny."

Destiny? Why had that word come to mind? Wasn't she beyond destiny? Free to live her own life? As if anyone were that free.

Rifkind picked up the finger.

Wilts said something; she didn't catch any of the words.

The sun had begun its descent to evening, but the longest hours of a summer afternoon had yet to unwind. There was ample time to return to the forest edge, to sit and study the shrouded castle.

The Glascards split apart to let her pass. No one said a word. No one followed.

The three Irdelmen didn't ride down the slope. Perhaps they were waiting for a reply, or perhaps, having delivered their message, they were just as glad to be done with their oath-sworn lord.

Rifkind was still up slightly in her *tal* and acutely aware of the Bright Moon hiding in the sun's overhead glare. She was aware of the dark moon, Vitivar, as well, skulking in the Bright Moon's wake. Rifkind would have had to pass through Vitivar's shadow, if she'd sought her goddess's counsel, which she didn't. She kept her thoughts close, focused on Gryphonage and vengeance.

Tyrokon braved her solitude. "Can I help? Can I do *anything?*"

Rifkind drove him away with a glance.

———

WHEN SHE LOOKED OUT OF herself again, the valley between the forest slope and Gryphonage was shadowed beneath dark clouds and thunder rumbled along the western horizon. *Lightstorm*, Rifkind thought reflexively and sought quick shelter among the hawthorns before remembering where she was. Not that Darian thunderstorms didn't command respect, but they didn't steal souls the way Asheeran lightstorms could.

Peering through the hawthorn branches, Rifkind watched as a lightning bolt grounded itself within the clouds surrounding the castle. Rifkind's eyes saw the lightning as a jagged silver-white streak, writhing and lingering like a struck serpent, but in her mind the silver was bloodred. Unhesitatingly, she leapt into her *tal* to find the truth of the two visions.

The truth was profound and unsettling. It wasn't that Illabin had woven wards around Gryphonage; she'd expected that from the beginning, or that they were every bit as complex as those that had surrounded his Merrinen forest tower. He was a powerful practitioner who knew how to hoard power in gemstones. No, what stunned Rifkind were the *colors* of the wards—iridescent greens and golds, reds and purples—and the way they reached up into the storm.

That can't be. Illabin's Merrinen wards had been plain amber. *Those are lightstorm colors*, she thought and rose higher still.

Rifkind rose beyond the ordinary limits of her *tal*, avoiding the storm, but soaring upward beside it. When she had risen as far as she could, she looked out and saw the world looming large and small at the same time. She beheld that it was *round*—not simply round as Darians drew their maps with a thin band of bright green around a dull brown Asheera, but shaped into a perfect sphere.

A sharp border divided the sphere. On the side of the border that faced an impossibly bright sun, Rifkind saw a half circle that looked remarkably like the western half of Daria as it was drawn on the best maps with white blots and streaks—clouds—obscuring about a quarter of both the land and the vast ocean.

On the night side—she guessed the border was the march of sunset— the sphere was scarcely brighter than the black between the stars, except for circle, a small circle compared to the size of Daria or the sphere itself. It was just to the east of sunset that bled red, purple, orange, and green in all directions, though the streamers faded where they reached into the sunlight.

If all her guesses about this strange vision were right, then the night-side blemish was a lightstorm, and not just any lightstorm, but the Death Wastes monster she had seen from Banin's back on their way to Epigos. Which was fascinating, but the Death Wastes storm was not the storm that had stretched her *tal* to its farthest extent.

Rifkind looked down between her feet—where her feet would have been, if she'd had feet or any other physical sense besides vision. The gray patches, all rough and angular, were surely the mountains of Glascardy and in their lee, green valleys, blue rivers, and an arc of white clouds.

The instinct that allowed Rifkind to recognize her face during those rare moments when she glanced at a mirror, informed her that she was looking down on the clouds that were above her body—though how the dark clouds of a thunderstorm could be so brilliantly white when seen from above was a question instinct would not answer. More interesting were the silver-white lightning flashes pricking along the clouds' length. Most interesting of all was the slender iridescent thread—undimmed by sunlight—that snaked briefly from the Death Wastes storm to one above Gryphonage.

The source of the color she'd seen in memory's eye? The source of Illabin's sorcery?

How many times since that night when she'd talked to Vendle in Hamarach's tent had Rifkind heard that the Wet-lands crawled with increasingly powerful sorcerers?

What had changed? Where did they get their power? Gemstones, such as the ruby Rifkind had once worn or Illabin's seven rings could *store* power, but not create it. A healer's power came from the Bright Moon—which Rifkind could neither feel nor see from her strange vantage above the world. In generations long past, men had drawn a similar power from the dark moon, Vitivar, and corrupted it.

Vitivar had been broken by what, whom, or when Rifkind didn't know. That was not among the secrets the Bright One shared with Her healers when She bestowed their crescents and Rifkind had never thought to ask. But *something* had created the Death Wastes where the giant lightstorm had taken root.

Rifkind would have given much to see the dark moon just then, but it was hidden behind the world. Instead, she watched the white storm above Gryphonage cast spider legs in all directions. None of them reached even halfway to the Death Wastes before they disappeared, but moments later, another thread, garish purple this time, shot from the night side and grounded itself in the Gryphonage storm.

How much more do you need to see?

Forget gods; they were, after all, done with her. Forget the lightstorm; even she would concede that it was too large for her to tackle. What mattered were those lightning feelers reaching out from the Gryphonage storm and the colored threads reaching back to them: Illabin drawing in the power to raise the dead, to mutilate her son—her foolish, reckless son, but *her* son all the more.

She could do something about Illabin.

Then do it!

That thought, which Rifkind would swear was not her own, nor the Bright One's, either, startled her out of whatever force had stretched her *tal* and held her at its farthest limit. She had a body and as sure as she was that her body was stretched out in the wet grass at the forest's edge, she was equally sure that she had a body that was cold beyond cold and falling.

How long did it take to fall from a height where the world was a sphere?

Long enough to see the white clouds dissipate and the sunset border to reach the sea beyond Glascardy. Long enough to decide how she would stalk and destroy her enemy.

Rifkind had transformed herself into a hawk when she'd spied on Illabin. It had proved a very useful disguise, but a hawk couldn't kill a man and she'd be satisfied with nothing less than the sorcerer's death. She'd been a ger-cat, once, and slain an emperor, but invading Gryphonage in ger-cat form would likely set her up for the same failure Cho had encountered.

She might pierce the wards in a hawk's form then change shape a second time and stalk the halls as a ger-cat . . . if she could change from one animal to another so far from her physical self . . . if she wanted to even try with so much at stake.

Or—the idea came to Rifkind while her feet were up and her head was down—she could be both hawk *and* ger-cat or something very close, some-thing very like the green gryphon on the Ballard's yellow banner.

Her head came around. What better form could her vengeance take than the Ballard crest?

Rifkind spread her arms. They became wings. She extended her arms a second time and they became a gryphon's forelimbs with fingers and thumbs and honed-steel talons. She drew her legs up, giving herself a ger-cat's haunches and its raking claws. The Ballard gryphon bore a bird's head with a hooked beak that could shear off a man's arm or leg; Rifkind gave herself the same. Then—because she was tumbling faster now and her wings could not steady her—she added the green gryphon's long tail with its heavy tuft at the end.

She flicked the tail twice. Her transformed self stopped tumbling. Her wings caught air. She stopped falling. The castle was below her, hidden within its cloud, but defined by its wards.

A gryphon was far larger than a hawk. She'd have to be careful, but Gryphonage was far larger than the Merrinen tower and Illabin's wards were loose woven. A few beats of the gryphon's heavy wings assured Rifkind that, though the chimeric creature was no graceful hawk, its patched-together body knew how to fly with no help from her.

32

Spiraling down to the castle, Rifkind found a gryphon-sized hole between two ribs of warding, then followed one of the ribs down to a parapet.

"Halt!" a guard shouted with just a hint of anxiety in his voice.

"Who goes there?" his companion asked in a similar tone.

They'd heard her hind claws striking stone or, perhaps, felt the air move as her wings fanned the air. For sure, they hadn't *seen* her. No Ballard man could have taken the sudden appearance of the family beast without raising a castle-wide alarm.

Rifkind considered slaying them to learn the gryphon's strengths and how it killed, but the men were simply doing what they'd been told and doing it properly. They didn't deserve death and in all probability the gryphon was as good at killing as it was at flying. She sat stone-still on the parapet, studying the wards while the men lost their wariness.

The ward ribs didn't ground themselves in any of the courtyards or the great hall, all places where she would have expected Illabin to anchor them. Instead they twisted into a shimmering rope that looped upward and disappeared in the fog.

Augemon's tower, Rifkind thought, raking memory for the names and positions of Gryphonage's many towers. There was, she recalled, a stairway winding around the outside of the uppermost reaches of Augemon's tower. She spread her wings and sprang from the parapet.

"Did you hear *that*?"

"What?"

The stairway was narrow and treacherous for a gryphon that had to scrabble frantically with forelimbs and hind to secure a landing. A handful of mortar bits went clattering down to the courtyard, leaving Rifkind more annoyed by her clumsiness than worried about its consequences. She climbed the stairs to a closed door that was pierced, but not damaged, by Illabin's wards.

Using the gryphon's dextrous paws, Rifkind opened the door, without—she hoped—overly disturbing the wards. Even with the door open, there wasn't much room for a healer to pass into the tower, much less a gryphon. She tucked her wings as flat as she could against her spine then crawled across the threshold.

When Rifkind was stretched out on her great cat's belly, some part of her wings brushed the ward rope that whined like a thousand angry bees and showered her with searing sparks. It was all she could do to remain stock-still until the wards, like the guards, calmed themselves.

If Illabin had come to investigate, she would have been helpless against him, but he did not emerge.

Staying low, because the gryphon's cat-like parts were its quietest and cats stalked their prey with serpents' skills, Rifkind eased down the stairs. From the landing, she studied the chamber where she had met with Ohlmer Ballard when she first came to Gryphonage. The chamber with its books and worktable made more sense as a sorcerer's lair than it had had as a lord's retreat.

She couldn't see the sorcerer from the doorway, but she could hear a man muttering—chanting—to himself in that part of the room that was hidden by the open door.

She could also see Lysse sitting primly on a painted stool. The child had eyes only for Illabin and if it weren't for the fact that she blinked every now and again, Rifkind might have mistaken her for a painted statue.

With perfect balance and exacting slowness, Rifkind extended one hand until one talon crossed the threshold. When that didn't trigger an alarm, she extended another finger, another talon, then the hand itself. She flowed forward, moving a hind foot at the very end, then started the stealthy process again with her other forelimb.

At the completion of that step she could see Illabin's back as he stood at the worktable.

She had made not the least sound. Lysse had not twitched on her stool. There was no reason for Illabin to have sensed a new presence in his chamber, but he did sense something and froze. His silence and lack of motion gave Rifkind a heartbeat to gather herself for her own attack.

But she was a shade too slow.

Illabin whirled around, rings ablaze with rainbow colors. He uttered a word and power rushed from him. It took Rifkind across the chest and hurled her against the wall. The upper bone of her right wing snapped like winter kindling. She screamed—an ear-splitting cry that surprised her and stunned him.

A half-dozen glass vials on the worktable shattered.

The sorcerer let the exploding glass distract him: a fatal mistake. Seizing her advantage, Rifkind launched herself across the chamber.

Stretched out, the gryphon was taller than the tallest man. Its weight bent Illabin backward over his table. With her forelimbs, she pinned his hands against the wood. Then she punctured his neck with her hooked beak while her hind legs clawed a race through his fine robes to his spine.

His organs spilled to the floor.

Illabin was dead before he could have known he was dying.

He'd never known who killed him or why, which suited Rifkind. She had her vengeance; she didn't need share it with anyone, even the son on whose behalf she'd exacted it.

Illabin's eyes were open. They were a startling shade of cornflower blue—the eyes of a beautiful woman. Rifkind did not trouble to close them.

Already the sorcerer's works were coming undone. The wards, grounded in bronze cauldron beyond the worktable, began to sizzle. Tiny strands of power popped loose, reminding Rifkind of Cho's braids on a sweaty summer's day.

The sorcery Illabin had wrapped around Ejord's daughter was fading, too. Intelligence and awareness flickered briefly in her eyes before she closed them. Her breath went out of her in a sigh and she slid gently to the floor, knees first, then shoulder and onto her side.

Rifkind strode toward her. She laid a gnarled, taloned hand on the child's cheek and gained no knowledge of her condition. Her healer's talent was locked in her true body. Until she could return to it, she was a gryphon, utterly and totally. A gryphon with a badly injured wing. Rifkind didn't need talent to know that the extra bone rising from her shoulder wasn't merely broken, it was displaced and shattered.

There would be no leaving the castle the way she came.

Men clambered on the tower stairs. "You first," someone said, and "Not me," followed by a sterner voice shouting, "Forward, or you'll taste *my* sword!"

A gryphon's hearing, it seemed, was not the best. She should have heard the men long before they got to the landing, should have realized that scream would have roused the entire castle. Men had to investigate, not willingly, perhaps, but with their commanders behind them.

Rifkind couldn't guess what they'd do when they saw Illabin slain by the Ballard gryphon. Maybe they'd drop to their knees in relief, or maybe not. She prepared for the worst, facing the doorway as she unfurled her one good wing and reared up on her haunches.

Flexing her talons, she screamed a second time, louder than before.

Two men in the front dropped their weapons, but someone in the rear had the presence of mind to hurl a spear. Rifkind dodged it easily, though not without cost. Rapid movement of any sort jarred her broken wing. Bone shards ground together and, though the gryphon did not experience excruciating pain as a human might, the room dimmed for a few heartbeats.

"Look at it!"

"Mohandru weeps!"

"What is it?"

"Can't you see? It's a *gryphon*!"

"The Ballard gryphon come to life!"

Rifkind advanced. The result was better than she'd dared hope: Men scrambled over each other in their determination to avoid her. One man—the commander, by the look of him—held his ground until she opened her beak and hissed. Then she had the landing to herself.

The tower stairs were a rightward spiral that had Rifkind's broken wing bumping against the outer wall on each step. She descended slowly and slipped more than once—her claws and talons were not meant for steep, slice-of-pie stone steps.

I'm a damned fool, she thought between steps. *Trapping myself in some creature's body like this. As damned a fool as Cho. It will serve me right, if this gets me killed. Damned fool—*

"It's coming!"

"Archers ready!"

Archers? She was the gods-all-be-damned Ballard gryphon! She'd freed the castle from the pall of sorcery.

"Aim for the heart!" a familiar voice shouted. "Don't bother with the head or any place else. It can be killed. Everything can be killed."

Ah—but she hadn't freed the castle from its lord. Ohlmer Ballard, who hadn't been born a Ballard, had rallied some of his men and arrayed them in the courtyard.

And if they killed the gryphon, what would happen to her? Would death undo her transformation and send her spirit shooting back to its proper body? Should she take the risk? Did she have a choice?

She should have had a choice. There was something she'd missed. Something she'd forgotten. There was no time to wrack memory in search of it.

To Rifkind's dismay, the gryphon could neither turn around nor go backward in the tight spiral of the stairwell. And, if it had, it was not as if Illabin's worktable offered a solution to her problems. Nor would the Glascards be racing to her rescue. Tyrokon could lead them to her rightful body, but he could not tell anyone where she'd gone. Jevan might guess, but guessing wouldn't be enough.

So it was down the stairs to arrows and whatever lay beyond. The gryphon's ears were bad, but its eyes were as good as any cat's. Torchlight as bright as noontime poured in through the arch at the bottom of the stairs.

"A purse of gold for the man who puts his arrow in its heart!" Ohlmer Ballard cried out to his men.

Rifkind had not included Ohlmer Ballard in her vengeance until she heard him offer a reward for her death. It was the arrows and her Asheeran prejudice against them, because offering a reward before a battle was something the Overnmonts had done many times.

At the foot of the stairway, Rifkind let loose with another gryphon scream. Despite the effort she put into it, the shrill sound was less effective in the open courtyard than it had been within walls. Still, it froze the men for a moment.

Rifkind's sharp gryphon eyes managed to pick Ballardskin's blond head out of the crowd. He was safely behind his men, at the top of a short flight of stairs. She approved of lords who commanded from the rear even less than arrows.

The gryphon lunged just as the arrows flew down from the walls circling the courtyard. Some of them, surely, missed their target and none of them struck her heart or any other vital spot, but they did strike her wings, flanks, and haunches. Each was more heavy than sharp, the feeling of hammer slamming a nail followed by numbness, not pain.

Pain would come later, if the gryphon lived that long.

Her left hind leg was as useless as her right wing when Rifkind reached Ballardskin's stairway. A man would have collapsed, but a man balanced on only two legs. The gryphon had four, one in each corner, and the momentum of its lunge to keep it moving.

So confident of his men—or so cowardly—that he had not drawn his sword, Ohlmer Ballard faced his death in slack-jawed horror. The collision was enough to topple him and the force of his skull striking stone was enough to kill him, though Rifkind took no chance and tore into him with every weapon the gryphon possessed: beak, talons, and claws together.

She wouldn't have long. Ballardskin's men were better than he deserved and the nearest ones had drawn their swords.

Rifkind felt the first thrust into her shoulder and the second ax-like cut against her spine. The third came between her ribs and, after it, she felt nothing at all. Her vision faded except for a single light in the distance that called her name and drew her forward.

Life or death?

She'd find out soon enough.

RIFKIND LAY ON HER STOMACH, half in, half out of a warm-water pool.
She was not in pain, not feeling anything at all except weakness and exhaustion. She was too weary to open her eyes, too weary to breathe. She
listened for the beating of her heart and heard nothing.

Not in my body. Not in my body. Not alive—

That meant— Rifkind was too weary to care what it meant, if it meant
anything. She was too weary to think.

"What am I going to do with you?" a woman scolded.

The voice was familiar. One of Tyrokon's mothers. Idi. The one who did
all the talking, all the scolding.

Rifkind ignored the question.

A breeze touched her cheek leaving warmth in its wake.

The crescent. Her crescent. Not Idi.

Damn.

"Is that any way to say 'thank you'?"

Warmth continued to spread from the living silver in Rifkind's cheek. It
reached her eyes; they opened by themselves.

She'd come to a place without color. The sky was so black it shone. The
stone on which she lay was powder white. The boot in front of her was
sewn from white deerskin, without a hint of buff or yellow. Even the sinew
holding it together was white, pure white.

A hundred questions or more crowded into Rifkind's awakening mind.

What had happened next?

Was her son still alive?

What about Reyna? Lysse? Ejord?

Would Cho recover without a healer?

The questions went on, but only one of them was worth asking.

"Did I kill him?" She mouthed the words; there was no air in her lungs
to give them shape.

The goddess laughed. "Why, yes, you did. Both of them. Ohlmer Aksel
preceded you, not by much, but you were, beyond doubt, the cause of his
death, and the sorcerer's, too.

"You could have willed yourself out of the gryphon. It didn't have to
come to this," the Bright One added.

Ah—that was what she'd forgotten.

But the gryphon hadn't been a dream.

She couldn't have awakened from it.

Warmth reached Rifkind's heart. It spasmed—painfully—then began beating. She took a breath.

"I'm alive."

"If you say so."

If anything, Rifkind felt wearier now that her blood was trying to flow into distant—oh-so-distant—extremities. She let lassitude wrap around her.

"You don't have time for that," the goddess said in Idi's voice. "You have a decision to make."

Alive—because she *had* said so—but not in her body.

"I'm tired," Rifkind said, speaking the words as they formed in her mind, not quite knowing what she would say next. "I remember dying. I was afraid, but there was nothing to be afraid of. Nothing. It was like being asleep. And I'm tired."

The goddess agreed, saying, "You've had two destinies."

"I haven't done so well without a destiny. Did you know that the world is a *sphere* and sunset is a line that moves across it? There's a lightstorm in the Death Wastes that isn't going away and Illabin had found a way to draw power from it. Before I killed him. Before I became a gryphon and killed him. There'll be more, You know. If Illabin found a way, someone else will, too."

Rifkind waited for her goddess to say something, but if the Bright One knew about spheres, lightstorms, or ambitious sorcerers, She kept it to herself.

"I go too far," Rifkind said to end the silence.

"That you do."

"It would be easier if I were ordinary."

"You?" The Bright One laughed. "You? Ordinary?"

"If I were—if I went back and was ordinary, then—then I could fall in love like my son has with that girl. I could have another child, and do better raising it. It was no good to be without a destiny after having had two. I need to be ordinary. Make me ordinary as You once made me a healer."

"I can't. You are everything that you have done. I can't undo that. I would have to undo time itself. Not all the gods together can undo time."

"Then I'll do it myself," Rifkind said. She closed her eyes. "I'll do it myself . . . I'll do it myself . . ."

RIFKIND HAD BEEN UNCONSCIOUS FOR two days.

Never mind that Reyna looked like a ghost, that her little sister was making things move without touching them, that they hadn't found a hair of that third girl Ballardskin had abducted, or that Cho's hand hurt worse than it had when Ballardskin took a knife to it—*Rifkind* was unconscious and the whole damned camp was tiptoeing around as if waking her up was a bad idea.

Lord Ejord had put her on a bed in his tent and surrounded her with candles like she was already dead.

It was worse than the old-time Gryphonage men burying that damn green gryphon in the castle crypt. At least once they'd buried it, they'd left it alone. Somebody had to sit beside Rifkind all day and all night, too, so she wouldn't be alone.

Lord Ejord had given Cho his choice of when to sit and he'd replied that he'd rather try to make Reyna smile again. They'd stared at each other long and hard. Cho thought that they'd come to an understanding without exchanging a word and that in someone's eyes, at least, he'd become a man.

Now, if only he could get Reyna to notice him. He'd taken her down to see the war-horses. That usually worked with Asheeran girls. She had put her hand on Tein's nose and given him a dainty patting. It wasn't much, but it was a start—

"Cho! Cho! She's moving! She's waking up!"

Tyrokon scrambled down the hill, arms flailing as he struggled to keep his balance.

Cho was tempted to tell his friend to shut up and slow down.

Nobody saw through Rifkind the way he did but he didn't want to start an argument, not with Reyna standing next to him.

Who knew, once she was awake, Rifkind might be able to do something for Reyna.

Bloody Bright, she could do something about Cho's hand.

So they followed Tyrokon up the hill—Reyna reached out to steady Tyrokon when he stumbled—and made their way to Ejord's tent.

Lord Ejord called him over. "Stand close. She'll want to see that you're safe."

Not a chance, but Cho bit his tongue and stood at his mother's bedside, next to Lord Ejord: a place of great honor in the crowded tent.

Rifkind's head moved from side to side, then her lips began to move. Lord Ejord bent close to catch her words. He stood up again.

"I don't understand her words. She's speaking your language."

Cho got down on his knees.

"Myself. I'll do it myself. I'll do it myself."

Of course. Was there any doubt? Rifkind never wanted anyone's help.

Cho stood and translated her words. He'd just finished when she opened her eyes. She looked straight at Cho and, for a heartbeat, he thought Lord Ejord was right and her first thoughts were for him.

He held up his bandaged hand, but by then she was finished with him—finished with Lord Ejord, too—and staring at the canvas overhead.

She'd never change.

Never in a million years.

She'd always be Rifkind.